THE
VOICES DOWN UNDER

BOOK IV OF
THE VOICES SAGA

WILLIAM L STOLLEY

iUniverse, Inc.
New York   Bloomington

The Voices Down Under
Book IV of The Voices Saga

iUniverse books may be ordered through booksellers or by contacting:

iUniverse
1663 Liberty Drive
Bloomington, IN 47403
www.iuniverse.com
1-800-Authors (1-800-288-4677)

ISBN: 978-1-4502-6317-7 (pbk)
ISBN: 978-1-4502-6318-4 (ebk)

Printed in the United States of America

iUniverse rev. date: 10/12/2010

Consideration

Very special thanks to Joan and Kevin Kelly for their continued support through the years. I would also like to thank Jody Kruse, another lifelong friend for her words of encouragement at just the right time.

I would especially thank my very good and dear friend Milton Gipstein for his sage like advice, his support, his wisdom, his expert tutelage, and his incredible sense of humor. Milton Gipstein is the Master Li that I created from fiction come to fruition. As Michael Tyler says to his mentor with a bow, "I open my mind to you."

Finally, I wish to openly express my love and appreciation for my son Michael, who works so hard at being a good teenager; my wife Lori, who has the patience of Job along with a beautiful sense of loyalty and dedication; and even my dog Duke. They give me so much love without measure, plus the safety net of family that we all need in life.

Contents

1. A search begins   1
2. Bad news travels fast   10
3. An unexpected voice   25
4. The major (general) and his minor, part 1   33
5. Encampment   39
6. Nightmare Walkabout   45
7. A note of urgency   51
8. Secret invasion   57
9. Morning pursuits   62
10. A portrait of evil   65
11. The professor's formula   72
12. Change of heart   79
13. Mangy men   86
14. A new awareness   91
15. Long distance connection   95
16. General changes   99
17. Stray   103
18. Our Australian agent   108
19. Connected   113
20. The major general goes whacko!   122
21. The community up-above   132
22. An oasis in the desert   139
23. Master Li's sanctuary – the library   147
24. Running Elk prepares   153
25. Dinner of ideas   157

26. PORTENTOUS VOICE   170

27. MACHINATIONS   175

28. ODE TO MIND SHARE   186

29. FAST FLIGHT   193

30. AT ALL COSTS   209

31. BLINDSIDED   218

32. ON THE RUN   229

33. A LONG DAY'S JOURNEY   236

34. A SENSE OF URGENCY   242

35. APPROACH WITH STEALTH   249

36. AN OLD FEELING   254

37. DEAD END   262

38. PERIWINKLE   271

39. DILEMMA   281

40. CHECK AND MATE   290

41. DESTINATION DESERT   300

42. THE MAJOR (GENERAL) AND HIS MINOR, PART II   307

Introduction

"Humanity evolved from creatures that adapted from two opposite worlds, one of light and one of darkness. We observe and quantify everything via its opposite: near and far, left and right, up and down, day and night... good and evil. While this pre-programmed fundamental thought process served primitive man for survival, this division of logical choices hinders our intellectual development and has become a detriment to our species, as it clouds our decisiveness." wls

"What is evil based on moral judgment? What about the morals of colonialists who enslaved millions of Africans? Or the morals of a church who tried to purge sin through the Inquisition? What were the morals of settlers who drove Native Americans from their land? What kind of high-minded morals did a government have when it purged its country of Jewish blood? What is evil in the face of such morality? When we apply moral judgment to what we do, we must first judge ourselves by the same standards as those we apply to others."

Master Li to the World Psychic Organization, Rollo, Kansas, October 2018.

CHAPTER ONE

A SEARCH BEGINS

THREE HUNDRED AND TWENTY KILOMETERS north of Adelaide (about 200 miles), not far from an area known as the Strzelecki Desert, a thin frail young man approached the front door of a nefarious establishment. The bright midday sun flared into his eyes and made him squint. Here, in this unlikely enclave of unthinkable mental squalor, he sought refuge from the heat and the type of person he could easily mold.

A young man of medium height, he casually sauntered into a dead-beat roadside bar. Bodily speaking, he was very different from the rotund crowd around him. This young man's clothes seemed to hang on his slim frame rather than fit it. With the door closed, he took a moment to brush the dust from his shirt while he adjusted his vision from the harsh dazzling sunlight to the dim interior light. In this part of the country, the oppressive heat drove many a man to drink, as the young man hoped it would. His sharp eyes quickly scanned the room.

Ice cold beer numbed the pangs of the hot desert air that pulled the saliva from the mouth like some great infinite sponge, which sopped up the last fragment of moisture and left one's mouth truly parched. Yet, the beckoning call of that ancient brew did not interest this pale shadow of a man, though he welcomed a few cold gulps of the golden liquid. He knew that alcohol dulled the senses and made his subjects susceptible to suggestion. With fecundatory purpose in mind, he sought men, big men, strong men, able bodied men; the kind of men who had no conscience and could help him carry out a devious plan.

He wanted to create an army of mercenaries, ruthless killers, men without hearts, men who shared his lack-of-regard for human life with the same voracity that he possessed. He needed expendable men, the kind no one

1

would miss, men without families, men without ties, corruptible men who would act in outrageous ways. He knew he could mold them with his expert tutelage to do his bidding.

Only a few days ago, he encountered a knowledgeable man who inspired him to plan a most despicable deed. After that meeting, he planned to bring about one of the worst catastrophes in the history of the modern world. In order to accomplish this goal, he needed to surround himself with strong, tough, and dangerous men to help him carry out his idea. The deserts of Australia breed tough individuals. What better place to start than a seedy bar with a notorious reputation, one he gleaned from the mind of the local constable – ten arrests for fighting just last week, his kind of place.

He paused to survey the scene of derelicts and degenerates before he pressed his way through the standing-room-only crowd. He did not wish to start a fight today, merely to observe and cut from this herd of cattle the prime beef.

"'scuse me, mate," his gravelly voice uttered as he pushed further into the crowded, smoke-filled room past patrons who had packed in around the bar. These beer-swallowing thugs sat mostly absorbed watching two rival teams of an Australian football game on television. Occasionally, they cried out together as a group when a "footy" either scored a goal or came close to one.

"… with a score of three goals and two behinds to six goals and four behinds, the Sydney Trawlers lead…" the announcer's voice droned on, barely heard above the noise inside the pub.

The young man pressed his way toward the back. At first glance, this frail creature, hardly a vision of masculinity with his thin arms, crooked nose, ugly gaunt face, and a few scraggy strips of hair dangling off his pointed chin, appeared more as a vagrant than a resident. One might describe his age as possibly forty years, judging from the dark circles under his eyes, sun-bleached blonde hair, and the strained expression on his face, though in actual years, he had just turned twenty.

The bar felt only a few degrees cooler than the outside air, with one window conditioner working hard above the bar and several slow-moving ceiling fans failing to spread its lone cool breeze about the crowded space. The pungent odor of perspiration was matched only by heavy plumes of cigarette smoke that hung in the air like a fog bank and tended to drift from one area to another. Few customers noticed or objected to the air quality as the vast majority generally smoked.

The scrawny young man worked his way through the crowd to the back of the room where some men gathered around a billiards game, while they watched the football match on another screen. No one noticed the pale youth take a seat across from the pool table. He watched the men and not the television. He carefully appraised their physical prowess and their mental capacity, or lack thereof, as he thoroughly probed each man's actions with a discerning eye.

"Beer," he called to the middle-aged buxom waitress who wore too much eye make-up.

She passed by the pool table with a tray full of empty bottles and used glasses while she hurried toward the bar with her orders.

"Are ya daft?" she shot back and started to add something flippant when the words caught in her throat.

She turned and stood still as she faced the young man. She obediently nodded and silently acknowledged his request. She set her tray down and headed directly to the bar for his beer while she ignored the other patron's requests.

"What's on?" the slender young man asked a large chap sitting nearby.

"Football!" the man growled out of the side of his mouth. When he glanced over and saw the disheveled youth, the very appearance of the lad nauseated him. "Whadya think we're doin?" he snapped. "Now shut yer trap or I'll shut it for ya!"

The man took a sip of beer and started to choke. In fact, he could not stop choking. He sat up and gasped for air while he placed his hands around his throat.

"Can't breathe…" he gasped as he turned to the thin young man who stared dispassionately at him.

The man's hands began to squeeze tighter around his throat as his face turned from dull red to blue. No one seemed to notice the man's dilemma. The other men stayed focused on the game. Eventually, his hands fell to his side as he slumped down in his chair.

The waitress walked up with a large glass of cold draft beer and set it down in front of the strange young man.

"Go away," he told her.

The woman picked up her tray, turned around, and headed back to the bar. She never said a word in reply or collected a cent for the beer. The young man glanced around and took in the scene. He saw men of varying size, description, and evaluated each one for his particular talents: that one for lifting, that one for shooting, that one for digging, and so on. He knew for certain that all of the men had to be fighters. One by one, he either approved or rejected them until he came upon a rather large man.

The hefty specimen was at least forty years of age he guessed, with a large square head, thick neck, broad shoulders, and big muscular arms that had bulging biceps. He wore a thin t-shirt that made his pectoral muscles on his chest bulge out as much as a woman's, though flat and chiseled. The man also had firm muscular legs, obviously the body of a weight lifter or body builder. His wide stance and closely cropped head stood a foot taller than the rest of the men around him, a titan amongst the rabble.

"Just the sort of man I need to lead a group in to battle," the slender young man thought. It only took him a moment to scan his mind. "Yes… he'll do."

He rose and walked over to the brutish fellow who gazed up at the television screen. The big man focused on the game while he waited to take his turn at the pool table. The skinny pale man stood next to him. He examined the large man closely, his face, his frame, the way he moved, and particularly his skull. The skinny man looked hard at the big man's head, as if his eyes could pierce the thick outer covering and examine the inner workings of the man's private thoughts.

The big man roared at the screen when his team scored. He waved his large, thick, sausage-like fingers in the air, clenched them in a fist, and vigorously pumped his hefty muscular arm up and down. No man in the bar had this man's impressive size or stature. The big man took in a huge gulp of beer, nearly half the glass in one swallow.

"Your turn, Girard," another man said to the big man.

Girard took his pool stick, brushed past the haggard young man as if he did not see him, and applied blue chalk to the end of his cue before he attempted his next shot.

"I'd go for the seven," the skinny young man said. He walked up to the edge of the pool table and into the light that shined down from the overhead lamp.

"What the hell?" Girard wondered. He reacted to the fact he had not seen the kid until just this second. "Who the bloody hell are you?"

"How long have you been out of prison, Girard?" the brazen youth asked. "Only a month and no work yet? Where did you get the money to buy beer and play pool? Are you hustlin' the locals or runnin' drug scams?"

Girard flipped the cue around in his hand like an expert at martial arts and held the thick end out like a weapon. His bicep muscles bulged and flexed as he walked around the table. His face wore a grizzled expression. Yet, the young man did not flinch or move.

"Give me one good reason why I shouldn't take this stick and smash your face with it?" the big man said.

"You can't," the smaller skinny man replied. "Try it. You'll fail."

Girard grinned at the prospect. He did not wish to violate his parole by starting a fight in the bar. He only wanted to get out of the heat and watch the playoff games like the rest of Australia. Earlier in the day, he visited an old girl friend and lifted some money from her purse while she took a shower after they had sex. Perhaps she reported it stolen. However, this arrogant pup represented no threat to him. He glanced around, still reluctant to start a fight. Yet he had a reputation of toughness to maintain. He bared his teeth to this punk, not in a smile, but as a grimace. This scrawny kid really pissed him off. He wanted to put the queer out of his sarcastic misery.

"Oh, what the hell," he said as he raised his hand, "it'll be worth it," he thought when he considered spending the night in the local jail. He only hoped his parole officer would understand why he smashed the punk's face in and cut him a break on early release.

Yet as he approached the defiant young man, about to bring the cue down on his head, his hand and arm stopped in the air, rigid and stiff. He could not lower the cue. As hard as he tried, he could not move his right arm, which he had raised high over his head. Sweat broke out on his face as he strained to move. He seemed frozen on the spot. He tried to rotate his head, yet it was just as stuck as if his blood had congealed. His eyes, the only thing he could move, darted to look nervously around the room. No one seemed to notice them. He thought it strange that he should have his arm up with the cue stick threateningly held over the smug skinny young man's head and no one even glanced their way.

"What's goin' on?" he whispered, almost afraid to speak. "What did you do to me?" the large man asked as he suddenly felt completely helpless by this strange power.

The young man moved closer and ran his long slender fingers along Girard's large muscular arm. The cold clammy touch of the young man's hand gave Girard the creeps.

"The body is so powerful," the kid muttered, "but the mind so weak."

The young man turned his back on Girard and walked over to his seat. He calmly took a sip of beer and looked at Girard with disdain.

"I told you," the young man said, half-smiling. "You can't harm me. It's impossible. I can control you and affect your memory, too." The young man stared at Girard with an expression that sent chills of fear cascading down the large man's spine. "Go ahead… move your arm… now," the kid said.

All at once, Girard found he could move his arm. He lowered the cue stick and gazed at his hand as if it were bewitched. He wondered why his friend did not react to his predicament and come to his aid. He leaned over and waved his hand in front of his friend's face. The man only stared up at the TV.

"Why don't they see me?" Girard asked as he turned to the curious young man. "Are you some kind of magician?"

"No," the scraggy kid told him and took another sip of beer. "I'm no

5

magician. But I intend to be the deliverer of their wretched lives," he said with such a sinister voice that Girard could not scoff at him.

"Are you some sort of prophet?" Girard wondered, skeptical. "I thought you guys were supposed to be holy and good. Somehow, you don't strike me as the pious type," Girard observed while he looked the young man up and down.

"Some will think I'm a god... the gullible ones, Girard," the young man said as he pointed around them, "the ones you and I manipulate. Once they see a demonstration of my power, we can convince 'em of anythin'."

"You know my name," Girard said. He put down the pool cue and moved closer. "I don't know yours."

"Cyrus," the young man said with a calm voice as he gestured to the chair across from him. "Cyrus Keaty."

"I gotta tell ya – Cyrus, is it? – that was some trick you just pulled. No man has ever bested me in a fight. When I say no man..." Girard started to say when Cyrus interrupted him.

"I know everythin' about you from your mind, Girard," Cyrus told him. He looked down his nose at Girard in a condescending way. "I know your personal history, 'specially your stint in the military with the friendly fire incident that landed you in prison. Your trainin' from there will come in handy. I also know about the women you've dated, your friends, family, and why you never married. I even know your style of lovemakin' with your girlfriends, which dey regard as rough, but a style I admire. I suppose not many women consider rape as love makin'," Cyrus added with a sneer. "You go through alotta girlfriends, probably why you've moved so often."

Girard gritted his teeth as he felt forced to swallow the young man's insults.

"I also know about the time you spent in prison," Cyrus continued, "and how once inside, you nearly killed a man with your bare hands, and why you felt justified... feelin' guilty about it and all. I know your lawyer misrepresented you at your trial. I happen to agree with your opinion of him."

"Whoa! Just a minute," Girard spoke up. "How the hell did you..."

"I told you," Cyrus once more interrupted as he sipped his beer. "I read your mind. Oh, and by the way, I also know that if you try what you are thinkin', you'll end up with dat stiletto from your boot stuck in your throat," he added as he drank his beer.

Girard stared at the lanky young man. Fresh nervous sweat broke out on his forehead and his stomach grew queasy. This punky kid completely unnerved him.

"This little dude either read my mind or he's a damn good guesser," he thought.

"I'm more than a good guesser…" Cyrus said as he put down the beer. "I just planted my comments in your head while I drank the beer, didn't you notice? I'm not speakin' to you… I'm linked with your thoughts… dumbass!"

Girard's eyes focused on Cyrus' mouth. He looked back up at the smug expression on the kid's face. He thought he'd better test that theory. He closed his eyes, thought about something, and then opened them.

"Go ahead, genius…" Girard started to say, when Cyrus cut him off.

"… of course I can arrange for you to meet her," Cyrus completed his thought. "We can discuss the model later. Actually, she doesn't live very far from here – about 100 clicks south, a suburb of Adelaide. I've never had any trouble breakin' into a buildin'. I'll arrange it so you can take her as much as you want. First, I have a business proposition. You need a job. I need a man of your stature. The job I have in mind will pay you better than any you've ever had," Cyrus told the big man.

"I don't' like the sound of that," Girard said. "Every time I ever heard that kind of talk, it meant I had to do somethin' illegal," he said in a low voice.

"Don't worry," Cyrus told him, "you won't get caught… this time."

"I've heard that promise, too," Girard replied.

Cyrus slammed his fist down on the table with such ferocity that it belied the smaller man's size. Its impact seemed to shake the entire room and the sound echoed as if they sat inside a deep canyon. Girard noticed that he was the only one in the room that reacted to the violent loud sound. Cyrus stared right into Girard's eyes and the big man squirmed as if Cyrus could see right through him, those steely gray eyes burned into his skull. The muscular felon uneasily leaned back in his seat to put some distance between them. Never had such an insignificant little man made him feel so deficient.

"Trust me when I say," Cyrus firmly told him, "that I can deliver anythin' and everythin'. I mean what I say… you've never met the likes of me," he spoke with ominous tones. "I have a project in mind, Girard. To complete this project, I need a small army of men… two hundred will do," he informed him. "I want men willin' to do anythin' I tell them. Some will do it for money, some for liquor or women. I'll do whatever it takes to entice them or intimidate them. You, my big friend, will lead and whip them into shape."

"How will you keep that many in line unless you can afford to buy them?" Girard asked.

"Don't worry, I can pay 'em," Cyrus told him, "and give 'em anythin' they want – cash, gold, you name it. But that won't be enough to keep 'em loyal to our cause. We must inspire 'em… you and I," he told the big man.

7

"You will be my second in command, in charge of deese men like a drill sergeant – a job, I believe, for which you're well suited. We will go west of here and live in the desert. I don't want to rouse any suspicion from any local authorities. I'll arrange for the support gear – trucks, fuel, food, water, tents, cots, and weapons – all the equipment we need to run a small army. I just need your help as my second. I'll reward you with anythin' you want. You name it," he promised. "Whadda ya want? A new truck, money, women? I'll give ya anythin'. Only you must show absolute loyalty and respect to me and do everythin' I order without question, even if it means *murder*," he said and emphasized the last word.

Girard did not reply this time. The man across from him might appear slight to most men, however everything that happened so far convinced him that Cyrus had some sort of power. He trusted Cyrus would deliver on his promise. He glanced over at the window. After the government released him from prison, he had no girlfriend, no job, and no prospects. He even contemplated suicide a few days ago. This man offered him a new life and power. What did he have to lose? After what he just witnessed, he believed that Cyrus could do anything.

"What will you have me do... prophet," the big man said with conviction.

Cyrus leaned back in his wooden chair, satisfied with Girard's reply. In a sickly display of fulfillment, his smile revealed a set of crooked, yellow-stained teeth. He nodded with his head to Girard's left.

"You can start by gettin' rid of him," Cyrus indicated.

Girard glanced over and for the first time saw a dead man sitting next to him. He glanced back at Cyrus and nodded. Then his face took on a hardened expression of determination and defiance.

"I want that woman today, not tomorrow, I want her in my bed tonight," he demanded, "and she must be willin' to do anythin' I say!"

"Not a problem, she's yours," Cyrus told him. "But havin' a woman is only the start, Girard," he said. "I promise you, much more will follow." He held out his slender white hand. "Deal?"

Girard took his hand, thinking at last, he had the chance to get back at Cyrus by crushing the kid's hand. Instead, Cyrus applied so much force to Girard's hand that he nearly broke the large man's bones. Girard's expression of confidence quickly changed to pain.

"Never forget who I am," Cyrus said as he squeezed the much larger hand while he stared Girard in the eyes. "I got great power and I'm not afraid to use it on anyone, includin' you." Cyrus let go of his hand.

"Yes... sir," Girard replied. He winced from the vice-like grip. Girard flexed his hand as he thought it was broken.

"That's more like it," Cyrus said with a sneer, "that's what I want to hear. Now, where do you suggest we find these men?"

Girard changed his attention from his hand to Cyrus.

"The best place to start is the parole board. Men fresh out of prison are the most desperate. We can find plenty of those," he said while he also thought, "I'm beginnin' to like this kid."

"I like your style, too," Cyrus sneered back.

Chapter Two

Bad news travels fast

A COLD WIND HOWLED ACROSS the fading darkness of the Kansas prairie. The advent of February's start brought terrible snow storms whose icy winds swept down the flat Kansas plain from Canada and covered the countryside with white oblivion.

A lone figure – dressed only in shorts, a t-shirt, and walking bare-footed in sandals – gradually made his way up Main Street devoid of winter's chill. Inside the protective environmental shield that kept the weather temperate and uniform, Chou's projection of energy made each day beneath its cover ideal – puffy white clouds slowly moved across an azure blue sky while a blazing sun disc shone light down on its residents at a proper angle as if it blazed 142 million kilometers (93 million miles) away in space. The light from the sun disc provided the proper amount and spectrum of energy needed for photosynthesis, yet would not harm a person's retina. The shield was one of Chou's first constructs from the fusor. Near the base of the shield's periphery, a person inside Rollo could look through the barrier and see the weather beyond its confines. As was the case today, it was the difference between balmy and downright frigid.

Zhiwei had confidence in his bearing and complete peace of mind in relation to his surroundings. As Rollo's head of security, winter was the least problem on his mind. No weather system could affect the little town. Likewise, no one from the outside could see Rollo or force their way in. In that regard, neither an invasion from the American military, nor some stray motorist concerned Zhiwei in any fashion. He had other considerations on his mind today as he walked from his office toward the massive five-story structure that towered over Main Street's opposite end. He looked up at the gargantuan manor house as he walked in that direction.

"What does Chou always say when he must see Master Li or attend a board meeting?" Zhiwei thought as he casually strolled along on the sidewalk that bordered the wide boulevard of Main Street. "Oh yes… any excuse to go the manor house is a good one," he thought and smiled until he glanced down at the black card in his hand. "I believe you had a better mission in mind, Chou, than the one I must make today."

Inside the great edifice, built as the headquarters for the World Psychic Organization, silence reigned. The beveled edges of the east-facing, cathedral-like, morning room's windows usually bent the sun's morning light and its rays burst into colors, an awe-inspiring sight illuminated the room – art versus practicality. The German philosopher Goethe once referred to architecture as "frozen music." The casual observer might say that the morning room in the manor house demonstrated the complexity of a symphony with the simplicity of a sonata, both fluid and expressive.

The white vaulted ceiling rose some 17 meters (over 50 feet) over the black and white marble parquet floor. Large, ornate, black wrought-iron support beams – inserted for their artistic decoration only – stretched upward to meet descending arches at various locations. Giant ferns, that did not resemble any current species, hung down from planters suspended in these arches. Tall massive trees – whose roots thrust down beneath the floor into special subterranean containers – emerged from great holes in several places, each surrounded by beds of different flowering plants. At the north end of the room stood a large open fireplace framed by a beautifully-carved pale marble façade. The room had sixteen, round, polished, black and white speckled, granite-topped tables supported with black wrought-iron legs. Each table had matching chairs that had a thick dark green seat, back, and arm cushions. The tables were scattered in no particular pattern about the large open space.

A centrally located glass tunnel connected the room to the north greenhouse. Butterflies and hummingbirds often flew up the open corridor to investigate the morning room's open blooms, their rapidly flicked tongues destined for an exotic flower's rich nectar.

The manor house's two permanent residents usually took their breakfast here while they reviewed reports that arrived daily from the World Psychic Organization members located all over the world. Master Li held out his black card, which he expanded to a larger 25 cm wide by 50 cm length (approx. ten by twenty inches) rectangular size to accommodate printed and visual reports compiled from agent's submissions. The expandable electronic object had the light weight and feel of thin yet stiff poster board.

"Here's the report from our sixteen-year-old Greek agent. Milo's guardians allowed him to drive a car on his own two days ago," Master Li mentioned. "He

11

thought it amusing and slightly ironic that he had to obtain their permission to drive a car, yet also had to thwart terrorists with stealthy precision."

"Hmm?" Han responded, not bothering to look up.

"Some of those inlets harbor the worst smugglers in the Mediterranean. On Kiran's advice and guidance, he built a monitoring station on the hill above the house," Li told Han.

"That's nice," Han said as he concentrated on his paper.

"Milo states that a Lebanese diplomat secretly met with the Syrian military council for two hours yesterday," Li linked. "Our Israeli agent, Sarah Reitmann, received a tip during her visit to the Knesset and asked if Milo could infiltrate the meeting. He's very good with disguises..." he added. "Tahir flew to Greece from Cairo, picked up Milo, and dropped him off for some WPO eavesdropping. Moments after that meeting, the terrorist organization Tannar claimed responsibility for rocket attacks into Hatay, Turkey."

"Israel probably knows more about the rest of the world than it knows about itself," Han muttered.

He finally took interest in Master Li's report. He lowered his electronic thin tablet and placed it on the table. When he did, the screen turned black and automatically shrunk back to credit card size.

"Do you think the Lebanese sought permission for a separatist attack?" Han questioned. "Did Milo say if the attack originated on the Syrian side or from somewhere in Turkey?" he asked Li for additional details.

Master Li did not lower his expanded card. Instead, he continued to listen as their youthful Greek agent, unable to halt the attack without direct infiltration of the military, described the bloody aftermath and how he helped with the wounded. Li admired Milo's courage to enter the battlefield and the progress the youth made with his new Greek guardians. He noted that Tahir, concerned about Milo's safety, flew him back to Greece shortly after the attack and insisted that Milo file his report from the safety of his home last night.

"Tahir looks out for Milo like an older brother... they get along well," Han commented. "I am so pleased with that young man's progress."

"Milo wants us to visit soon. He says his stepfather is a good fisherman, his stepmother is a great cook, and we have an open invitation to dinner," Li told him, absorbed in the report.

Han smiled, shook his head, and picked up his card, which instantly resumed its expanded size of 25 cm across by 50 cm in length, its flow of information resumed where he left off.

"I see in this morning's Tyler Foundation report from Tahir's Middle East division that our programs in Africa have reduced starvation by 37%," Han informed Li.

"Seel write those reports?" Li questioned.

"Hmm," Han chimed in. "Poverty levels have dropped, too," he added. "Tahir placed sixteen of those commercially available fuel cell boxes in Mali last month." Han paused and looked around the spacious room. He had the same problem Cecilia had when Michael first proposed the grandiose idea of building such a large structure – excessive opulence. "I feel so guilty… It's just that our level of comfort sometimes make me…"

"Yes?" Li wondered and looked around his paper.

"We have all this stuff… it's a shame we can't do more," Han said with some frustration in his voice.

"Remember that all this stuff, as you call it, cost us nothing… zero… the fusor created everything for no cost… not even the energy to run the device. If we tried to share the fusor with them, you know what they'd do with it," Li pointed out.

"Create the most lethal weapons… make human clones… manufacture money or illicit drugs…" Han linked as he recalled the logic of this old argument. "I know the project also helped our locals with increased discipline and gave them a sense of accomplishment. They feel bound to this place, which is what we've wanted from the start…"

Master Li reached over the table and touched his friend's hand.

"I understand how after reading that report you'd feel frustration, guilt, even remorse over our lifestyle compared with others…" Li linked all the sincerity he could muster. "We must do things their way… the hard headed human way. That is why we have the foundation, to alleviate ignorance, poverty, disease, and malnutrition," he stated and leaned back. "The foundation pumps billions of dollars toward this effort every month. Unfortunately, the moment we have success in one area, greedy fools rush in and break things down… declare war… run off with funds… impose martial law… it's one thing to fight the intangible. It's far more difficult to fight greed, lust, and ignorance. We can't impose a solution on them. We can't stand over humanity with a stick in our hands and demand they behave. You and I both know life on planet Earth doesn't work like that."

"I believe they call that a dictatorship," Han commented and sighed. "No matter how hard we try, humans seem to muck up our best efforts to help them," he linked. "But should we just give up and throw in the towel?" he wondered.

Master Li said nothing in return. Han assumed that Li thought his question redundant. They had this debate many times in the last two and a half years. Seeing that Li largely ignored his question, Han gave up and used the tongs on the nearby platter to retrieve a fresh piece of Running Elk's delicious pastry. He placed one on each man's plate. He drooled over the prospect of sinking his teeth into the sweet poppy seed delight.

"With Running Elk back in the kitchen, no one will starve in this house," Han thought as he focused on the tender poppy-seed-filled morsel. "Still, I'll contact Tahir today and speak to him about ramping up our efforts in Africa and other needy places."

"He and Seel know the exact amount of money needed to flow into an area without making an imbalance," Li reminded. "Let Steven Harper, Sir Charles, Tahir, and General Liong worry about the foundation's disbursement. You, my learned friend, are here for your specialty – strategy."

"Yes, Master Li," Han quietly replied as he reviewed the financial news. "I will make suggestions…"

"…and they will be appreciated, Han," Li linked and finished his thought. "How is the poppy seed pastry?"

"I'm about to find out," Han linked back with a slight smile of anticipation.

Hours before anyone else rose from their beds, Running Elk started her daily ritual of baking. Although she could have used Chou's fusor to create any food substance known to man, she only used the device to create basic ingredients: flour, sugar, yeast, eggs, butter, and so on… and not just any flour or sugar, but usually hearty strains based on samples taken from every part of the globe. Ever since she returned from Paris, she preferred to make her own preparations. She had hundreds of recipes regarding varieties of freshly baked goods that included pastry and decorative loaves, which she proudly displayed every morning on their table.

When Master Li and Han promptly descended the main staircase at 0700 hours, the smell of fresh baking met the happy men on their way to the morning room. Running Elk usually stood at the bottom of the stairs to greet Master Li and Han.

"Good morning, sirs," she said and respectfully bowed.

"Good morning, Running Elk," they chimed in return.

"Today's breakfast originates from the eastern Mediterranean," she informed them. "I have khubuz (pita bread), labneh (cream cheese), dried, cured, and sliced leg of lamb, fresh garlic cloves, fresh olives, olive oil, sea salt, dried smoked fish, tahini, dates, fresh figs, a type of granola served with goat cream, spun honey, and I made some poppy seed pastry… just for you, Han," she said and smiled, although she glanced over at Master Li before she walked to the kitchen.

Master Li usually added some private thought of thanks to her as the two men headed up the hall to the morning room. Han never knew exactly what transpired between them, although he occasionally noticed Running Elk in a very good mood after she and Master Li had their exchange.

The two men, having reviewed some of the daily reports, set down their "electronic papers" which collapsed back into small black cards while they filled their plates from this morning's choices. A decorative tea cozy covered a nearby pot of green tea. Master Li removed the cover with his mind. The pot lifted into the air and poured an equal amount of the pale brown liquid into porcelain cups.

After the two men nibbled on a bite or two of this and that, Master Li expanded his card and resumed the reports. Any food they did not consume, Running Elk recycled through the fusor.

"Tahir informs me that he and Seel have made it official," Li mentioned. "She is now a Level IV psychic. He monitored the transition locally while I sort of looked over his shoulder from a distance."

"A powerful new member," Han muttered as he looked over the ripe figs. "After that bombing caper with the pirates, I should have known that…"

"…she was one of us?" Li finished.

"No, that you would keep the knowledge of her psychic powers hidden until Tahir became involved with that gulf business and the American bombs at sea," Han commented as he split open the fig. "Thank goodness you converted her at the last minute and she helped him or else…"

"Tahir was also pleased with the flyer Villi provided," Li cut him off. "It came in handy when they tricked the pirates," Li informed Han. "First time Villi made one that could fly and go under water."

"Villi is versatile… I have to give him that," Han muttered as he dabbed his mouth with a napkin and then expanded his card.

Li touched a corner and moved onto the next report. Only he could hear the talking head of Sarah Reitmann, their Israeli agent, as she faced him and spoke. She discussed the Turkey business and made the same speculations Han made only moments ago. He smiled when he thought how well the new members worked together.

With his left hand, Han picked over the dried and cured fish fillets, the same type used in the desert by the Bedouin, while he held his card in his right. The smoky aroma from the fish made his mouth water.

"Pastry bread… fruit… hearts of palm… fish…" Han muttered with delight as he looked over the platter, "and goblets of fresh squeezed purple grapes along with our usual pot of green tea… bless the maker…"

"I wouldn't call her the maker…"

Han laughed at Li's reference to Running Elk.

"General Liong will be in Shanghai this week," Li mentioned as he watched the general's report. "One never knows who will join our ranks next," he commented.

"What's that?" Han said, distracted by the food choices.

"Madam Liong sends you her greetings," Li continued.

"Hmm," Han hummed agreement as he returned to his paper and focused on operational reports, such as the one Seel submitted on hunger and poverty, two prime aspects of human difficulties that the WPO and the Tyler Foundation pledged to eradicate.

Master Li switched to the next member: Kiran Meshwari in India.

"Kiran has such a lovely face, don't you think?" Li thought as he gazed at the smiling young woman. "The Indian legislature is contemplating funds to build nuclear submarines… Pakistan agents discovered this and filed a protest with the United Nations… I thought after the two nations teetered on the brink of nuclear war in 2015, the Indians wanted peaceful solutions to things…" he sighed. "She says she is trying to discourage their development, but states the same problem with Milo… lack of time or ability to infiltrate the military hierarchy."

Her colorful and three-dimensional image jumped out from the flat surface. She told Li how she looked forward to another Rollo visit after her trip last fall. She loved her new apartment in New Delhi. While her family soon forgot about her after her disappearance, she quietly continued to provide for them, thanks to funds she received via the WPO. At some future point in time, she intended to open a branch of the Tyler Foundation in the capital city. She regularly reported to Zhiwei's team on the Indian government and often left special messages for Chou, whose scientific jargon in mathematics and physics which she expressed even baffled the great Master Li, who barely understood them. The two advanced technologists often exchanged ideas remotely. Thanks to Kiran, Chou worked out how to launch WPO satellites into space, a project he planned to start once he built the catapult devices that Kiran designed.

Li changed the paper to reflect other members. The Russia report followed as Leni expressed concern over Chinese troop movements and Russian military exercises in the Arctic Circle. She finished with a personal message for her brother. She couldn't wait for Villi to visit again. She complained she had no one to mind share and missed her brother. Master Li touched a different part of the screen and sent the lengthy familial portion of her message to Villi's station in the hanger complex. Villi could then send his own message to his sister via his black card. Although they could not mind share via a black card, Villi could keep in touch and even make a special visit as long as he arranged it in advance.

"Mind sharing has become an important outlet," Master Li sighed.

He could not indulge in that level of activity with the other psychics as his mind's imagination would overwhelm any psychic on a lower level and possibly harm them. He did not feel left out as he had other local mental pursuits, such as his interaction with the Native American community and Running Elk.

Han reviewed Steven Harper's the latest market outlooks, while Li watched Catherine Olsen explain Washington's next legislative agenda. Su Lin, the genius of Rollo's psychics in that she studied more subjects than any of them, often helped the east coast agent on points of law. Catherine had special notes for Su Lin and other alerts for Zhiwei regarding security changes at the White House, FBI, CIA, Homeland Security, Pentagon, and other government agencies.

Catherine's personal relationship with Steven Harper remained an open one. Both psychics dated "regular" people in their local jurisdictions. However, they maintained a cordial if not involved relationship when Catherine returned to her New York residence. As with other psychics, the open mind sharing bound their friendship together which was impossible to describe in "normal" terms.

Li sailed through a report from Jonathan Showalter. He and Maria Mueller shut down the terrorist network in Europe last year after the incident in Luxembourg. They spent the months that followed by rounding up most of the agents and transporting them back to their homelands. The couple virtually eliminated Europe as a source for their funding. However, Europe turned out to be a hot bed of spy activity as some families with close government and military ties actually made a living at it. Lately, Zhiwei directed the couple to infiltrate government spy organizations in Germany, France, Italy, Spain, Sweden, and Poland.

Master Li touched the corner and turned the page.

Meanwhile, inside good old Britannia, Sir Charles finally announced his retirement from the BANX board in England. In the power struggle that followed, he managed to maneuver his best friend James into an upper-level broker position. William decided to follow his father's footsteps. He dropped out of his partnership with the law firm and began work for the newly formed Tyler Foundation branch in London. The freshly converted William used downloads to brush up on corporate and business law while his father left a key position on the Tyler Board for his son. Charles quietly prepared William to take over the reins of the London branch once he set up the philanthropic corporate infrastructure.

Master Li saved the final overseas report from Camille in France. Li gazed affectionately at her image as she smiled and spoke candidly while she paced back and forth inside her office. She announced her plans to eventually run for public office, if no one within the WPO objected. No mortal man, or woman for that matter, could resist the charms of the angelic French industrialist. Even the great Master Li was not immune to her beguiling feminine beauty or her incredible wit. He patiently took his time while Camille discussed her large corporation's interaction with the French government and her place within the European Union. When she finished her report, his card shrunk in size and he put it in his pocket.

"How refreshing," Li absently sighed and reached for his cup of tea.

"I wonder if Camille had that sort of reaction in mind," Han quipped.

Master Li glanced up as he sipped his tea. His face held no expression.

"I don't know what you mean," he blankly stated.

"Although," Han added, "I'm inclined to agree with your assessment. I find her... wonderful."

Master Li did not respond. He pursed his lips and blew across his teacup.

"What do you hear from Sir Charles?" Han wondered. "I understand he worked with Seel and Tahir to create the Middle East branch of the foundation."

"Last month's news..." Li reminded. "I believe he took Elizabeth and William with him at the time," he pointed out. "Tahir gave them a personal tour of the pyramids. He started to explain the mystery of the..." Li suddenly stopped his link. Both men turned in their seats. "Zhiwei is coming," he observed, "and by the state of his mind, I'd say with unpleasant news."

Han's paper suddenly flashed an alert story from Indonesia. A ferryboat sank with three hundred and eight-two people aboard – all drowned. He quickly changed the read out. He did not want that bad news to cloud his thinking. He would have Kiran investigate the incident, when she had time, and offer solutions so it would not happen in the future, if they could help it.

"I'm not in the mood for more bad news today," he thought as his card shrunk and he pocketed the device.

"We don't have a choice," Li retorted. "Our head of security is here and eager to share some rather gruesome details."

As Zhiwei crossed the piazza and headed for the massive front doors, they parted and opened for him. He charged into the foyer and headed to his left.

"Sorry to disturb your breakfast, gentlemen," Zhiwei linked as he crossed under the great rotunda and walked up the hall toward the morning room, "I have something important to report. It's urgent and cannot wait. I would have linked the situation over to you. However, I believe this required personal interaction."

"Come in, Zhiwei," Master Li linked and took a sip of tea. "We're just having a light breakfast this morning. Join us?" Li offered.

"No thanks," Zhiwei linked as he approached the room.

"What would you like to tell us?" Li asked.

When Zhiwei stated "situation," Han glanced expectantly at Li.

"Is this serious?" he wondered.

"I thought I should bring the matter directly to you," Zhiwei linked; the smell of Running Elk's delightful fresh pastry filled his nostrils as he entered the magnificent huge room. He paused before the two men seated at the table. "You call that feast a light breakfast?" he questioned and smiled. He knew the fusor could produce a ton of food in seconds and recycle it just as quickly. Like the other psychics, it galled him to think they could do so much for the world... if only the world would let them.

He shook his head as he looked at the two men, so content in their surroundings. Compared to his Rollo Security Station, always abuzz with youthful music and activity, this was a serene and peaceful setting, almost like a painting that depicted the perfection of tranquility. Zhiwei had Jennifer and Selena as his noisy yet efficient security assistants. His helpers finally graduated from Su Lin's school and considered their position in security as permanent. So they voted to remain in Rollo.

For the past two and a half years, ever since the psychics sought the local Native American's for help, these young women monitored coded security information from governments located around the world. Zhiwei had Zinian expand their living space inside the new security building where they remained on alert twenty-four hours a day. Zhiwei's Native American girlfriend tolerated the situation as she trusted her "life mate" and knew the two girls had more interest in Villi's crew than in Zhiwei.

He took in a deep breath and tried to ignore the distracting mound of food. Although his mouth watered for one of the tempting treats, he pressed on with his terrible news.

"I wish they'd invite me to breakfast some morning," he thought before he realized that he stood in the presence of the greatest psychic in the universe.

Master Li cleared his throat and gazed at his head of security.

"This house is open to every member of the WPO twenty-four hours a day, Zhiwei," Li linked to him. "However, if you wish a formal invitation... how would you like to come tomorrow morning for breakfast?" Li asked. "Bring your staff."

Han smiled expectantly and nodded his approval before he decided to pull his black card back out and resume his review of news and financial reports. He wanted Master Li to finish with his part before he took over as master strategist.

Zhiwei would have welcomed the opportunity to bring his staff for breakfast in a heartbeat. Only upon consideration, he recalled previous commitments.

"I'm working with my team on some new security protocols tomorrow," he said, the disappointment on his face obvious. "I'm afraid I'll have to take a rain check."

"Too bad," Li mentioned, "Running Elk will be disappointed, too. I believe she said she was making breakfast from Belgium tomorrow – variety of jams, jellies, yogurt, brioche, waffles, chocolate pastry, and hot cocoa… that sort of thing. Han?" Li said as he glanced over at Han. The strategist mumbled agreement with his head behind the expanded screen. "You must make it soon," Li said to Zhiwei.

"We will," Zhiwei replied. He drooled over the prospect of taking one of Running Elk's delicious fresh pastries, piled high on a large plate.

Han sensed Zhiwei's feelings. He put down his expanded card, reached over, took a clean plate, and with a pair of tongs, took the best three pastries off the tray for Zhiwei to take back to his station.

"Would you like coffee instead of tea?" Han offered. "We can make it to go?"

"Make three to go," Zhiwei requested, "with cream and sugar."

Han mentally called one of the house staff and made the suggestion. After working for the past six months in the mansion, their Comanche staff often interacted with Han and Li in this manner. They were not surprised when one of them "spoke" to their mind. Li gave any locals willing to help in the WPO headquarters building extra compensation. Han passed along an elaborate request. The to-go order list surprised Zhiwei. As soon as he sensed Han completed the order, Master Li addressed their head of security.

"You wanted to tell us something, Zhiwei?" he asked.

"Oh, yes," Zhiwei responded as if he suddenly woke up. "As you know, our office scans world communications for any trouble spots or disasters. However, we also monitor for any references made to Rollo, Kansas – just part of our routine security protocol. One of my assistants came across an internal police memo in Adelaide, Australia that struck us as very strange. The local police flagged a murder for special review. After an Australian's crime lab attempts to decipher the autopsy results proved too puzzling, they requested America's top FBI forensic team investigate."

"Go on," Han said as he lowered his expanded card. Any murder mystery intrigued the strategist.

"They called on the FBI because… well, someone found the body of a young woman who turned out to be an American tourist. She washed up on the shore during a high tide with her body relatively intact," Zhiwei explained.

"She'd been staying at a hotel on the beach, but about 150 kilometers from where they found her body. Some person, or persons, thoroughly molested and then brutally strangled the twenty-two-year-old Caucasian female. That is not the weird part. The autopsy revealed her actual cause of death as a crushed trachea…"

"That often happens in cases of strangulation," Han commented.

"True, but not internally crushed without any bruising found around her neck," Zhiwei added. "In fact, the young woman had no marks on any part of her body; no sign of a struggle, period, except for genital blunt trauma which reflected the possibility of molestation but was doubtful. DNA tests were also inconclusive since seawater diluted the samples. The autopsy results baffled the local coroner in Adelaide. He wondered how some form of inward pressure could crush the entire trachea without any external sign. He called in one of Australia's top forensic professionals. Her autopsy report stated, 'In addition to the possibility of sexual assault, a source of unknown origin, possibly due to a vacuum as in an applied interior force, caused the trachea cartilage to collapse, which resulted in suffocation.' Since they could not determine if an actual crime had been committed the Adelaide police were all set to ship the body back to America. However, after they read the report from one of Australia's top labs, the local police department requested a forensic specialist from America perform an additional autopsy on the body. The FBI requested they ship the body to San Francisco where they could complete the investigation prior to family notification. Those statistics alone would be interesting enough, right Han?"

"Mmm," Han hummed as he stared at Zhiwei.

"Here's the really weird part that caused the computer alert," Zhiwei pressed on. "It seems the young woman was on vacation and that her parents have substantial income from an insurance settlement. The police said her identification listed her present address in Oklahoma…"

"… and the weird part? Please, Zhiwei," Li interrupted.

Zhiwei glanced between the two men. "When the FBI performed a background search, they found an actual certificate that listed her birthplace as Rollo, Kansas, a town that does not exist. The moment an agent filed the report electronically, our computer system instantly alerted us to this anomaly. We thought we had destroyed all references to Rollo on every computer in the world, thanks to a special virus created by Chou that infected all known systems. We eliminated Rollo from local maps and any printed after 2016."

"What are you saying?" Li quickly responded. "You mean that the FBI has an open case that indicates a woman comes from a non-existent southwestern Kansas town?"

"Evidently, this one slipped through the cracks," Zhiwei replied. "The

FBI found an old hard copy of the actual birth certificate and literally put the information back into their data base."

"What action did you take, Zhiwei?" Han asked.

"Naturally, we immediately altered the data electronically, which changed her place of birth back to Oklahoma," Zhiwei told him. "I alerted the Washington branch. Catherine Olsen graciously changed her plans this morning. She slipped into the FBI headquarters and destroyed the hard copy file. Afterward, she left a bug for me."

"A bug?" Han asked. "A listening device?"

"No, Chou's bugs are far more sophisticated," Zhiwei explained. "We call them bugs because they can move around, slide between walls, and go places where a cockroach, for example, might go. His device will seek out and find their internal communication systems and send us all the frequencies within the building so that we can tap into the government's computers… should the need arise."

"Of course," Han replied sarcastically.

"After that, I sent Michael on an errand to check the other former residents and see if they had any files in any county courthouse. He found none," Zhiwei told them.

Master Li glanced over at Zhiwei's black card that had expanded and showed the autopsy results. The ghostly figure of a woman, laid out on a stainless steel slab, stared outward, her gaze permanently fixed. Her remains had been carefully sliced open and given a thorough review by the pathologist. With his mind, he closed Zhiwei's card and closed his eyes, that horrible image now forever stuck in his memory.

"That poor unfortunate young woman…" Li openly thought as he regarded her picture and Zhiwei's report. He scratched his chin, deep in thought.

Zhiwei's eyes expectantly traveled back and forth between them. He waited to see what Han would suggest. Unlike any other person in the group, Han used obscure facts, such as the ones he presented, to correlate connecting coincidences into theories, hence his informal title, Master Strategist.

Han's eyes unfocused for a moment as his mind swiftly sifted through the data and rapidly concluded the obvious to him.

"Seems clear to me…" Han uttered without hesitation.

"Mmm," Master Li nodded. "I'm forced to agree."

"What?" Zhiwei asked. Unlike Li, he could not penetrate Han's block.

"When all other possibilities are eliminated, whatever remains, however improbable, must be the truth…" Han paraphrased the old axiom of a fictional character.

"Sounds like a quote. Who said that?" Zhiwei wondered.

Han turned his head toward Zhiwei with a slight smile on his lips.

"I'm surprised, Zhiwei," Han said, "and you being in security – those are the words that Sir Arthur Conan Doyle put into the mouth of his best character, Sherlock Holmes. He said that after you analyze a problem and you've eliminated all the other possibilities, whatever is left, however odd or strange as it may seem, must be the truth."

"What truth did you uncover, Han?" Zhiwei wondered.

"Master Li? Do you wish to answer that?" Han asked as he addressed his friend.

"Do you believe your suspicions are correct?" Li wondered.

"With relative certainty," Han answered.

"I'll be forced to test your theory," Li countered.

The two men turned their attention toward Zhiwei. The head of security could not read their stone faces or penetrate their blocked minds.

"Would someone please let me in on this revelation?" Zhiwei requested.

"The answer is obvious, Zhiwei," Han pointed out. "Only one kind of person on the planet could have killed the girl in the manner you describe. Her origins are simply a matter of coincidence – fortunate for us they were flagged, unfortunate for the victim. She happened to be vacationing in the wrong place at the wrong time. The physical evidence here is more important than her link to Rollo. It points to a subject Master Li has feared since this operation started two and a half years ago."

"…and that is," Zhiwei wondered.

"We have a new potent rival… in Australia," Han stated and gave Li a brief glance. "Unfortunately, if he psychic – and it is highly likely that he is in this case – then he has murdered young women for sadistic pleasure, which means he developed his power independent of Galactic Central, not an easy feat for most psychics, and has gone rogue. He is the most dangerous kind of psychic – over confident and self-absorbed with power. For all we know, he is at least a level III," he speculated, "based on his ability to manipulate psychic energy to such a finite degree. I would assume that Master Li will…"

"We should leave for Australia at once," Zhiwei interrupted.

"Not exactly," Master Li finished. "We cannot rush over there without knowing who he or she is… however, with internal molestation involved, we can be certain the rogue is male. *I* will be paying Australia a special visit first to perform some reconnaissance before we send in a team. Zhiwei, I'd like you to see if Adelaide or nearby communities have reported any unusual cases of missing or molested strangled women over the past year. Also, notify our agents in India and China. Have them check local news and security outlets for any suspicious criminal activity. Particularly, have them look for trouble within their governments. If he is ambitious and seeks power, he may already have a network of spies working outside Australia."

"On the other hand," Han spoke up, "he may only be a pervert and have sexual assaults on his mind."

"We should take every precaution," Li told him. "Thank you for this information, Zhiwei. You were correct to bring this news in person."

"Yes, Master Li," Zhiwei said as he knew a dismissal when he heard it.

He neglected the three filled pastries on the plate with new orders that preoccupied his mind. Yet, as he marched toward the front door, a member of the house staff flagged the determined young man down and handed over a bundle that included a complete breakfast for three inside along with large coffees and an entire plate of fresh pastries. He thanked her and headed back to the security office with the large bundle.

"Are you really going alone to Australia?" Han linked to Li. "That's a long flight to take with Villi."

"Who said anything about flying," Li answered and tapped his temple with his finger.

Chapter Three

An unexpected voice

NEARLY NINE MONTHS AGO DURING the late spring of 2018, Master Li traveled around the globe and converted psychics in New York, England, Germany, Greece, Israel, Egypt, India, China, and Russia, which added new members to those previously converted in France and Mali. Unlike the Motambou's whom he only converted to Level II, Master Li wanted strong agents abroad to help form a better coalition within the World Psychic Organization. Therefore, he converted the new psychics to Level IV and brought them back to Rollo last summer where they trained with the first nine to increase their proficiency, especially in the manipulation of energy to form bubbles, feats psychics of lower levels could not perform.

2018 seemed a year of great significance. Psychics emerged from divergent places all over the planet, except two continents, South America and Australia. Han and Li ruled out Antarctica altogether, since it had no indigenous population. However, the lack of psychics in the other two major locations puzzled the Rollo analysts. They did not understand why psychics did not develop in these regions, despite their large population numbers.

Once the new alliance formed, the expanded membership took a great deal of Han and Master Li's attention. Instead of twelve psychics to monitor, Li had twenty-six, if you included Seel Owatu, Tahir's fiancée, who converted in the fall of 2018. While Camille and the Rollo psychics had two and a half years experience, most of the remainder Level IV psychics had six months or less. This presented a problem to Master Li when it came to requests for assistance in general events that required or called-for humanitarian interventions, such as assistance after an earthquake, a flood, a hurricane, or some other large scale disaster. The psychics' charter specifically stated a pledge to help humanity during times of extreme need. Eventually, Michael and the other Rollo psychics hoped that the world network could be onsite to any disaster in a matter of minutes.

However, something about this rogue business puzzled Master Li. He wondered if Han picked up on it. Within a few moments of Zhiwei's departure, Li recalled how his cousin in China covered his psychic signature so well that Li could not detect him, even when the villain was less than ten kilometers away. He did not sense his presence until the man launched his assault on Cecilia.

"Do you think this rogue has masked his signature?" Li questioned.

"I wondered about that," Han linked into his open train of thought. "Just as your cousin did…"

"…you were not there at the time," Li related to Han.

"I'm familiar with the story. Michael and Cecilia told me everything. Your cousin was a powerful psychic," Han linked as he recalled the details, "some said he could have been your rival. Perhaps that is why you reacted in the manner…"

"I don't wish to discuss that," Li cut him off. "I simply wanted to point out that this psychic may have learned the same trick or method… a way to mask his psychic signature."

"A natural form of blocking?" Han wondered.

"Perhaps," Li concurred.

"If one rogue psychic can mask his presence, perhaps others can, too," Han suggested. "We may find rogues in many places, even South America where you've said none exist."

"Possible," Li linked as he mulled the problem. "I've tried to remain vigilant…"

"Vigilant?" Han questioned when Li referred to his constant scans of the globe. "Excuse me, Master Li… I'm afraid we must be more than just vigilant. We should have a system that seeks out individuals from birth…"

"How do you propose we do that?" Li questioned.

"I don't know," Han replied, stumped. "Perhaps we could examine statistical data, farm it from each country…"

"No computer is that large or complex," Li countered.

"Not yet," Han commented as he glanced in the direction of Chou's lab. "Don't forget you have links to some of the greatest technical minds in the universe," he reminded, "and one of them lives right across the street."

Although Chou worked on many projects, building an all knowing intelligent computer was one of his last priorities. He had too many smaller projects in this new growing community with so many needs than to spend his precious time on creating the ultimate computer. Kiran was likewise as busy in India, a country with over a billion people and she was its only psychic, thus far.

"What if I redouble my effort?" Li told a skeptical Han.

Han shrugged his shoulders at Li's humorous film reference.

Having made the mistake of missing an emerging psychic, Li was determined to resolve his error in judgment. He decided that he would not delay any longer and take a mental trip to the land down under. After they finished their breakfast, Li pushed away from the table.

"Where are you off to," Han asked, "the land down under?" Master Li imperceptibly nodded. "I'm still trying to explore this new house," the younger man told him. "I believe I'll start with one of the museums. Good luck on your journey. Happy hunting... it's night there... no better time to enter a man's head than in his dream state, when he's susceptible."

"Then I best start right away," Li replied.

Master Li walked toward and then through the large double doors that parted before him and closed behind. He made his way up the long wide hallway, deep in thought, strolled past the library until he stood under the rotunda. He paused, tipped his head back and looked up at the nine golden stars around the center of the great dome overhead. They stood for the nine original members and reminded him of how far they come in such a short time.

"You were right to build this place, Michael," he thought. "Perhaps we shall need such a fortress before this ordeal with humanity is over..."

He continued onward up the grand staircase, past the first landing and took the right-side stairs toward the south wing. The stairs wound around to the second floor with his bedroom the first door on the left. The tall door to the massive suite dwarfed the little white-haired man who sauntered in. He headed directly to his prayer rug in front of the large east-facing window where he often meditated. He closed the heavy draperies to shut out the light.

In the darkness, Li recalled that the victim had vacationed in Adelaide.

"Australia..." he thought and began to reach out from his location as only a master psychic is able. "To the land down under..."

Beyond the plains of Kansas, over the Rocky Mountains and the wide deep Pacific Ocean, Master Li's mind flew over New Zealand and finally arrived in Australia. He searched for the town of Adelaide, nestled in behind Kangaroo Island and facing the Gulf of St. Vincent on the southern side of the great island continent. He hoped to find additional clues as to the origin of this rogue psychic.

"What's this?" he wondered as he halted his mind journey and alighted on a strong source. "This is unintended," he thought as he encountered a dilemma. "Could it be? We not only have a possible rogue, we have another aspect to this case, a fact I'm certain Han will find interesting… perhaps a potential problem." He took in a deep breath as he realized the scope and distances within Australia. "This continent is larger than I thought. My power obviously is not adequate to continually scan all of the activity on the planet. This monitoring system will need to change soon if we are to maintain a viable organization without the external corruption of emerging rogue psychics," he thought.

As much as Master Li tried, he could not locate any other psychic signature than the one closest to him. He took nearly three hours and carefully combed several major cities for any additional signs of psychic activity before he eventually came away with no other source. After Li had nearly exhausted all of his energy, he finally returned to his body in Rollo and absorbed some much needed psychic energy from their Native American friends.

Although the Comanche did not possess the needed portal for further psychic development, the Native tribe produced more psychic energy than practically any other source on the planet. Michael Tyler chose well when he picked Rollo as their base of operations. Once they began to form a community, the psychics understood the need to keep and maintain a close yet necessary relationship with the Native Americans, as if the two were meant for each other. The tribe understood this, too.

The psychics not only brought prosperity, but they expanded the tribe's level of awareness, and most certainly influenced their level of intellectual development. No person in Rollo was more acutely attuned to this symbiotic interaction than Master Li. Every time he returned from some journey abroad, he gratefully basked in the glow of their energy. Li never borrowed psychic energy from Running Elk. She was different. Like Star Wind and John, they possessed "rudimentary levels of being psychic" Li explained to her one day. She always knew when he left and when he returned. She could feel it.

Running Elk was in the kitchen reading a cook book, when all at once she put the book down and called to one of her kitchen staff.

"Master Li is back," Running Elk said.

The girl looked at her as if the woman was insane. How could she know that? What did she mean, "He is back?"

"Did you hear me?" Running Elk said and raised her voice. "Prepare tea!"

No one refused Running Elk. The girl jumped to fix a tray. Inwardly, the great matriarch smiled. But on the outside, she was all business as she pitched in to help make a proper "tea" for her lord and master… for that is how she saw him from the moment he cured the little girl, as she would always see him.

As Master Li recovered, he thought about his observations and tried to emulate the process Han used. However, his attempts to wade through that form of logic evaded the master psychic. With all of his power, he did not know everything.

"I'm no strategist," he finally thought and reached out to his friend. "Han! I need your help!" Li linked to him.

A startled Han nearly hit the ceiling of the museum room and flipped a fossil up in the air out of his hand when Master Li's strong link came through to his mind. Han was in quiet repose. He had only seen two of the manor house's ten museums since they moved last fall and hoped today presented some quality time for his chance to study. He stopped the object in midflight before it crashed on the floor and pulled it back into his hands.

"Want something?" Han asked as his shaking hand put the fossil down.

"May I call you away?" Li asked him.

"I suppose you wouldn't call me if it were not important," Han replied.

"Sorry for the abrupt link, Han," Li apologized. "I've contemplated this since I returned and cannot grasp its significance. I thought I'd let you know... I sensed only one source in Australia," Li informed him.

"So? What is wrong with finding one source? Does it bother you? Were you thorough enough? I thought you were going to spend the entire day there?" Han wondered.

"It took too much energy," Li explained.

"Can't this wait until we meet for dinner?" Han suggested.

"Sorry my friend," Li resumed, "I thought you would want to know right away. True, I could locate only one source of psychic power. But a new development has arisen and the evidence seems clear, yet I find it disturbing. I can only come to one conclusion – Australia *must* have two psychics," Li told him.

His words had an immediate chilling effect on Han's preoccupation.

"Are you certain?" Han put to him.

"The evidence points to that conclusion," Li suggested.

"This could be bad," Han responded as he rose from the display case. "We should meet now and call Running Elk for lunch. Have you identified the source?" Han asked.

"I have," Li told him. "I sent the new information to Zhiwei for a background check. He compiling a file as we speak. Perhaps he can give us a complete dossier on this man."

"I believe we should invite Zhiwei for lunch," Han suggested. "This case grows in complexity."

"Zhiwei said he was swamped with several things," Li stated. "I'll send for the information by courier. Meet me in the library."

Master Li cut his contact with Han and linked with Running Elk.

"I fixed a tea," she spoke to his mind.

"I appreciate that… Han may wish lunch instead," Li informed her.

"I'll have it ready for the morning room," she replied.

"Thanks," Li answered.

For a moment, the two held a brief joyous interaction, for Li did like her, perhaps he loved her… only he found it difficult to let go of his late wife. Their marriage lasted nearly fifty years. He broke contact with Running Elk when Zhiwei's thoughts requested a link.

"Yes?" he thought.

"I've sent Selena with the file," he told Li.

"That was fast," Li linked back.

"Why didn't you obtain the information from this psychic's mind?" Zhiwei wondered.

"I could not penetrate his thoughts," Li replied. "He's had some problems lately which produced very strong emotions that presented difficulty for me."

"I hope you find what you need in the file," Zhiwei told him.

Master Li paused to draw in additional energy as he parted the drapes. Sunlight streamed into the room. He pressed his fingers onto the sides of his nose as he gradually replenished his depleted psychic reserves. He reflected on the immensity of the planet and Han's fear that he could not penetrate every mind or sense every emergence of psychic activity. He sensed the latest group from Europe and the Middle East only after they began to evolve on their own. Perhaps he was already too late in other instances. He may have missed not one or two, but dozens of candidates. They could be isolated in mountain communities, lost in jungle villages, or could even be scattered within major metropolitan areas like New Delhi.

"Perhaps I'm too old…" he briefly considered.

After several minutes of contemplation, he rose and headed toward the library where he sensed Han's presence. Gradually, he made his way back to the main floor and opened the library's large double doors when he approached, only to discover that Han sat alone at the opposite end in near total darkness, reading the documentation that Zhiwei compiled and provided via Selena. The pretty young courier rushed the papers to the manor house via a hover-scooter.

"I see you have the file I requested," Li stated as he moved into the dark room.

"I met Selena at the front door…" Han muttered. He never took his eyes off the file.

Li could have crossed this room blindfolded. As in Han's case, Li had been in less than a third of the manor house rooms, although he knew this room quite well. He altered the original blue prints to create the current configuration. He quickly maneuvered around the center table and walked toward the large fireplace at the opposite end where Han sat.

"Found anything interesting?" he asked Han.

The other man pored over the documents. His eyes rapidly scanned each line and took in every detail. Just as Master Li walked up next to him, Han closed the file and looked up at Li.

"Could you..." Han asked and gestured toward the large fireplace.

Li understood his request. In an instant, a huge illusionary fire burst to life inside the giant hearth, its orange-yellow glow illuminated the two men. Li sat in one of the nine high backed chairs that faced the fire. It gave off no heat but provided Master Li a means to contemplate his thoughts while he stared at it.

"What did you find?" Li asked. He could have probed Han's mind for the answer. However, he learned to have patience when dealing with other psychics.

Han tossed the folder over to Li and stood up. He began to pace back and forth, deep in thought.

"Zhiwei was extremely thorough," Han began. "I believe I have a complete understanding of this... this Major General James Montgomery Pollack. Actually, I feel I know him well enough to make an informed opinion," he stated as he paced. "He is a product of traditional English schools and good manners. James Pollack is a man whose family had connections with other upper class, socially conscious, English families. They arranged his marriage, his promotion through the ranks, and his position in Australian society. Rest assured, the general didn't commit those atrocities on the beach," Han explained with confidence. "His history and profile do not meet the criteria for this crime. He isn't the type. Trust my judgment in this. I know that to be a fact without ever having met him."

Han paused a second and cleared his throat, which gave Li a chance to speak or link before he continued. Han always amazed Li when he performed this quick analysis, as he knew of no one who could take obscure facts and draw conclusions as quickly as Han could.

"If the general did not commit these atrocities, I need to find the person who is responsible," Li linked to him. "I could not penetrate the man's mind the first time I encountered the general. He's having some emotional difficulties at the present and worry ways heavily on his conscience. Perhaps I need to return to Adelaide and attempt a deeper probe of the general."

"You have a worse dilemma on your hands," Han continued. "You've got two psychics in Australia. One of them has an obvious psychic signature, and yet he is still relatively unknown to us. The other man knows something about stealth, is a powerful psychic, and possibly a serial killer!"

"I did not sense another psychic," Li said to him.

"Eluding master level psychics seems to be a growing specialty of rogues," Han said. He smiled and offered his hand to Master Li. "Perhaps we should discuss this over lunch. All of this running up and down corridors has made me hungry."

"I can't believe I missed him," an exasperated Li admitted.

"It's happened at last," Han said with a sense of smugness, as the two men turned toward the room's entry.

"What?" Li asked.

"Someone has outsmarted the great Master Li," Han grinned.

"The effect is only temporary, I can assure you," Li returned the jest.

"All is not lost. One thing you have going for you is surprise," Han put to Li. "I don't believe he is aware of us...at least, not yet. That can work to your advantage. If he is an egomaniac... if he believes he is unique as he looks around and does not sense another psychic, he might believe he is alone. Perhaps we can lure him into a false sense of security while we examine his aspirations for the future, if he has any..."

"We?" Li questioned.

Han laughed in response. "Let me rephrase," he linked as he continued to lead Master Li from the room, "while *you* examine his aspirations... and please share your information with me, of course."

Li privately called his special chef and informed her that, as they had discussed, they would have lunch in the morning room. She had it ready for them.

"That was fast," he linked to her.

"In some things I am very fast," she thought back to him.

Running Elk met the two men in the hall outside the library and informed them lunch would arrive soon. When they walked into the great room, they noticed that she changed their table's location closer to the fireplace. Beyond the powerful force field that protected Rollo, they could see snow falling on the Kansas plain in the distance. With a thought, a fire sprang into the room's hearth as the men sat and waited for their lunch.

Han brought the file from the library, as Master Li had not yet read the case.

"You should read up on this man before lunch," he suggested.

"I don't want to read that," Li nodded toward the folder. "You have a way of seeing between the lines of the written page. I know full well that you've created a scenario in your mind. Tell me what you know, Han, about this James Montgomery Pollack."

CHAPTER FOUR

THE MAJOR (GENERAL) AND HIS MINOR, PART 1

As best he could interpret from Zhiwei's document, which was considerable, Han told Master Li the story of the general and his bride.

"His story begins in Australia…

Major General James Montgomery Pollack was born July 14, 1953 in Adelaide, Australia, eight years after World War II ended. Early in his life, his family sent the young lad to England for a proper education. The Pollack family enrolled James into the Duke of York School, a preparatory academy for boys with over two and a half centuries of tradition. James studied classic Greek and Latin along with mathematics, archaeology, history, economics, French, philosophy, music, and literature. During breaks from school, he lived at his grandfather's estate in the English countryside. Lord Pollack introduced young James to many famous political and military leaders that visited during summers in the late 1950's and early 60's. His grandfather instructed James in lessons of shooting, hunting, and strategy. By age 14 in 1967; he was a crack shot, an unsurpassed marksman. These skills proved useful in James' career.

Upon prep-school graduation, his grandfather, being Lord Pollack and a House of Lords member, made certain the young robust lad attended only the best military school in England, which satisfied James' wish to emulate his father's career. He enrolled in the Royal Military Academy at Sandhurst, the oldest, most famous military school in the world where he took highest honors and graduated at the top of his class in 1975. Even at the age of 22, he held a commanding presence.

Unfortunately, Lord Pollack died shortly thereafter. He left a large estate equally divided between his two heirs: James' uncle, Stephen Pollack, and his father, William Pollack. Stephen took over the estate and kept control of the shipping business, while William maintained his service career in the military out of his sense of duty, despite his large inheritance. James began his commission in the Australian Army as a second lieutenant, although given an unassigned status thanks to his father's influence.

While James' family came from Chelsea-Kensington, Penelope Hawkins was born and raised in Clapham (London) August 4, 1957. Her grandfather Arthur Hawkins had money that went to six heirs on his death. Unfortunately, most of the family fortune was spent within Penelope's lifetime. Her father, Col. Fitzhugh Hawkins was a career officer of the British Army. As a boy he attended Harrow and later also attended to Sandhurst. Penelope learned about the life of a military wife from her family experience. In the early 70's, the family moved into military sponsored barracks and had to leave behind the family home, sold at auction to pay debts. Sandhurst hired Col. Hawkins to teach at Sandhurst in 1971.

Five years earlier, Col. Hawkins met Lt. Col. William Pollack during a joint military exercise. The two men enjoyed one another's company and kept in contact now and then. Eventually, they renewed their friendship when William flew back to England to attend his son's graduation from Sandhurst. To his delight, he discovered that Col. Hawkins had been one of James' instructors. The two men sat together at the ceremony as presenters, since James had the honor of being awarded top cadet in his class. William Pollack looked out on that sea of faces and easily found his son in the front row.

"This is a proud day for you," Hawkins quietly commented to his friend.

"It would be prouder still if James told me his intentions," Pollack replied. "Study and work," he said, "that's all the boy knows. You'd think he'd find time to have a hobby or be interested in a young lady... not this one. Career, that's the only thing on his mind!" he wistfully spoke.

"Well, if that's what's troubling you on this perfect day, let me offer a solution," Hawkins eagerly stated, which roused William's curiosity. He half-smiled when he saw Pollack's face. "I have a daughter who would be perfect for your son," the colonel intimated. "We can introduce them at the Officer's Ball this evening... let nature take its course."

William agreed to the meeting with one provision, that if the couple should become engaged, he, and not the father of the bride, would pay for the wedding. He knew Hawkins' financial state, a man who lived solely on his officers' meager salary, whereas, William's family could well afford a grand affair.

"You drive a hard bargain, Will," the colonel eventually relented. "I accept your terms."

The two men shook hands on the deal.

"Agreed!" they said and grinned over the prospect of being in-laws.

The two fathers were right to bring their children together, as if fate decreed it so from the very beginning. From the moment James met Penelope, the two fell in love, despite the arranged meeting. They affectionately took to each other and made their courtship a short one. They announced their engagement after only two weeks of dating. However, on the advice of their parents, the two continued to date socially for nearly a year before they finally wed, which forced James to scrub his adventurous plans and remain on staff in England throughout this period.

Unfortunately, during the year of their engagement, Penelope's mother, Lady Esther Hawkins, grew ill and passed away, which nearly spoiled the planned ceremony. However, Col. Hawkins insisted the couple proceed with their nuptials as planned. The wedding actually instilled a bit of hope into his life, though when he gave away the bride, Penelope turned around to kiss her father and could not find a dry eye in the house.

The new bride took charge of the household arrangements, a no-nonsense kind of young woman, having lived in a military family. She helped James organize their finances with a little help from Stephen Pollack, as he made some important investments with the endowment they received from William.

After James spoke to his father about where he should serve, the newly commissioned officer met with his new bride and suggested a possible move for the sake of his career, one that would impose on Penelope's feelings. When James explained his reasons for returning to Australia, Penelope readily agreed, knowing what it meant to his career, though she would miss her father. She made the transition a smooth one.

Just three years passed when James quickly worked his way into the rank of captain. When only another four years passed in the Australian Army, his commanders promoted him to the rank of Lt. Colonel Pollack, matching his father's retirement rank. He achieved this honor after his brilliant move in saving an entire company of men during the Afghanistan campaign.

A riot and terrorist attack resulted in a stolen nuclear weapon. It never went public, but this act forced the government of Pakistan to secretly ask the international community for help. A group of concerned governments asked the Australian government to send in an emergency strike team, which had trained for this purpose. James headed that team and his actions led to his promotion.

During the decades that followed, James continued to work his way up through the ranks until the summer of 2018, when he received his latest promotion to the rank of Major General and head of his division. At that point, James Pollack had been in the military for over forty years and should have retired a few years earlier. During that time, he earned the respect of his peers and the men under his command as being tough, yet fair-minded and even-handed. However, James refused retirement packages offered from the military six times. Although after his troubles of late, retirement began to appear more attractive.

Throughout their marriage, Penelope and James created a life and a reputation for being some of the most likable people in Adelaide. In addition to their membership in the Affendale Sunset Country Club, James belonged to the exclusive Digger's Club, an invitation-only establishment for high-ranking officers with field experience. Penelope worked hard on her social standing within the Sunset Club located only a few kilometers away from their house in Dover Gardens.

Digger's was established after the first world war by officers as a place to relieve stress. Two or three times a year, officers from around the nation stopped by the obscure building to celebrate their military careers and exchange thoughts, ideas, and stories. While the younger officers preferred the exclusive suburban country club set and newer establishments, the Digger's Club represented a shuttered secret world of power that certain officers in the military privately sought. The Digger's Club might be in the worst part of modern Adelaide, but the men behind those walls held positions of authority within the military establishment, where no lieutenants, captains, members of the press, or any outsider had access.

Membership required more than just a royal crown on one's sleeve. This club was available by invitation only. Officers of that rank and higher from all over Australia traveled to Adelaide and often met at the exclusive retreat. Many internal conflicts within the military were settled there. Membership required officers serve in at least one active military campaign, were decorated, and promoted to at least the rank of Lieutenant Colonel. When men gathered in the bar to discuss their past, "they'd better damn-well have something to talk about," General Stipden told James Pollack when he received his invitation after achieving the base rank.

That first day he arrived, he saw his father's name on the wall of honor with his name on a new plaque underneath. James recalled his hazing well, as the other officers forced him to reveal details he never shared with anyone else about his tours of duty, right down to the stench and rashes from lack of proper hygiene, or the time his company ate grubs found in the rice they obtained from local villages because "when toasted, it added more flavor."

His fellow officers wanted James to tell every juicy morsel and roared with approval when he provided them. Others shared similar stories from wars far more brutal than James Pollack ever saw. They talked about sleeping in trenches filled with water mixed with the blood of their comrades; or eating rations out of necessity while they recalled seeing friends blown to bits. Their ghastly details made his troubles pale in comparison.

Lt. Col. Pollack suddenly realized that these men made this club exclusive for a reason. A tight bond of trust existed between them, which allowed a level of frankness, honesty, and openly shared feelings. He knew this act of sharing allowed the men to cope with the terrible memories of their field experience. Unlike enlisted men, these officers had too much pride to have a military psychiatrist treat them for PTSD, Post Traumatic Stress Disorder. They relied on the emotional support they received from other officers and found that undying loyalty at the Digger's Club... without question, without prejudice, without hesitation. Here men who loved their country above all things could be open with their opinions and not worry about them being repeated elsewhere.

Most of the club's membership simply enjoyed the peace and solitude away from their offices and families. These men considered the Digger's Club their last refuge from humanity, while a staff of lesser officers, like Sergeant Beery, the man usually assigned to the front desk, pampered their needs with drinks, cigars, newspapers, light luncheons, and solitude.

... and that's his life in a nutshell," Han finished.

"You derived all of that from those files?" Master Li questioned.

The master strategist did not speak or link. His opinion was not necessary. He simply stared back at Master Li. The facial expression from Han in this manner made his feelings clear – everything he stated was true.

Master Li pushed away from the lunch table. He had much to contemplate. He said nothing to his friend. He looked down at the floor as he wandered away from the morning room and walked up the "glass" covered hall toward the north greenhouse. Han knew better than to disturb Li when he meditated on a problem.

Inside the north greenhouse, the large domed structure held a myriad of plant varieties from trees to shrubs, bushes, flowering plants, fungi, mosses, and grasses. Some animals and insects roamed freely about the spacious 200 meter wide space with a small pond at its center. He passed the young Native American botanist assigned to manage the two greenhouses. Su Lin gave her private lessons for two years in preparation for this task, which she relished. She waved back and started to speak when she noticed the serious expression on Master Li's face and allowed the elderly man to pass through the space undisturbed. Li had his favorite bench where he would eventually sit while he contemplated his next course of action.

Li thought back to his luncheon with Han and what the strategist revealed about James Pollack. Han spoke words that described the man beyond the facts.

"Han certainly has a way to discern subtle details from general facts," Li noted as he closed his eyes. His mind began to wander from the greenhouse, across the prairie, and soon sped over the wide expanse of water to a land down under in search of two men: one obvious, one hidden.

CHAPTER FIVE

ENCAMPMENT

GIRARD STOOD ALONGSIDE THE LEAD vehicle, his large frame nearly equal in its size. He looked the role of a military sergeant with his tight, olive-green t-shirt and khaki colored shorts along with his slouch or bush hat, his bulging muscles clearly visible as they stretched out the fabric. He gazed up the row of vehicles behind them. Their motors churned and burned up precious petrol while they awaited orders to depart, three hours to dawn. They had a long road of rough travel ahead. Girard met his "leader's" goal and obtained 200 men, plus or minus a few inescapable casualties in the process. He and Cyrus drugged some of the men in the back of those trucks to ensure they did not escape. Cyrus' actions convinced Girard that the scrawny young man did something to many of the men, which made them cooperative. Otherwise, he thought, why would they be here, as several men left wives or girlfriends behind?

"They aren't exactly a volunteer army," he thought as he looked up the line. "They'll do. What Cyrus doesn't accomplish by scaring the hell out of them, I will when I whip them into shape. They won't be lonely for home when we get to the desert," he thought. He tried to advise Cyrus that their training area in the Flinders Ranges was beginning to attract attention. Yet, he discovered Cyrus knew that fact and had been preparing a more permanent base camp, where they were about to go.

Satisfied with the group leaders he trained over the past few weeks, Girard knew they would help him with discipline once they reached the new base in the dessert region west of Warburton. He glanced over at the front passenger in the lead car. He patiently waited for the young man who sat still with his eyes closed. He knew better than to speak out when he saw Cyrus preoccupied this way. He also knew that Cyrus would simply read his mind

39

to obtain any information he wanted. Thus far, Girard had no complaints with Cyrus' treatment.

At least the boy delivered on his first promise, to give him a date with Susan Daley, the aging ex-model and part-time actress from the billboard that he first noticed on the hill outside his prison cell. He drooled over her picture for a year during the last part of his brief four year confinement. He found his "date" with her direct and to the point. Cyrus dispensed with dinner and flowers. When Girard arrived at her house, Susan answered the door naked. She simply took Girard's hand and directed the big man to her bedroom.

While she did not object to anything Girard did to her, the encounter with the perfect model turned out very different than he imagined. When he left, Girard no longer held such a high opinion of woman so willing or so dispassionate to do anything he proposed. Over the course of two hours, he repeatedly brutalized the woman without even a whimper from her, which took the thrill away from his assault. He did not wonder why for very long. When he left her house, Cyrus stood next to their car with a broad grin on his face. He could tell at once that Cyrus had somehow watched them the entire time.

"Huh? What did I tell ya?" he put to his large friend. "Wasn't she great?"

"She's just like any other woman," Girard grudgingly told him, "a piece of meat I can use how I want, when I want."

Cyrus also delivered on ridding Girard of his prison record troubles. He eliminated the parole officer, by having the man destroy Girard's records. He left a nonsensical written message and put a gun to his own head. Girard had nothing against the man, just relief knowing he did not have to return to prison for violating his parole.

As their time together continued, Girard gradually became more calculating, similar to Cyrus in the callous way he thought of other people, with an increasing level of arrogance and disdain. He knew that no matter what he did, Cyrus would always have his back. Therefore, he made certain that no one would ever harm Cyrus.

"Say the word," Girard said finally as he swung his legs into the driver's side.

Cyrus glanced up and took in a deep breath. He had to pause while his energy gradually returned. It took him time to regain his psychic strength. He had been busy during the night, altering thoughts, changing minds, whipping his force of men into shape so they would be ready and eager to depart. The process drained him.

"Let's get to the campsite," he finally said. "I estimate we'll have enough fuel reserves for the next few months. Then we'll need to raid some town or village… should be easy enough. We also have enough food and water in the supply truck for about three months, if the men don't go hog wild," he added.

"I'll ration those," Girard chimed in. "We'll have enough."

Cyrus glanced over at his second as Girard pulled the truck forward and the other vehicles fell in behind them. They managed to rendezvous to this obscure point in the country without arousing any suspicion, just as Cyrus predicted. The one thing he could not control would be military flyovers. Fortunately, they did not occur on a regular basis. He thought about bringing down a jet, but it would take too much energy, at least he thought it would. He never tried it.

"How far to this… encampment," Girard asked.

"Ha! You really don't remember, do you?" Cyrus said to him and smiled.

Girard hated that sly smile. He knew it meant that Cyrus had entered his mind and erased another memory, something he did earlier and then revealed to Girard he had.

"I don't remember," Girard insisted.

"You and I set it up two weeks ago," Cyrus said as he opened a small thin computer. "You and some other men we employed worked very hard to whip the place into shape. I rewarded you with one of the local girls…"

"Was it fun?" Girard asked. "I mean, did she and I have a good time?"

"Oh, yes, my friend," Cyrus said, "until you got carried away and strangled the poor girl as you finished her off." He glanced over and saw the expression of angst on Girard's face. "Don't worry," Cyrus reassured him. "I took care of it. She was a slut. She died happy," he said, chuckling. "We dumped her in the ocean where we put the rest of them."

Girard concentrated on the road for the next few miles. Yet, the actions of Cyrus bothered him. What had the girl been like? Was she pretty? Was she homely? Did they have sex? Was it good? Or did Cyrus just say those things to get under his skin? Perhaps Cyrus watched them. He cringed at the thought. He would not put it past the perverted leader to do anything. He knew that Cyrus sometimes watched him when he took a shower. He did not know if he admired him or lusted after him. He shuddered to think the later.

"I wish you wouldn't do that… erase my memory, I mean," Girard spoke up. "I want to remember those things, especially if a woman is involved… even if they were bad. I like women… *prefer* women."

"I don't want you to remember certain things," Cyrus angrily shot back. "If she blabbed to someone in her town about us… or worse, if the military ever caught and interrogated her… or even you, then you got nothin' to tell them. Nothin! They can put you on the best lie detector in the business,

41

and they won't find a thing," Cyrus insisted. He saw the disappointment on Girard's face and knew he had to keep his second a close ally. "Look mate, I'm trying to protect you," he told him as he changed his tone to a sympathetic one. "This is a dangerous business we begin…" he said and lowered his voice. Girard glanced over as Cyrus finished his words. "I have an ambitious plan… yet, the rewards will be great, for both of us."

Nevertheless, despite those reassurances, his words rang hollow with the big man who treasured moments with women after his experience in prison. He wanted to remember he was straight and not forced to use a man as he had once done when he felt desperate in prison. A man once propositioned him. He beat the fellow prisoner senseless and then raped the poor young man. He got isolation for that. But to Girard, it was worth it.

Instead of Cyrus's words giving him inspiration, they made the little twerp sound superior, condescending, and patronizing at best. Girard wondered why he ever agreed to this bargain, although he knew he had little choice when it came to Cyrus. Yet the more he considered it, he still had not seen the riches that Cyrus promised. The experience with the model turned out to be a rather hollow and unfulfilling act. At least, he still had that memory. He would have to bargain for something more valuable next time.

Cyrus suddenly laughed aloud as he gazed down at his laptop's screen. Rather than ask, Girard waited for the "leader" to inform him.

"The military wonders what happened to their supplies, all those vehicles, food, weapons, and equipment," he smiled as he spoke. "They launched an investigation. It wasn't difficult to turn one general on another," he told Girard. "Their minds are filled with petty jealousies. This General Sanders is an idiot. He pits other men in his division against each other so he can get ahead. Then he goes in and takes credit for solving messes. It was easy to manipulate his mind when we drove up next to the base outside Melbourne three weeks ago. I simply had his men drive over what we needed to meet us."

"They did?" Girard cut in. "I don't remember…"

He waited for a reply. He glanced over in time to see Cyrus make an "oops!" expression. Cyrus shrugged his shoulders, smiled, and put his hand over his mouth.

"You erased that memory, too?" Girard complained.

"I needed the practice," Cyrus mumbled.

"What other memories have you erased?" he requested.

This time Cyrus glared at Girard, as if by questioning his actions or decisions, the big man had challenged Cyrus' authority to do what he wanted, when he wanted.

"I can force you to do anything I want and then take that memory away," he said through his teeth, hissing like a snake. "I don't need you to question my authority, Girard," Cyrus reminded him. "I need your muscle to keep the men in line and report any problems that arise to me. Is that understood?"

"Yes, sir, or should I address you as prophet?" Girard mumbled. "It's what some of the men are saying."

"You can drop that stuff," Cyrus said as he leaned back. He saw that he made his point and it sunk in. "You and I both know I'm no prophet, saint, or holy man, far from it. Just Cyrus or sir will do," the scrawny young man said as he returned to his attention to the computer screen. The report he read pleased him. "The general is tryin' to cover up his error. He's pulled every trick he can recall to keep the army from findin' out where he misplaced trucks, weapons, and supplies."

"How can you..." Girard started to observe.

"The general gave me every secret code in the military," Cyrus stated as he completed Girard's thought. "I can access their system remotely. My problem now is surveillance," he muttered. "I could alter the paths of their jets, except it's pretty complicated," he complained. "It doesn't matter. I programmed an alert if it happens. I'll catch it in time. Meanwhile..."

Cyrus closed the screen, took in a deep breath, and sighed.

"I think I'll have that woman I saw from the village north of us, tonight," he said as he thought about her and not the road or Girard. He quickly glanced over at Girard and laughed. "You see? I do *prefer* the female sex... most of the time!" He laughed a hysterical kind of laugh that unnerved the big driver.

Yet, Cyrus' statement that he liked women sexually came as a relief to Girard. After he saw the way Cyrus looked at him, he feared that Cyrus may have done something sexual with him and then removed that memory.

"At least the guy's straight," Girard realized. "I was beginning to wonder what I'd done with him and he had erased."

"Why? Are you still used to that sort of sex from being in prison?" Cyrus suddenly popped into his mind.

"No... sir," Girard answered as humbly as he could muster. "I never wanted to do anything like that, even in prison... sir."

"Good, because when we finish this day, I was going to reward you with a woman, too, if you want one," Cyrus said to his second.

"Yes, sir!" Girard answered, a bit cheered at the prospect.

"This time, Girard," Cyrus advised, "try not to kill her in the process!"

The sadistic little psychic did not confess his involvement. It was Cyrus who obtained the girl when they passed through Adelaide on their way to the camp. She had the great misfortune of being a pretty face in the wrong place. They brought her to the camp and the men brutalized her before they returned her to Cyrus. In the privacy of his new tent, he strangled the girl when he crushed her larynx with his mind, not Girard, and afterward had her body dumped in the bay north of Adelaide when they returned. She was the recent corpse that brought the Rollo psychics into the picture.

The convoy of military vehicles spent the next sixteen hours driving north and then west. At one point the road ended, and the column of vehicles continued due west across the countryside for another hundred and fifty kilometers into a region that had no settlements, the middle of the desert. With only twilight remaining, they finally arrived at their destination, far removed from any witness or any civilization.

"Up ahead," Cyrus indicated.

A shallow dry gorge opened up before them with only the southern way in by vehicle. The north end of the gorge had a steep incline, too steep for their trucks. Cyrus had his tent at the top of the north end so he could look out on his men.

As Girard peered through the twilight, he noticed several bivouac style buildings, the temporary kind made from large steel poles and canvas, laid out in organized fashion. Obviously, someone took a great deal of time and effort to previously set up such an elaborate encampment for them, tucked away within this small shallow canyon. Three of the buildings appeared larger and more complex in their structure than the others did.

"You created a military style encampment," Girard said as his head turned to Cyrus.

"We built it the way you wanted it," Cyrus told him, "you and some local urchins that we didn't need afterward," he added in a low voice. "Anyway, the mess hall is back there, the showers and latrines over there. Take me to the right. I have the large bungalow on the north end," he gestured as he spoke. "You have the smaller one further down the hill. Your favorites can go into that central area," he indicated a place in the middle. "They'll have the best cots and supplies. Put the rest of the men over there," he pointed to the left.

"And the ones that disobey?" Girard asked.

"Easy," Cyrus stated, "We kill them in front of the men as examples."

CHAPTER SIX

NIGHTMARE WALKABOUT

OLD MAN OODGEROO TOSSED AND turned for three sleepless nights. He did not dream about anything in particular, no specific nightmare plagued his dreams, and no one single worry struck his heart such as overdue bills or an impending illness. A voice troubled poor old Oodgeroo, a pleasant voice actually, but a voice none-the-less that called out his name through the night. After he awoke from his restless sleep, the memory of those dreams troubled him all the next day.

"Was it an ancestor?" he wondered. "Perhaps a long lost relative... or even some god like being that roamed the universe and tried to impart some wisdom. It could even be a warning of some terrible event..."

"What?" his wife yelled from the garden. "What are you mumbling about?"

"Nothing!" he called back, "nothing."

Without a good-night's sleep, the tribal elder became increasingly irritated with the smallest offense. Unlike his usual jolly self, lately Oodgeroo would snap at just about anyone who spoke to him casually about his health or the weather.

"G'day, Oodgeroo!" a friend said when he passed him on the street.

"Not for me, it isn't!" he snapped back.

He did not bother to explain his problem. Instead he stomped along, muttering incoherently as if his offense to others did not matter.

By the third day, every person in the village caught wind of his latest affliction and avoided him. If they saw him walking along the street, they would cross to the other side. Even his wife of forty years informed their friends not to bother the old man. They had argued over everything and nothing for three days.

"He's so moody! If he doesn't improve, ahm not gonna wait till he gets better," she angrily told one of her closest friends. "Out he goes!" she exclaimed, followed by an obscene gesture.

Yet, this old man could not be so easily disposed. Oodgeroo led the local Nungah tribe of Indigenous Australians, referred to in the past as Aboriginal Australians or Aborigines. Every man, woman, and child in the village respected the old man. He strived to set a good example for others. He maintained his good health at his age by eating the right food, taking long walks, and was usually very good natured… until recently. Down through the years, he became the kind elderly sage that every person in the village trusted to give out good advice. At seventy-eight, he moved, looked and sounded better than other indigenous Australians half his age. That is why this sudden mood change bothered nearly everyone in his village.

Oodgeroo felt determined to have a fine night's rest on the fourth night. His wife compromised and wisely offered to sleep at her sister's house. He drank warm milk, a drink he detested, and even took a sleeping aid. Having the bed alone, he stretched his limbs wide without his wife's elbows and knees poking into him.

"Ah!" he exclaimed as he took a deep breath. "Rest at last!"

He settled down to a nice quiet night with no interruptions.

For a few hours at least, Oodgeroo had his wish. He fell into a deep sleep and rested peacefully. However, the voice that plagued his dreams for the past three nights returned and brought him out of his tranquil slumber.

"Oodgeroo!" the voice spoke. It came through so loud and annoyingly abrupt that the old man figuratively hit the ceiling.

"What?" he shouted as he looked around the room for the source of the sound. However, he soon discovered he was no longer in his bedroom. He floated in the middle of space, surrounded by stars, with no bed, no room, and no landmarks. "What's this?" the old indigenous man asked. "What's going on?"

"Oodgeroo," the strange voice spoke harshly to him.

Determined this time to figure out the source of the voice, he asked it questions.

"Is that you, Grandfather Chadley?" he wondered.

"No! I am not your grandfather!" the voice quickly replied. "I am a special voice, here to warn you that… the… the sky… is falling."

"Very funny," the old man grumbled. "This must be a vision."

Now this whole time, old Oodgeroo actually lay asleep in his bed. Yet, he was not aware of that. He thought that he was having a vision. In the tradition of the Nungah, an ancient prophecy foretells of visions that bless the minds of some men. The intensity of the dream made Oodgeroo feel he was having one.

"How do I return home?" he asked. "Why am I in outer space?"

"You are not in outer space, you stubborn old man! You are at home and in bed!" the exasperated voice told him. "You think this is a vision?"

"Yes?" Oodgeroo answered, uncertain.

"Oh… of course… that is exactly what this is. This is a vision!" the voice insisted.

"Oh…" Oodgeroo mumbled. "Well, why didn't you say so?"

"I'm trying to tell you that now. So… if this is a vision, then you must listen to me. Look over at that region of space," the voice instructed. Off to his right, he saw a big dull object that barely reflected the light of the stars, a large slowly rotating rock that floated aimlessly in space. "See that rock?" the voice asked. "Well… that rock will fall from the sky," the voice indicated.

"That rock?" Oodgeroo questioned.

"This is a very special kind of rock… this rock turns to fire as it tumbles to Earth," the voice said.

"You mean this asteroid will become a meteor?" he asked.

Silence followed, as if the voice were contemplating his remarks.

"I did not know you were aware of asteroids or meteors?" the voice replied.

"Oh, course! What do you think I am; some kind of backward bush idiot?" Oodgeroo responded.

"Never mind!" the voice shot back. "This meteor will cause great damage to the Earth if allowed to enter the atmosphere. I can show you," the voice spoke.

The scene changed to where Oodgeroo had a clear view of the planet Earth from space. A flaming meteor struck the Earth in the East China Sea. A wave of destructive energy cascaded outward from the impact zone and engulfed southern Korea, Japan, and most of coastal China. Strangely, because of its location between the land masses, the destruction did not spread to the rest of the globe.

"This is terrible," Oodgeroo exclaimed as he watched.

Oodgeroo rubbed his eyes. When he pulled his hands away, he stood alone in absolute darkness, everything else vanished around him. For several seconds, he could not speak. The vision made the old man weep. Finally, he sniffled and tried to reason things through.

"Will this happen?" he wondered.

"It may never happen, if you can act soon," the voice told him.

"Act? Who could stop such a thing from happening?" he asked.

"A man might be able to intervene in time," the voice requested, "if you

47

can find and warn him. His name is Major General James Pollack. You will find him near Adelaide, in Brighton. Go to Brighton, specifically, to the Digger's Club on Dover's Square off Yarmouth Road."

"Are you kidding? I am a black man. That is probably a white man's country club. They won't even let me near the place. How will I get in?" Oodgeroo wondered.

"You will find a way," the voice said.

"How do you know such details? I never heard of a vision like this before?" the old man grumbled. "… and Adelaide… How will I get there? I have no car and Adelaide is over two hundred kilometers away!"

"Walk," the voice told him.

"Walk? Are you crazy? I am an old man, a walk that far will kill me!" Oodgeroo exclaimed.

"You must go, Oodgeroo. The world will end if you do not act," the voice put on him. "You must leave in the morning," the voice insisted.

"My wife will think I have flipped my lid," Oodgeroo replied, dismissive.

"Go to Major General Pollack and deliver that message. Then you will have done your part and can join your ancestors in their heavenly estate," the voice assured him.

"This isn't a put on, like some kind of reality show, is it?" he asked the voice.

The voice laughed before it resumed its composure.

"No, Oodgeroo. I have come to you, because you are the only person in Australia with whom I could speak. You must pass this message to Major General Pollack, or the planet will suffer a terrible fate," the voice told him.

The old man began to toss and turn.

"I knew there was a reason why I felt so uncomfortable. Very well, I will do as you request. It will be difficult for me, but I will find a way," Oodgeroo said.

"One more thing…" the voice added.

"More! What else?" the old man demanded.

"Another man is part of this scheme. He lives in the desert of Western Australia, a difficult journey that will take many days to reach," the voice explained.

"Don't tell me… you want me to walk all the way to him as well," Oodgeroo blurted as he began to grow frustrated.

"No… that is not your responsibility. You must tell Major General Pollack about this man," the voice advised. "He will take the necessary action to assemble a strike team before this man can use his power to bring down the great stone in the sky."

"You mean the meteor?" Oodgeroo questioned.

"Yes! Yes! The meteor!" the voice impatiently replied.

"You make no sense, Grandfather Chadley," Oodgeroo said as he shook his head.

"I am not your grandfather!" the voice insisted.

"How can a man affect a rock in the sky… I mean, an asteroid?" the old man asked.

"I do not know. This man is very evil and powerful in strange ways," the voice explained. "Pollack must become aware of this evil man or it will be the end of our world and the beginning of his. No person can stop him once he carries out his plan."

"Major General Pollack cannot stop him?" Oodgeroo asked.

"… with help he can," the voice said.

"What kind of help… not that any of this matters. This is all such a silly dream. I can't believe I'm having this conversation," Oodgeroo stated with disbelief.

"The general has yet to discover his power," the voice informed him.

"This is even more confusing," Oodgeroo insisted. "First you tell me a meteor is going to strike the Earth. Then you tell me to go to Brighton and speak with a Major General Pollack. Why should he believe an old black man like me when I tell him a story about stopping some crazy person in the desert? This is absurd and I've heard just about enough. Goodnight, Grandpa Chadley," Oodgeroo said and rolled over.

"I am not your grandfather!" the voice declared.

"Whoever you are, it's been nice talking to you," the old man said. "Please don't wake me any more with this nonsense."

Oodgeroo's body lifted up out of his bed and floated high into the air.

"Hey!" he cried, as he feared the heights. "What's going on?"

"You must believe me," the voice said.

Oodgeroo saw the meteor again, falling to Earth, this time from a closer perspective. He stood on the shore not far from a large city as he watched the blazing stone of fire crash into the South China Sea. A great destructive wave of ocean water spread outward from the impact and came toward him. In that moment, Oodgeroo realized how horrible it would be if this ever happened. The entire city behind him, full of millions, would be destroyed. He could feel the rush of the wind and moisture on his face. He winced at realism.

"Stop!" he cried out.

Oodgeroo blinked his eyes and sat up in bed. He looked around his room as sweat trickled down the side of his face.

"What a terrible nightmare!" he said as he wiped off his face. "I'm glad that's over."

He had never left this room or his bed. Yet, his pajamas were soaked with perspiration. He felt the bed and pinched his skin to make certain he was not dreaming any longer.

"One thing about having a vision," the old man mumbled, "much better than reality television."

Chapter Seven

A note of urgency

Oodgeroo was right about one thing, his wife strenuously objected to everything he told her about last night's dream the following morning.

"You saw what?" she demanded.

"I'm telling you I saw the earth from space!" he pointed up.

"Did you break into the ceremonial wine last night?" she asked, frowning.

"No, I didn't drink anything last night," he said as he struggled to pull his backpack down from the hall closet.

"What do you think you're doing with that?" she asked.

"I must go to Adelaide," he said and returned to the bedroom. He opened his drawers and threw several pairs of socks into the bottom of the backpack.

"Do you think this Major General Pollack is going to believe an old aboriginal man…" she started.

"Indigenous," Oodgeroo corrected.

"Alright, indigenous then," she said as she moved to block his way. "First of all, I don't care if it is 2019 and we are all supposed to be equal," she directed to him, "those officers ain't gonna let you into that private all-white country club."

"Aren't gonna…" he interrupted.

"I'll speak as I like!" she bellowed. "Second, no white general is gonna believe some old crazy black man. Third, you'll be dead before you get to Adelaide!"

"I'm still going. I witnessed a profound vision. I swear I saw a meteor strike the planet from space," he pointed out. "Why won't you believe me?"

"From where?" she asked, still skeptical. "How did you get into space?"

"I floated up," he casually answered as he raised his arms.

"Oh, you're nuts!" his wife blurted, exasperated by his behavior.

"Probably, but I still must go. Excuse me darling." Oodgeroo said as he moved around his wife and finished packing his knapsack.

"If you want to make a fool of yourself, you do so without me!" she yelled.

His wife stormed out of the house, and poor old Oodgeroo never had the chance to say goodbye to her. She left without telling her husband where she was going or if she would be gone for good.

For a moment, he stared at the door before he finally shrugged off her comment and continued to pack. The old man packed clothing along with food in case he grew hungry. The food added even more weight. When he finally finished a few minutes later, he stood in the doorway and swayed as the heavy backpack threw off his balance. He wondered how far he could walk with this bundle he created.

"If my forefathers did it, then I can do it," Oodgeroo nodded while he adjusted the straps and tried to stand upright.

He could feel the strain on his lower back. Drooping, he bent his shoulders forward. He closed his eyes, made it down the front stairs, and took the first few steps toward the road. The morning air felt hot and dry. A sudden breeze kicked up swirling little dust tornadoes around his feet as the old man proudly walked in a southwesterly direction away from the village. He heard some of the villagers comment as he strode up the street.

"Where's he going?" a woman said.

"What's that crazy old man up to now?" a man commented.

"I'm going on a vision quest!" he shouted back over his shoulder.

They could see him struggle with pack's weight and bulk. Yet, no one offered to help. Oodgeroo fought with the burden on his own.

The coastal city of Adelaide was hundreds of kilometers away. He would need to make many stops and rest his weary bones if he were to survive. At that rate, the trip could take him weeks, Oodgeroo realized. He decided to follow the road, better than walking through the countryside with hazards like scorpions, venomous snakes, poisonous spiders, and other nasty creatures.

The breeze turned into a powerful wind that threw a fine powdery dust into his face. Oodgeroo stopped long enough to wipe his eyes out. He could hardly see which direction to go. He had only arrived on the edge of the village, when he already felt lost and wanted to turn around. The old man started to cry from the frustration he experienced, also because his eyes and back hurt. He only wanted to fulfill the request from the vision.

"Beep! Beep!" a car horn blasted into the air, which made the old man jump right out of his skin.

"What in blue blazes?" he muttered.

"Get in, you old coot!" a woman's voice yelled.

A small car pulled up next to him. Through his watery eyes, Oodgeroo made out the face of his wife.

"Where did you find a car?" he asked as he blinked away the moisture.

"It's my sister's cousin's husband's car, but it'll get us to Adelaide, so's ya don't have to walk!" his wife yelled at him. "Your grandfather Chadley might haunt my dreams next if I make you walk!"

The old man did not know which he should do first, laugh or kiss his wife out of gratitude.

"Get in!" she yelled at him.

Startled, Oodgeroo slung his knapsack into the back seat.

"What about fuel?" he asked her as he put his hand on the door.

"The owner says we have enough to get there and back," she explained.

"Well… couldn't you find one that had air conditioning?" he asked.

"If you say one more word to me between here and Adelaide, I'll push you out the door and make you walk the rest of the way!" she yelled.

Oodgeroo swallowed hard and decided to follow her suggestion. He sat quietly while his wife drove the very long distance to Adelaide. Neither had ever been to a city this large. However, since the vision gave Oodgeroo such explicit directions, they thought they could not possibly become lost.

On arriving in Adelaide, they immediately became lost.

Normally, the journey to Adelaide from their location in Australia would take a couple of hours. However, at only forty kilometers an hour, their fuel-efficient car practically crawled across the southern continent island. Therefore it took them nearly five hours just to reach the outskirts of the city and another two hours to reach the location of the officer's club, which made the time late in the afternoon.

How fortunate for the aging couple that Major General Pollack decided to stop by Digger's after work that afternoon. He'd been under a great deal of strain lately and needed to unwind before he went home.

"Are you sure the old man gave you the right directions? I think we're lost," the wife said as she craned her neck to see.

"The last time we asked for directions, the man said to take a left on Brighton Road, then turn at the fourth street on the left. Well? We're on Brighton Road, aren't we?" Oodgeroo gestured.

"Humph," his wife grunted. "That's three," she said while she counted the number of streets they past.

"Lewis Street," Oodgeroo noted. "The next should be Yarmouth."

"There it is!" his wife pointed. "Finally!"

The next street on the left was Yarmouth Road. She turned up the street.

The directions from the old man in the dream guided them the rest of the way.

"… when you arrive at Dover Square," he told Oodgeroo. "You'll find the Digger's Club."

"What's a digger?" the wife asked.

"How should I know?" Oodgeroo replied as he shrugged his shoulders. "They have these pet names for each other. They're the military! That's how they do things."

"I'll bet honest money you never make it in the door," his wife said and slapped him on the back.

"Thanks for the vote of confidence, dear," the old man answered. Fearful, he swallowed hard which hurt his parched throat.

They pulled their car into Dover Square and found the old brick building with a small brass plaque outside that read: "Digger's Club – Member's only." Hardly noticeable unless one knew it was there.

The old woman nudged her husband and laughed. "You'll never get inside."

He waved her off and stepped out. The surrounding buildings, all seemingly connected, resembled this brownstone structure, except that this building was wider and not as tall. The streets had no traffic and no foot traffic. Several parking spaces were marked, "reserved" with only a few luxury cars parked in them. No one stood outside at the front door and no security cameras pointed down at the street.

He walked up the steps and tried the handle. The door was unlocked. Cautiously, the old man pushed the heavy solid wood door open and went inside. A man with broad shoulders, short cropped hair, and wearing a military dress uniform sat at a reception desk. He busily reviewed some screen in front of him, when he looked up and saw Oodgeroo walk into the building.

"Member's only, chum. No locals allowed," he spoke abruptly.

"Sorry to interrupt," the old man spoke softly. "I wish to speak to Major General Pollack, if he is in."

"What did you say? Here now! This here's a gentleman's club. None of the likes of you allowed in here, old man! Now you just run along and don't be botherin' the major general," the soldier said.

"You must tell him I wish to speak to him," Oodgeroo insisted.

"Didn't you hear what I said?" the man raised his voice and came around the desk.

At that moment, a word popped into Oodgeroo's mind.

"You must tell the general it has to do with 'periwinkle.' He'll know."

The sergeant pulled up short. He stood much taller than Oodgeroo by nearly half a meter. He stared down at the cowering smaller black man who grasped for an ounce of courage while he defiantly stood his ground.

"Here! What do you know about that? Is that some sort of code or something you just said?" the authoritative man said as he searched over the black man's face.

Oodgeroo felt too scared to speak or do anything else except nod up and down.

The sergeant scratched his chin for a moment while he never took his eyes off the old man. He had been in the military for many years. He had interviewed terrorists first hand. They had steely lying eyes that tried to cover up their intentions to commit harm. He saw no such guile on this man's face. He felt this man would not have the cunning to deceive him and might be a messenger with some sort of coded message. The general would want to know the message immediately.

"Periwinkle, eh?" the man said with a lower voice. "You'd better wait over there. Don't speak to anyone and none of your messin about! We've got security cameras in here pointed right at you! If you try anything, we have it on video," he said and gestured toward a small black globe on the ceiling.

Oodgeroo again nervously nodded, turned around, and obediently headed over to sit on a nearby bench. As he sat, he spotted a drinking fountain nearby, the kind with a refrigeration unit built into the base to make the water extra cold. He licked his dry lips and waited until the sergeant left the room before he made his move.

As soon as the large man left, he swiftly moved toward the public conveyance. Oodgeroo lowered his head, twisted the handle on the side, and ice-cold water shot into his very dry mouth. Oodgeroo didn't spill a drop as he sucked out the cold liquid refreshment. His mouth pulled the fountain's water right out of the spigot. Oodgeroo heard footsteps. He whirled around and plopped down onto the bench while he tried to catch any droplets of water that ran off his chin. He burped just as the major general rounded the corner.

The first thing Major General James Montgomery Pollack did when he laid eyes on Oodgeroo was frown.

"What's the meaning of this?" he bellowed, angry with the sergeant. "I thought you meant this man was a member of my regiment? I've never seen this man before in my life!" He stomped up to Oodgeroo and stood before him. Major General Pollack towered in height even taller than the sergeant, hovering over the smaller black man.

Poor Oodgeroo. He had just enjoyed his swallow of fresh cold water when this big boisterous man wanted him to cough up answers and he had none. He tried to speak, but he became so intimidated by the presence of the two military men, nothing came out.

"Come on! Out with it, man! You're wasting my time!" the general demanded.

"The sky is falling," Oodgeroo timidly spoke.

"What?" the general bellowed as he turned to the sergeant. "Is this some kind of joke? Did General Sanders put you up to this?"

Even the sergeant appeared upset now. Oodgeroo cleared his throat. He had to quickly spit his words out before they threw him into the street.

"The vision told me to tell you. It said you'd need help to stop the meteor. He said you will know what to do, soon," Oodgeroo worked up the courage to say.

"Have this man escorted from the premises. Now!" the general yelled, clearly upset. He shouted his orders to the poor sergeant standing next to him. "Visions! Meteors! Poppycock, indeed!" The major general spun around on his heels and left.

The sergeant started to grab Oodgeroo to throw him out of the building when the old man put up his hand.

"Please, sir. Don't manhandle me. I promise I will leave and never come back," Oodgeroo told him.

"See that you don't!" the sergeant barked. "Botherin the major general with that nonsense…" he mumbled as he headed to his duty position.

Oodgeroo walked out of the building with his dignity intact. He was not certain if he had accomplished all he set out to do, but left the building satisfied he delivered the message. Yet a feeling came over him that made him stop when he noticed the military insignia on the car parked in its designated spot. He saw the word 'major general' in the window. He went to his wife.

"See? They gave you the boot, didn't they?" she grinned.

"I had a large cold drink of water," he bragged.

"And you didn't bring me one?" she cried as she licked her parched lips.

"It was a drinking fountain woman!" he told her wrinkled face. "Do me a favor. See if there's pencil and paper in the car. I need to write a note," Oodgeroo said as his mind considered the words to use.

The old woman mumbled her unintelligible reply as she shuffled through the crowded glove box in the front seat of the old car. Oodgeroo knew he would complete his obligation once he left his note for the general to find, while more thoughts flooded into his head.

As he scribbled away, he wondered what the general considered as a "breakthrough." Personally, he did not believe the pompous windbag deserved anything but failure. He felt the general treated him badly in the lobby. He did this more for his grandfather, Chadley. Though as he wrote the note, he could swear he could hear in his mind, "I'm not your grandfather!"

CHAPTER EIGHT

SECRET INVASION

"STAY OUT OF MY DREAMS!" Cyrus yelled so loudly that his voice startled his bodyguard on duty nearby. The shrill cry shook the guard from his sleep.

Not wasting a second, the security guard swiftly moved inside the tent having heard his boss's shout. Yet, upon arriving in his sleeping quarters, he saw no one else but their leader as the young man sat up in the bed, breathing hard, with a wild-eyed expression on his face. He surmised at once that the young man some called "prophet" had another bad dream.

"Sir, are you alright?" the bodyguard asked.

Cyrus wiped the sweat from his face. This had been the third intense and troubling dream this week. The men around him began to talk about his fear of the night. They spoke of "madness" setting in.

He had to put a stop to these rumors. Despite the fact he wore nothing at all, he ignored the presence of the guard, rose from his bed, and crossed to the table where an old fashioned ceramic pitcher of water sat inside a washbasin. Although he had his own shower and sink, he poured some out water and splashed his face.

Cyrus gazed at his reflection in the mirror that hung on the fabric wall. He saw a thin pale man with a haggard appearance and dark circles under his eyes from lack of sleep, stare back at him. He took out a towel and dabbed the cool liquid from his sunken cheeks. He scratched at the scraggy growth on his chin and inspected the blackheads on his crooked nose.

The guard looked at this skinny nude boy with detached emotion. In his heart of hearts he saw a pathetic weakling whom he felt he could break in an instant, but knew better than to dwell on such thoughts, as it seemed their leader could read the minds of his comrades. He had seen that power in action and rightly feared it.

The nude young man stretched out his slender pale frame. His steely gray eyes glanced over at the curious bodyguard who watched him. He did not bother to search the man's mind. He really did not wish to know his thoughts, as most men regarded him with skepticism. As long as they feared him, which he felt the guard did, the rest did not matter.

"Send in Girard," he ordered as he straightened.

"Yes, sir," the man said. He spun around like a good soldier and exited the large tent.

When Girard returned a few minutes later, he did not find the shaken leader of their newly formed army, which the bodyguard reported to him. Nor did he find a man filled with fear and trepidation. Instead, Girard walked in on a young man who impatiently waited for him with grizzled determination and an insane affect to his reasoning. Cyrus wore his "fatigues" that hung loosely about his slim frame.

"Thump," a large, very sharp, pointed dagger pierced the table in front of him, its dull black color reflected none of the lantern light in the room. "Thump," again the tip of the blade poked through the map lying on the table. Cyrus dug it out and threw the blade back in at the exact same point, his accuracy was undeniable.

"Do you know what time it is?" Girard asked. "This is the middle of the night," he said, disgruntled.

"*He's* havin' his breakfast," Cyrus uttered under his breath.

"Who's havin' breakfast?" Girard wondered.

"What?" Cyrus said, distracted by Girard's voice. He glanced up and stared at the large man standing in front of him. "Shut up!" he growled. "I don't need your advice. I'm thinkin'."

A hole began to form on the world map in the location of the ocean between China, Korea, and Japan, known as the South China Sea. Cyrus, seated at one corner of the table, threw his knife precisely into the exact same spot repeatedly, never once missing or straying from his target. Each time he leaned over, retrieved the knife and then precisely threw it at the exact same spot. Girard watched him as Cyrus repeatedly did this, although he never said a word. Several uncomfortable seconds passed before Girard spoke again.

Rather than make a comment about Cyrus's bad dreams, he proceeded with other matters.

"Since you are awake, sir, I'd like to give you this evening's report," Girard requested.

Cyrus stared off into space, acting as if he did not hear his second.

"Sir? Did you hear me?" Girard asked.

"What? Oh, yes… go ahead, report," Cyrus said as he threw the knife again.

"A sentry on the eastern end of our perimeter states that a jet flew near our position, about ten miles east. Not enough for a visual, he believes, but close enough to spot activity on his scanners," Girard told him.

Cyrus paused, his knife hand poised dangerously in the air, still aimed at the table.

"Well? What do you want me to do about it?" Cyrus growled.

Girard shifted uncomfortably in his seat. He did not like to press urgent matters. However, Cyrus acted oddly at times, as if he could not make sense of facts from a military point of view. Girard constantly had to press him into action.

"Make it go away with your mind, Cyrus, just as you did with the others," Girard requested.

"It's just a fly, a speck, don't let it bother you…" Cyrus told him.

"Yes, but they could report our position, send in an airstrike, or worse…"

"I told you to forget it!" Cyrus yelled at his subordinate. "Besides," he added in a calmer voice, "if it bothers you that much, move the camp twenty kilometers west to the secondary site. We'll be out of their usual flight pattern. We have enough men to tear down and rebuild the camp faster than the four days it took us to build this one. We also have a few disposal men we can use to impress the others. There's another washout gorge, similar to this one, we can use. We said if anythin' happened, we'd use it as a fallback position."

He stared at Girard. The large man wanted things neat and tidy. He did not like the idea that the military might send jets against them and spoil his commander's plans. For once, Cyrus had to agree with his second.

"I give, Girard," Cyrus finally said. "Use whatever excuse you like with the men, I don't care. You handle it. I will support you. If you wish, I will divert the next jet or you can move the camp or both. I'm… I'm preoccupied with somethin' important… for once, you decide."

"As you will, Cyrus," the man said and started to bow his head.

"None of that, no bowin'… I don't like bowin!" Cyrus objected. "I'll have none of that!" he yelled at Girard.

He took the blade and threw it directly at Girard. He barely missed the big man's head by a matter of a few centimeters. The point of the blade lodged its sharp point deep inside a nearby wooden pole. He threw the knife so quickly with such precision that Girard did not have time to react. He considered himself lucky when he saw how deep the knife imbedded into the wooden pole.

"Did you understand my directive?" Cyrus bellowed. He leaned back and propped his feet up on the table.

Girard understood this man all too clearly. He witnessed Cyrus' cruelty

59

over this past week when he made men commit suicide in the most gruesome ways. It certainly impressed the men and made Girard aware of his boss's extensive power.

"Yes, Cyrus!" the man snapped to attention. He saluted military style, turned, and stepped outside.

Cyrus could hear Girard shout commands in his name as he strode down the hill and walked into the encampment. He hated to deal directly with any of his followers, except when he had to make a speech and rouse them to anger. He reveled in their hatred, their fear, their wasted emotion that he learned some time ago allowed him to soak up their energy like a sponge. It sustained him, gave him additional power, as if he absorbed rays from the sun and turned them into electricity. He liked the feeling of power that coursed through his body. This energy made him tingle all over, better than a woman made him feel. These men freely gave off their energy in droves during such moments. He didn't care if he could not hear their thoughts when they were extremely angry or fearful, he could read it on their faces.

"Break down those stoves!" he heard a man yell.

"Pack your stuff!" another assistant to Girard added.

"Tear this down. We're movin' the camp tonight!" another ordered.

Commotion broke out all across the encampment and spread to the other side. He heard the clucking of chickens and baying of the goats. Girard convinced Cyrus to bring in fresh meat and some women to tend the animals and cook. By "tend the animals," Girard also intended they give the men pleasure. Cyrus made certain the women knew their jobs and performed them without protest. The men kept them very busy.

"Breakdown all the tents and gather the animals for transport! We're movin' twenty clicks to the west by dawn. Hurry!" Girard yelled.

Reluctantly, Cyrus rose from his large handcrafted chair, with its leather seat and wide arms. He went to the pole and dug out his knife. He spun around and threw the knife across the room, which drove the point into the table at the same location on the map.

"That is where you will strike, my lovely big rock," the psychic said with a devilish grin, "and not that nosey oriental old man or anyone else can stop me once I make the energy bounce off its side."

Cyrus pulled the knife from the table. He closed his eyes and threw the knife again, this time he buried its point in the pole farthest from him. His accuracy with weapons increased immensely over the past year since he felt his power grow. Whether a gun, a knife, it did not matter. He had lethal accuracy with any weapon.

Even jet aircraft no longer troubled the leader since he learned the art of altering thoughts. A military jet flew over their position when Cyrus first brought his group into this desert compound. He entered the pilot's mind and turned the jet around. He found he could remotely fly the plane if given enough time to learn the controls. Instead, he sent the pilot away with no memory of what he saw.

As a psychic, he had progressed quickly on his own without guidance from other psychics, in the same manner as Master Li's cousin did in China and other rogue psychics had, such as the women who supported his cousin. While Galactic Central tried to dissuade Cyrus from independence, he ignored their advice and shut them out. He threatened to harm his voice if it ever tried to contact him again. The voices could not close his portal without Master Li's guidance and Li could not perform that operation remotely.

By the time Master Li finally broke through to Cyrus' mind, the Australian's voice in Galactic Central could not make a link with its Earth counterpart. Unlike the Oman subject, whose portal Li and the voices closed, Cyrus managed to partially convert his own area of the brain and could block any signal coming from the distant galaxy. To attempt such a procedure now, even in sleep, Cyrus might reverse the process and send the particle back into the main chamber, which could result in the death of a voice – a first in its 400,000 plus year history. Therefore, Li decided he had to contend with Cyrus on his own. He began by invading his dreams, or rather, his nightmares.

CHAPTER NINE

MORNING PURSUITS

MASTER LI SPENT THE MORNING in the library alone. He tried to concentrate his power on a long distance journey that did not involve the conduit in his mind. He could travel to distant stars with relatively little effort, especially when he walked the timeline. Whereas, when he tried to reach around the planet, the effort seemed the more difficult experience somehow, as if he had to stretch every energy resource to its limit. He could not explain this obstinate duality, as if part of his brain prevented him from reasoning it out.

With as much power as he could muster, he attempted to influence Cyrus from this distance. However, his plan to affect or disrupt the other psychic met with continual frustration on his part when the rogue easily blocked him. As he made yet another attempt to invade the rogue's mind, he sensed Han enter the library and move toward him.

"Did you find out anything this time?" Han asked as he tapped into Li's thoughts. "You said you had trouble trying to stay inside his mind."

"After I read the morning's reports, I concentrated on reaching my power over to Australia," Li responded.

"… which is never an easy task, especially when one considers that all WPO members except for you can only extend their influence a matter of meters and scan an area a few kilometers wide around them, let alone the several thousand you attempted," Han linked. He sat in the chair next to Li and noticed that Running Elk prepared tea for them, or at least for Li.

"Distance is more of a problem than I considered," Li confessed. "Evidently, that is the reason I had trouble sensing him in the first place. Australia is about as far from us as any point on the planet," he pointed out.

"Too far for the great Master Li?" Han sarcastically put as he reached to uncover the tea cozy. "I find it difficult to believe that you have trouble with anything."

"I do in this instance," Li expressed. "I can hear his thoughts at times, but I cannot affect him or dwell in his mind for very long. My energy level is too weak at that distance and he can easily block me."

"What about using Galactic Central?" Han suggested.

"He's permanently locked them out," Li told him. "He threatened to harm his voice if it should try to contact him again. I've told the voices to stay away from any abusive rogues and not monitor their activity," he told Han. "Rogue psychics will be our responsibility. Because of our ability to generate our own psychic energy, Earth psychics are the most powerful in the collective. We are stronger sources of psychic energy than any evolved creature yet discovered. No telling what kind of damage Cyrus could inflict if he wanted."

"Safe for the voices, difficult for us to track rogues," Han offered as he took a piece of cake. "Evolution could spring many surprises our way."

"For the moment, let us concentrate on Cyrus. I've entered his dreams a few times and tried to unsettle him," Li said as he accepted a cup of tea from Han.

"You don't need to tell me how it's affected him," Han interrupted. "You managed to leave an impression but the experience has taxed both of you. I can see it in your face. You won't be able to sustain those intrusions much longer without the energy drain affecting your health."

Master Li took in a deep breath.

"You're right, of course," he replied. "I must let him go."

"I sense something else," Han stated as he felt Li held more news.

"I also managed to locate our candidate," Li told him.

"You mean the real candidate? So Pollack *is* a psychic with a conduit!" Han exclaimed.

"Yes, but he tuned out his voice long ago, in the same way many of us from that time period did. I tuned out my voice, and Sir Charles did the same thing in his youth," Li explained.

"All three of you from around the same era of time... the only survivors from that tumultuous period..." Han commented.

"...that we are aware," Li interjected. "If a sudden surge of births occurred around the time of Second World War or shortly thereafter, I suspect that another took place sometime around the last decade of the twentieth century. I wonder if World War II killed most of the psychic children. Millions died. Perhaps some still survive in isolated pockets. We don't know and we don't have time to send Villi and Michael on some global scanning mission," Li told him. "We'll just have to deal with them as they show up," he linked as he added a slice of lemon and drizzled some honey into his cup of tea.

"Did you try direct contact with general…" Han began.

"No, I could not link with him either," Li finished his thought. "However, after I roughly scanned the continent, I did find an aboriginal man receptive to suggestion. Oddly, the man has a similar psychic trait to Running Elk. These native tribes, in Australia and America, may represent some failed line of evolutionary development in the psychic area. All I know is that they generate more psychic energy than we do and we'd be lost without them. At any rate, I sent this aboriginal man on a mission to Adelaide after I spoke to him in his dreams," Li informed his strategist.

"That only leaves one very flimsy alternative for us…" Han reasoned as he mapped out their strategy for Australia.

"At least Cyrus revealed part of his goals," Li spoke up.

"… and that's all we have to go on?" Han finished the thought. "Time to assemble a team…"

The two men nodded as they made mental assignments and lists of things they would need on a trip to Australia.

"I find only one weakness to your strategy, Han," Li pointed out.

"What weakness?" Han demanded.

"We know… you know nothing about this… Cyrus Keaty!" Li stated. "He is an unknown! How can you possibly conceive a strategy based on my sparse knowledge of his intent?"

"Put Zhiwei on it. He can find out anything about anyone," Han said.

The two men continued with their tea in silence, although Master Li seemed far too tired for Han's sake. Han figured he should contact Cecilia and have her examine Master Li as soon as possible. Li picked up his thoughts.

"I don't need Cecilia," Master Li linked to him.

"At least, lie down and perform some healing meditation after tea," Han requested.

"I think I'll skip lunch today…" Li linked as he put down his cup.

"Skip…" Han started and paused when he saw the pained expression on Li's face.

Master Li slowly rose and made his way out of the library. He sensed Han's worried eyes follow his form.

"I will do as you ask and rest," Li linked. "I suggest you advance our ideas on how to stop Cyrus."

"Why suggest it?" Han retorted as the door closed. "You know I would anyway."

Chapter Ten

A Portrait of Evil

Cyrus Keaty led a sheltered life. His father died when he was five. He lived with his mother until the teen began to make "bad" things happen around his home town of Whyalla. Once he discovered he could manipulate the minds of others, he "got into all sorts of trouble" as his mother put it, when she noticed a sudden change in her son. He began to bring teenage girls to his room and afterward, they could not remember being in his house. Soon, people in his neighborhood started to ask questions about Cyrus and the "strange goings on." Ashamed to face his accusers, his mother would only go out at night to shop. Rather than expose his power and have to answer for his crimes, he chose to drop out of school and left Whyalla. First, he robbed a local convenience store for some cash before he struck out on his own.

"Easy pickings," he thought when he saw how easily he could come and go without notice. No one seemed to miss Cyrus after he left, including his mother.

Without so much as a goodbye, he packed his belongings, stole a car, and drove straight to Adelaide. Outside the city, he abandoned the car and paid for an apartment with the stolen cash. He spent the last of his funds on some meager furnishings for his apartment. Short on money, he began to rob stores around Adelaide the next day. Sometimes at the end of a long day, he did not have much power left within him. Depleted of its source, the weakened Cyrus quickly made his way home before he passed out, sometimes with piles of stolen money scattered around in the same bed with him until he slowly recovered.

Cyrus found and dealt with one eager pawnbroker who took particular interest in his goods. The man soon realized that Cyrus was probably the "silent robber" as the press dubbed him. The news stated one peculiar thief left no trace and baffled local investigators on how he continually disabled security systems. The pawnbroker did not question Cyrus' source of items, as the man quickly changed most of the expensive fenced jewelry into its basic elements. He removed the stones and melted the metal parts of the jewelry into pure elemental bars. Cyrus' continued business represented more money than any source he ever had. Therefore, when the police came around with questions, the pawnbroker looked the other way and said he knew nothing. He quietly accumulated wealth from the strange scrawny young man with an uncanny ability to steal anything undetected.

On one occasion when Cyrus entered with his weekly round of goods, Cyrus took the pawnbroker, whose name was Sidney, by surprise with an entire jewelry store heist. He pulled up his satchel and poured out some expensive pieces. Sid could hardly believe his windfall – gold rings, bracelets, chains, two large sapphires, and a 4-carat diamond solitaire worth more than half his shop of trinkets.

"Not bad…" he muttered and took out his loupe to get a closer look. He had seen many fakes. This stone was genuine. He pulled the loupe out of his eye and whistled.

"See? I've got some nice stuff for you today, Sid," Cyrus said with pride.

The pawnbroker's eyes lit up with glee. However, he felt this inexperience kid needed some guidance. He wanted Cyrus to rob bigger places, since the "kid" had a knack for it. He was just as greedy as Cyrus.

"You got lucky this time, kid. But you're going to need a gun if you intend to rob anything bigger than a small neighborhood jewelry store," the pawnbroker quipped.

"Just give me my cash, Sid," Cyrus told the man behind the safety cage.

As usual, the man weighed the gold jewelry and handed over to the nineteen-year-old a small percentage of the stolen goods' actual value. Yet, Cyrus considered it a large amount of cash.

"I have a large selection of handguns…" Sid pointed out.

"Guns?" Cyrus questioned as he counted his money. "I don't never need no gun," he commented. He looked up at the puzzled man's face. "First of all, I don't need to threaten anyone who gets in my way," the youth bragged. "Second, a gun can't do what I can do."

"A gun could stop you in your tracks," the pawnbroker scoffed.

"No gun can stop me," Cyrus said with sinister tones. "Guns are for idiots."

"Everybody needs a gun," the man insisted. "Even I have a gun," he said. He pulled out a large caliber handgun. He pointed the barrel at Cyrus while he fingered the weapon, mostly to prove he would not hesitate to use it.

The moment the pawnbroker threatened him with that gesture, Cyrus decided he did not like Sid. In fact, once he took the time to look into the man's mind, he saw how the pawnbroker had actually robbed him of his fair share over the past year and a half. He glanced down at the gun in Sid's hands.

"Go ahead, try to shoot me," Cyrus told the man. "You'll find it's impossible. No one can harm me!" he bragged.

"Get out of here, you stupid little brat," the pawnbroker said with a grin. "You may be a good thief, but you're the one who's an idiot!" he said and laughed.

"Don't you laugh at me," Cyrus told him.

"What are you going to do, you scrawny little bastard? You can't even swat a fly!" the pawnbroker pointed out.

"You'll be sorry you said that," Cyrus muttered.

The smile on the pawnbroker's face faded. He reached over and activated the switch to open the security door. Cyrus stepped through the door and watched as Sid took his handgun, placed the barrel to his head, and blew his brains out. Cyrus pushed his carcass out of the way. He destroyed the security system and cleaned out the shop's coffers.

When he opened Sid's safe, Cyrus realized he hit the jackpot. He would not have to rob any more stores. Sid had enough valuables in his safe so that Cyrus could live in comfort for a long time: diamonds, watches, bars of platinum, gold, and silver, rare coins, and lots of cash. He found two large gym bags in the back and filled them so full, he could hardly move them. He took Sid's car keys, threw the bags in the trunk and started the car.

Cyrus walked back inside and turned on the gas stove that Sid used in the winter months for heat. He cracked open a back window and left, using his mind to lock the door from the inside. In the alley behind the store, he lit a cigarette and took his time smoking it. He looked over at the barely opened window and sensed the time had arrived. He stepped into the car, started the engine, and backed up the alley several meters.

"Let's see how good my aim is," he whispered.

He flicked the cigarette butt into the air. The hot tipped stub flew with incredible precision and entered the window just as the gas reached the opening. The shop exploded, caught fire, and burned to the ground. Later, the police autopsy determined the pawnbroker had committed suicide. After that day, Cyrus added murder to his list of atrocities.

As he sat in the car outside his apartment, he contemplated his next move.

"What am I doing?" he thought as he considered the two bags full of loot. "This amount of money is nothing compared to what I could make. After all, who can stop me?" he thought. "Why should I settle for petty theft, when I could own a treasury?"

By the time December of 2018 rolled around, Cyrus – now living in a large house under an assumed identity – grew bored with his life in Adelaide. He decided to "look in on his mother," whom he hadn't seen in a very long time. He didn't know why, but he thought he might drive past his old house in Whyalla.

"Maybe I'll pay a few bills for her," he thought. "I suppose I owe her that much."

After he drove around the bay to Whyalla and discovered she had moved away – the small house where he grew up was abandoned, ruined, and boarded up – he headed back to Adelaide. All during his drive, he thought about what he could accomplish with his power. He felt he needed to widen his scope and create some grand scheme that involved a much larger target.

"I am the only one in the world with this power," he thought. "No one can stop me."

His inflated egomaniac mind raced with possibilities as he headed around the bay toward Adelaide.

Just north of the city, he noticed a homemade sign along the side of the road that pointed to some large gathering in an open park. Several people, some with campers, had set up for some celestial event.

"I wonder what's going on?" he questioned as he slowed down to investigate.

Curious, he pulled into the roadside park where he encountered a large group of people setting up several devices. People were scattered into smaller parties that stood around certain complex apparatuses he had never seen. He wondered what they were.

"Astronomy meeting tonight," a sign stuck in the grass read, "all are welcome."

He did not know a thing about astronomy or even what a telescope was. He had never seen one. Science never interested Cyrus in school. Yet, for some reason, the subject and the devices aroused his curiosity. He parked his car amidst the trucks and trailers camped out on the site. Dozens of people formed "tailgate" parties. Smoke rose from grills cooking food while people shared stories, ate and drank while they waited for darkness. He noticed a few people had large and nice telescopes, while dozens more brought their own smaller versions. Cyrus walked over to a young man seated at a table, which had a sign "Help our club" on the front. Most of those people attending the event had already arrived.

A freckled-faced young man with reddish-blonde hair, no more than 16 or 17 years of age, sat behind a table with a cash box collecting a "donation" admission fee for new observers who wished to participate. He started to ask Cyrus if he was a club member. Instead, he changed his mind and stared straight ahead. Cyrus moved along side, already linked into his brain, and shared the young man's thoughts.

"What are you doing here?" Cyrus mentally inquired.

"Stargazing," the young man's thoughts told him.

"Stargazin?" Cyrus questioned, "Explain."

"Do you know what a telescope is?" the youth wondered.

"I think so..." Cyrus replied. However, he found the device and its purpose in the young man's thoughts. "How will you use them?"

"We use telescopes to look at different celestial objects... most people like to look at Jupiter, Saturn, certain nebula... Tonight, we're trying to spot object 6847 (2009) ER," the youth told him.

"What is that?" he asked.

"An Alinda asteroid," the teen replied. "It is the largest celestial object to pass this close to the earth in the last ten million years. It's nearly 2 km across. It's orbit will take it between the earth and the moon! Isn't it exciting?" the youth's enthusiasm betrayed his emotional attachment to the subject.

"An asteroid?" Cyrus thought. "Why should anyone be so excited over a big rock in space?" he considered.

"Don't you know?" the young man's brain answered. "If that asteroid hit the planet, it could cause a terrible ecological disaster," he relayed to the psychic. "Granted, it isn't as big as the one that wiped out the dinosaurs, but this chunk of rock could do some serious damage if it struck one of the continents," he informed Cyrus.

For a few moments, Cyrus pictured the thought in his mind. He imagined the chaos that would follow such an event... just the kind of diversion that would allow an opportunistic psychic person to take advantage of the situation.

"Paul, is it?" Cyrus asked.

"Yes," he responded, "my name is Paul."

"What would happen if it struck the ocean?" he asked the teen.

"I suppose it would depend on the depth of the ocean. Water would certainly cushion the impact, but still result in a huge tsunami that would engulf the coastline of any nearby landmass," Paul told Cyrus.

Cyrus held the young man prisoner inside his own mind. Paul had no choice but respond to Cyrus.

"Where would it do the most damage?" Cyrus wondered.

"The Gulf of Mexico..." Paul speculated, "or the Caspian Sea... oh, yeah, I'd say the Sea of China would be the best spot or the worst."

"Why there?" Cyrus wondered.

"It lies between Japan, South Korea, and the east coast of China… probably a billion people would be affected," the teen guessed.

"Would you say it would disrupt the world's economy?" Cyrus wondered.

"Economy?" the lad retorted. "The meteor's impact would devastate China's coastal cities, including Shanghai. That would wipe out her export business, and probably a third of her population. Half of Japan and South Korea would be under water. Banks around the world would collapse…"

"Good," Cyrus thought. "I have chosen the place where the asteroid should hit," he thought.

"You can't just land an asteroid in one spot," Paul's voice broke in.

"Why not?" Cyrus angrily shot back.

"For one, you'd have to move it, adjust its speed…" Paul pointed out.

"How does one move an asteroid into a collision course with the Earth?" Cyrus asked.

"It would take a huge amount of energy… unless," the intelligent teen thought.

"Yes?" Cyrus asked.

"Well, if the asteroid was still far enough out in space, a simple nudge is enough to change its trajectory," Paul reasoned. "But you'd have to apply the right amount of energy on a specific date and time to have the asteroid penetrate the atmosphere and land exactly where you wanted," the teen explained.

"How do you do that?" Cyrus wanted to know.

"I'm not an expert…" Paul told him.

"What I need is an expert. Where is the nearest…" he thought as he searched the young man's brain, "…astronomer?"

"Dr. Gerald Gordon is giving a lecture on astrophysics at the university in Adelaide this weekend," the knowledgeable teen replied.

"Perfect timin'," Cyrus thought.

"Paul?" a voice called out.

One of the young man's friends started to walk toward the table, curious about the man who stood next to Paul. Yet he noticed that neither said a word. Cyrus turned that person way. The day had finally given way to the evening as twilight faded to darkness.

"Good bye, Paul. You've been every useful," Cyrus said as he turned away.

The teen stood frozen for a moment, before he rolled his eyes back into his head, his eyelashes fluttered, and he fell over backward to the ground.

"Look everyone!" someone yelled.

Cyrus nervously glanced around.

"It's the space station!" the person said as he pointed skyward.

Most everyone looked up. For the moment, no one noticed poor Paul's condition. Cyrus took advantage of the distraction and returned to his car, deep in thought as he pondered over this new information. He suddenly had a new goal. He needed to seek out one other person to help him create a plan of attack, an expert in how to move an asteroid. At last he had a purpose, something worthy of his talent, one to which he could aspire. He would be great. No, he would be the greatest man who ever lived. A new grand plan began to percolate inside his brain.

"I must seek out this... Gerald Gordon," he thought. "I should return to Adelaide and find this astronomer." His ego soared with excitement at the prospect of being... *the most powerful person in the world.*

CHAPTER ELEVEN

THE PROFESSOR'S FORMULA

AFTER CYRUS LEFT THE ROADSIDE gathering, he recalled the words of the amateur astronomer and thought about what it could mean for his future. Now that he had a goal in mind, he needed help to achieve that goal. He needed an expert.

"Dr. Gerald Gordon is giving a lecture on astrophysics at the university in Adelaide this weekend…" he heard Paul's voice.

As he drove back to the city, he began to map out the details of his plan after the disaster. Once the asteroid hit, he would move into China and take over command of what military infrastructure remained… after he affected the path of the asteroid… if it could be done, an ambitious goal. He would need help with that, too. He would need a team of military experts, a group of fighting men, expendable men, who would protect him and help him achieve his goals. They would sneak into China just before the asteroid struck and infiltrate the military infrastructure. When confusion reigned supreme, he would surprise his rivals, Russia and America, with a pre-emptive nuclear strike. After that, he would rule over humanity with his power to manipulate minds.

Once he arrived in Adelaide, he headed straight for the university and continued to make more ambitious plans in his mind.

"Perhaps I can broadcast my power through the television," he considered. "But first, I need to move an asteroid. Then I'll surround myself with a small army of men… enough to supply me with all the energy I need…"

He knew how to absorb energy from others as long as he remained close to the source long enough. He also knew that if he were to attack an object as far away as a remote location in space, he would need many men around him with heightened emotional states to quickly replenish his energy.

"I'm going to need my own private army," he thought.

He thought about where he could find them, too. He heard of a small town north of Adelaide that lent itself to the criminal element. He would scout locations for his camp one afternoon and wander around the desert. Perhaps he would find the kind of place to suit his needs. He would do this after he visited this professor. Cyrus' mind raced with possibilities as he drove faster and faster toward the lecture hall. He checked his expensive watch. He hoped he hadn't arrived too late.

"First thing first," he thought as he turned into the parking lots outside the lecture hall. "I must pay this professor a visit and persuade him to cooperate."

He parked his car and entered the front door. He found the lecture hall and quietly entered the back of the auditorium. The professor had already given the bulk of his talk on astrophysics and was summing up. The packed room surprised Cyrus, as he wondered why so many people showed up for such an obviously boring subject.

"I had no idea anyone would find such a dull topic so interestin'," he mused.

Cyrus did not realize Dr. Gordon's importance in the astrological community. Gerald Gordon published one of the greatest papers of the decade when he presented his Grand Overall Theory of Cosmology. He had been nominated twice for a Nobel Prize in physics. Cyrus didn't care about his credentials. He only wanted someone smart enough to work out a solution for his plan and felt Dr. Gordon could accomplish it.

Dr. Gordon continued to speak. So, Cyrus decided to listen…

"… and if we pull back from the local group into an even larger picture of galactic clusters," Gordon spoke, "we begin to see pathways between clusters of galaxies. These skeins may represent routes of energy that connect great clusters," the professor said as he gestured to the large screen on the wall. "We believe these conduits hold great significance in the overall theory of how energy in the cosmos interacts," he explained. "The universe contains many unfamiliar types of energy and hidden forces…"

"You got that right, professor," Cyrus thought. "If you only knew how connected those clusters are," he thought.

"… when we understand the purpose of the conduits and the overall interaction between the clusters, then we will not only understand the powerful forces of the universe, but perhaps gain insight into its creation," the professor finished. The lights came up. The room broke into applause.

As soon as the lecture ended, Cyrus worked his way through the exiting audience up to the podium. Surrounded by admirers and the curious, Dr. Gordon slowly wound his way from the stage toward an exit off to the side that led to his car. He had other appointments to keep. So did Cyrus. He considered his life a busy and important one, too. He wasted no time in clearing a path to the astrophysicist and soon eliminated the competition.

"Dr. Gordon," Cyrus said as he drew nearer.

The professor's conversation with a young woman suddenly halted when she abruptly turned around and walked away. The puzzled man realized that everyone around him had also left, except one man who stood before him. Gordon artificially smiled at this man possessed with the strange stern expression and piercing eyes.

"We must talk," Cyrus said briskly. "This way," he said and gestured.

Without so much as a wave to his friends across the room, the professor and this stranger slipped quietly from the auditorium and out the side exit door. As soon as they stepped outside, Cyrus directed the professor to the back of the building. The smaller parking lot directly behind the auditorium seemed deserted.

"I hate to be in a hurry," Cyrus began, "but I need some answers and I need them now. I'm still not very good at probin' memories but here goes."

Cyrus scanned the man's mind without disrupting too many blood vessels or memory banks. This time he slowly moved through the brain and managed not to break any as he had with the amateur astronomer Paul. He found a vast storage file filled with personal history, current facts, and of course, Gordon's cosmology theory. Simply because he beheld the thing did not imply he understood it.

"I don't know what this means," Cyrus thought. "I suppose I'll have to revive you."

Cyrus pulled out of the man's mind. For a moment, Gerald Gordon stood still, blinking as he stared all around him and wondered how he moved from the auditorium to this place in what seemed like an instant to him. In fact, it appeared as if everything had changed around them by Gordon's perspective.

"Where am I?" he asked. "Who are you?" he wondered as he engaged Cyrus. "How did we suddenly move here?"

"Never mind that for now," Cyrus stated as he dismissed his question. "You are safe but I am in command. If you don't think so, mate, I can make you strike your own face any time I wish."

"Try it," the professor goaded.

"It's your face," Cyrus said as he completed the thought put to action.

Dr. Gordon formed a fist and started to smash it full force into his nose. It stopped just barely a hair's breadth from the skin. He'd clenched his eyes shut in reaction and then opened them as he stared cross-eyed at the fist hovering in front of his face.

"Please don't test my resolve again, doc," Cyrus told him. "I am not a patient man and am liable to do somethin' terrible. For now, I will let you live if you give me the information I need," Cyrus threatened.

The professor, still staring at his fist, gulped.

"May I have my arm back?" he asked.

His arm fell limp to his side. When he regained control, he held up his hand and examined it as if it were a specimen.

"Amazing power," he said quietly.

"I can do a lot more," Cyrus informed him. "Right now, Dr. Gordon, I need information. Then I'll let you go."

Gerald Gordon turned to the obtrusive man with the strange face. He'd seen a face like that once, on the wall of a post office. That was the face of a killer.

"What do you want to know?" Gordon wondered.

"I want you to calculate how much energy it would take to move object 6847 (2009) ER," Cyrus requested.

"Are you with a government?" Dr. Gordon asked him.

"Who I am and what I will do with this information is none of your damn business doc. Can you make the calculation or not?" Cyrus pressed his question.

"Yes, if you give me a moment," Gerald responded.

"In your head?" Cyrus asked.

"I do all my calculations in my head," Dr. Gordon told him.

"Alright then, go ahead," Cyrus stated.

The professor began to visualize the asteroid. He knew the number classification very well and the asteroid's history. The infamous object was once thought to be part of the extinction event maker; only to put off doomsayer's predictions by having its projected path miss the earth, albeit barely. As he prepared to do this, Cyrus dropped in on his thinking process. He watched how the professor calculated the asteroid's weight, speed, its current trajectory, and mass.

"First, I'd like to know how you propose to alter its course," he asked Cyrus. "I won't ask why because, well, frankly I believe it's a futile gesture."

"I'll be usin' a special kind of energy," Cyrus told him.

"And how will you focus this energy away from the planet and into space? The further your energy travels from Earth, the more likely it will diffuse and spread apart, which would make its impact very small, if felt by the asteroid at all," Gordon told him.

"That was my next question. My mind can produce a great deal of energy. How can I focus enough of this energy to move the object?" Cyrus wondered.

"You could try to bounce it, if you had a mirror source. It would have to be a very large mirror," Gordon told him.

Cyrus suddenly recalled the last thing the person shouted at the astronomy meeting... the space station! He had seen depictions of it, with its large shiny panels that stuck out from its sides.

"How about the solar panels on the space station? They could reflect a beam and I think they have energy in them," Cyrus pointed out. "Would they be enough to boost a signal from Earth?"

"They're certain large enough and have considerable power," Gerald Gordon told him. "However, they are at the wrong attitude. You'd have to turn the station on its side. Changing the position of a vessel that large will not be easy."

"Then what?" Cyrus asked.

"Well, then you'd need to focus your beam at this panel and aim it in the right direction, of course. Because of the power in those panels, they might help amplify the signal, thereby giving it additional power to... actually, this kind of preposterous," the professor chuckled. "Energy from a person's mind..."

"Can you do the calculation?" Cyrus asked.

"Yes, but I won't. On some strange chance that what you propose might be possible, I won't be party to this," Gordon told him.

"To what?" Cyrus responded as he had tried to not tip his hand.

"Whatever it is you are planning?" Gerald said, stepping back. "Why are you changing the course of this asteroid? I can think of only one reason."

"You are correct, professor. That is indeed what I intend," Cyrus said.

"You read my mind?" Dr. Gordon asked.

"I am in your mind now. Look at my lips carefully," Cyrus said as he stepped into the light from the nearby overhead streetlamp.

"They do not move," Gordon observed.

"Our minds are linked through a special connection," Cyrus explained.

"Are you some sort of mutant?" the doctor of astronomy inquired.

"You might say that," Cyrus admitted. "Now I'd like that calculation, if you don't mind."

"But I do mind," Gordon told him as he took a step backward. "I will not help you in this harebrained scheme of yours."

"You have no choice, doc," Cyrus told him. "I see you working at the Sliding Spring Observatory. I see your son, your wife, your brother... you've told me where they live in Coonabarabran, their habits, addresses, phone numbers. I see everythin' about 'em. I can find your son at school and hurt him in terrible ways that you would not like. As I hurt him and your wife, I can make you watch. Eventually, I can wipe out every member of your family and all the friends you ever knew, professor. I would leave you alone to think about what harm you caused them by not givin' me the information I want. Now… give me that information now!" he demanded.

"What's to prevent you from doing that anyway?" Gordon replied in a shaky voice. He realized that this man had no scruples.

"I don't like to use force unless I have to. Tell me what I want, and I will let you go. I've already told you I would do this," Cyrus told him.

"Alright," Doctor Gordon sighed. "I will give in to your demands. I don't wish any harm toward my family. If I give you your information, I only ask one thing in return."

"What?" Cyrus said impatient. He had waited long enough.

"When do you plan for this catastrophe?" Gordon asked.

"Oh, right after that asteroid hits the planet," Cyrus told him.

"Then you must affect the asteroid's path approximately six weeks from now or it will miss the planet," Dr. Gordon replied. "It will take a great deal of energy…"

"I have the energy. Start your formulas," Cyrus directed.

"Very well, I will make the calculations. Here is your information," the professor said.

A flood of calculations poured from the scientist's mind: the angle of the solar panels, amounts of energy required, the precise location and timing of the strike all entered Cyrus' brain. He took note of everything. He did not have to write anything down. He had developed an incredible capacity to remember everything. Even if he didn't understand the formulas, he could write them down and have a computer figure the calculations.

As soon as Dr. Gordon finished, Cyrus turned and started to walk away.

"Please…" Gordon called to him. "I must know…"

"What?" Cyrus stopped with his back to him.

"Why?" Dr. Gordon called after him. "Why do you wish to kill all those innocent people?" he helplessly pleaded.

"Power," Cyrus whispered to his mind with his back still turned toward the doctor. "When this is over, I will be the most powerful man in the world."

"It's always the same, isn't it," Gordon shouted after Cyrus. "As men gain power, it corrupts them to the point they believe nothing can stop them. Why not use your ability to do something good?"

"Good?" Cyrus said as he turned around and glared at the professor. "Soon, the whole world will look up to me as a god to perform miracles for them. I will be their savior. Mankind will worship me for centuries as the greatest human that ever lived. Everyone will know my name and do my biddin'."

"And when you have this world in your grasp, what will you do with it?" Gordon asked him.

"Do as I want," Cyrus stated with a serious face.

"That's it? That's your goal?" Gordon wondered.

"What more is there?" Cyrus responded.

Professor Gordon carefully asked this next question about his own fate.

"Will there be a place for scientists in this world of yours?" the professor put to Cyrus.

"Definitely," Cyrus stated. "I need you to invent new stuff for my amusement. Goodnight, doctor."

The image of Cyrus vanished into the darkness as Dr. Gerald Gordon stared at the space where his form had been. Without regard for his friends, the shaken doctor ran to his car. He no longer cared about the Nobel Prize or anything else except the safety of his family. He also knew he had to move his family far away from Australia. He had friends in Europe. He would go there and find a position.

He hurriedly entered his car, started it and zoomed off without putting on his seatbelt. As he quickly drove up the road, a voice spoke to him, the voice of that crazy man.

"You can run from Australia as far as you want, Dr. Gordon," the voice spoke to his mind. "I can still find you… Gerald!"

Distracted, Dr. Gordon momentarily stared off at nothing. He did not see a student walking back to his dorm. The student absent-mindedly stepped into the road, thinking about Dr. Gordon's lecture. At the last moment, Gordon swerved to avoid him only to strike a tree along the side of the road. Even with airbags, the doctor's body, unrestrained, flew through the windshield and rolled on the ground. As he took his last breath, he saw to his horror, the image of an asteroid striking the planet.

"What have I done?" he cried.

Then Dr. Gerald Gordon was no more.

CHAPTER TWELVE

CHANGE OF HEART

SERGEANT HENRY BEERY LOVED HIS job... and why shouldn't he? He no longer worried about strenuous physical labor as he inched his way toward retirement, ever since his old commander, Major General Pollack, brought him over to the Digger's Club where he worked the front desk. As social secretary and head of security, Beery kept the members of the club happy. He made certain their favorite chair remained unoccupied should they drop by. He had their favorite drink ready when they did walked in, and had a current newspaper on a nearby table, or a sandwich ready should one of them request it.

He and his staff of three corporals stood ready at the officers' disposal. If he was not pulling duty at the Digger's Club, Sergeant Beery might be the maitre d' of a famous trendy restaurant. He made certain operations at the club ran smoothly. The aging sergeant enjoyed his quiet secure position at the club. He took it very seriously.

When the old aboriginal's entry embarrassed the sergeant, he wanted to make up for his blunder in the major general's eyes.

"My car, sergeant," Major General Pollack requested as he walked up to the desk about an hour after the incident. The sergeant pushed the button for the corporal acting as valet that day.

"Yes, sir!" a voice came through the intercom.

"Major General Pollack's car," the sergeant ordered through the device.

The general stood by impatiently as he waited for his car. Although only parked up the street, he liked having his car ready for him at the front steps when he exited the club. When the corporal stepped out, he noticed a folded piece of white paper stuck up under the wiper.

"Sorry, sir," the corporal said and started to grab it when the sergeant yelled out.

"I'll take that!" he ordered. He reached over and snatched the paper from the windshield. He was about to tear it to pieces, when the general stepped forward and put out his hand.

"Beery!" the general barked. "Hand that note to me," he demanded.

"Yes, sir," Sergeant Beery said. He snapped to attention as he handed the note over.

The general did not bother to open the note. He slipped the paper into his right pants' pocket. He noticed the strange handwriting on the outside, and the printed word, "Periwinkle." He knew not to open it in front of anyone present; although, he guessed that the sergeant had a vague memory regarding the name.

"Strange they left it on the outside of the car," he thought. "That's taking a chance."

The general glanced around to see if anyone else might be watching them as he moved into his car. Very few people knew the origin of that title. He wondered how the old aboriginal man knew about Code Periwinkle, unless a breach in security happened and someone exposed his secret file. He wished now that he had retained the man for questioning instead of letting him go.

"I hope this wasn't a set up... that I played into Sander's hands," he thought.

As the general drove out to his home in the country, he wondered what the note would mean and what secrets it would contain.

"A shame I can't raise Penelope," he thought as he drove through the city. "She's at the hospital today with the women's auxiliary, performing volunteer work, looking in on veterans. If I call her cell phone, she'll let me have it for disturbing her."

He swelled with pride when he recalled her work for various charities and community projects. However, on days when she volunteered so much of her time, she would not be home to cook. Penelope did all the cooking. That meant the general had to reheat leftovers, or microwave some frozen product. No delicate flavorful home cooked meal this evening.

The hour turned late in Australia, where summer months occur in December, January and February. By the time the general pulled into his driveway, the sun sank below the horizon. The first evening stars began to shimmer in the growing twilight. He parked the car in the garage and walked through the empty house. His children left the nest years before, grown, with families of their own. On holidays, they came to visit... the grandchildren eager to see Grandpa... if he was available. James was seldom at home and missed many birthdays, sports games, graduations, and concerts. As a devoted public servant, the military was his life. Penelope accepted that even if the children had difficulty accepting it. For all his success, the general only wanted close companionship in his senior years. Penelope satisfied all of his needs. Even after all the years he spent with her, the arguments, the threats, the angry words they exchanged in the past, he had many more pleasant memories with her than unpleasant ones. He still loved her very much and she did him.

Seeing her picture on the bar, he sighed, "We made this far, Pen... guess we'll stick together to the end, eh what?" he commented.

Fumbling in his pocket, he felt the note and pulled it out. Rather than read it, he tossed the note onto the bar at one end of their living room. The general enjoyed a stiff drink now and then, as did his friends. He didn't like to drink too much at the club, as he drove home afterward. But now that he was home and recalled the disastrous day he had that ended in total chaos, a drink sounded good to him.

He walked around the bar and poured out some whiskey in a glass with a few chunks of ice. The general preferred English whiskey to any other spirit, usually just straight up at the bottom of a glass. Some men his age preferred gin and tonic. Not the general. His grandfather introduced the older teen to fine aged whiskeys years ago when he attended Sandhurst and returned to the estate when granted leave. He never once saw his grandfather inebriated. The sage taught him temperance, something he kept his entire life. Tonight, he tempered the whiskey with a bit of soda water. He raised the glass toward the family portraits that lined one area behind the bar.

"To you grandfather... father... you were my rock," he said and tipped his head back.

He nearly drained the glass and hesitated to pour another. Despite his day being a long and difficult one, if he drank too heavily, he'd have a headache in the morning.

"More bureaucratic paperwork to push," he commented when he sat in a large comfortable chair. He kicked off his shoes and took a sip of what remained in his glass. "This new project is a pain in the ass!"

His commanding officer ordered his area to undergo an overhaul in the computer system along with its programming, a monumental task, considering they would replace every piece of equipment and install all new programs. That meant retraining his staff, too. Today, some sort of glitch in the system resulted in either misplacing or losing a large amount of military equipment. It fell on his division to modernize the procurement division so that this sort of thing did not happen again.

"A bloody waste of time," the general thought. "I wish we'd settle on one damn system instead of having to improve and change them every five years!"

His staff grudgingly voted to pull double duty during the week, to have the new system up and running. Additional hours along with all the changes made life in his operations department very stressful. They also had the burdensome task of locating this missing shipment of parts and vehicles in the inventory. They wouldn't mind a few missing vehicles, but the weapons were another matter. He had to send staff investigators from his office to scour warehouses manually as the main storage buildings were scattered between bases in Sydney, Canberra, Melbourne, and Adelaide. The process left his office short on workers and supplies with several divisions crying for parts and vehicles.

By the end of the week, the general longed for a field command, like the older days in his youth.

"Field commands are for the younger officers, not the old men," he thought as he finished off his whiskey. "Funny," he considered. "I don't feel old. I can still do push-ups, sit ups, and run as fast as most of the office geeks in my building," he mused when he thought about the personnel under him.

As he stared at the empty glass, he realized he did not put in enough. That was when he noticed his aged hand. He firmly gripped the glass and knew that at one time, he could have shattered the glass with his brute strength. He knew better than to try that any longer.

"They don't want an aging major general in the military," he said as he tipped up the glass to his lips. "You're hair is turning gray. You have old-fashioned opinions. You haven't been educated in a state college the way these new officers have," he echoed the sentiment of his superiors. "You have the stiff boorish manners of the upper class. That sort of individual doesn't fit in with the new group," he thought as he took in the last drop. "You know the difference between Keats and Byron, Hayden and Handel, Newton and Russell... you can speak Greek, Latin, and French... but these new officers don't give a rat's ass about any of that stuff! They consider you pretentious and overbearing. I'm a social bore. Well, to hell with them... and to hell with supper!"

James rose to refill his glass. If Penelope were coming home late, then he would drown his sorrows with a few more drinks before he went to bed. He no longer cared about eating. He didn't even care if he rose tomorrow with a headache. He went to the large southwest-facing window. The bright lights of Adelaide burned in the distance.

The sun had set and still no word from Penelope, not a phone call, not even a text message. The general poured out another double whiskey over his melting ice before he glanced down at the folded paper he dropped on the bar.

He set down his drink and picked up the message. He opened the folded paper and noted the handwriting. A shaky hand scribbled the following rather long note in English:

"Dear Sir: I am a man who must care for his village just as you care for your men. I have never traveled far from my village. Two nights ago, my ancestors visited me. They told me the sky is falling, which, as we both know, is silly..."

"You've got that right," the general commented. He read on.

"However, my ancestor also told me of a man in the outback of Western Australia, somewhere west of Warburton, intent on some devilish path. A large number of followers surround this man, whom they consider their leader. They are armed with stolen weapons taken from a military base. You cannot fight this evil in any normal way. No military power can destroy him. To stop this man, you will need the help of those located in America. Good luck, Major General Pollack. Oodgeroo."

First the words, "...stolen weapons taken from a military base," bothered him. "I wonder how he knows that to be true." Then the words, "No military power can destroy him," struck a familiar chord in the general's mind. He had all kinds of weapons at his disposal, tanks, artillery, cruise missiles, and even airborne sorties. Why would this aboriginal man think the Australian Army could not take out a few little flies in the desert?

The general returned to his comfortable chair, sipped his refreshed glass of whiskey, and read the note three more times before he finished his second whiskey and fell asleep in the chair.

"James," a voice spoke.

The general heard a soft calm voice in his head. Was he dreaming?

"Yes?" he answered.

"James, wake up. It's me, Penelope," his wife said.

He felt a finger poking into his chest. He blinked his eyes and glanced up.

His wife's lovely face came into view. Like James, Penelope Pollack began to form gray hairs in her once beautiful auburn hair. She felt fortunate. Most of her friends had dyed their hair for years. She put off dying hers. While she did not "let her body go," she began to take on that doughy appearance older people acquire. Yet, her eyes still sparkled with kindness and understanding, as they had all of her life.

"Penelope? Oh, yes," James sputtered. "Sorry, dear. I must have fallen asleep." He wiped the sleep from his eyes as his wife came into focus. He smiled up at her. "Must have been dreaming... fought a campaign in the desert against a formidable foe. Then I..."

The general noticed the note from the car had slipped from his hand. He searched the floor for it.

"Looking for this?" Penelope said as she held up the note. "Who is Periwinkle?"

James cleared his throat and sat up straight. Penelope knew that when he acted this way, he usually had to lie to her about the true meaning of things like Periwinkle. She knew he never told anyone, not even his own wife about certain military secrets.

"It was a nickname from the men…" he began.

"No, it wasn't," she shot back while she shook her head. She knew when he lied to her. "I suppose I don't need to know," Penelope said as she glanced down at the note, "Do I? But, what's all this nonsense? I called the club to see what time you left. Sergeant Beery informed me that an old black man asked to see you. He laughed and said the man told you the sky is falling." Penelope did not smile. "At first, I thought it was absurd, until I read this note. I'm no military expert, but this sounds like a warning."

The general's eyes fell on the note and then he glanced back up at his wife. "Now you're the one sounding queer, Penny," he said, dismissive. "That's just the ranting of some old man."

She gave him a familiar expression of concern. She stood her ground while she waited for an explanation.

"Honestly!" he said, in denial. "This note is absurd. It doesn't make sense."

James stood up from the chair. He took the note from her hand and tore it to pieces, throwing the pieces into a waste paper basket inside the bar.

"That's the end of that!" he said as he brushed his hands.

Penelope's eyes went to the wastebasket. She decided that an argument was not worth their time, and turned away as she intended to head upstairs.

"How was your day?" he said as he tried to change the subject.

"Oh, you know, the usual stuff," she stopped to reengage. "The retirement center is at full capacity. I checked on the condition of the veterans that we know and looked in on a few that I've never met. They do so look forward to our visits. I particularly enjoy seeing General Stipden. He has such a great sense of humor after all the terrible things that happened to his family… wife died of cancer, his only son killed in action. He faced a lot of personal adversity through the years and still manages to smile and tell jokes. I don't know how he does it."

"I actually miss seeing him at Diggers…" the general softly reminisced.

Penelope glanced back at her husband for a moment and realized he no longer paid attention to her. He stood at the bar and stared out the window. His gaze seemed unfocused as if another subject occupied his thoughts. After being married for this many years, Penelope knew her James better than he knew his own mind. She could tell that when his thoughts drifted away like this, he usually had a good reason.

"I'm going up to shower," she said and left him alone.

The general set down his drink and walked over to the window. Their house sat up on a hillside with a nice view of the bay in the far distance. The twinkling lights of Adelaide lay all around the rim of the inlet bay.

The general's eyes wandered up to the stars. With the city lights so close, he had difficulty making out many celestial bodies except the main constellations, a few bright stars and planets. Something caught his eye. One particular star twinkled bright blue, its brilliant light and color seemed out of place.

"That's a bit odd," the general remarked. "I never noticed that one before."

At first, he thought it might be a jet or a plane, even a satellite. Yet the more he gazed on the celestial object, the more he found he could not take his eyes away. The star seemed too pretty and captivating. All at once, he began to feel dizzy. He thought it might be the alcohol. Yet, this sensation transported him away. He wondered if this was the beginning of a heart attack or a stroke.

"Oh, my," he said as he began to weave unsteadily.

He thought of calling out to Penelope for help, but the words he wanted to say caught in his throat. His lips moved but nothing came out. He reeled backward, lost his balance, and fell to the floor. His eyes rolled back into his head. He lost consciousness as he stared up at the ceiling and the room began to fade.

"Am I dying?" was his last thought.

CHAPTER THIRTEEN

MANGY MEN

"GET IN A STRAIGHT LINE you filthy scum!" Girard barked as he walked down the line of ragged men standing before him.

He turned away from them and walked toward the front. In the oppressive heat of the mid-day sun, sweat trickled down the sides of his face and from under his arms. He wanted to strip off his damp t-shirt, but felt that since he made the men work out in their uniforms, he should set an example.

The men in his best two best companies had to suppress a smile. They knew Girard looked out for them and fought for their best interests. Unlike the way they feared Cyrus, these men admired Girard and held him in higher esteem than their so-called leader. Girard had a sense of pride in the way the men in companies A and B responded to his command. For the first time in his life, he had a feeling of accomplishment.

"You look like soldiers," he thought as he walked along their line.

The two front groups were in great physical condition. Their uniforms exuded good clean sweat from a hard workout, just as his did. They stood at attention in perfect rows. In a relatively short time, they became harden soldiers. They took command without question. He molded them into a fighting force that would make any military commander confident in his troop's abilities to carry out missions. Girard knew most of these men by their first names and trusted them. They were smart, worked well in teams, and relied on each other for support.

"I could take these men into battle and win," he thought.

The front two groups slept in the preferred area just below his bungalow. At night, he walked among them and took their personal requests to Cyrus, who usually fulfilled them. Some of the men wanted a change in women, while others wanted money for families back home, or special food items. Cyrus could usually find a way to procure and fulfill their requests.

Yet, as Girard looked past them toward the back, his confidence waivered until he noticed a distinct difference, the sloppy dress and lackadaisical attitude on the men's faces within his last two companies. He wondered how Cyrus would behave if he saw some of these men. They resembled the kind of men he saw in prison... undisciplined, uncooperative, and unruly.

"Company's A and B!" he yelled out to the group of one hundred men. "You have done well!" he told them. "You will receive special bonuses. Give my assistant your list. Dismissed for the day!"

The men broke ranks, smiled, and hit each other.

"Girard has trained them well," Cyrus thought as he watched through field glasses from his tent. "He hesitates with the second half," he observed. "Perhaps he fears my wrath... as he should."

The two companies broke apart and scattered into the center section, which could accommodate four companies of men.

Andrew Lissen, an assistant to Girard who handled messages and managed some of the logistics, ran up to the big man and whispered something to him. Cyrus heard what the assistant said, though he sat in the shade over a hundred meters away. Like other psychics whose power grew with time and use, Cyrus could hear and see distant things with increasing clarity.

"I caught two men fraternizing last night, sir," the assisted said and nodded toward them. "I informed Cyrus, as he asked me to watch for such activity. He told me to have you address it, sir. He wants you to make an example."

Girard nodded when he heard the news, and glanced over in Cyrus' direction to receive his approval before he acted. Cyrus raised his right hand and pointed up, which indicated Girard should proceed. He knew what was coming next, and actually looked forward to it.

"Company's C and D," Girard began, "I understand some of you have behaved less like soldiers and more like animals." He walked over to where the two men in question stood side by side. "That sort of behavior will not be tolerated here!" he barked at them. "You were hired to be professional soldiers. If you have needs, you must address them through Lissen," he shouted. "I'd rather have a completely straight command; and, I don't care if you prefer men over women... just not each other! We're soldiers, not whores! We need to maintain discipline! Are we clear on this?"

"Yes, sir!" the men responded.

Girard began to walk up the rows of men and looked them over as he walked.

"Our leader will provide those needs for you when necessary and only *if* you have gained merit. You gain merit by working hard, hitting your targets, and carrying out orders without question. If you train properly, you will be rewarded!"

Andrew Lissen walked behind Girard to gage the reaction of men after he walked past. These men called his assistant "Lezzy," or "Less man," but that was as far as the teasing went. They knew better than to test Girard's patience. Although Lissen was clearly a suck-up, Girard trusted Lissen as the man who demonstrated the most prowess of any man in A or B Company. He earned his spot as Girard's go to man.

"Do you understand me?" he yelled at the two companies.

"Yes, sir!" the men shouted back.

"You will return to the lesser barracks until further notice. If necessary, I will take the best of Company C and D to make a new company. I don't want to do that. If you see a man bringing down your company's rating, it is your job to put a fire under his ass! Is that understood?"

"Yes, sir!" they shouted back.

These men had the most problems with discipline. Some refused to work out in the heat, or fire weapons as instructed, and so on. Most of the men in these two companies had problems with attitude and authority as well.

"Some of you men feel you should not be here, or that you are being treated unfairly," Girard said. "I will let our commander, Cyrus, address your concerns."

Girard turned and faced the main tent at the top of the camp. He looked toward the shadow area in front of that tent. He knew Cyrus always sat there. Girard pulled the lip on his cap down over his eyes and did not move. He stood at attention and waited for Cyrus.

"Come to attention for Commander Cyrus!" Girard yelled to the men behind him.

Most of these men already stood at attention, while others did not. As they stood in the hot sun, sweating profusely, they wiped their faces and wanted to head for the shade as the other men did.

All at once, Girard could feel these men shift as Cyrus slowly made his way from his large tent. The moment the men saw him rise, they jumped to attention out of fear. Girard kept his focus ahead. He ignored the heat. He slowly breathed and patiently waited for Cyrus to make his way down the hill.

"Thank you, Girard," Cyrus said in a low voice to his second. "You worked hard today. I have more than one reward for you. I believe you will be pleased with them both. One is inside your tent… a blonde. She is both young and willing. As to the second reward, it is parked out behind my tent. I hope you like it," Cyrus told him.

Girard raised an eyebrow and wondered what he meant by that.

"Companies C and D ready for inspection, sir," Girard yelled.

"No, they are not," Cyrus said as he moved past Girard and walked over to the first line of men. "Despite your best effort to help these men, Girard," Cyrus continued, "some of them do not wish to cooperate," he said.

From the middle tent system, the other men dismissed earlier, lined up to watch the show. They knew that Cyrus was about to administer punishment. As much as he rewarded, he could punish as well. All of them had seen it.

"You... fatso!" Cyrus barked to one lazy man. "Step up here!"

The man nervously stepped forward.

"Cyrus... sir, I just wanted to..." the man started.

"Shut up!" Cyrus yelled. "It's too late for excuses. I watched you all day. You had your chance to prove your worth."

"You!" he pointed to another man. "You in the striped shirt, come here!" he said as he pointed to the man standing next to the chubby man.

The soldier ran up but did not speak. He stood at attention.

Cyrus glanced over at the line of men who watched him with fascination.

"Strangle that man to death!" he yelled, "Do it slowly, so that as he dies, he will realize I mean business. The rest of Company C and D... I want you to watch and know this is your fate unless I see some better effort on your part!"

"We would with better food!" one man in the back shouted.

Cyrus spun around.

"Who said that?" he called out.

The men did not respond. Cyrus smiled.

"You believe you protect him. Your silence cannot hide the traitor. I know who said it. I wanted to see if you would give him up. I don't need your help to find him. Watch!" he said.

Cyrus turned away from the lines of men behind him. A man in the back row of company D took out a pistol, put it to his head, and pulled the trigger. His brains spattered all over the soldier next to him. No one in the camp spoke. Cyrus spun around and carefully watched the faces of the men before him to judge their reaction. He turned his attention back to the two men who still stood at attention.

"Now," Cyrus said using a calm and cold voice. "Carry out your orders, soldier," he told the man in the striped shirt.

The entire group watched as the man slowly strangled the fat man to death. The fat man did not struggle, as Cyrus prevented it. When he finished, the man in the striped shirt let go of the fat man. The plump soldier's body slumped lifeless to the sand.

"Company C will bury this man," Cyrus ordered and indicated the fat man. "Company D will bury that man. When you are finished, both companies will dig four new latrines south of camp," Cyrus told them. "They are yours to use. Carry on," he ordered. "Come to my tent when you are finished," he directed to Girard.

Cyrus glanced up at the row of men still watching him from the base camp. He lifted up his arms and called out to them.

"Work hard for me and I will give you everything," he yelled out. "Work against me and that will be your fate!" he succinctly spoke and pointed at the fat man on the ground. "The choice is yours."

He turned and walked casually up to his tent. He stopped half way.

"If even one of you thinks of shooting me in my back or slitting my throat the middle of the night, I will know it. If you want to shoot a bullet into your own skull, or slit your own throat, then I suggest you keep thoughts like those out of your head, for I know what every man here thinks. If you don't believe it, challenge me!" he dared them. He turned around and stood with his arms wide. He pulled his shirt apart while he bared the skin of his scrawny chest. "Go ahead... shoot me!" he shouted. This time his words reverberated and echoed through the canyon as if he yelled through a megaphone. No one moved. "No challenges?" he spoke with defiance as his eyes traveled through the men. "Good! Carry on."

Every soldier eyed Cyrus with fear. No matter what Girard said, when Cyrus walked among them, the men only had good thoughts about their leader. The scrawny man buttoned his shirt. He walked over to a large chest that sat next to his chair. He opened the lid. The interior contents reflected yellow brilliance in the midday sun.

"Lissen! I want you to give a solid gold coin for every man in A and B Company!" Cyrus cried out as he stood before his tent and indicated the box.

A hundred gold coins! A great murmur passed through the men in the main tent. Cyrus turned around and entered his tent. He left the box open. The men could see the golden light reflected on the back of the lid. Behind Cyrus he heard a great cheer rise from the main tent, follow by a chant.

The men rhythmically shouted, "Cyrus... Cyrus... Cyrus... Cyrus!"

Girard grinned wide as he looked around him and felt nothing could stop them ... nothing in the world.

He joined the men, "Cyrus... Cyrus... Cyrus!"

CHAPTER FOURTEEN

A NEW AWARENESS

JAMES MONTGOMERY POLLACK DID NOT die on the floor of his living room from a heart attack or lose his mind to a stroke. In fact, he was perfectly healthy. Instead, the major general underwent an experience that few humans on Earth would ever endure. A conversion took place inside his head that reconfigured his previous brain structure into a new one.

Unable to breakthrough his staunch military training, and having consulted with the WPO's Earth-bound authority, the great organization known as Galactic Central, located hundreds of millions of light years away in another galaxy, decided to authorize his initial conversion via a green light approval from Master Li. He had performed remote conversions such as this one when the situation called for such action back in 2016. He converted the three psychics in Paris with that method when he sensed them on the verge of psychic self-awareness. Had he not intervened, they may have become rogue psychics. However, he would rather be present personally during conversions, as he felt instruction afterward more important than the physical process performed by the voices.

An eerie silence fell over the Pollack household while the general lay on the floor of his house. He underwent a procedure perfected over four thousand millennia ago by those who performed this function as part of their duty to the Intergalactic Psychic Collective, made up of 105 worlds that stretched across seventy different galaxies. Connected via the voices in Galactic Central, this community of worlds traded thoughts, ideas, cultures, and information. Now the general involuntarily joined that collective along with his earthbound counterparts.

Master Li linked with the newly converted mind and spoke to him.

"Welcome to the World Psychic Organization, Major General James

91

Montgomery Pollack," the soothing voice informed him at the end of the conversion.

Unfortunately, James did not hear Master Li. As he lay on his living room floor, his mind opened like a flood gate to hundreds of memories that suddenly poured in from his past...

"James, you must listen to me," he heard his father's voice echo over the span of time. "The place for rapid advancement is in Australia, not England. Who knows how high you'll rise or how quickly if you return? England has too much competition. You must convince your wife!"

"Then I will take your advice, father, and bring my new bride to Australia," James said. "If she approves..."

"If she..." his father started to protest.

"This is the twentieth century, father," James reminded him. "I cannot throw her over my shoulder and force her to leave England, especially when her father is still trying to cope with the loss of his wife. If Penelope wishes to leave, then we will go."

"I will wait to hear from you," William said to his son, "and pray Penelope has enough sense to let her husband do his duty."

When his father left him, James wondered how long it would be before they spoke again, especially if Penelope said no. Fortunately, he did not have to wait long. She gave him her answer that afternoon.

With his father-in-law's considerable influence, Lieutenant James Pollock would begin his military career in Australia, the place of his birth. However, the newly commissioned officer had yet to prove his worth. Therefore, he volunteered for active duty the moment he started his career with the Australian Army. While Penelope did not relish James going into some war footing on foreign soil, she knew the life of the military and accepted all of its risks, including the possibility that her husband would not return.

The moment James arrived on the southern continent with his wife, his father, Lt. Col. William Pollack, welcomed James into the Australian Army fold as he held a position open within his regiment. James could still see his father's smiling face when he first stepped inside the Digger's Club, though the young untried officer did not yet have an invitation to join. The opportunity to advance would come soon, thanks to his father.

"To my son and his success," his father toasted with the other members present.

"To the son!" they echoed.

Two years later, James and two other strike teams volunteered for a secret mission inside Afghanistan – retrieve a stolen nuclear weapon. He had just four days to nap the culprit who was supposedly making his way south along the

Sulaimān Range. They promoted James to captain the day before his company flew at night from Australia to Pakistan and then into Afghanistan. Of the three teams sent in, only James' company returned without any casualties, a feat no other officer accomplished and why James rose so quickly in the ranks – political expediency. Nothing breeds promotion like success.

A year following his achievement in Afghanistan, his father-in-law grew ill. Penelope returned to England where she found her father practically living in squalor. He had fallen into a deep depression and neglected his surroundings after his wife's death. Penelope stayed in England for six months and wrote to James often during that period. He replied but said nothing about his own feelings, because he felt lost without her. Once she felt her father was stable enough to leave on his own, she returned to Australia. Shortly after her return, Penelope became pregnant with the first of three daughters she bore him.

"We're going to have a daughter," she told him. "… a daughter… a daughter…" her words faded away.

Those were happy years for James, golden years, memories he cherished.

As James Pollack lay on the living room floor of his house, his mind replayed memories he nearly had forgotten: the history of his family, the day he met Penelope, the years of their fruitful marriage, his career in the army, and his aspirations for retirement. A lifetime of memories returned with remarkable clarity, as if they took place yesterday. Power surged through his body. Via an infinitesimally small singularity referred to as a conduit, aliens altered paths of blood vessels, changed the brain's internal structure, and differed the mix of chemical composition to create an entirely new area inside his mind that he could access and utilize once he awoke.

During this brief nostalgic reverie, James recalled the most remarkable memory of all – a voice he heard as a teenager while in prep school once more took precedence in his mind. Back then, the voice puzzled him, frightened him, and made him react with anger. He learned to suppress it. In time, it went away. However, when he heard it during his conversion, the memory came back sharp and clear, impossible to ignore.

"It was you!" he cried aloud. "I heard you at boarding school!" His commanding voice echoed around the living room, although his body remained supine and his eyes closed. Had his wife heard him shout those words, she might have come down the stairs to investigate.

Upstairs, and oblivious to his condition, Penelope took her time in the shower during James' conversion. If she delayed her shower by a few minutes, she might have heard him cry out when he fell. She would have rushed to his side, witnessed the event, and probably called the paramedics. They most certainly would have taken the general to the military hospital in an ambulance. She would not understand that her husband had nothing wrong with him, or that his new destiny lay along a path that included the most exclusive club in the world, far more selective than the Digger's Club. Had he undergone a CAT scan during the conversion process, no telling how it would have turned out... it might have killed him. Master Li seemed willing to take that chance.

Fortunately, James conversion proceeded smoothly and he gradually resumed a conscious state.

"James? I know it's late. Do you still want to go out tonight?" Penelope called from the bathroom as she toweled off. "Fedder's is still open. We could call Charlie and tell him to throw a steak on the grill for us," she loudly commented as she pressed the soft cloth against her flesh. "I wouldn't mind sharing if you order it medium... James? James!" she called once more. "Are you there?"

She wondered why he had not followed her up to the bedroom as usual.

"He's probably out on the deck, smoking one of his obnoxious cigars," she thought. "Perhaps he isn't hungry after all. I'll take my time then..."

James' body lay very still. His heart faintly beat in his chest. The thoughts in his head swirled about like a ship caught in a whirlpool, drifting away until even his conscious thought slipped back into oblivion.

CHAPTER FIFTEEN

LONG DISTANCE CONNECTION

HAN WALKED INTO THE MANOR house's huge library and discovered the room in near total darkness, not even the usual bright fire burned at the end of the room. Why he and Master Li preferred the room in near darkness most of the time, he could not say. The only time any light ever penetrated the great room seemed to be in the late afternoon, when the west facing windows allowed thin shafts of orange light that forced its way past tiny slits in the tall, heavy, dark green, velour drapes.

"Doesn't anyone ever turn a light on in this room?" he thought.

At first, Han assumed he was alone as he did not sense another psychic present. When he headed into the room, he reached out with his mind to turn a lamp on and sensed a strong psychic's presence materialized across the room. He delayed the action while he peered through the darkness at the distant figure.

"Li?" he surmised. He noticed an arm protrude from one of the nine chairs in front of the fireplace. "Where were you?"

When Master Li did not answer, Han did not pursue any further questions. He quickly surmised the truth to his question when he sensed a strong block. He recalled that he and Master Li discussed the conversion of Major General Pollack as an imperative.

"Ah, he's performed the conversion," Han correctly guessed, especially when he sensed Galactic Central as part of the same connection. He did not need to question the viability of this remote procedure.

"Probably carried out his plan with the new candidate in Australia," Han considered. The thought of a new mind in their group excited him.

He quietly withdrew from the library, knowing he should not disturb Li during something as delicate as a conversion.

"Michael won't like this," Han thought as he closed the library doors with his mind. "He likes rules, regulations, codes, oaths, pledges, that sort of thing. He likes it when people follow them and becomes upset when they don't. I can hear him now; 'I thought you said no more remote conversions!' for I am certain that is what Michael will say."

Instead of waiting in the library for Li to finish, he walked up the hallway toward the elevator on the north wing. He wanted to inspect Master Li's latest collection of extinct insect specimens from the mid-Paleozoic Era, about 350 million years ago. One scorpion measured well over a meter in length with huge pincer claws and a great stinger. Li joked he had to dodge back and forth before he finally subdued the creature. Han raised his eyebrows for only a second upon hearing that fabrication.

"Master Li?" a strong psychic voice came through, which caused Han to pause outside the elevator.

"What is it, Michael?" Han replied in Li's stead.

"Zhiwei informs me, we have an urgent problem in Russia that may require WPO intervention," Michael cut in. "He's been trying to reach Master Li. He thought I should try. Leni requests an immediate audience. She states her information is highly classified and requires Master Li's level of skill."

"Master Li is busy with a new conversion," Han informed the man who currently acted as head of the World Psychic Organization, though Master Li was certainly its most powerful member. The membership unanimously elected Michael a few months ago when they opened the manor house to the entire membership in a grand ceremony.

"New conversion?" Michael questioned. "I wasn't aware of this. Regulations of the new charter specifically state that remote conversions are best avoided until the board can properly..."

"Sorry, Michael," Han interrupted. "Master Li must have considered the matter urgent and proceeded with a conversion... without the need to start a WPO board consultation."

"Where is the candidate located?" Michael asked.

"I believe Australia," Han informed him.

"What? We don't have a branch in Australia," Michael pointed out. "This will be the first contact in the region. We have protocols in place now, Han. Master Li should have contacted me..." he protested.

"Again, I'm sorry, Michael," Han apologized once more, "this came up only recently. I should have linked with you sooner, only you were very busy with Chou and Villi. Zhiwei should have informed you as well. He came to us with some new information about an attack in Australia. The evidence from the autopsy points to the work of a rogue psychic."

"A rogue psychic in Australia..." Michael considered as he mulled over this information. "Do you mean to say Master Li agreed to accept a new candidate under these conditions and this rogue is undergoing conversion?" Michael questioned.

"No, we believe there is a second psychic..." Han started to explain.

"Wait a second, we have two new emerging psychics in Australia," Michael inquired, "and one is a rogue?"

"I believe so..." Han told him and then hesitated. "Just a second, Master Li has completed the conversion. His mind is free for linking. I'll link with you later, if you need me. Han out," he linked.

"Thanks, Han," Michael linked back and changed his connection.

Han took in a deep breath, grateful Michael did not admonish him for not keeping the tall young man informed of the affair. He stepped into the elevator that quickly whisked him up three floors. The doors opened across from this wing's museum.

Like a bright iridescent glittering jewel, a large freshly preserved beetle rested, not inside the display case, but on top with a note attached:

"Knowing you would want to closely inspect this, I left it out. Enjoy. Li."

Han smiled as he picked up the large extinct yet intact specimen with his mind and began to examine it with a nearby tool. He gazed with awe at its size and complexity. At that moment, one of the large hairy forelimbs moved. Frightened, Han tossed the beetle into the air, only to realize that he triggered an autonomic response – not that the beetle might still be alive. Master Li waited until the specimen expired and preserved it in stasis to keep it fresh. Han caught the specimen with his mind in mid-air before it struck the floor and gently returned it to the top of the case. Being alone in these museums with such strange objects began to unnerve the master strategist. He took in a deep breath and tried to relax.

"If he ever brings one of those back alive, he won't have to wait for old age to do him in," Han thought as he carefully placed the large creature back on top of the display case.

Inside the manor house library, the fireplace roared to life as Master Li leaned back in his chair and took in a deep breath. He returned to his body and drew in the necessary nourishment they referred to as psychic energy. He sensed Han rising in the elevator on his way to the museum and Michael eagerly awaiting acknowledgement.

"Hello, Michael," Master Li linked once he completely revived. "I wondered when you'd drop in. We have much to discuss," he began. "First, I must apologize for not keeping you informed about recent changes. It seems we've both been very busy. I know you communicate with our members on a daily basis. This is a special case, which I don't wish to discuss in an open link. Come to the house for a private consultation. On your way, tell Zhiwei that I will link with Leni in Russia at once. Li out!"

Michael hesitated with his response. He wanted to remind Master Li of the new WPO charter and what his responsibilities were as its leader to enforce those rules. He shrugged off the notion that he had to remind Li of anything and linked briefly with Cecilia instead. He headed off to the manor house by crossing the street that separated their houses.

"I'm taking a meeting with Master Li," he linked as he slipped out the front door.

"Anything serious," Cecilia linked back.

Dr. Beaton-Tyler worked daily in her clinic at the opposite end of Main Street. Today, she had to repair a work related injury, a rare occurrence after Zinian changed work safety rules.

"I'm not certain... but, something new has come up and I... I may be tied up for awhile," he linked to her.

Her patient looked up in time to see Cecilia stop and stare at the wall. The Native American's knew that when their psychic friends had that far away look on their faces, they were probably in conversation with some person or being. Cecilia blinked and refocused on her task.

"What is it?" Cecilia's patient asked. "Nothing serious I hope."

"Let's hope not," she whispered. "Now where were we... making new bone..." she continued.

CHAPTER SIXTEEN

GENERAL CHANGES

AFTER PENELOPE PUT ON SOME casual evening wear, she exited the bathroom and glanced over at her bedside clock. Too much time passed. She knew the general must have changed his mind. Content that some important matter occupied his mind, she took off her outfit and changed into a nightgown for bed. She removed her make-up and pampered her face with some pricey skin product in front of the mirror. When she glanced over at the clock, she realized the general had usually retired by now. He would either watch their bedroom television or stand out on the upper balcony and smoke one of his expensive obnoxious cigars.

"James?" she called out.

Penelope rose from her settee and went to the balcony door. It was locked, the upper deck dark.

"James?" she called as she turned around.

Silence. She thought he might be in another part of the house. As she started for the stairs, a strange thought occurred to her that James might be incapacitated by a stroke or heart attack. She flew down the hallway to the top of the staircase.

"Papa!" she affectionately cried out.

When she heard no reply, she rushed down the stairs, her eyes searched around for him.

"James?" she cried louder.

No answer. She started toward the kitchen when she saw his head sticking out from behind the sofa on the floor.

"James!" her voice shrieked.

She feared the worst had happened. She went to his side on the floor. However, her scream actually startled the general awake. He immediately sat up. He sputtered and blinked his eyes as he gazed up at her with a puzzled expression.

"Penny? Sorry, love. I must have fallen asleep," he began. "Strange. I don't remember how I got down here?"

With his conversion complete, he did not yet realize that he had changed into a completely different person with amazing abilities. Due to his prolonged dream state, Master Li broke off contact after the conversion. He could no longer maintain the connection.

"Oh, you old goat," Penelope thought, relieved. "I was scared to death something happened to you." She put her hand up to his head.

James Pollock stared up at his wife as he sat on the floor.

"I see no need to call me names, dear," he said to her. "I must have dozed off. That's all."

He started to rise, but his head hurt so badly that he felt weak.

"I didn't say a word," Penelope said as she placed her arm around his shoulders and the other in his hand, trying to help him up off the floor.

"Why you did, too," he insisted. "Just now, you called me an old goat!" he said to her as he struggled to rise.

"James, I didn't say a word... so help me," Penelope snapped back as she helped him to his feet. She stopped and stared at him with a queer facial expression. "But I did think it."

He stood there at her side and regarded her honest face.

"What's that supposed to mean?" he said.

"How should I know you pompous old bag of wind?" she thought.

"Now, *really* Penelope," James said as he tried to be understanding. "You've never used that kind of language around me before. What would your father say if he heard you speaking like that," he cautioned.

"I never said a word," she spoke up. "What did you think I just said?"

"I don't know as I care to repeat it," he said and started to turn away, upset with his wife.

She reached out, took his arm and firmly held him.

"It's important, Papa," Penelope asked, her eyes searched his. "Tell me what you thought I said."

"You called me a pompous wind bag," he muttered the words. He did not wish to repeat them.

Penelope sucked in air and gasped.

"Oh, James," she said as her eyes widened. "What has happened to you?"

"What are you talking about?" he replied. He had a puzzled expression on his face.

Penelope put her hands on her hips.

"Darling, something has changed about you. Perhaps it was the fall. I believe you're in for a bit of a shock," she said as she peered at his head.

"What is it? Spit it out!" he demanded.

"I believe you're reading my mind," she told him straight out. "You could never do that before." She put her hand to her chin. "I wonder if that old tribal man put some kind of curse on you."

"Surely, Penelope, you don't believe in such things!" James said with growing concern.

"Of course, not," she threw back at him, "but I never actually saw anyone read minds either!"

"Quite," he relented. A moment of silence passed. "Now what do we do?"

"Can you do anything else?" she asked him.

"Like what?" he returned.

"I don't know. Think," she requested.

"I thought that thinking too much is what got me into this mess," James asserted.

"No silly," Penelope said as she relaxed. "Concentrate on something."

"Like what?" James wondered.

"Like… that ash tray on the bar," she indicated.

"What should I think about?" he retorted, seeking direction.

"Think of it traveling across the room," she told him.

"I think you should stop this nonsense right now and go to bed at once," he firmly spoke as he started to take her arm.

Suddenly, Penelope's face unfocused. She turned and walked up the stairs.

"Penelope? Penelope! Where are you going?" he insisted. However, his wife continued to move and did not respond. "Penelope?" he asked softly.

The general followed his wife up the stairs. She walked straight to the bed and slipped under the covers with her housecoat on. She sat in the bed and stared straight ahead. He walked over to her and waved his hand in front of her face. She did not seem to see him in front of her.

"Penelope!" he shouted, inches from her face.

Startled, she blinked her eyes as if waking up. She shook her head and stared at him.

"How in blue blazes did I get here?" she asked.

"I said, 'I think you should go to bed,' and you walked up the stairs and went to bed!" he told her.

"Really? Incredible! You have such power?" she questioned. "So, you don't just read minds; you can influence them, too. I'll wager you can do more, as well. Something *has* happened to you, James, something very profound and very significant."

"Be careful 'bout what you say, my dear," he cautioned.

"You are the one that better be careful," she retorted. "When you become forceful, you might unintentionally order someone to 'go jump in the lake' or worse, 'go shoot yourself!' and they'll do it!" she pointed out.

"Good heavens! Perhaps I should call off work for tomorrow," he suggested.

"That's probably a good idea," she agreed, "until we know more about what's happening with your mind."

"Do you think it's safe to be around me? I don't wish to cause you any harm," he wondered.

"In all the years we've been married, you never once threatened or yelled at me, at least, not in the harsh way some husbands do. I trust you implicitly. I believe I will be safe. Come here... come snuggle with me tonight," she said as she patted the area of the bed next to her.

"Should we call the doctor? I have a terrible headache," he told her.

She knew a thing or two about impending stroke signs from having volunteered in the hospital for the last twenty years. She knew many physicians as friends. She looked into James eyes carefully and felt his pulse.

"Close one eye. Now the other. Grab my two fingers and squeeze," she offered. "Close your eyes and touch your nose with your index finger. Stick out your tongue and move it side to side, then up and down."

She finally gave him an overall appraisal before she made up her mind.

"Personally, you seem as fit as a fiddle," she told him. "I doubt the doctor can peer into your mind, though. Besides, this might disappear by morning. Let's see what tomorrow brings first, shall we?" she suggested.

"Very well, Penny," James said as he relented to her request.

"I'll get you something for a headache while you change," she said as she rose and walked toward the bathroom.

"Yes... I'll change," he replied. He removed his tie and unbuttoned his shirt. "Please, make the dosage strong!"

James changed into his pajamas, took the two pills that Penelope offered, and joined her in bed.

"In the morning," she said as they drifted off, "everything will be normal. It's stress, that's all."

Exhausted, James soon drifted off to sleep in her arms. However, Penelope stayed awake awhile longer. She wondered what really happened to her James, and how this might affect their relationship with all their friends in the community. Eventually, even with all of her worries, she drifted off, too.

CHAPTER SEVENTEEN

STRAY

"WILL YOU LOOK AT THAT damn fool," the station owner Harry said to his friend, Spike. "Looks like that guy wandered in out of the desert," he continued.

"How do you know? You've seen that before?" Spike asked as he rubbed the grease off his hands onto a shop rag.

He sauntered into the front office from the garage as Mrs. Tisdale's car was nearly finished. Spike looked with squinted eyes against the bright sunlight, having left his sunglasses in his truck.

"Oh, I've seen it many times," Harry replied.

He did not move from his spot in the clustered front office. Harry had his sunglasses on, or else his eyes would not have penetrated the midday glare of the Australian sun as it blazed down on the hot white sand that surrounded them. A young man with two days growth of beard on his sweaty filthy face, staggered toward them. He had walked for nearly two days without much rest or sleep.

For the first three hours of his journey, he ran away from the base camp until he could run no more. After that, he walked through the night. When the sun came up, the cool night air quickly changed over to the oppressive heat of the desert. His container of water ran out a few hours after that. He continued to walk until he came upon some tracks in the sand, followed by more tracks. All of them headed north. He followed them for another day when he finally found a grated road and continued along that until he eventually came upon the service station where the rough grated road ended at a flat gravel street.

He could not believe his eyes – civilization – food, water, shelter, and help. He walked nearly forty kilometers in two days. Exhausted, tired, thirsty, hungry, and desperate, he headed for the first sign of real people he had seen since he left Adelaide weeks ago, not the fanatics in the camp he left behind him.

The man named Harry, the man who ran this isolated service station for over twenty years after the last owner, glad to be rid of it, sold him the property, stared at the disheveled young man with dispassionate eyes. While business was definitely slow, Harry did not mind the pace. The occasional motorist, though becoming increasingly rare, usually needed some of his precious and rare petrol from time to time, and sometimes they needed his other supplies of energy, too.

Harry had them all: a tank of natural gas, replacement solar panels, even a windmill in the back that generated electricity. He had an array of tire sizes, water, coolant, and many car parts. Harry was an opportunist. You name it, Harry had it. Few other service dealers around the area were comparably equipped. They often referred repairs to Harry's shop. Knowing this, he charged twice as much. Harry could take advantage of the stranded strangers and usually cleaned out their bank accounts. His mechanic friend, Skip knew this, too. The friends had become partners, thanks to Harry's ingenious way of squeezing out every pound of flesh.

"Hey, do ya remember that fellah came from China," he related to his rotten-toothed friend, who often munched on hard candy. "He thought he had one of these off-road vehicles that would never break down, or so he thought! He had lots of money! Took us a week to fix that thing, remember?" Harry recalled. "By the time we got through with him, he wanted to go back to China real bad!" he grinned. "This fellah don't look in such good shape," he said as he scratched his chin.

As he approached the station, the young man's hopes of survival rose. He could not believe his luck.

"At last, some help!" he thought. "Water... and some food."

He stumbled along the edge of the grated rough road and fell over sideways through several prickly bushes that scratched and tore at his clothing. His nose, cheeks, and the back of his neck were sunburned. He could barely move his hands. His feet throbbed from trotting over the hot desert sand. He stumbled across the gravel road that separated him from the service station.

He fell upon the front door and found he did not have the strength to turn the knob.

"I'd better help him," Spike said and started toward the door.

Harry reached out, grabbed his mechanic friend by the wrist, and pulled him back.

"He made it this far, didn't he?" Harry stated. "Let him come in and tell us his sad story. Then we'll find out how much money he's got and go from there."

The untidy young man looked through the window of the service station front door. He sought sympathy from the faces of the two men inside. Instead, he only saw removed curiosity on their faces as they watched to see if he could open the door.

"Dollar says he caint open it," Spike muttered.

"I got that dollar," Harry muttered back.

Determined, the young man used two hands to turn the knob. He finally pushed to open the door, only to realize he needed to pull on it instead. He nearly fell over as he pulled back, twisted around, and then stumbled inside.

"Damn!" Spike declared and handed a dollar over to Harry.

Seeing a tall drinking fountain, the kind with an electric cooler inside, the thirsty young man stepped up to grab a quick drink

"Hold on, stranger," Spike, dressed in bib overalls, said as he stepped in front of him. "Who are you?"

"Blake..." the man tried to speak, his mouth so dry, his lips so cracked, and his voice so parched that he could only manage the one word.

Skip glanced over at his boss. Harry smiled back to his friend and shook his head, which meant they would not get much from this man. Harry gestured at his clothes as if to say, "This man has nothing of value."

The man who called himself Blake fell upon the tall square metal drinking fountain and pressed the front bar, expecting water to shoot from the curved head on one corner. Nothing came out. He pressed the bar again, and again, and again, until he realized it was not working.

The two mechanics laughed and pointed to the machine next to the wall that took money for a patron to pay for bottled water.

"You gotta pay for stuff around here," Harry said. "We don't give out anything free. How do you expect us to make a living, out here in the desert, if we gave away water that costs us an arm and leg?"

Blake stood there wavering a second. He had been inside this building less than a minute and already he hated this scruff ugly man who had his feet propped up on his desk. Blake reached to his belt and pulled out his gun.

"Water..." he managed to say. He cocked his gun and pointed it at the man's chest.

"Shit!" Harry exclaimed as he sat up. "That guy's gonna kill me for a bottle of water!" he said to his friend.

Blake's hand started trembling on the gun, as if any second he would fire.

"Here!" Harry said as he opened the front of the dispenser and pressed a secret side button that he and Spike used when they wanted a cold drink.

"You gotta help me..." Blake struggled to say. "He's after me..."

"Who's after you?" Spike said over Blake's shoulder.

Blake nearly dropped his gun. Harry wanted to grab it but stopped. He still had not pulled out a bottle of cold water from the pay dispenser. He glanced over at the bent down young man and waved at Spike to keep his mouth shut.

"He's a murderer," Blake managed to speak as he gathered enough spit to speak. "He'll kill you, too..."

"Sure he will," Harry said as he tried to reassure the man with a gun.

Before Harry could give the weak young man his bottle water, Blake spun his body around toward the door, uncocked and holstered his weapon. He held out his right hand. As if he knew what Blake wanted, Spike tossed him a spade shovel. The young man caught it and marched out the front door. Harry and Spike seemed to stare with blank faces at the air in front of them.

Blake stumbled around to the back of the service station and started to walk in away from the building until he came to a large scrub bush. He pushed the shovel into the sand and began to dig. For several minutes, he used every ounce of strength he had to dig a hole. He dug down deeper and deeper until he stood waist deep in a hole. He tossed the shovel to one side and turned back toward the station.

A desert vehicle pulled up behind the service station. A thin scrawny young man with bleach blonde hair stepped out. He was quite alone. Although the man in the hole might be weak from his trek through the desert, he was nearly twice the size of the ghostly figure that stood over him. He spat on Blake's face.

"You made a lotta trouble for me," the skinny kid growled. "Take out your gun," the pale lad ordered. "Put it to your head and pull the trigger."

Blake did not hesitate. He had no mind. He had no will. Someone else was in charge of his body now.

Inside the service station, Spike took out the rag from his back pocket. He wiped his hands as he walked into Harry's cluttered office.

"You can call Mrs. Tisdale," he said. "Her car is finished."

Harry looked down at the floor.

"Whadda ya trackin in sand for?" he demanded. He gestured toward the floor that had white sand all over the area near the front door.

"I didn't track in no sand," Spike shot back. "You probably did it."

Harry glanced up at his mechanic friend out of necessity.

"I ain't been outside... so you musta done it!" he declared. "I'll call Mrs. Tisdale. Go get a broom and sweep that sand back outside."

"Crack!" a sound penetrated the quiet air.

"What was that?" Spike asked as he looked around. Harry did not reply. Spike glanced over and noticed his shovel missing. "Hey! Where's my shovel?"

Harry did not bother to respond. He was too busy with a parts catalogue in his hands. He wished he had more money to buy car parts.

"Who knows?" he said, absently. "Now, will ya sweep up that sand?"

CHAPTER EIGHTEEN

OUR AUSTRALIAN AGENT

THE MORNING AFTER HIS CONVERSION, Penelope urged her husband to call off from his work. His commanding officer, Lieutenant General George Sanders, "Georgie" to Penelope, called the house twenty minutes later. He inquired why the general had called in sick, for the very first time ever in his career.

"James is all right, isn't he Penelope?" the skittish man asked.

"Just a bit under the weather today, Georgie," she told the man on the wall screen. "He'll be right as rain tomorrow."

"Sounds like he needs a doctor," General Sanders offered. "I've never known James to have a sick day in his life."

"If he does need a doctor, George, I'll ask James' doctor to come by. He only lives up the street. He's very familiar with the general's health. Well, goodbye," she said and started to disconnect.

"You aren't trying to pull a fast one on me, are you Penelope? Where is James? Why can't I speak to him?" the general asked as he glanced over her shoulder.

"I don't know what you mean, George," she said as she moved closer to the camera to fill the picture. "Pull a fast one, indeed. You've been watching too many American films. Besides, James is asleep. He had a high fever last night and a severe headache," she insisted. "I'll have him call you when he rises, if that will make you feel any better. Now may I say goodbye?" Penelope asked sweetly.

"At his age, I suppose he can be sick a day once in a while..." the general admitted. "Very well, Penelope, take good care of him, goodbye," the general said.

Without further adieu, Penelope turned off the wall-communicator. She placed the phone in message mode to stop the flow of outside calls.

"You'd think the world couldn't go on unless you went into work today," Penelope said as she turned to her husband across the room.

"We are behind in that new systems project, dear," James said. "They expect me to fix another mess again, I suppose."

"Oh, forget all that nonsense for today," she insisted. "Let's return to our little experiment," she said with a tinge of excitement in her voice. "Do you feel anything new since last night?"

"Yes... I..." he hesitated.

"Please, James, what is it?" she asked.

"I spoke with a China-man last night... in my dreams, I suppose," he confessed.

"A man from China?" she questioned.

"Well, I thought he was from China... that is what I felt," James confessed.

"What did he say?" she asked him.

"A pleasant fellow actually," James told her. "He said he was part of a group of people in America with similar traits as mine. He said he was glad to have me on board, and all that," the general explained to his wife. "I'm supposed to contact my voice at Galactic Central, right away," he said. His tone dropped in volume as the last part embarrassed him.

"Voice?" she questioned. "Galactic Central? What was that?" Penelope wondered.

"Dear, if I could make any sense of this, don't you think I would have by now? I just thought it was a silly dream, that's all. It did seem awfully real though. And it fits with what the note said... those in America," James pointed out.

"Did this Chinese gentleman have a name?" she asked him.

"Li Po Chin," James told her.

"Li Po Chin. This is most peculiar. I wonder if I went on the Internet, and searched the Chinese database, I could find Mr. Chin," she wondered.

"I'll wait in the rec room. I'd like to smoke and play a game of billiards while you search," James said as he started to turn.

"No need to search, Penelope," a voice spoke to both.

Penelope gasped. She turned and looked at her husband. James spun around as if someone broke into their house. He started to challenge his intruder when he froze, his mouth stuck open as he stared off at nothing. Penelope thought his actions seemed queer.

"James?" she said as she waved her hand in front of him.

She tried to say something further but discovered she had no voice. She massaged her larynx and did everything she could to speak, but nothing came out.

"You must forgive me for this intrusion, but I must speak with both of you," the calm voice spoke. "I am the voice in James' dream last night. I am Li Po Chin. I was a Chinese poet and scholar until about two and a half years ago, when I received my conversion from Galactic Central, just as General Pollack did last night. You can hear my voice because I am using the general's mind to transmit thoughts into both your minds. He can hear me, too. Go ahead, Penelope. You can speak to me and ask questions," the voice told her.

"What do you want of us, Mr. Chin," Penelope asked. "Is my James alright? I mean, he isn't injured by any of this, is he?"

"You and James are now part of a very special group of people," Li explained. "Very few humans have the ability to transform into a psychic being. Last night, a group of alien beings, able to bend space and time, sent a packet of energy and information via a tiny conduit in James' brain that transformed a portion of his mind. He is still the same James you've always known and loved, Penelope, only now, he has new abilities," he spoke reassuringly.

"Like what?" she asked.

"Actually, James should contact his voice at Galactic Central to find out that information. His voice will tell him everything he needs to know," Li told her.

"His voice?" she questioned.

"James brain has a special conduit which allows him direct contact with an ancient race of alien beings that live in a distant galaxy. We call them voices, their true name is difficult to pronounce. Very few humans on the planet Earth possess this conduit. Consider us a new type of human, slowly emerging around the planet. The aliens in Galactic Central can facilitate communication between worlds," Li informed her. "About three years ago, the Earth joined the Intergalactic Psychic Collective, a system of intelligent worlds scattered about the universe."

"How does he turn this…a conduit, you said? How does he turn this conduit on or off?" she asked.

"I tried to explain that to him that last night, but he kept insisting his experience was nothing more than a dream," Li answered.

"I know you are real, Mr. Chin," the general broke in. "I realize now this is not a hallucination."

"That is correct, general. All you need to do is think about your voice at Galactic Central and they will hear you," Li instructed. "After awhile, the process becomes easier."

"Once I contact Galactic Central, what happens next?" James wondered.

"You will be given the freedom of choice to use the power as you will," Li explained. "However, our organization requires that you use restraint when exercising this new power in public, such as interfering with the natural progress of humanity, or revealing your power to others. You cannot tell anyone else you are psychic, nor influence humanity in such a way that draws attention to this ability. We act and move about in secret using stealth. That is our way."

"We all impact history, just by being who we are," Penelope observed.

"True, but in the case of a psychic, he or she must not use his power to influence others to do things that are radically different. For that person will eventually discover the distinction," Li further explained.

"Are there others like you and James out there?" she asked.

"Yes, we are scattered around the planet. Currently, the largest concentration is in America and Europe. We have formed a group, which we call the World Psychic Organization. We drew up a charter that contains rules to which we all agreed should govern our ethics. Someday soon, we will transport both of you, Penelope and James, to come here for advanced training. You will stay in our new headquarters. Meanwhile, you must continue with your lives as if nothing has changed."

"America seems like an interesting place," Penelope stated. "I would enjoy a visit."

"That's an invitation I will hold you to, Li Po Chin, poet," the general added.

"Remember, general, you must not reveal your power to anyone. If you do, terrible consequence will result, not just for you, but for your entire family. The world does not understand us, or our power. Should they discover your psychic ability, you could place your entire family in terrible danger. If you need me for any reason, you have but to say my name. I will try to respond as soon as I can. Goodbye for now, Penelope; Good luck, Major General Pollack, Li out."

"Nice to have spoken with you, Mr. Chin. Goodbye," Penelope said.

The general, finally able to move, glanced over at his wife. Penelope looked back at her husband with increased concern in her eyes. She wondered what Li meant by "terrible consequences."

"Papa," she said quietly as she moved closer. "What do you think Li meant by terrible consequences for our family? What does he believe would happen?"

James could not look his wife in the face and respond. He had seen the military and the government do terrible things to people. He feared the worst.

"It seems this is my destiny, Penny," the general explained. "I have changed in ways that might frighten some people. What Li is trying to do is protect us. He believes most people would consider us a threat. They might take us prisoner, kill one of the children, dissect their brain, and subject the rest of us to endless batteries of tests. Li hopes to circumvent any misunderstandings by making us aware of how others would see us. People fear the unknown," he said in a low voice. He turned to face his wife. "I'm sorry, Penny. Li is right to advise us. We can't mention this to anyone… not a soul, not even the children." He pointed toward the wall screen. "They'll kill us!" he whispered with such fierceness, it alarmed her. She knew he meant the very military that provided their livelihood for the past four decades.

"I understand," she replied, "your ability must remain our secret. We've kept secrets before," she went on, "it won't… kill us to keep this one."

He relaxed to see how she remained calm and how well she handled this new aspect to their lives. She crossed over to him.

"You have other powers, too," she said as she moved to him. She pressed her face up to his, her lips next to his lips, "powers to command…"

He smiled at her humorous implication.

"Does this mean you have to do what I say from now on?" he asked with a slight grin.

Penelope smiled back, "I've always been yours to command."

"Oh, Pen," he sighed as he placed his arms around her. "I must confess, for the very first time in my life…"

She kissed him on the mouth to prevent him from saying he was afraid. He kissed her back. They held each other for a moment before he broke away. This action puzzled her. He went to the window and transferred the rest of his sentence to her mind.

"I believe that for the first time in my life, I'm frightened," he thought to her.

She came up behind him and wrapped her arms around his shoulders.

"I hear you clearly. Seems I have a bit of that stuff in me, too," she thought. "We'll save a bundle on telephone bills," she said, jokingly.

He turned around and took her into his arms.

"Don't worry," she continued. "We'll get through this together, just as we've tackled a hundred problems in the past."

"I love you," his thoughts echoed in her mind.

"Yes," she said as she kissed him. "For the very first time in over forty years, I am convinced you do."

CHAPTER NINETEEN

CONNECTED

As he promised Master Li, James Pollack decided to contact Galactic Central. However, uncertain as to what he would say, he kept Penelope nearby as his inspiration. The two sat in the living room, the general with a stiff drink, and Penelope with a cup of tea, though privately, she wished it was the other way around. While the general seemed nervous at best, Penelope tried to remain calm, at least on her exterior, for neither knew what to expect.

"Hello? Voice?" James inquired.

"Are you speaking to them yet?" Penelope asked.

The general shot her an expression as if to say, "I've never done this before... how will I know?" The general shrugged his shoulders. "I wonder if it's the same voice I once heard years ago..." he privately wondered.

Penelope shrugged her shoulders back in silent communication. Both of them felt intimidated to discuss their true feelings, which amounted to confusion and frustration.

"Mind if I fix some lunch while you speak with the little green men?" she quipped.

The general rolled his eyes.

"I don't believe they're creatures from a science fiction movie," he replied sarcastically. "They probably look like you and me?"

"Oh, then they are from Earth," she shot back.

"I'll keep trying," he said as he closed his eyes.

"...and I'll take that," she said and took away his crutch of a drink. "You should drink tea and not something that will cloud your judgment."

"Humph," the general muttered as she lifted the drink from his hand.

Penelope took that as her cue to leave the living room and head for the kitchen, mumbling on her way out, "perhaps they'll tell us how to fix things around the house... that will come in handy."

The general kept his eyes closed and concentrated on listening. He did recall a voice, one he never confessed to others that he heard, from a very long time ago in boarding school when he thought his classmates were pulling a prank.

"Hello? Are you there? I do remember you now... you sounded so rough with your metallic tone... scared me to death... I booted you out back then... I might have been too hasty," he thought. "You can return, if you like. I'm ready to speak with you now."

The general turned his head left and right as if aligning his head might change the reception.

"James Pollack!" a strange metallic voice boomed into his head.

"I say!" the general replied as he nearly fell over out of his chair. "Could you tone that down a bit!"

"James..." the voice answered with less intensity.

"That's better," the general stated. "Now this Li fellow..."

"Li Po Chin?" the voice cut him off.

"Yes..." James confirmed.

All at once, the general detected that he and this other party were not alone. In fact, he felt the presence of hundreds, perhaps thousands of minds linked up with their conversation.

"What is going on?" 'James asked.

"The Galactic Central collective is interested in all matters that concern Mast... Li Po Chin," the voice related.

"Oh... as I was saying, or thinking to you, rather," the general began once more. "This Li fellow wanted me to contact you, says you know what to do, and how I'm supposed to think, that sort of thing."

"Yes, James, or do you prefer to be called 'general' by us?" the voice asked.

"Actually, I'd prefer general. I do like the title, worked hard for it, if you don't mind," James requested.

"We will consider this contact your first, general," the metallic voice started. "I will begin the first lesson with a brief explanation of how your ability works and what Galactic Central can do for you. We will let Li instruct you on Earth's protocols," the voice informed him.

"This Li fellow... is he important?" James asked.

"Yes," the voice replied, succinct.

"That's it? No other explanation?" James asked.

"We will let Li explain his position on your planet," the voice said.

"Ok, fine," James acknowledged, "I probably understand certain ground

114

rules already… no overt use… don't interfere too much, that sort of thing. What I want to know is why didn't this desert fellow have to follow the same rules? Why does he do bad things and get away with it?"

"Unfortunately for your planet, not all psychic minds require a conversion from Galactic Central to perform certain abilities, general," his voice explained. "What Li refers to as a rogue psychic can use his power to gather and concentrate psychic energy. For example, you returned with your company of men intact because they followed every command without hesitation, did they not?"

"Come to think of it, I've never had a soldier question an order!" he suddenly realized.

"You are blessed with a unique and rare gift," the voice confirmed. "Some of your species have developed a special trait that is extremely rare in humans. In the case of this rogue, he possessed the same physical qualities from birth that you also possess. Unlike this man in the desert, however, you have certain advantages."

"Like what?" James asked.

"Conversion reorganizes the mind and allows greater latitude in manipulation. Your present level of ability has far greater capacity to absorb and use psychic energy in a disciplined fashion than a rogue can achieve through trial and error," the voice explained.

"Discipline, you say," James responded. "You beings in Galactic Central have worked out a very clever system of enticements," he pointed out. "I notice you use colloquialisms, quite a distinction."

"You may apply your powers of observation by using your new abilities to achieve greater comprehension of your world, general," the voice pointed out. "Once we terminate this lesson, you should contact Li and he will help you further."

For another thirty minutes, Major General Pollack kept open his link with his counterpoint alien voice across millions of spatial light years. He learned about the Intergalactic Psychic Collective, the library on Artane, how to travel off world via his voice, and how to use his voice as a learning resource to enhance his level of understanding. When the conversation finished, he lay back in his chair and stared at the ceiling, overwhelmed by all that transpired between them.

"I thought perhaps you'd like to…" Penelope started to speak as she entered the living room with a tray in her hands.

The moment she saw James with that far-away look in his eyes, she quietly set down the tray of sandwiches and cold drinks. For a few minutes, she sat and carefully observed her husband for any new changes. She saw a man deep in thought. Finally, James blinked and glanced over at her. His eyes swam with moisture. She could see he was obviously moved by the experience.

"Are you back with me?" she asked and waited for his reaction.

"Most amazing, Pen," James sighed. "I never dreamed that such creatures existed," he said to her. "We are most certainly not alone in the universe. Not only is there a great tower on a large planet which these beings call Galactic Central, but over a hundred worlds with millions of minds like mine speak to each other every day via this place," he said with such conviction in his voice that it alarmed his wife.

James' revelation challenged everything she knew as a fact – that there was a heaven and a hell, that god existed somewhere out there, and that the people of Earth were chosen to be special in the universe. They were not unique. Heaven and hell might exist, but beyond the confines of the universe. If God were out there, it must be beyond space and time as well. She struggled to grasp the significance of what he said.

Yet, if what James just revealed *was* true, then the planet Earth was not special. They were just another planet along with many others that had intelligent life. Her mind raced with questions. Was this Galactic Central a threat? Could they come to Earth inside spaceships and take over the planet? As she grappled with this age old conflict of wide spread paranoia, she could not fathom the great distances which separate systems and made such travel both impractical and ridiculous. She did not realize that Galactic Central was hundreds of millions of light years away and what that meant.

Instead, Penelope retreated from this internal conflict. She could only find safety and refuge in her routine, call it a housewife's peace of mind. She had to disregard anything that threatened her simple but joyous life of purposeful predictable monotony. She had a husband to support, to love, and nurture. She had a house that needed constant attention. She had her garden. She had her organizations and friends. Nothing would change. Her world needed to go on.

"Have a sandwich or something cold to drink," she suggested as she forced smile on her face.

She did not realize that the general could see through this artifice. It saddened him that he no longer lived in the same ignorant bliss. He heard her internal dialogue and watched how she skillfully suppressed this news.

"We've bit the apple, Pen," he thought. "The tree of knowledge revealed too much… no going back."

"What?" she asked and tilted her head.

"Didn't you hear what I just said… about Galactic Central?" he asked her.

Penelope stared back at her husband. James never lied to her. If this

116

was the new truth, the new religion, she could either embrace it, or run screaming from the room. She was a military brat, which in her mind was not a derogatory word. Being raised around the military made her practical and quick to adapt. They had many friends down through the years who died in battles. Their families had to cope. She took in a deep breath. The general patiently waited for her to reason it out. For a second, she glanced up at the ceiling and tried to envision this off world place before her eyes fell back to Earth gazed across the room at her husband's.

"You realize that any sane housewife might argue with her husband, tell him he lied, or at best made up stories to increase his importance in the eyes of others. I have heard of such cases," she said with the precision of a lawyer. "They might accuse their husbands of trickery or of being mad. Some wives might even leave their husbands or worse, have them committed," she said as she moved closer. She put her hand on his, as if to reassure him. "Those wives would be in denial if they behaved that way... with you. While all of this is fanciful and difficult to accept..." she said and took in a deep breath, "I can tell you this... I believe in you, James. I believe something wonderful has taken place, call it a blessing, but definitely not a curse. If you tell me that the universe is full of intelligent and marvelous people who speak to each other with their minds instead flying around in space ships, and they've been doing this for thousands of years... well, let us just say that I believe you. Oh yes, my darling, I do. You don't have to make speeches or put your words on trial. I've known you practically all of my life. I know you speak the truth. I'm convinced," she spoke, and with such conviction, James nearly burst into tears.

"Oh, Pen," he responded with building emotion.

He squeezed her hand and pulled her over on top of him. The couple embraced while exchanging a long and tender kiss. When Penelope finally broke free, she straightened her hair and her clothes, and turned to her tray.

"Now," she said and tried to relax, "how about that sandwich?"

James nodded his answer. Penelope set up a wooden tray with his sandwich, drink, some chips, a dill pickle and a napkin. James could not wait to explain or share the rest of what he experienced with the voice.

"They informed me that I am a level three, Pen, whatever that means. I can absorb psychic energy from other people without harming them. With that energy, I am capable of doing many things, such as moving objects. Watch," James excitedly said. He focused on a glass container with straws that rested on the bar. It rattled around for a second before it flew through the air and smashed into the wall behind the bar, scattering straws everywhere.

Penelope gasped at first and suppressed any smile when she saw the disappointment on James' face.

"Sorry," James apologized right away, "I didn't mean to…"

"Well, that's something you'll have to control," she said as she rose to clean up the mess. "I can't go around the house picking up broken things all day. Is that understood, James? If you must make something fly, then I suggest you take that power outside!"

She spoke with such perfunctory, James agreed without argument. For a second the couple just looked at one another. Then they burst out laughing. Whether it was a nervous release or not, neither would admit.

"Quite!" James said finally, a bit ashamed. "But Penny, look here. I can do this, too. The voice said to enter the mind of those around you and…"

Penelope watched as the general spoke. Suddenly, he disappeared.

The effect startled Penelope to see her husband sitting before her one second and then vanish in the next.

"James? Whatever you did, I'd like you to reverse it at once. You're scaring me," she said as her eyes searched for him.

"I'm right behind you," he said as he grabbed her shoulders and made her jump.

"Oh!" she exclaimed. She took his hand and squeezed it to make certain he was solid. "What made you disappear like that?" she asked, more curious now than frightened.

"I never disappeared at all," he explained. "I altered your perception of me in your mind. I simply made you believe I wasn't here. Interesting, wouldn't you say?"

"How did you do that?" she asked.

"The voice said to enter the visual cortex of people around me and block part of the signal entering their brain that put me inside their visual range. It's a kind of nerve stimulation. The whole thing seemed easy once I tried it," he explained.

"Easy for you…" Penelope thought. "That means you can go just about anywhere you want. That's a tremendous power, James, being completely invisible to others. I'll wager you have other abilities just as amazing. I wonder if these people are thinking about taking over the world?" she wondered aloud.

"You mean Li and the others in America?" James questioned.

"Mmm," she said as her mind raced with possibilities.

"I doubt it! You heard Li. We aren't to interfere with the rest of humanity," James began.

"Did you hear what you just said?" she interrupted. "You said 'we' as if you were apart from the rest of humanity. Does he place himself above the rest of us? I wonder," she conjectured.

"I don't think he meant anything like that," James explained.

"I know what he said, but what's to stop him?" she argued. "That native said in his note, 'no military force could stop him.' If that is the case, what government could stop this WPO organization from taking over the world? Perhaps they are recruiting members and biding their time until they are in strategic places and then, whoosh! They enslave the human race!" she exclaimed as she waved her arms in the air.

She faced her husband and breathed hard, as the idea she concocted in her speech astounded her.

"Poppycock!" James objected. "Li said they followed a strict moral code. If anyone violates it, their psychic ability is rescinded," he told her.

"Rescinded! How do they do that?" she questioned.

"I think he said the process could be messy. They have to break some blood vessels in the person's head, erase memories, that sort of thing," he told her.

She considered that statement a second or two before speaking.

"That is strict," she reasoned. "I guess you'd better watch what you do. Though, I'm glad they don't want to control the rest of us or anything else. Can you imagine if someone evil got this power? They could…"

Penelope stopped her line of thought. She noticed that James suddenly developed a serious expression on his face.

"Oh, my goodness," she declared as she realized the same thought, too. "The man in the desert… referred to in the note!"

"That's why the old man chose this time to deliver it, my dear," James said as he completed her thought. "Master Li must have been the ancestor the old tribesman heard in his dreams. They knew my time had arrived to convert. I suppose they're leaving it up to me to stop this madman in the desert. Remember? No, military power can stop him? Now we know exactly what that meant. He could make soldiers shoot each other, or jets that flew overhead pass by without seeing him. The only way to stop him is for another psychic to go out into the desert and meet him head on," he said with a far off look in his eye. "Well, if that is the case, then I'm their man," he spoke with determination.

In that moment, Penelope realized her husband considered going off into the wilderness to stop this man on his own. She moved over to her husband and looked into his eyes, right in front of his face.

"You can't do this alone. Remember what the rest of the note said? You must contact, Li. They'll send help from America. Promise me, James," she begged him. "This desert madman has a whole following out there. He might be very powerful. One person against him with this power may not be enough. No soldier would go into battle without some kind of rear guard.

119

Think like a soldier, like the general that you are, James, and not like a foolish hero," she sounded a note of caution.

The pleading quality in her tone showed the general how much she meant to him. She first recognized his ability to lead men long before his first promotion, when she made him believe in himself. She trusted his judgment and instilled in him the same level of self awareness she had. Penelope was the only person in his life who had that kind of blind faith in James. He had to trust her judgment this time as well. She would never steer him in a wrong direction. James nodded and that sent her the message, he would do as she asked.

"I'll contact Master Li," he said.

"You've used that expression once before a second ago," she said. "Why do they call him Master Li? He isn't going to enslave you? Is he?" she wondered.

James chuckled, "No, darling. Michael Tyler, the head of the WPO, gave him that title out of respect years ago when they first met. He wanted Li to be his teacher in the psychic arts, if there is such a thing. You see, Li wasn't really a poet. He was a language arts and literature professor who taught at Harbin University for fifty years. He never wanted to be called 'master.' However, once Michael started to address him by the title, the others in their company followed suit. They recognized qualities in Li that lent themselves to being masterful. He is, after all, a very wise and powerful man."

"Who is Michael Tyler?" she asked.

"About three and half years ago, Michael Tyler was the very first human converted by the voices in Galactic Central. After a year on his own, he went in search of Li and made his conversion possible. The voices said that Michael is not only a powerful psychic but a natural leader, too. He insisted from the start on the provision of non-interference and restraint. Ever wonder why you never heard of the Tyler Foundation until only recently, when it started showing up on public television and other charity events?"

"You mean these people are responsible…" she started.

"Yes," James said as he interrupted to explain. "They use the free market system to obtain money. Through this foundation, they help people and work silently behind the scenes through the system."

Penelope sighed as she thought about all of the donations made by the foundation over the past two years that helped a variety of causes she supported.

"I may have misjudged your WPO," she said as her face took on a kind expression. "I've worked with representatives of the Tyler Foundation for wounded veterans. They showed up at a charity event in Sydney only a few months ago. The representative was a retired oriental general. He brought his wife… I'd say they are very good and generous people. They gave the largest donation the veteran's home every received. Come to think of it, I never met such understanding people…"

She stopped and gazed at her husband. She realized that she probably addressed psychics that knew how to fulfill her needs without speaking. They read her mind.

"I'm sorry I didn't attend the event," James said.

Penelope straightened her dress and smiled at her husband as if she had resolved whatever conflict she felt a moment ago and it somehow passed.

"Tell the psychics in America," she said, "we want this… Master…"

"Master Li," James filled in.

"Alright, Master Li," she agreed. "We want him to come here. Perhaps with all that power on our side, you can beat this rogue at his own game. We can discuss the whole thing over dinner this evening. Where is this WPO located?"

"Rollo, Kansas," he stated.

"Rollo, Kansas?" she echoed. "Never heard of it. Are you saying that the whole enterprise is in some small Kansas town?"

"Some live in America," James confirmed, "the rest are spread all over the world."

"Go ahead…" she pointed to his head. "Call them."

"Oh, quite right," he answered as he closed his eyes. "Calling Master Li… Master Li…"

CHAPTER TWENTY

THE MAJOR GENERAL GOES WHACKO!

THE DAY AFTER MAJOR GENERAL Pollack called off ill for the first time, he reported to work as usual bright and early the next morning. He cheerfully walked into the building, whistled as he walked along the corridors, which was highly unusual behavior for a man that usually bore a grim expression of determination. He strode into his office complex buoyant and exuberant; two words that hardly ever described the general.

"Good morning!" he happily stated to the guard when he entered his section.

He had a spring in his step and extra energy. For being a man supposedly at death's door the day before, he seemed as chipper as a chipmunk in a bed of seeds. Any old wounds or pains that he used to experience in the past, no longer bothered him. Even age did not slow the general in his movement. Since he learned to absorb psychic energy, the power surged through his body. It renewed his spirit, healed old aches, and made him feel recharged, revitalized, and youthful. He shared some that change with Penelope last night. She told him that he had not satisfied her that way in years. She sent him out the door with a swift pat to his back side. He felt terrific since.

"Good morning, Sandra," the general called out as he practically skipped into his office.

"Good morning, sir," his surprised secretary said when he bound past her desk and headed for his office door. She stood up at attention. "Are you feeling well?" she asked, curious where his high spirits originated.

"I haven't felt this good in many years," he told her. "Yesterday was simply a fluke. I'm back and ready to put a few ideas to work. Do you have your pad?" he asked.

His secretary had a thin electronic pad that connected her to anyone in the office complex, via phone, email, or special messenger. She could either use it as a keyboard or use a special pen to write notes down. She reached over and took the device off the top of her desk, lifting the pen at the same time to take dictation if necessary. He motioned for her to follow him into his office.

"First, I want all six division heads and their support staff called to my office in one hour," Major General Pollack began as he spoke to her over his shoulder. "I want them to bring their latest reports. I am especially interested in information regarding trouble spots. The one thing I do not want this morning is excuses. Is that clear, Sandra?" the general told her.

"Yes, sir!" she said with big smile.

"We are going to have this new system up and running today. Glitches? Never heard of them. Crashes? Not on my watch! Now, let's get cracking! Don't worry about coffee or anything silly like that. I'll order our breakfast and have it sent in by messenger. Please send those orders out at once, priority one!" he told her and added a smile at the end of it.

Sandra saluted and the general gave her one of those expressions like, "that isn't necessary." She smiled and backed away.

"Good to have you back, general sir!" she told him as she returned to her desk. She picked up her communicator and began barking a few orders of her own.

"It's good to be back," the general thought as he picked up his phone to order coffee and other items for their meeting. "... yes, I'd like steam tables and settings for twenty-four... eggs, sausages, bacon, beans, toast, muffins, marmalade, chutney, juice, fresh fruit, and some extra pastries, no donuts... oh, you'd better add two large pots of strong coffee... cream and sugar," he told the person on the other end, "and mark all of this urgent! I want it here and set up in one hour... can you do it? You can? Great!"

He leaned back in his chair, propped his feet up on his desk and placed his hands behind his head, very uncharacteristic for the staunchly conservative general. He grinned like a schoolboy with a secret crush on a girl, not that he would tell anyone that he and Penelope made passionate love, or that she probably had more orgasms from this one encounter than any in their entire marriage. James felt like a man on top of the world, confident, supported, loved, and in charge.

He sat up when he sensed a large group of people start through the complex and head his way. When he called the meeting to order that morning, he quickly picked up on everything in everyone's mind – suggestions, ideas, ways to solve problems, things no one shared out of timidity. All at once people connected, freely exchanged opinions without feeling challenged. Everyone sensed a difference in the air that spread like an infection from buoyancy into enthusiasm for their work.

Not only did James Pollack perform his leadership job well that morning, he never left his desk to break for lunch, as had been his usual habit. He found no frustrations to drive him away from his desk today. Little did others in department realize, the general knew exactly what any soldier or officer thought about him, or about their jobs, and about the project, including important suggestions on how to integrate the new computer software and streamline the supply process. Therefore, the general found he could cut through the "bull" and get to the point, which at first startled his staff, until he encouraged each them "to do better" with uplifting rhetoric.

"Now I believe we understand what to do. I suggest you go out there and make things happen," he told them when the morning meeting ended.

"You know," one junior officer whispered when he leaned over to his friend as they walked from the meeting, "I believe his illness is the best thing that ever happened to this department. Perhaps it's contagious and we'll all catch it."

"I only hope that's the case," the other officer replied.

As the day progressed, positive reports started to flow back from all the divisions. The general's secretary reported positive updates. His plan to implement the new system and streamline their department worked. The general stayed on his phone and communicated with his division heads while he worked out minor details and offered suggestions for solutions to problems that arose. He even received reports from the investigators and had them change tact, which resulted in new information. He worked straight through and kept his secretary by his side all day without a break. Finally, around 2:30 in the afternoon, he went out to her desk. He watched her for a second as she relayed the latest memo in military terms.

"...that the second divisional process, while making a substantial increase in tertiary budgetary restraints, could make additional subsections to the addendum..."

"Do we really sound like that?" he asked as he interrupted her.

"That's military linguistics," she shrugged. "What's up, sir?"

"You haven't taken one break today, Sandra," he told her. "I want you to close up shop and go home early today," he suggested.

"And miss out on all the fun?" she replied. "Not on your life! Besides, I ordered sandwiches which should be here any minute," she told him. "I'm staying... and if that means disobeying an order, then consider this mutiny, sir," she said not knowing how he would respond.

His face did not betray his real feeling toward her, admiration. He moved closer to her desk.

"Carry on, then… lieutenant… first grade," he said as he turned.

She was 2nd L.T., second grade. First grade meant a promotion and more money.

"What did you say?" she asked as she rose up out of her chair and came around the desk. She held out her arms to give him a hug.

James held up his hand to stop her.

"First of all, I'm a happily married man," he said with kindness, "and secondly… this promotion is long overdue, Sandra," he told her. "Tell me when those sandwiches arrive. I'm done with coffee. I could use a spot of tea! Make it iced tea!"

"Yes, sir!" Sandra replied as she smiled. She saluted and returned to her desk.

"Tell the department heads I want a three o'clock meeting and some results from our intervention today. Will you do that?" he requested.

"You won't have much time to enjoy that sandwich," she commented.

"I'll have to eat it during the meeting," he told her. "Get to it!"

"Yes, sir!" she said and again saluted.

The general felt proud of his division. They did an outstanding job on the project, having worked out all the problems that previously plagued them. By the end of the day, they resolved every single crisis that had plagued them for months. They put through rush orders on equipment, parts, and activated the new computerized system, making it fully operational in every department. The entire base was abuzz with the activity coming from Major General Pollack's division. He inspired his staff with his sudden burst of creativity and ingenuity. His innovation did not go unnoticed. A few "spies" purposely planted in key positions on the base telephoned reports back to Melbourne and Canberra.

Shortly before one o'clock, Lt. General Sanders' secretary stated he had an important call from the Chief of Staff on line one. The head of the army located in Canberra, capital of Australia, got wind of the major general's improvements. When Sanders picked up the phone, General Wallace started in on him as if he had been sitting on his hands all year. He demanded to know why his office detected this sudden flurry of activity from one of the general's subordinates.

"I want to know what's going on over there," General Wallace demanded of General Sanders. "Seems the whole army is singing Major General Pollack's praises today. They say his Adelaide division has completely streamlined the parts division, the ordering department, and the shipping department. My secretary said she heard that as a result of his division's actions, they saved the army millions in appropriation money. I don't want a report about his activity next month, I want you to go over there and investigate this today, George," General Wallace told him. "I want you to find out what's going on and get back to me," he ordered. "I know it's late in the day, but I want you to fly to Adelaide and find out what you can, then call me. I'll take the call at home if need be. Understood?"

"Yes, sir," Sanders reluctantly replied. When he hung up the phone, he did not seem pleased with the progress made by his underling. "Get my car!" the general called to his secretary. "Have a jet waiting for me at the airstrip. Seems I must pay James Pollack a visit," he mumbled.

About three forty-five in the afternoon, a knock arrived at the general's office door, right in the middle of James' departmental meeting. The general did not take the time to look up from the table. He was too busy reviewing reports as he munched down a cold corned beef sandwich and drank iced tea.

"We need to shore-up this part of the supply chain," James said to his division heads. He pointed to a display screen that showed a variety of charts and graphs. "With this new system, we have the power to move people and parts around with 40% greater efficiency, you realize. I'd like suggestions. Brad?"

A second, louder knock sounded on the general's office door.

"We're in the middle of a meeting!" the general barked as he returned his focus to one of the division heads, Bradley Cummins. "Sandra!" he called out. "I really don't have time for any interruptions," he said. "Tell them to go away."

"Not even for your commander?" General Sanders asked as he pushed open the door.

The entire room stood to attention including General Pollack.

"General, sir," James said as he jumped to his feet and saluted. "What brings you to Adelaide? If you'll pardon the intrusion."

The general returned the salute as he glanced about the room. He took particular interest in the charts and graphs on the wall screen. His eyes narrowed on the display of changing figures and the flashing upward arrow marked "40%."

"At ease," he said as he walked around the table. He noted the stacks of papers and electronic notepads in front of each person. "You've certainly been busy today, general," George Sanders said as he made his way to toward his old nemesis James Pollack. While he pretended to be James' friend, in reality he was responsible for making his life miserable. "You should have more days off, if I'd known you were going to show up and go gun-ho like this when you returned," the general observed. "I hear you turned this whole department around completely in just one day. I congratulate you," he said as he nodded to the general.

"It wasn't me," James said with all modesty. "My team is responsible. They worked hard today. They deserved the credit, sir. I only made a few suggestions," he said as he gestured around the room.

The moment he said that, the entire team began to protest. They pointed their fingers at the general and said he was the person responsible for the turn around.

"Such loyalty is admirable," General Sanders commented. He turned his focus back to James. "Well! It's nearly four o'clock, old boy," he said as he pointed to his wrist and rubbed his hands together. "Let's go to Digger's for some tea," the general suggested and winked as James knew he meant cigars and brandy.

Surrounded by his subordinates, James Pollack had been in the middle of instructing them on a complete reorganization that would streamline the pipeline with any future projects of this nature. His eyes traveled from one staff member to the other, questioning that decision offered by General Sanders.

"Go ahead, sir," his departmental assistant Lt. Col. Bradley Cummins finally spoke up. "We've done wonders today, sir. We'll finish up," he reassured him.

The other team members concurred and added their approval.

James realized that Sanders wanted to pump him for information. However, he could not disobey what amounted to a command from his superior to leave his job. He straightened his tie and reached for his jacket.

"I'll be with you in a moment, sir," James told General Sanders. He leaned over next to Brad Cummins and whispered a few things in his ear. As he pulled his head back, he mouthed, "I'll call you later," to him as he left.

The lieutenant colonel smiled back at the general. If anyone in that room could take over after the general retired, it would be his right arm, Bradley Cummins. The general felt relief when he sensed Brad plunge right in and take the same assertive stand to lead and inspire confidence in his staff.

Outside the building, Lt. General Sanders called for his car and ordered the driver to take them over to the Digger's Club. While not a limousine, the upper echelon of the military had such perks as a driver so they could work in the privacy of a car to and from their assignments. On the way to the Diggers Club, George Sanders spoke with high praise in regards to Jame's efforts, while he said nothing about the phone call from Chief of Staff General Wallace in Canberra.

Sanders had not been to Digger's in a long time. Normally, he was stationed at the base outside Melbourne. He rarely made an appearance at the Adelaide base. He had many major generals under his command at bases in Sydney, Melbourne, Canberra, and Brisbane. He considered James Pollack just another subservient operations officer that he could manipulate as he did with so many men under his command. He planted spies on those bases, officers loyal to him. They reported on the base's activities and often performed "pranks" that caused problems for other officers. Sanders wanted to be Chief of Staff and he would not allow any other officer to stand in his way. Ambition blinds some men to reason.

James had to suppress a smile when he heard the clarifying broadcast of the general's true thoughts come from the man's mind sitting next to him.

"Amazing work your team did today. Outstanding," Sanders commented. "I don't understand how they solved so many problems so quickly. But I have to say, you're looking good to the old man upstairs," the general informed James.

"Thanks, George," James beamed.

("Yes… you're really such an ass, James… making me look bad to General Wallace… I hope this doesn't slow my promotion," George thought.)

Privately, James set aside his formal self and relaxed while in the company of a man he knew for many years; a man he knew as his superior and occasionally met on a social basis when he and Penelope attended Army functions. It seemed to James that his relationship with Lt. Gen. Sanders suddenly changed. Just last week, Sanders practically threatened him with a demotion. The supply chain had bottlenecked through bureaucratic red tape and deliveries fell weeks behind schedule. The Army oversight office listed several supply items missing from different warehouse locations. Some of the pricier items included vehicles and advance weapons explosives. Additionally, new project designers found communication difficult between departments. Implementation of the new computer systems dropped in priority while Maj. Gen. Pollack's division scrambled to find the missing items. Several different program applications fell behind schedule as a result. With so many problems to address, and investigative teams combing bases, suspicious that one of the division heads ran a fencing scheme, James' team ran around in disarray, much to his frustration but Lt. General Sanders' delight.

Now, in one day the general seemed to have fixed every single problem that threatened him only yesterday. He implemented the new programs, he streamlined the ordering and procurement processes, and he discovered only minutes ago, what happened to the missing items – someone pilfered General Sanders' base warehouse outside Melbourne. James did not let on he knew, because Sanders acted as if James was his best friend. The threats he made last week seemed a thing of the past, to be forgotten. Someone in top command today must have ordered the lt. general to investigate their progress, James reasoned.

"Why else would Georgie bother making a special trip at the end of the day?" James privately wondered. "... and why Diggers? He seldom went to Diggers any longer... considered it stodgy. The other members did not like Sanders. They thought of him as a pompous ass."

"Just how did you do it?" Lt. General Sanders asked. "Turn your department around in one day, I mean."

James suddenly realized that he had the ability to find the truth in General Sanders' mind. This time, instead of searching for the right thing to say, he probed the general's thoughts for the answers. At once, James could feel the tension between them. Had he really wanted him to fail? He sensed the general upset because James improved his position within the ranks so quickly. He made a quick pass of Gen. Sander's mind.

Secretly, General Sanders feared that James Pollack might pass him by with the ultimate promotion – that of command general. There were only five in the whole country, with General Wallace being the fifth and chairman of the joint forces, second only to the Prime Minister. He actually hoped James would fail in the assignment. He purposely slowed the supply chain and placed his own staff members in key places to create problems for James' division. Eventually, he hoped that when James could not solve the supply or program integration messes, General Sanders' own team of experts would solve the problems and he would take credit. Afterward, Sanders planned on the promised promotion he felt his due after all his years of service.

Unfortunately, General Sanders had no one to blame for the problems he created. He could not take credit for solving the problems when he went before the joint chiefs' meeting in Sydney next week. James accomplishment filled the general's head with feelings of jealousy and envy, not the sentiments he expressed aloud.

As James heard these thoughts, his feelings changed, too. He no longer looked on "Georgie" as his friend of twenty some years who offered to help him from time to time. He saw him as a fierce competitor, but one that held no scruples and followed no code of ethics.

"Well? Are you going to tell me?" Sanders demanded after he waited for the reply.

"I'm sorry, George," James said as he blinked and put on a phony smile. "What did you ask? I'm probably tired from such a long day."

"You have not explained how you merged the computer programs and straighten out the supply lines. I hear you managed to move a long list of backlogged equipment to its intended destination." Sanders commented.

"The same way you would have, George," James told him. "You see, I read their minds. I gave them just what they wanted. I promised my civil servants a fat raise if they hustled faster and they did just that!" he kidded.

The response brought a hearty laugh from General Sanders. Yet even as he laughed, he eyed the general with suspicion. James felt more at ease. He truthfully answered the general and pulled off his reply with such confidence, George decided to drop the matter for the time.

When they arrived at the club, Sergeant Beery acted on the information James' secretary gave him. He had an isolated quiet area prepared for both men to relax.

"Welcome to Digger's Lt. General, sir. Haven't seen you around here for awhile," Beery remarked when General Sanders walked in.

Beery's brash comment caught Sanders off guard.

"Yes, um, been meaning to stop by for a drink," he lied.

Beery saw through the shallow comment but had everything ready for them as James' secretary called him and warned of their impending arrival. General Sanders usually drank Brandy and smoked a domestic cigar. Beery knew that Maj. General Pollack usually drank Darjeeling tea at this time of day. He preferred his whiskey later in the evening and then enjoyed just a few puffs of a Caribbean cigar out on his upper deck just before bedtime. That way, when he returned home from the club, he did not smell of liquor and tobacco on his breath when he kissed his wife. Penelope appreciated that note of consideration, since on occasion, their kiss led to other pursuits.

The two men sat in their chairs. James opened up his paper. He did not see any mention in the news of a "madman" in the desert.

"The man's operation would be clandestine, wouldn't it?" he considered.

"Is that the Post?" George asked.

"Would you like the sports section?" James replied.

"How the devil did you know that?' George asked as he stared at his subordinate.

"As I said, I've been reading minds today," James told him honestly.

George frowned at James, and then he smiled when he thought James must be joking.

"If only that were the case, old boy," Gen. Sanders responded. "Do you know what that would mean for the service? Here, I'll take that."

He took the section of the paper James offered. He grimaced at Pollack for a second before he settled down to read his section on the Kensington Cricket matches.

In his mind, Gen. Sanders thought: "Pollack's a bit wacko on this mind reading stuff. Perhaps if he brings it up again, I'll suggest he tone it down. Don't want to give the enlisted men any advantage, talking about their superiors."

"I'll make a note of that," James thought. "This has been a great end to a very productive day," he added as he thought about his accomplishments.

He bonded with his wife in a way he had not felt in years. He successfully completed a project that had bogged down his department for the past three months with procedure and threatened his job. He formed a new yet cautious alliance with his superior officer, and he spoke with aliens from a distant galaxy. If only the members of his club knew that a few hours from now, Major General James M. Pollack would reach across hundreds of millions of light years from earth to an alien species and further enlighten his mind. When he finished the "download" experience, he would rise a new man filled with increased knowledge and awareness. He felt vastly superior to anyone he knew, except his wife of course.

Berry brought their refreshments.

"Ah," he sipped his tea with confidence and spoke aloud, "I believe I'll overhaul the entire civil service system tomorrow," he quipped.

General Sanders peered over his paper and stared at General Pollack, afraid to take him at his word.

CHAPTER TWENTY-ONE

THE COMMUNITY UP-ABOVE

A LOVELY DEMURE YOUNG NATIVE American girl moved down the basement stairs with deliberate purpose as she carefully walked toward a solid wall of masonry. Rather than stop, she bravely continued her forward stride and easily passed through the impenetrable barrier. The wall recognized her cellular structure and allowed her entry. Had another person approached at her rate of speed, they would have a very sore nose about now.

"Recognize Star Wind," a voice chimed.

What appeared to be solid stone pieced together with a bonding agent, such as cement, was instead a façade, meant to fool the uninitiated. Not Michael or even the great Master Li could pass this way without Chou's approval. Only Star Wind, Chou's wife of just four months, could pass through the powerful barrier created by magnetic forces strong enough to reflect a nuclear blast at point blank range.

Thereby, Michael considered that in case of a nuclear attack, should that scenario ever play out, this was one of three completely safe places in Rollo where the community could flee, in case the worst happened; the sub-floors of the great manor house and Villi's underground transportation center being the other places completely safe from attack.

When Michael brought up his security concerns about being locked out of Chou's lab, the young scientist whose lifespan Cecilia froze at 19 years of age, defended his security measures.

"First of all," Chou explained in a general meeting, "no one is going to drop a nuclear bomb on a place that doesn't exist," he pointed out. "Secondly, each house has sufficient stopping power to withstand a nuclear blast from say… seventy kilometers away, such as Dodge City. Third, some of my projects have devices that in the wrong hands could…"

"This is a morbid line of thought," Michael responded. "We recognize the necessity of your wall. Let's drop this matter."

Today, this afternoon, as Star Wind stepped through the illusionary space that gave way to her molecular structure, she moved into an area that still mystified and marveled her sense of awe.

One could only describe the space on the other side of the barrier as immense. Chou built an enormous subterranean cavern with multiple levels and specialty areas, carved out and supported by walls made of super strong substances created inside Zinian's construction-sized fusor. The lab spread out into a vast space beneath the surface of Rollo and spread downward the same height as a twenty story building would extend if constructed above ground and occupied an area of about four city blocks. Two years ago, Chou proposed this space and Zinian's crew with special devices, dug out this subterranean cavern to house Chou's ever growing sophisticated laboratory. The size equivalent of many giant warehouses combined, he created this lab for the sole purpose of providing enough room to house a variety of devices intended to improve or enhance the life of the WPO's membership – everything from ground vehicles to airships to new building materials and other experiments. Chou created and tested hundreds of new inventions in this gigantic underground space.

Chou reasoned he could safely test objects and ideas while not having to worry about harming his wife or anyone else in Rollo. The walls that made up the top, sides, and bottom of this structure were of made from a lightweight yet super strong material that nothing short of sustained nuclear fusion could penetrate. Chou located his house over the middle of the lab. Only the manor house's sublevels and Villi's transportation structure sunk deep into the ground but not to the extent that Chou's lab did.

In this space, Chou could experiment to his heart's content. Once he realized he could create other fusors from his first device, he made several copies of varying sizes and placed them in different parts of his lab. Simplified mechanical robots ran fusors every hour of the day, churning out products and starting experiments while he rode around on a special hover car that followed a magnetic track. Shortly after Star Wind moved in, she had to drag the excited youth out of his lab or else he would not ever stop to bathe or eat. While Chou protested, he privately enjoyed her attention and intervention on his behalf. Only partially psychic, Star Wind, with Chou's assistance, took special nighttime knowledge transfers that he monitored and soon she worked as a valued assistant for her brilliant husband.

As Master Li once told him in China – a moment that seemed ages ago instead of the thirty months that elapsed since that time – "You will be the greatest technologist the world has ever known." His invention of the fusor helped to make their new life possible. Since that time, he continued to crank out marvelous devices.

Star Wind had grown into a beautiful young woman during the past two and a half year period. Sixteen when the psychics first landed, she left behind her lanky awkward teen body and matured into a curvaceous Native American woman with large brown eyes, long black braided hair, and bronze skin. While Chou could not take psychic energy from her, such a move is considered an attack between psychics, she gave him so much more in their relationship, including a healthy boost to the geek's libido. She found Chou attractive from when they first met. They respectfully kept their distance and remained in a cordial relationship until last spring, when Star Wind turned 18 and insisted she move in with Chou.

When Running Elk returned from France for a visit, she found a different daughter, nearly as transformed as she was. She approved of her daughter's relationship with Chou and gave her blessing. The two were officially wed at the manor house opening ceremony in October 2018 that also included the gathering of the WPO members and the writing of the charter. That was over three months ago.

As she stepped forward into her husband's lab, a remarkable platform safely and gently lowered her down to the very bottom of this enormous internal structure. A rail rose up out of the platform's material and molded under her hand. She dropped nearly a hundred and fifty meters toward the dark floor below. Once she reached the bottom, Star Wind guided the platform that hovered about ten centimeters over a special "glide path" in the floor toward a distant light.

She maintained her glide path toward the single light source in the distance. An arrow moved along on the lab's floor to indicate Chou's current location. The man seated within that distant light did not believe in wasting energy. Yet, she did not have to stumble around in the dark. A soft glowing bluish light directed her path along the way and kept her immediate environment faintly lit. She passed by a variety of objects, some huge, others small and complex, shelf after shelf came and went, items stacked on tables or shelves, some measured over fifty meters high.

As she grew nearer, she could see the ever-young Asian man. His hard work and long hours over the past two and half years had not left one line on his very youthful face. As he intently bent over a workbench, his current project occupied his attention to the extent he did not sense Star Wind's approach until she appeared out of the darkness. A yellowish cloud floated inside a force field which Chou hovered over like a protective parent.

"What is that?" Star Wind curiously asked as her platform stopped.

"What do you think it is?" Chou replied, having finally sensed her.

He delicately adjusted the edges of the cloud, carefully using a probe that appeared to be a very long needle attached to a robotic arm. A billowy moving object with no discernable edge, about 14 cm tall and 4cm wide in places, rotated as Chou Lo, Rollo's master technological genius, pushed and prodded the object, until each area he touch took on an extra golden glow. That additional illumination meant the object had reached its ideal and stable state.

"Is it some sort of miniature cloud?" Star Wind asked.

"Yes…" he replied expectantly, "and no. This is a just model. The real one will be slightly different in configuration."

"It must represent something other than a cloud," Star Wind guessed. "If it is not a cloud, which is usually very massive and fluid, then it probably is something completely opposite, a very tiny object."

"Excellent," Chou said as he sent her a furtive glance. "I believe living with me is beginning to pay off handsomely for you," he pointed out.

"That and your mind transfer lessons," she managed to link back.

Chou smiled when she did, for of all the non-portal psychics they had encountered, Star Wind represented the most developed of that line. He was very proud of her.

"You were right to suppose it represented something very small," he told her. "This is a single molecule," he indicated. "These are atoms," he pointed to the fluctuating edges. "I'm entering this structure into the memory of the fusor. I have a list that is constantly growing," he said as he pointed to a flat panel screen next to the machine with a long list of formulas. He turned his attention back to the model.

"Is that protrusion at the end of the probe, an atom?" she asked him.

"Yes," he answered absently, his concentration focused on the probe.

"Look at it move," she said, "as if each atom had some magical source of power."

"That's what most scientists think, too," Chou said as he shut down the manipulating arm. The molecule continued to vibrate and appeared solid while it glowed with a golden color.

"Atoms derive their energy from their intrinsic structure," he explained. "They are surrounded by an EMS (electromagnetic spectrum) that affects everything in the universe."

"When you said you created these molecules for the fusor, did you mean you created formulas for all of them?" she wondered as she gazed on the molecule.

"Oh, yes. All I need do is enter the molecular formula into this device and all the fusors in Rollo will be able to duplicate it," he further explained.

"Which molecule is this?" she asked.

"Something your mother will need tonight in abundance… butter," Chou said with a certain amount of pride.

"That's butter?" she asked.

"Uh, huh," he said as the arm pulled back. "Churned cream, but not just any cream, your mother made specific demands… requests." He took off his safety goggles and took in deep breath. "She wanted the unsalted organic butter made from specific cows that grazed along the banks of the…"

"You don't need to explain what my mother wanted," Star Wind chuckled. "Since she went to cooking school, she's become quite particular about her ingredients. Mind you, I believe that's a good thing as long as you can tolerate…"

"Far be it for me to question Running Elk," Chou said with a smile. "At least that's done," he said as he sat up straight. "When do the guests arrive?" he asked.

"Villi flew in members from China and India last night. He made a special trip for Leni. He intends to give General Liong his own flyer during this visit…"

"That's overdue," Chou commented.

"…Tahir will fly the Mediterranean group here this afternoon," she told him. "I believe Sir Charles intends to fly the group from Europe via Villi's recent present to him. Villi went to central Africa this morning to pick up Salla and Filla."

"I wonder why Master Li has called for the entire membership to gather," Chou considered. "Perhaps he has some grand mission in mind… that would mean I'd have to leave Rollo," he worried. "I have projects…"

"As you often say, reading Master Li is difficult," Star Wind replied. "Michael gave his approval. That's why I am here. He told me to tell you to shut down for a few days and join the festivities."

"Well… I suppose we should go up and prepare for Running Elk's marvelous feast," he said as he anticipated a masterpiece meal from the world's greatest chef. "Alexander," Chou called to his personal computer, "continue projects 11,668 through 11,773 in automated status."

"Acknowledged," the male computer voice answered.

"Convert communication standard to my ring," Chou ordered.

"Understood," the computer stated.

"Perhaps we'll all wear such devices some day," Star Wind commented about Chou's special ring.

He took such things for granted.

"Not a bad idea… I could create a piece of jewelry that could contain…"

"Not now," she said and kissed him on his cheek.

Chou pushed back from the workbench. The seat automatically put distance between his body and the devices, and removed the safety equipment placed in front of him. The equipment shut down under its own power.

He took his wife by the hand and the two stepped aboard the entry platform that brought Star Wind to him. Minutes later when they walked out through the barrier outside the laboratory, the security wall sealed behind them.

"Let any intruder try to penetrate that," he told Zhiwei the day he completed the entrance.

"I must admit," Zhiwei said as he ran his hand over the stone wall, "you surpassed my recommendations."

"You can thank Master Li for increasing my level of concern," Chou replied at the time.

Master Li feared if any of Chou's devices fell into the wrong hands, they could wreck havoc with humanity. Therefore, Chou made the lab so secure, only he and Star Wind could enter it. She once started to tell her mother, Running Elk, about the marvels inside the lab when her mother cut her off.

"If Chou needed others to know," Running Elk stated, "he would have advertised."

"But mother, you should see…" Star Wind started.

"Sometimes, daughter," Running Elk told her, "it is best to be silent about such things."

Star Wind took her mother's counsel after that and never mentioned Chou's laboratory. As a matter of fact, Zhiwei made certain she was the only Native American outside her mother that knew of its existence.

"Ready for the big night," Star Wind asked as she adjusted his bow tie.

"Yes," Chou replied as he watched his image in the mirror over her shoulder. "I look forward to seeing Sir Charles, Camille, and the others," he told his wife. "Most of all," he said, "I'm thankful for any excuse to go into the manor house. I do love to visit Master Li and Han."

"You helped build the house," Star Wind said.

"Well, we all helped… and you decorated the interior," Chou said as he gazed at her with pride. "However, after working in a dark place like the lab all day," Chou said as he beheld his wife in her evening gown, "even a diehard technologist like me looks forward to being surrounded by beautiful things. It only takes one visit to realize — the manor house is the most magnificent dwelling on the planet… and it didn't cost a dime to build, not one red cent."

"I'd have to agree," Star Wind said as she moved closer, "my handsome husband."

"You look beautiful," he said as he kissed her on the lips. "Shall we?" he said as he offered his arm.

The couple emerged from their house and joined the other couples and guests that headed up Main Street to eat dinner at the most incredible domicile in existence. While their Native American friends gathered at the civic center across from the medical arts building for a sumptuous feast Running Elk prepared earlier, the most gifted and powerful people on planet Earth gathered in what one can only describe as the most exclusive club in which no one speaks a word, a place where an outsider would feel isolated.

CHAPTER TWENTY-TWO

AN OASIS IN THE DESERT

"IT WAS MICHAEL'S IDEA," MASTER LI protested.

"It was my idea," Michael relented when he first proposed the project during a meeting, where Cecilia objected to both its size and ostentation.

"I hate to remind you," she spoke with all seriousness, "the world is full of starving and diseased people and we are building a big glitzy mansion... hardly a show of sympathy for the poor and misbegotten."

"Might I remind my esteemed colleague," Zinian rose to Michael's defense, "that we are not spending a single dollar on this structure, that all the materials are being made from dirt, and that the Tyler Foundation will give fifty billion dollars this year alone to charities around the world!"

"Point taken," Su Lin echoed as she bid her friend resume her seat. "Like Cecilia, I feel the plans over the top..." she offered, "however, like Michael I look at our future and see how this represents more than a symbol of wealth... it stands as the epitome of our understanding... a place that will house the greatest treasures of the world and dedicate itself to preserving the history of the planet earth," she said on the border of pomposity. She glanced over at Cecilia, "If I were the architect, it would be twice the size. I'm sorry," she linked to her friend. "I must support Michael."

Since all votes must be unanimous, Cecilia crossed her arms and looked around the room. The others wondered if she would block the project. She took another look at Michael's three-dimensional rendition.

"We'd better double our efforts to end poverty and disease," she said and aimed her comments directly at Master Li. He nodded and glanced over at Michael.

"I can't pour any more of money into the world than we have going out Cecilia," Michael reminded her. "We would disrupt the stability of every currency by inflationary spending." Before she could object, he continued, "but I will do my best to make certain we end all world poverty and disease within the decade."

Cecilia closed her mouth and silently relented to its construction, which began not long after Zinian revamped the village of Rollo. For two years, his crews assembled millions of pieces until in the fall of 2018, they finally finished the interior spaces...

Rising like some great colossus above the flat Kansas plain, originally designed by Michael Tyler, brought to fruition by Zinian's architectural plans and built by his crew – which consisted of nearly every able-bodied man or woman in Rollo – the great edifice created as the headquarters to the World Psychic Organization and the home of Master Li rests on the grassy plot that once occupied a vacant field at the eastern end of Main Street. Simply known locally as the manor house, the building is so large that it casts a shadow over nearly the entire city of Rollo until after ten o'clock most mornings – only the far north or south ends of Rollo are spared this daily eclipse.

The visitor to the manor house first passes through a large yet open-gated entry whose wide base is made up of huge natural granite stones carefully pieced together. Out of their top springs lengths of black wrought iron twisted into creative shapes that arch upward on either side until they meet and surround three large cursive golden letters: **WPO** at its pinnacle. This massive gate stands alone with no connection to any fence or barrier around the property.

Moving on, the visitor walks up the white stone drive that spreads further apart until it forms a large piazza with a multi-figured water fountain in its center. Each god-like naked muscular or feminine figure perpetually sprays water from a variety of openings; their writhing shapes reach skyward or passionately stare at passing visitors. Twenty large, white, beautifully carved, crystalline colonnades form the great front façade spread out in a semi-circular entry. The top of their seventeen meters of height measure the location of the first story's interior ceiling with an additional four levels of floors that rise above them. Each subsequent floor measures eight meters of interior height, except in the center of the structure under the rotunda, which is open inside. Topping the massive structure is a large white dome with eight ribs that stretch down from its peak. Lifelike statues of eight original members wearing tunics face away from the base of the dome, each one precisely aligned to a compass direction. The figure of Master Li tops the dome. His statue faces way from the front entrance. He looks toward the east. Each day, his statue catches the first rays of the sun disc as it rises above the artificial horizon.

On the opposite or eastern side of the building, two "glass" hallways at ground level lead diagonally toward north and south "glass" domed arboreta that house specially designed ecosystems. The clear material that Chou invented used throughout Rollo instead of glass is stronger and harder than a diamond by a factor of ten thousand. Despite its clarity, the incredibly strong substance can only be destroyed by the interior of a star.

At the start of the project during the subterranean excavation phase, Master Li marveled over the size of the substructure that would hold the mass of the building about to rise five stories above the ground level. He called on Michael one morning to explain once more the intricacies of monstrosity. As the two men watched Native American workers place the first support beams of the infrastructure into the large excavated hole, it appeared as if the sheer size of the beams would be impossible to handle. The crew's ease at moving them about belied their ability to carry significant loads of weight. Although very light in weight, each beam measured four meters wide and deep while being 64 meters in length. Zinian spread a gooey like substance at their base which locked the gigantic beams into the bedrock. Spaced evenly apart on the north and south wings, the crew could begin to attach the cross beams to these anchors. A middle gap of 60 meters at the center had to attach the supports for that part of the building with one great curving piece (actually made of four curved parts) that wrapped around the back of the grand staircase and connected the north wing to the south wing. From there, workers extended a lattice of horizontal and vertical supports that spread the overall load bearing capacity to the large vertical beams.

Master Li stood on the street next to Michael and watched, along with other village members, this massive skeletal structure rise into the air in just one day. He linked to his pupil.

"I asked for a meager house, Michael," he commented.

"You have a meager house," Michael replied as he referred to Li's current house behind them. "You'll soon move into one worthy your station."

"Is this a house or an office building?" Li wondered. "What do you intend for its final size?"

Michael pulled the figures from his head as he had memorized the exact dimensions. He worked over the schematics with Zinian for two months before Chou's large fusor on the south side of town started to churn out the lightweight numbered parts that eventually be glued together.

"The headquarters is 400 meters (1312 ft) wide, 250 meters (820 ft) in depth, and over 65 meters (213 ft) in height if you count the ornate carved marble railing around the top of the mostly flat roof. Since it will never rain on the WPO headquarters, we added gargoyles at the corners for decorative purposes only."

"Its interior consists of five stories," Michael continued, "four wings, fifty bedrooms, sixty full-sized bathrooms, an Olympic-sized swimming pool, two greenhouses, ten museums, and twenty showcase galleries. On the main floor you'll have a morning room in the north wing, a dining room in the south wing adjacent to the huge kitchen. We designed it according to Running Elk's requests. Finally, the first floor has a very large and quite magnificent library, which I might add, you modified. We had to extend the dimensions of the entire first floor just to accommodate your library!"

"I did make those changes," Li concurred. "Didn't I?"

Michael continued, "The front has an expansive foyer entrance with a connecting grand staircase in the center of the house. Each floor has over eight meters of height of interior clearance, with the first floor entry taking up over seventeen meters of interior clearance, except for the area of the central foyer rotunda surmounted by the dome."

"Would you remind why we need a dome on top of that?" Li wondered with raised eyebrows.

"Of course," Michael answered with a smile. "We had to top the outlandish with something even more outrageous. By the way, the dome adds another eighteen meters to the top, which brings the total height to 83 meters. When we add your statue, it will put the top at 86 meters," he pointed out, "Personally, I believe it will be the greatest domicile ever created."

"I can't make you change your mind," Li commented. "Living inside this... monstrosity... will only make the occupants feel small."

Michael turned to his master.

"The world group, such as its size currently is, voted unanimously to create a headquarters for the WPO in Rollo. We also thought it would make a great residence for the head of that organization... which, by the way, is you," Michael pointed out. "This structure represents the culmination of our knowledge and experience with Galactic Central."

Li shook his head and sighed.

"In that case," Master Li replied as he rubbed his chin, "to honor such a historic place, I'll have to journey through time and collect some of the greatest treasures from history to fill it."

Those words bothered Michael.

"I understand how you could peer backward at the past via your time ribbon," he pointed out. "But I've never understood how you can physically go to a place that no longer exists and bring an object back from what you describe as shadows of the past," Michael wondered.

"Let me simply say, I have the capacity to interact with the past... in a physical way," Li told him.

"You mean you could date a famous woman from history..."

"I hardly had that in mind," Li retorted. "That's a young man's pursuit."

Michael gazed off at the horizon, as he tried to visualize what Li described, though no psychic other than Master Li could actually travel into the past. Michael tried to mentally apply what Li revealed as to how he conceived the timeline worked.

"I've always wondered… did you ever meet…" he started.

"Yes," Li answered. "Like most figures of history, the stories about individuals are grossly exaggerated. Most people are quite ordinary and do not resemble the beautiful people portrayed in paintings or media recreations. People are not models or actors with perfect skin, perfect noses, and wear makeup. They are real, Michael, like you and I. What makes people famous is their ability to affect change on a large scale. If they do, no matter the method, history remembers them, the good along with the bad."

"Will I be able to have this capacity someday… traveling into the past?" he thought to Li.

"I'm sorry," Li told him. "I cannot reveal that information to my pupil," he linked and saw the disappointment on Michael's face. "However, you'll see the results of my journeys soon enough," Li smiled. "As Su Lin suggested, I intend to make this place a treasure trove of human and natural history."

After two years, Zinian's work crew finally completed construction of the five-story mansion with three sublevels underneath the main floor that could house the entire community if necessary. As Michael promised, Zinian's crew topped the structure with a large dome and life-like statues of the original nine. Resting upon the wide expanse of a dusty flat Kansas plain, the enormous structure acts as the focal point, not just for the psychics, but for the Comanche helpers who glued those millions of pieces together. They felt a sense of pride and accomplishment. Only two years earlier, the tribe lived in run down government trailers and squalid conditions. Today, each tribe member lived in a grand home and had contributed to the transformation of this dusty little village into an isolated world class oasis surrounded by a desert of little dusty prairie towns. No grand structure in Vegas, Paris, Dubai, or Shanghai could complete.

When guests first arrived, they walked through the main entry marked with two, tall, massive, wooden doors, each with a large ornate hinged golden knocker on the outside. Inside, the floor of the foyer consists of polished white marble tiles with real, radiant-cut, 40-carat gemstones of diamond, emerald, sapphire, and ruby, one inset at each of the four corner joins. The workers laughed when Zinian directed them to pocket the extra gemstones as Chou created bags of them, more than were needed. The men and women on the crew kept them as souvenirs or made them into rings. The entry floor sparkled and dazzled the eye of the visitor.

"Too bad we can't spend them," one of the men said as he stuffed a forty carat diamond into his pocket.

"If you went out and started throwing around 40-carat gemstones, their value would plummet," Master Li reminded them. "Remember, they're just a stone... granted a pretty stone, but worthless compared to what we have here," he said to them and swept his arm toward the direction of the village. "We can create a thousand diamonds... but there is only one Rollo."

Some of the crew gave them to their children, while Li warned that the stone's sharp edges could injure young children and instructed caution.

Having finished his rounds and hearing rumors spread of the infamous floor, Michael showed up to investigate. The workers proudly pointed to their precision.

"Seems a shame to walk on it," he commented when he entered. "I don't want to ruin the polish."

"That floor is sealed with a clear material that will last longer than us," Chou proudly pointed out. "You could tap dance on it for a month and never scuff the surface. It never needs waxing. That perfect sheen will last forever."

The workers chucked and everyone started stamping their feet, which even made Master Li laugh and join them as he performed an old-fashioned soft shoe dance.

"Forever is a long time, Chou," Michael pointed out as he danced around.

"We may test that theory one day," Chou responded via a link so the crew would not hear. They were not aware that the psychics could, theoretically at least, live for hundreds of years.

Stepping past the large open foyer, the eye automatically follows the grand staircase with its sweeping upward curves. A thick dark green carpet partially covers the rising mahogany wood and its fancy balustrade to the first landing where the stairs divide and lead to the second floor corridors of the north and south wings.

From the second floor landing, the bifurcating staircase led up to the third and four floors. This creates a huge open space in the center of the house. On the fourth floor, the staircase swung back and disappeared into the fifth floor which formed the circular opening around the interior base of the dome. For those less ambitious, the house had two elevator systems at the opposite ends of both wings. An additional rear elevator from the kitchen connected to all the floors for the delivery staff should anyone request room service.

High above the main staircase atop the center of the house stood a massive dome that crowned the structure. The inside of the dome was painted sky blue with puffy white clouds around the edges and a circle of nine golden stars. Windows rim the entire periphery of the dome near its base to cast sunlight inside its interior.

On a long massive chain made of some super strong material, a 25-tiered crystal chandelier hung suspended from the dome's center. Its surface glistened with hundreds of faceted tear-drop crystalline forms. When the morning sun shone through the windows above the first landing, the light struck the chandelier's crystals and filled the open space with shimmering rainbows that cascaded down every surface.

Once Zinian's crew finished construction, the task to decorate the inside fell to Star Wind, chosen by the nine psychics for her artistic propensity. Master Li helped by providing many of the items she requested.

"What do you think... a large vase on either side," she pointed to the first floor landing.

"Done," Li said, "Go on."

Star Wind gave him lists every day, and every day he brought priceless objects to her, more beautiful than she envisioned. No one questioned where Master Li obtained these rare objects of antiquity that showed up during the decorating phase.

However, the vases she requested turned out to be two large Greek urns, some two meters high, and each covered with detailed pictures of naked athletes engaged in some sport. Inside each urn she placed large exotic dried plants that Li brought from the Paleozoic Era. Shortly after their arrival, Michael and Zinian showed up and closely examined the urns. The two men stood at the base of the staircase and watched Star Wind direct some crew to hang a tapestry on the wall of the first floor landing between the two vases.

"They are in perfect condition, as if someone brought them back from Greece over 2500 years ago," Michael commented to Zinian.

"And who's to say they weren't," Zinian commented as Star Wind directed workers. "Where did you get those?" he asked her.

She pointed to Master Li, just as he walked up behind Zinian and Michael. The two startled psychics turned around, surprised they did not sense him.

"Do you like them?" Li asked with his typical soft voice. "In terms of aesthetics, they were years ahead of the Chinese," he added with admiration in his tone.

"Oh, yes, Master Li," Michael and Zinian chimed in together.

"I like them. Trust me, they won't be missed," he informed them. "They were commissioned as commemorative pieces to celebrate the first nude Olympic Games in BCE 720. An earthquake in Olympia caused a column of marble to crush them. I felt I should save the work. Don't you?" he put to them.

"Oh, yes, Master Li," the two men chimed back.

The elderly man shuffled off toward the library.

As Michael and Zinian watched him go, Michael linked, "Why the first nude Olympics?"

"I just wondered how he carried them through time," Zinian commented. "They're huge!"

"I suppose it's best not to ask," Michael muttered. He hoped Li would not overhear his remarks – but he did.

Two white marble statues of partially clothed women, each baring a basket of grapes or olives, symbols of fertility, flanked the bottom of the staircase. Each statue rose approximately four meters in height and rested on a marble base, carved by an unknown Renaissance sculptor. The detail was remarkable, right down to the texture in the skin. Villi speculated Michelangelo created them. However, Michael argued for Bernini, or perhaps students of these masters.

With the help of Master Li, Star Wind used her artistic affinity to transform the great house into a living museum and gallery, dedicated to all that is wonderful and glorious about the planet. The original artwork on the walls in the hallways and bedrooms was a mix of ancient, classic, and modern (depending on the location). Li provided artwork from cultures and civilizations long extinct, even paintings thought lost in fires during World War II. Su Lin marveled at their perfect condition when she first walked through the house.

"May I bring my classes here?" she asked of Li.

"Every room in the house is open to anyone day or night," Master Li told her, "except one room."

"Your bedroom?" she asked.

"No," Li told her before he walked away.

They soon discovered which room Li felt to be the most precious and reclusive when the first child tried to enter on their own.

Rooms on the other floors located throughout the north and south wings resembled displays from natural history museums or art galleries, where visitors could view preserved extinct species and artwork preserved from different eras of time. Li filled cases with rare tablets covered with forgotten runes, golden goblets, crowns befitting a king or queen, rare paintings, pottery, glassware, a variety of clothing, armaments, and other remnants of ancient cultures in perfect condition as if skilled hands created them minutes ago, along with dozens of preserved biological specimens.

Nevertheless, Master Li saved the rarest most precious specimens for the library.

CHAPTER TWENTY-THREE

MASTER LI'S SANCTUARY
– THE LIBRARY

THE WPO HEADQUARTERS HAD MANY parts to it: the expansive well-equipped kitchen made specifically for Running Elk, the ornately decorated dining room, the sunroom on the main floor with its beautiful mosaic tile floor and towering ceiling. On the far eastern side, north and south greenhouses filled with exotic flowers, a variety of plants, and even some rare forms of wildlife. Some of the different floor museums contain priceless objects and preserved rare biological specimens. Zinian designed every room with great care to bring out attractive features in their exquisite detail. However, one room in the mansion stood above all the rest, known more for its character than intrinsic beauty.

In addition to the collection of rare books, the library is perhaps the most magnificent room in the mansion by virtue of the rather valuable, interesting, and extremely rare artifacts held within. It was an integral part of this grand and complex structure. Master Li took particular pride in designing the room and filled it with as many remarkable items he could locate throughout the history of the planet. Anyone who sought to find Master Li could usually locate him here.

Large towering stacks of extremely rare books covered the entire eastern wall on two levels that extend upward to the ceiling of this huge open space. Li's design placed the ornately decorative ceiling some seventeen meters (55 feet) above the floor. A very thick, faux-virgin-wool, woven, Persian carpet covers most of the floor. The Chou-created rug stretches out some twenty-five meters wide by eighty meters long and leaves two meters of floor space around the periphery of the room bare to reveal polished wooden planks, except in front of the fireplace where tile replaces the wood.

Li rescued two original antique Tiffany lamps from bombardment during World War II. One lamp adorns a large flat rectangular mahogany table near the center of the room, where Li often performs experiments much to Han's dismay. Across from the table near the front windows, Star Wind arranged a seating area that consisted of a sofa, six large over-stuffed chairs with ottomans and a coffee table with floor lamps next to each chair, an inviting enclave for readers.

The second Tiffany lamp sits atop a large roll-top desk in the far northwest corner between the fireplace and western wall of windows. This desk is usually cluttered with ancient books, charts, maps, diagrams, and other important works Master Li leaves out for reference. A very large dictionary rests on a wooden stand nearby, while stacks of books with markers sticking out of them, sit on a table next to the desk. Small drawers contain items like Brutus' knife that stabbed Julius Caesar, or the telegraphed message received by Hitler that the allies landed at Normandy, or the set of laurel leaves Napoleon wore for his portrait, along with many other tidbits of a similar historical value.

Li kept the member chair arrangement the same as he did in his first house: nine, large, high-backed, dark-green leather chairs with ottomans, set in a semi-circle face the room's enormous open fireplace, whose inner hearth measured some six meters wide and nearly three meters high. The fireplace was framed in rose-colored carved marble with a large mahogany mantle that extended beyond either end of the fireplace. Small marble-topped tables separated the chairs. Whenever Master Li or Michael Tyler called a meeting to order, the original nine members sat in these chairs to discuss matters. Now they stood for the WPO's governing board.

Nine tall windows rose in parallel along the western wall that faced out the front of the great house on its northern wing. At the top of each window is a Greek letter formed in green stained-glass outlined with solid gold. These letters symbolize one of the original nine members, Li, Michael, Cecilia, Zhiwei, Zinian, Chou, Su Lin, Villi, and Han. Heavy dark green velvet drapes with gold gilded ties and gold-tasseled valances top and frame each window. Master Li generally kept the drapes closed during the day to protect the books on the opposite wall from exposure to afternoon sunlight. The curtains were sometimes pulled back for evening meetings.

In the southwest corner of the room, a large realistic globe of Earth slowly turned to represent the position of the actual planet. Tiny lights on its surface indicate the supposed location and the level of psychics around the planet. White lights represent psychics at levels one through four. A single yellow light represents the only Master Level psychic (Master Li). Currently, five continents have blinking lights with Australia recently added. Only Antarctica and South America remain dark. Thanks to Chou's marvelous flat communication cards, Zhiwei can track the location of each WPO member and place their locations on this globe.

Before Zinian's crew completed their work on the rest of the headquarters, Master Li brought back books he obtained via his time travels. Han assigned each book a place on the shelves – although he did not put a mark on any book – and placed them in order whenever they arrived. Master Li constantly contributed additional books. Han was never surprised to find new books resting next to his chair with a note: *"Please add these to our collection, Han. Thank you, Master Li."*

Although every edition appeared new, publishing dates or types of book gave away their origin. Some books were hand-written, made centuries before the printing press, created from cultures that obtained the knowledge of paper making, yet their civilization or language may have long since vanished Master Li pulled all dust, mildew, bacteria and mold from the room daily to prevent any deterioration of the paper.

"Generations from now," Li told Han. "Our great-grand children will enter this room as adults and thank us."

Michael walked in one day to inspect the completed room prior to the grand opening. He had little time to inspect every room in the vast expansive headquarters building, however this room fascinated him the most. He often perused the overwhelming variety of first editions. No one in their organization could top his ability to speedily read through an entire book in minutes and retain its imparted information the way Michael could.

Upon entering the library on this occasion, he noted a new area, a large cubical built into a section along the wall about waist high, subdivided into smaller cubicles; each contained a few scrolls of rolled thick paper. He wondered how Zinian changed the wall made of a substance that wasn't supposed be vulnerable to any saw. Chou must have developed a tool to cut through the substance, he surmised. He made a comment to Master Li...

"This wasn't in the original design," Michael observed.

"That is correct. Zinian altered the wall for me a week ago," Master Li answered, "I admire that man's flexibility... and yes, Chou developed a new cutting tool."

Li stood at the center table in the middle of the room, examining an ancient specimen of insect via a stereoscopic dissecting microscope. As he examined the dead specimen, he drew an amazing likeness on a sketch pad next to him with incredible subtlety and detail.

"What are these scrolls?" Michael asked Li as he poked at one.

The preoccupied elderly gentle man did not reply. Li was too busy drawing while he used a delicate probe to move the creature's appendages.

Michael picked one scroll up to examine it more closely. The sturdy yet primitive rolled paper had the appearance of being quite old by its design, its edges rough-hewn. He noticed a hand written note in black ink made with a quill on the exterior of the thick papyrus. He could not make out the language of the writing. He untied the twine wrapped around the two ends and opened the scroll. Hieroglyphics covered the paper in neat columns. However, next to the hieroglyphics, someone scribbled a series of Greek letters, as if it were a translation.

Michael studied the letters and symbols for a few seconds before he gave up.

"My Ancient Greek is a little rusty," he confessed, "but I believe this scroll tells a story," Michael observed as he linked to Li. He glanced across the room at Master Li and wondered why Li did not respond.

Again, Li linked nothing directly back to Michael, but mumbled something about his specimen, "…this is a strange way for nature to attach an appendage… no wonder they're extinct…"

Michael returned his attention to the scroll. He marveled at its newness. He ran the tip of his finger over the dried ink. It had a thick raised quality.

"Master Li," Michael asked as he admired the craftsmanship, "where did you find such excellent reproductions? The papyrus is so perfect, as if someone had the formula for making paper from the Egyptians." He held up the open page in his hands closer to his face. "They seem almost genuine."

"They are genuine, Michael," Li finally linked to Michael, as he probed the recently expired giant beetle.

"What do you mean by genuine? Where did you find these scrolls?" Michael asked.

"A recent acquisition from the Library in Alexandria," Li continued, not looking up.

"But, Master Li," Michael protested, "the Romans burned the library to the ground nearly two thousand years ago. It no longer exists. The parts that remain are under water."

Li finally stole Michael a glance, and shrugged, "Nevertheless, that's where I obtained some of them. That one did not come from the library. Imhotep originally wrote the one in your hand. He had an idea for a story and scribbled something down in my presence. I passed the scroll on to Aristophanes who later, with the help of some Egyptian librarian, performed the translation to Greek."

Michael looked at the scroll and chuckled, "Imhotep died in the first dynasty, long before the existence of the golden age Greeks. How could Aristophanes obtain an Egyptian document that old?"

"As I said… Imhotep gave it to me as a gift. I showed it to Aristophanes," Li met Michael's eyes. Li tried to explain. "He and another Egyptian scholar labored over the text for several days before they finally agreed on a translation to Greek, which they wrote in the right margin." He glanced back down at the beetle. "I know I cannot alter history but it closely resembles 'Lysistrata' although I could be mistaken. Imhotep was quite the pacifist, you know."

"That's impossible, Master Li," Michael declared.

"Whatever you believe," Li muttered his attention refocused on the unusual creature.

"I mean, if Imhotep wrote this scroll, then that would make it nearly four thousand years old! In order for paper to survive that long, you would have to preserve it in something. Nothing stains this paper. It is as clean as if someone made it yesterday! Mold, fungus, humidity, dryness, all destroy paper," Michael lectured as his frustration grew. "It might last a few hundred years maybe, but unprotected paper, just lying out in the open for over four thousand years? I don't think so!"

"Who said they're four thousand years old?" Li went on examining his specimen. "I said I acquired them recently."

"Oh, come on, Master Li," Michael grinned. "If that were true, this would be the most valuable piece of paper on Earth," Michael mused. He waved the scroll over his head and tossed it into the air like a baton before he caught it. "This looks brand new!"

Master Li glanced over at Michael throwing the scroll up over his head and winced. He rose from his chair with a swiftness that belied his age. He hurried over to Michael, reached up, and gently took the scroll from Michael's hand.

"If you are correct about its value, I'd better be more careful with it, shouldn't you," Li said.

He gently placed the scroll into the rectangular opening in the wall with the other scrolls.

Michael glanced over at the wall. Nearly a hundred scrolls lay on their sides, many marked with a ceramic tag that hung by a piece of leather cord wrapped around a wooden dowel through the middle. He noticed the tags had either Greek letters or crude numbers carved into them.

Michael twisted his head toward Master Li and then returned to stare at the scrolls. He glanced back at Li again, and then examined the scrolls more closely, frowning the whole time. When Michael searched Li's mind for the truth, the master psychic revealed that he took this scroll and other samples from the library long before the Roman's accidentally burned it.

For a moment, Michael longed to question Li further.

"What was it like inside the library?" he thought to him. "Was it as beautiful as the historians say it was?"

However, Li seemed too preoccupied with the prehistoric specimen to answer. Michael decided he would ask him later. On a quiet evening a month later, Li favored Michael with several stories on his time travels over hot tea and cakes provided by Running Elk, the head of the household staff and their principle chef.

That experience in the library left a profound impression on Michael. As he walked from the manor house that day, he sent the story mentally to Cecilia. She passed it along to Su Lin. She linked it to Villi, who told Chou, and so on.

After that, the community buzzed with curiosity about the other items lying about the library. Master Li, however, made it clear he meant his collection of ancient artifacts for every member of the Rollo Community to use and enjoy whenever they pleased.

Passing through the large double doors at the south end of the library, the fireplace lies opposite the entrance, the focal point of the room. A thick, wide, polished, mantle-piece crowns the front of the open hearth and awaits Master Li's magic to create a realistic fire that burns day and night without a log ever being consumed or giving off heat. Pictures of community members sit on the mantle.

Master Li placed rare artifacts from his travels around the world upon the fireplace mantle, too. Eventually, some of these extremely rare items included a jewel-encrusted solid gold statue from the Aztec civilization, a fur-line solid silver crown that holds a large ruby in its center, and a large golden ring with an enormous green emerald in the middle of it along with strange runes on the band. Li's piece de resistance rests near the mantel's far right corner, its sparkling brilliance is clearly noticeable from any part of the library.

A very large diamond, an oval as big as dinosaur's egg with hundreds of facets, sits on this corner in a special holder. Tipping the scale at over 3000 carats in weight, the natural rock, taken in raw form during the early stages of the planet, is worth untold wealth. Li informed the group during one meeting that a grateful jeweler in Amsterdam cut the diamond in 1847, when Li provided the man with another diamond large enough to make the cut. The giant diamond caught any light in the room and sparkled with amazing brilliance.

Those entering the library – friends and guests alike – enjoyed the priceless objects that Master Li scattered about the treasured space.

CHAPTER TWENTY-FOUR

RUNNING ELK PREPARES

"I LOVE THE IDEA THAT this house is filled with so many wonderful things," John commented as he moved about the dining room. "Chou created a beautifully carved table, didn't he?" he said to his mother, Running Elk, while he continued to help lay out the place settings for this evening's activities.

Running Elk dismissed her kitchen staff and gave them the day off. Rollo's Native American crew planned a big party that evening at the town's civic center, where she spent the first part of her day preparing their feast. When she returned to the mansion, she called upon her son for help in serving the membership.

"I'm sorry you'll miss the tribe party," she said as she practically twisted the tribal leader's arm to stay.

"I don't mind, mother," John replied. "We both owe him a great debt," he added in reference to Master Li.

Tonight, the headquarters would come alive when WPO members from around the globe would meet in a one of these rare gatherings at the bequest of Master Li. He and Han held an informal affair last night for the Liong's, Kiran Meshwari, and Leni Velitnik. While she provided a wonderful meal, Running Elk promised a formal banquet in the dining room this evening.

"Chou can definitely work miracles with his machine," the ex-tribal matriarch spoke when she regarded the table. "The furniture, place settings, even the candelabra are magnificent," she commented. She placed the last of the cut crystal goblets on the table. "In Europe I saw many fine castles and great estates, the Palace at Versailles being one. For all of their gold gilding and cherubs, they pale in comparison to the quality of this great house. Michael Tyler designed it. Chou provided the materials. Zinian and your crew built it. Master Li filled it with exceptional treasures; extraordinary things I never saw in Europe or anywhere else. Who could top that?"

"The collections on the upper floors are unlike anything I ever saw in Wichita or Kansas City," John commented.

"I have news for you, Li brought in museum pieces unlike anything in New York, Paris, or London," his mother echoed. "Take the library," she pointed out. "Did you ever see a library with artifacts or books like those? I picked up one book and noticed that the author signed it personally, "To Li, the wisest man I'll ever know," she stated. "Now why would a man like Sigmund Freud write a thing like that inside the cover of his book?"

John silently shrugged his reply as he opened the buffet drawer to set out the dinnerware. He held up one patterned spoon to his mother, the polished, yellow, metallic surface puzzled him.

"Brass-ware?" John asked.

"Brass?" Running Elk laughed. "Those forks, knives, and spoons are 24 karat solid gold! Chou put a thin, clear, hard coating on the outside to prevent nicks or bending."

"Gold!" John exclaimed as he held the weighty spoon closer to his face. "Did you say solid gold?"

"Yes, Master Li requested Chou make them from solid gold. He told me that way they would never need to be polished," she said as she took the glistening object from his hand and placed it on the table. "He's right, of course. Pure gold never tarnishes… only other metals mixed with it do." She moved the spoon into its proper position. "Pretty!" she declared, which caused John to scoff at her over simplified assessment.

"What else besides cooking did you learn in Europe?" he asked.

"Oh, je parle un petit Francais," she rattled off.

"Anyone can say they speak a little French," John shot back. "Is that all you learned in the twenty-four months you spent at Le Cordon Bleu?"

"I know what mirepoix is," she told him, "and how to make a roux," she added. "I can create a soufflé as light as air," she continued. "I placed a first in pastry. They awarded me the Grand Master Chef's Award. They've only honored three people with such awards over the past fifty years," she spoke with pride as she rubbed a smudge from a glass. "I took a first in sauces, entrees, and soups," she smiled as she gazed at her reflection in the glass. "I took seven second place awards in creatively serving meat, fish, vegetables, poultry, eggs, fungi, and another first in desserts," she added when she turned to John.

"Who took the first in those catagories?" he asked.

"Oh, I did not mind losing to Henri Rothschild," she mused. "He is probably the greatest chef in Europe, or the world for that matter… and one that few will ever taste his cuisine. He goes to the Cordon Bleu to find new chefs for his restaurants around the world. After the first year, we became great friends. He invited me to dine at his estate on several occasions, especially when Camille was out of town. He taught me a great deal about wine, cheeses… and many other things," she added with a wistful tone. "He was a tremendous flirt for being 62. Those potent Frenchmen… ils peuvent certainement balayer vous désactiver vos pieds dans la chambre (they can certainly sweep you off your feet into the bedroom)," she sighed as she leaned against the table, lost in some reverie.

"That time you lost me," John commented.

Running Elk cleared her throat and straightened her posture. She changed her focus to finish the table settings.

"I thought Li would be jealous…" she muttered. "I should have known better. He's not the jealous type – far too understanding."

John shook his head as he watched his transformed mother move with such grace and balance. He never pictured his mother as an international celebrity, let alone someone so cosmopolitan. She returned from France completely transformed from the woman he knew in that small house where he grew up. She lost the jeans, doughy figure, and frayed graying hair which she had always kept in a ponytail. She showed up with perfectly coiffed brown hair, rejuvenated skin, and wearing fashionable clothes. She even wore make-up, something she never did. John marveled over her metamorphosis.

"Magnifique!" she declared as she looked down the table. "A setting fit for the likes of Master Li and his honorable guests," she proudly declared, "a group whom I consider more worthy than presidents, prime ministers, or royalty."

"You certainly set a fine table…" John pointed out.

"Apercu!" she declared as she interrupted his thought. She ran into the kitchen. "I must check my roast!"

"Why?" John called after her as she ran through the kitchen's swinging doors, "What's for dinner?"

"Meatloaf!" she called back.

"What?" he replied, aghast.

Running Elk, not wishing to stain the fresh apron she just put on, grabbed two mittens and opened the oven door. She lightly touched the rotisserie of turning meat before she closed the oven and shut off the heat. She smiled when she came back through the double doors and saw the disappointment on her son's face.

"It's an old joke," she told him. "When I first started to cook for Li and Han, I only knew very simple dishes like meatloaf." John looked surprised. "Have you forgotten? Darling, I raised you on dishes like macaroni and cheese.

That type of simple cooking was all I knew. I burned my meatloaf five times in Li's fancy oven. I threw out seven undercooked versions, and only served it once before I realized the men would not eat one bite. Li convinced me to visit Camille in Paris. If I hadn't made bad meatloaf, New York City might be in shambles," she told John. "It was on the flight to Paris that Master Li and the others noticed the 2016 hurricane headed toward New York City."

"What are you saying? They were responsible for the sudden dispersion of that Category Five hurricane?" John asked. "I thought the scientists said a sudden rush of cold ocean water was the reason."

"How do think the cold water suddenly showed up? Chou invented some sort of device that churned up the Atlantic. It was the only way they could shut down the storm," she explained. "If they hadn't decided to accompany me to France, the psychics would not have noticed the hurricane. As it was, Li and the others stood on the seashore and fought the storm at its height with only the power of their minds. He said a huge wave nearly washed the whole group out to sea!" she told her son with admiration in her voice. "How brave they were that fateful day when they stood side by side on that rocky shore and faced nature in all its fury…"

John stood before his mother with his mouth open as he listened to her.

"Why didn't you ever tell me what really happened?" he asked her.

"Sorry," she said as she pulled him toward the kitchen. "It never came up."

"Never came…" he started. "Mother, that storm is one of the greatest events of the century!"

"Listen," she said to him. "We must be ready to serve in about twenty minutes, as soon as the last guest is seated," she pointed to her diamond studded wrist watch. He had not noticed the jeweled masterpiece. "That means you must quickly escort and seat our guests the moment they arrive," she told him and waved her arms toward the dining room entrance. "Oh, and John…"

"Yes?" he said as he paused.

"Thank you for helping me tonight," she said and kissed his cheek.

John smiled as he turned and sprinted to the room's entrance. The tuxedo that Running Elk brought back from Paris fit him perfectly. He tugged at its bottom as the first guests approached.

CHAPTER TWENTY-FIVE

DINNER OF IDEAS

TWENTY MINUTES BEFORE EIGHT O'CLOCK, Master Li and Han descended the grand staircase to greet their guests as they arrived from the community and the rooms above them. The two men wore traditional clothes that Li had hand-tailored from silk merchants in Eleventh Century China.

Master Li wore a finely-woven silk, pale yellow tunic underneath an open black silk ceremonial robe trimmed in green that also had a matching green Chinese dragon hand-sewn onto the back. Han wore a red full-length silk tunic trimmed in black. His black robe trimmed in red had a red Chinese mythical figure that cast lightning bolts from his hands. Both men wore small tasseled caps of golden silk.

When the two men met at the first landing, they had the same first reaction. An incredible odor wafted up the staircase from the direction of the dining room. They swiftly descended together and cautiously approached the large archway of the dining room. Once they beheld the magnificently displayed dining room table, they knew this evening's meal would be special.

"The place setting is… quite beautiful," Han observed.

The white orchid centerpieces, polished candelabra, sparkling crystal glassware, exquisite plates, and the gold-ware dazzled the eye in the candlelight. Han glanced over and noticed Master Li allowed the smallest smile of satisfaction before he turned around.

"Sir Charles!" Li exclaimed, "You look handsome this evening," he complimented and shook his hand. "William… so glad you could come, please," he added as he motioned them toward the table while more guests advanced on the center of the house.

William Bickford, Sir Charles' son, converted last fall when Master Li returned to England and performed the ceremony. William graduated from Oxford earlier in the year and had started his law practice in London.

"Camille!" Li sighed, as the tall French woman wearing a long glittering gown of woven pearls glided toward them. "Beautiful as always… please… Maria… Jonathan… glad to have you," Li nodded his head to the recently converted couple from Germany. Li warmly greeted the next couple, his favorite "homeless" pair from New York City. "Catherine Olsen!" Li said as he smiled. "The cheapest lobbyist in Washington who fights for the foundation. You've been very busy this year. Thank you for taking the time to come," he said to her.

"I wouldn't be here if it wasn't for you," she said. "You know my date, of course."

"Steven Harper," Li said, shaking his hand, "The CEO of the Tyler Foundation, formerly known as Michael's trust. How are the markets these days?" Li asked yet knew the answer.

"Master Li," Steven bowed out of respect. "I wish to open…"

"Not tonight, Steven," Li stopped him. "Everything is informal tonight. All minds are open. You know Camille, Sir Charles, Maria Mueller, and Jonathan Showalter…" he said as he made introductions. Steven and Catherine joined the rest of the diners, escorted to their seats by John.

"Are they a couple?" Han privately linked.

"Romantically?" Li finished the thought. "I never pry in such matters."

Han wanted to cry foul and instead kept up his warm exterior welcome smile.

More guests of the WPO came down the grand staircase: General and Madam Liong from China, Milo Tabor Drasmus from Greece, Sarah Reitmann from Israel, Tahir Wadi al-Jamil from Egypt along with his wife Seel, Kiran Meshwari from India, and Leni Velitnik from Russia. Salla and Filla Motambou from Mali filled out the last of the international contingent. The room positively buzzed with psychic energy as open-minded members freely linked. John escorted each person to his or her place at the long table and took drink orders at the same time.

Everything and everyone in the dining room came alive with the free and open flow of psychic energy. Whether it was the soft light from the old-fashioned incandescent light of the chandeliers overhead, the candle-lit tapers that burned on the table, or the gush of emotional sharing that easily passed back and forth across the table, no one could honestly say. Earlier, Running Elk placed a gold placard with each member's name engraved on the front in the person's native language as well as English. She kept the permanent place markers, one for every member of the WPO, in a nearby drawer.

John stood near the table wearing his tuxedo uniform and white gloves.

"Everything is splendid," Han linked to Li in the reception line. "I sense a general feeling of satisfaction and optimism in the room. Running Elk went over the top," he privately commented.

"Oh, yes, Running Elk," Li said as he watched his guests enjoy the splendor of the setting. "It's so good to have her back in Rollo. She was away far too long," he added.

"Speaking of guests," Han linked as he nodded toward the front door.

From the local group, Villi and Su Lin arrived first, the young couple handsome in their formal tuxedo and dress. Li could not recall Villi ever wearing a tux except at his wedding.

"You look very nice this evening," Li commented as the big man approached.

"I like the dragon," Villi mentally commented. "I won't ask which dynasty you robbed," he added.

"I had them made," Li quipped back.

"Oh, my," Su Lin reacted as she craned her neck toward the distant dining room. "How sumptuous," she linked to Li, "... and how fortunate you are to be in residence here," she told Han.

Master Li smiled and embraced her. He blocked out Han and anyone else within sensing distance when he leaned over and whispered in her ear.

"I did not wish to come off too ostentatious. Personally, I'm pleased you like it. We did overindulge a bit here and there," Li confessed.

"Any time you wish to trade residences..." Villi hinted to Han.

"Be my guest," Han gestured. "It took me ten minutes yesterday just to find the room where we have breakfast," he jokingly complained.

"I thought you were psychic?" Villi kidded back.

"Not *before* breakfast," Han shot back.

Villi and Su Lin slid past the short reception line, eager to mingle with the rare visitors from around the globe. They proceeded to their seats in the dining room.

"Look," Villi commented, "the French Stateswoman, Camille Ossures... isn't she..." he hesitated, "the second prettiest woman in the room."

"Good observation," Su Lin said as she took his arm. "William Bickford is quite dashing. I hear he's single!"

"Drinks?" John requested as he moved up on the opposite side of Su Lin.

"Sparkling white grape juice," Su Lin requested. "I believe I'll go vegetarian tonight."

"Green tea," Villi stated, "hot, lemon, honey, Master Li style."

"Very good," John noted verbally as he had no discernable psychic ability.

The psychics did not drink alcohol, which included wine, although the WPO only loosely enforced this rule. Camille insisted on being able to at least sip French wine occasionally. Sir Charles usually took a nightcap of cognac. Maria and Jonathan enjoyed an occasional beer or wine as did others. Most of the psychics agreed that inebriation was out of the question.

Zinian and Zhiwei arrived without their Native American escorts. Their girlfriends wanted to attend the party at the Civic Center and excused their husbands for the evening. Zhiwei suspected Li privately arranged their eagerness to join the other party. Chou and Star Wind followed the two young men. Finally, Michael and Cecilia arrived at the door. Michael wore a new tux and Cecilia had on a Parisian evening gown. She asked Camille to bring them from Europe.

"You look lovely," Han commented to Rollo's physician.

"Why thank you, Han," Cecilia smiled and turned around. "I like the robes... Master Li brought them through time?"

Han nodded as Michael spoke up.

"What's that delicious aroma?" he asked as he looked over Master Li's shoulder. "Running Elk create another masterpiece?"

"I'd say you smell about three million Tyler Foundation dollars and the knowledge of the Cordon Bleu," Master Li quipped, which brought a smile to Michael's lips.

Cecilia took Michael's arm as he led her toward the dining room. At the entrance she stopped once more. She took note of the ivory tapers lit in front of each table setting with dozens of white orchids.

"Michael," she linked, "this is so lovely!"

"Not bad," Michael noted. "Do you feel the energy in this room?"

"Everyone is here. The entire rooster of the WPO is under one roof," she commented. "Do you realize that because of our ability, people from many nations with different cultures, different religions, different races, ages, sexes... interact, socialize with perfect communication and no misunderstanding!" she finished.

Michael smiled at her lengthy observation and steered Cecilia to the last two seats. Han and Master Li sat at opposite ends. The couple sat with Camille Ossures on one side and Sir Charles on the other. Stephen Harper and Katherine Olsen sat across from them.

"White..." Cecilia started, when Michael made a hand signal.

"Two red grape juice," he requested because he knew Running Elk had prepared beef tenderloins and they were not going to eat vegetarian. Cecilia patted his hand before she turned to Camille, the two women quickly engaged in repartee.

"More drink orders," John called out as he ran into the kitchen. Running

Elk was busy preparing the first course on trays. Her son John was the only local besides Running Elk allowed to use the fusor, although John could only use the one in the kitchen. He quickly exited with the last drink orders.

Li held few organizational dinners as grand or as elaborate as this one. Chou recreated the elaborately furnishings that topped the table: table cloth made from the finest Irish linen, Chinese Imperial porcelain (Yuan Guan Yao), Waterford crystal (Colleen Encore stemware line), along with Clifden cashmere napkins, even sterling silver toothpicks according to Running Elk's specifications. Lying on the charger plate, each person had a hand written menu on parchment paper. Not only had Running Elk learned French during her stay; her English improved a great deal, too.

This was Running Elk's hand-written dinner menu:

Appetizers: Potato Pancakes Vonnas with fusor Pacific smoked salmon, topped with crème fraîche, and/or fusor Beluga caviar; fresh dill garnish w/side sauces; or grilled tropical fruit w/fresh mint & bourbon glaze for vegetarian guests

Soup choices: Bouillabaisse, or Chicken (w/chicken stock), or Spinach Velouté (w/ vegetable stock), or Vichyssoise

Fruit ice (raspberry) to clear palate

Opening main entrée: Beef Bourguignonné or Pit Roast Filet with herbs w/ side dishes – grilled asparagus, fresh buttered pasta, stuffed mushrooms, onion butter on flat bread

Opening main entrée vegetarian: Ratatouille or Baked Pissaladière w/ side dishes – grilled eggplant brushed with roasted herbs, seven bean & mushroom cassoulet

Fruit ice (lemon) to clear palate

Closing course: Special chef's salad (made to order from fresh greens and herbs)

Dessert: Apricot Soufflés (a la flambé and/or a la mode optional)

The fusor made such rarities as salmon or caviar a treat, especially when no animal was harmed in the process. Running Elk made certain Chou duplicated every subtle nuance to their delicate flavors.

After John filled the drink orders and took the guest's order preference, he and Running Elk burst from the kitchen with large serving trays of appetizers.

"I will serve," Li announced.

As the chef and her son passed each guest, that member's particular dish floated down in front of them and landed with perfect precision. When the expeditious couple had served every guest's appetizer, the assembly turned to

Master Li. He stood up and the group followed suit while they eagerly awaited the words from a master poet.

"No man or woman is better understood than at this table," he eloquently spoke, "for we who set out to improve our lives, will someday affect the course of humanity with the same measure. Let it be said, from this moment onward, that this natural change by means of subtly, will help guide those who are lost and search for answers, that we may provide some ray of hope in an hour of darkness," he said as he raised his glass. "I give you, 'Ad Astra per Aspera,' which roughly translates as 'may we reach the stars, though life may be difficult.' By the way, it is the state motto of Kansas!" he smiled as he took a sip.

The others followed suit, and returned to their seats. Li picked up his outside fork and took the first bite. The restrained gathering burst into conversation as people began to mentally converse while they ate.

"C'est magnifique," Camille declared upon tasting the first morsel. "I would say Running Elk is the pupil extraordinaire, come home to boast, no?"

Sir Charles, who appreciated the pun, privately linked to Camille.

"She has yet to outbake herself," he added to the humor.

The other guests did not argue the point. Most added their affirmation that Running Elk served fine cuisine.

"This is outstanding Running Elk," Villi openly linked after his first taste. He craned his neck to catch a glimpse of the cook and pay her a compliment.

However, no one saw Running Elk. After she and John first served the appetizers, she returned to the kitchen and would not show her face. She meticulously examined each serving tray before John took away the next course and made certain each plate's presentation was identical. An hour and ten minutes later, when the guests had devoured every last crumb of dessert, the satiated diners called for the chef but she did not or would not appear.

Master Li rose, which caused all the heads to turn in his direction. The great arched wooden doors to the dining room swung shut and sealed off the room. He tapped the side of his glass to quiet the guests before he resumed his seat. Every member kept an open mind while they centered their attention on Master Li.

"I'd like to address some private concerns," he started. "As you know, we try to convert new psychics when they appear ready. To that end, we add their wisdom and difference into our inclusive organization," Li began.

"Since our inception, we have expanded into a global network," he continued. "Psychic intelligence reaches into every government. We are privy to that nation's most guarded secrets while we quietly keep humanity on a course that will avoid mass extinction," he told them. "For two and a half years, we have heard no stirrings from Australia, although agents from India and China recently traveled to Sydney and Perth. In their reports, they detected no psychic activity, nor did I… until last week," Li informed them.

This news brought a stir among them as Li had not shared his recent findings with the other members.

"Tonight, I can announce the inclusion of our twenty-fifth member, Major General James Montgomery Pollack of the Australian Army," Li informed them.

"Did you say James Pollack?" Sir Charles Bickford spoke up.

"Do you know him?" Han asked as he glanced over at Zhiwei.

"I knew his father-in-law, Fitzhugh Hawkins. He passed away a number of years back. He was a good man and one hell of a commander in the British Army," Charles muttered. "He was also a member of my club," he continued. "I believe his daughter, Penelope, married William Pollack's son, if memory serves. That must be James."

"Your memory serves you well, Sir Charles," Zhiwei linked in. "After they married, the Pollack's moved to Australia, where James rose through the ranks to major general," Zhiwei informed him.

"I see," Sir Charles noted and mentally added that information to what he remembered of the family. "I also recall the Pollack family involved in shipping… there was a Lord Pollack who ran an import/export business… automobiles, parts, and other goods," he said as he searched his mind. "That was his grandfather. I recall that when Lord Pollack died, James and his brother eventually sold off the business and spread the holdings through the family. He must have gained considerable capital from that transaction. I wonder why he stayed with the military. I understand Stephan Pollack has extensive business holdings and is quite wealthy."

"Perhaps for the same reason you remain in service to your crown," Camille spoke up, "he had loyalty to his country and his troops." She turned her attention to Master Li. "I sense that you hold back additional information which you are reluctant to share with us. Please continue your report, Master Li."

"As usual, Camille, you are very perceptive," Li nodded in her direction. "She is right, of course. In my ignorance, and perhaps complacency, I believed that my power circumnavigated the globe. I ignored Australia because I thought that I would sense the rise of any new psychic. I did not know that another psychic emerged over the past few years and that he had the capacity to remain hidden," Li said.

"I detect more to it than that," William Bickford linked.

163

"What is it?" Maria Showalter spoke up. "I sense something terrible happened," she added as the shared feeling passed around the room.

Master Li shifted in his chair, took a sip of tea, and looked from face to face.

"Something terrible did happen," Master Li informed them. "We received a report recently that has bearing on this development. Before I proceed any further, I want Han to explain what we uncovered. Han?"

Unlike Master Li, who could easily block out a room of such strong psychics, Han could not. It was all he could do to calmly link while a room full of inquisitive psychics bore down on his mind.

"Please allow me to explain," he requested and held up his hands. The other psychics backed off and listened. "Just over two weeks ago," he began, "Zhiwei showed us a report that someone in Adelaide Australia sexually assaulted an American young woman. The assailant crushed the woman's trachea, yet left no outward sign, such as a bruise, which perplexed authorities. After they performed an extensive autopsy, they called for an FBI forensics expert to investigate."

A murmur spread through the room as several quickly concluded, just as Han did, that the perpetrator must be psychic. This realization brought a general expression of disgust. Before anyone could comment, Han continued his report.

"In analyzing the autopsy results," he linked, "Zhiwei, Master Li, and I came to the same conclusion… that only a psychic could have performed this maneuver on his victim during rape. The pathologist gave no explanation, other than injury by 'unknown external source.' They labeled it, 'collapsed trachea.' Concerned for the populace, Master Li scanned Australia and searched for a psychic signature. At first, he only found James Pollack…"

"I don't believe it!" Sir Charles quickly objected, "not for a second…"

"Easy, Charles," Han cautioned, "Please allow me to continue."

Sir Charles calmed his emotions. Camille put her hand on the top of his.

"When we researched the general's life, we could not find any instance when he ever used psychic power prior to this incident," Han explained. "On the surface, James Pollack should be our prime suspect. However, during his communication with the general, Master Li did not detect the act anywhere in his mind, which the general readily held open after Galactic Central finally broke through. This contact confirmed our hypothesis that we had another psychic in Australia, a rogue psychic, one who used his power to commit heinous acts," Han related to the group and glanced over at Sarah Reitmann, who started to interrupt with a question. "We know the person is male," Han explained, "because *he* was not afraid to leave traces of semen behind."

Silence filled the room, as every member contemplated the evidence that Han laid before them, although Sir Charles breathed a sigh of relief. Han had finished the presentation of his evidence and returned the focus to Master Li.

"Han and I have concluded that we may never know when someone evolves if they keep that aspect bottled up and guarded inside their mind," Master Li stated. "I have tried to monitor for this kind of activity. However, his distance from me prevents continual observation, and I cannot be everywhere around our planet to watch for others who might emerge at the same time. It seems our numbers grow with each passing year. As the organization expands, we must expand our awareness of emerging psychics. Every psychic in this room must therefore be vigilant. One rogue can expose our existence and spell the end our organization."

"What is *his* goal?" Tahir asked.

"He wants to rule the planet," Li stated, which brought a few chuckles

"He wants to rule the planet?" Jonathan spoke up, sensitive to such a ridiculous goal. "Are you certain he isn't German?" he quipped which brought chuckles from Camille and the Bickford's. Maria shot him a frown.

"Is the man mad? That kind of logic is absurd!" Maria chimed in.

"He actually believes he can succeed," Li told them. "He has an ambitious agenda mapped out," he added.

"How could he possibly attain such a goal from Australia?" General Liong questioned.

"He plans to crash an asteroid into the China Sea," Han linked in. "If allowed to carry out his initial action in space, he might be able to accomplish this goal. Such an act could disrupt the entire region…"

"…destroy many cities, kill many people," Madam Liong added.

"Disruptive would be an understatement," Tabor put in. "He could wipe out the entire country of Japan. Think of the loss…"

The members stirred over this horrific news.

"I don't understand. You are the most powerful psychic in the universe," Camille interrupted. "I've never heard you describe such power to us. How can he do this?"

"I'm not certain of his plan's exact details," Li explained. "I tried to discern those details on three different links that I managed to make with him during sleep. Currently, I am too far away to affect much penetration. At this distance, he can easily block me out. I only saw the results of his plan in his mind, which he likes to play over and over in his head," Li stated.

"You must move closer to him," Karin suggested, "or send one of us to Australia," she added.

"I cannot risk your involvement," Li countered. "We do not know the extent of his power. Instead, I propose we send a task force to Australia and determine how far along he has progressed toward making his goal a reality. Most of you have been psychics for six months or less. If he takes advantage of your inexperience, he could cause havoc in our ranks. We need a team of experienced psychics capable of acting in crisis situations. Naturally, I speak of the Rollo psychics... however, this mission should be voluntary. To take on such a mission means assuming a great deal of risk. Since this part of the globe does not directly involve anyone's territory, I would not expect other agents to participate in this effort."

"Nonsense," Sir Charles said as he echoed the room's sentiment.

"If it's a global threat, Li, then it affects every member here... experienced or not!" Leni spoke up.

Others chimed in their agreement until Master Li held up his hand.

"I applaud that sentiment... and acknowledge you have one of the highest acuities in the martial arts of any member," Li proudly acknowledged. "Yet, I also know every psychic in this room and their agendas: the Motambou's are very busy starting a new hospital in Mali; Camille has decided to run for the French assembly; our European and Middle East agents actually broke off engagements with field operatives to attend this meeting; Charles is helping William in London; and finally, General Liong has begun to form a new network in China that will search for new psychics in the world's most populous nation. Leni actually ducked out of a crisis to be here. I knew all of your itineraries before you arrived," Li said as he looked about the room. "Everything you do is important for this organization. You form a vital link that makes this planet a virtual ring of psychic awareness. However, I also know that none of you can break away without grossly affecting your current projects," Li observed. "Except..."

He looked over at Michael, Cecilia, and the other local psychics.

"... except the psychics in Rollo, who have nothing on their agenda other than to build and maintain this psychic community. Part of our purpose was to establish a base of operations. When problems like this arise, we can fly a qualified team of specialists around the world on quick notice and intervene during times of crisis, without disrupting our integrated village."

As Master Li spoke, the other eight local members linked their approval.

"Can't you reveal anything else about this rogue?" Camille asked.

"I'm sorry, Camille, I wish I could. We know very little of this man," Li began. "He is very clever. He managed to erase much of his personal history. What I know I gleaned from our brief encounters. His name is Cyrus Keaty. Han figures he has been rogue for at least two, possibly three years or longer. During that time his power has grown strong. This independence warped his sense of morality. I suspect he has sadistic tendencies and is responsible for killing several innocent people, with women prominent among his victims. A large group of followers surrounds him. They keep his level of psychic energy fully charged. They've encamped in an isolated outback region of Western Australia, partly to avoid arousing suspicion. I suspect he is trying to form the basis of what will be his initial army."

"Master Li," Michael quietly broke in, "what about this Major General Pollack? Will he help us?"

"The answer to that question is... yes," Li began before he turned to Han.

"James Pollack is very receptive to Master Li," Han explained. "Li and I feel we can fly a strike team to Adelaide and use the general as a guide. We'll work our way inland and create psychic bubbles to shield our presence. This should catch Cyrus unaware. We can eliminate the threat before he can carry out his space project."

"Excuse me," Su Lin spoke up. "How is it possible to divert an asteroid without some kind of very expensive and elaborate space based operation?" she questioned. "This could simply be some fantasy in his mind. Don't you think so, Master Li?"

"Chou?" Li asked.

The young scientist had nearly fallen asleep. After working long hours in his lab and being satiated from the large meal, he started to drop off.

"Chou!" Star Wind whispered and nudged him awake.

"What?" he asked as he sat up and rubbed his eyes.

The psychics either smiled or chuckled at poor tired overworked Chou, whom every man and women in the room respected as their technical genius.

"The question on the table is this," Tahir offered. "How does one change the course of an asteroid?"

Chou glanced over at Han as if the young strategist could clarify Tahir's question.

"Is it possible to divert an asteroid millions of miles away from earth? Is it possible to accomplish with psychic energy?" Han asked him.

Chou cleared his throat. He and other scientists throughout the psychic collective have extensively studied the various applications of psychic energy. Chou even gave a lecture on Valos VII on this subject.

"One of the ideal qualities of space is that it offers no resistance to the transfer of energy. Unless you travel too near a black hole, a star or even some large planets the size of Jupiter, gravity wells could cause deviations. Otherwise, energy usually travels in a straight unimpeded line," he stated.

"What does he hope to gain by diverting an asteroid?" Zinian asked. "Why does he want to destroy the planet?"

"I'm not familiar with the asteroid," Chou replied. "Master Li?"

"The asteroid in question isn't powerful enough to destroy the planet or even most life on the planet," Li told them. "However, it is large enough to cause general damage should it strike the planet at a vulnerable location. Cyrus wants to disrupt the world in such a way as to take control of a government in chaos, such as China's government would be after the disaster," Li said. "I believe the asteroid is a diversion. Han thinks his real goal is to take over a military base. The Australian continent might provide some of the manpower and weapons he needs. However, the real power lies in a place where he can create havoc. With its security system in chaos, Cyrus reasons he can step into China and take over," Li explained.

"If that is his goal," General Liong spoke up, "he may be onto something. We will look into China's disaster response program when we return."

"We would appreciate input from any member," Han added.

Li glanced around the room at the drawn faces. The evening had taken a somber turn. The news of a rogue psychic, a man who might disrupt or even destroy the work they started, bothered everyone.

"We have much to consider over the next few days," Li told them. "First, I would like to thank you for taking the time to attend this meeting and thank Running Elk for all her hard work..." Li conveyed to the group before he folded back the great dining room doors and released the kitchen door.

"...and it's about time, too," Running Elk said as she uncharacteristically burst through the kitchen doors. "...all this talk about the end of the world, my goodness," she declared. "It's enough to give a person indigestion! No one will want to come back! Shame on you, Master Li!" she said as she wagged a finger in his direction.

Her comments broke up the room into smiles and laughter. Even Li laughed.

"You must forgive me, Running Elk," Li apologized.

"Yes, he is such ungrateful clod," Camille chimed in. "Well, I appreciate your handy work dear lady," Camille said as she rose and clapped her hands.

The others in the room joined Camille and applauded Running Elk. The middle-aged woman bowed to everyone before she made a hasty retreat. Camille let the smile fade from her face. She turned to Master Li as did the others. The members in the room understood the gravity of the situation. Each one, without speaking, bowed to Li and made their way out of the dining room.

The invited guests went through the house to the library. Sir Charles promised to group share amusing stories while Running Elk delivered hot tea. The original nine founding members of the WPO stayed in the dining room.

"What now?" Cecilia asked. "When do you suggest we should start to plan our trip…"

"We cannot waste a single hour," Li interrupted. "We must begin preparations at once. Every member of the team should contribute."

"Master Li," Michael interrupted, "I'll need time to organize…"

"Michael," Li addressed him and the entire group, "we have run out of time. We must leave as soon as possible, perhaps within the next two days. Start your preparations now. Our next stop is Australia!"

With that brief statement, Master Li headed off to mingle with his guests in the library. Han went to his bedroom on the second floor. The rest of the Rollo headed toward the front door and home. They knew they must begin to analyze what they needed for the journey ahead. However, despite the pressure to begin their mental lists, Villi and Su Lin along with Michael and Cecilia had odd sensations pass through them on the way to their homes that night… sensations they had not felt since they first declared their love for each other. Like teenagers in heat, the two couples snuck off to their bedrooms to enjoy what had become a rare interaction between the busy pairs lately. They did not understand the impetus behind this sudden impulse, but blindly followed its lead, as if compelled.

In the library, Master Li dropped a curtain of silence over the room, and shared with the group a vision of their future, one that he could not share with his Rollo friends.

"The time has come to reveal a secret… one you must swear to keep…"

CHAPTER TWENTY-SIX

PORTENTOUS VOICE

THE CLOCK NEAR THE BED said 2:17 am. Penelope watched James as he slept. About twenty minutes ago, he woke her up when he started to cry out words in his sleep. She tried to wake him, yet no matter how hard she poked him, he would not stir. He settled into an uneasy rest, his eyes stayed closed while he tossed and turned, as if under restraint. Propped up on one elbow, she gazed down upon her husband's face. She knew every line, every blemish, every facet of that face, both familiar and comfortable to her, like a pair of old slippers. It troubled her to see him stressed.

"What is happening to you, James… or should I say to us?" she wondered. "Are you on some other planet; or do you occupy the mind of some exotic being I will never know?"

As James began to sweat, she pulled back the blanket. She worried about his state of mind and felt helpless to do anything for him. She could not call the doctor on this one. She knew that James experienced some internal struggle. Yet, knowing the general as well as she did, he never gave up without a fight. She only feared his defeat, especially if he tried to match wits with this desert madman.

James Pollack walked in a dream world he had never seen. This was not the usual kind of dream, where the environment is vague and images of things come and go quickly, seldom with purpose. This world seemed all too real, yet this place had no defining borders. He gazed out on an endless landscape of thick swirling clouds. He heard voices speaking, distant voices, troubling voices, anxious voices. One voice in particular stood out. He seemed inexorably drawn to it, like a moth to a bright light. The surrounding air pressed in on him and squeezed him with a crushing atmosphere. He felt he could hardly breathe.

"What is this place?" he wondered.

"This is the landscape of a psychic's mind," a sinister voice uttered to him.

"Who are you?" James asked. "If this is my mind, how did you get in here?"

"I might ask the same question," the gravelly voice replied, "as you are in my mind as well."

James heard and felt a cold, indifferent, cruel voice; a voice that did not have the qualities of mercy or empathy in its tone that James sensed when Master Li occupied his thoughts. Nor did it have the analytical qualities of his Galactic Central connection. This psychic had vulgar repulsive thoughts. James felt as if he had somehow lassoed the devil and could not let go.

"Where did you come from?" this wicked voice asked him. "I thought I was unique and alone in this country... now I sense you... you must reveal your true nature to me... I must know if others like you and I exist in this place... if I can control you, I can control them... I can take them... use them..."

James realized in that moment that he had linked with the psychic from the desert and the man could hear his thoughts.

"I know you," James confessed. "You're that maniac fellow in the desert with his followers."

"How did you know that?" Cyrus challenged him. "Where did you get that information?" Cyrus wondered. "I sense familiarity around you. Who the hell are you?"

"That's classified stuff, old boy," James insisted. "Strange, I never realized we could pop into each other's mind like this."

James innocently wandered about this psychic landscape. Neither his voice nor Master Li had instructed James Pollack on blocking technique. Yet even Cyrus was not aware of advanced blocking technique, only rudimentary elements of it.

"I'm tired. I cannot do battle tonight. I'd prefer you did not disturb my sleep," Cyrus told him. "Go and leave me in peace."

"I think you have it the other way around," James told him. "You popped into my head."

"Wait a second," Cyrus hesitated. "You aren't the distant powerful one that's been bothering me..." He made a sudden revelation that the world had not just one other bothersome psychic, but more... how many, he did not know. He only knew that this bumbling fool was not the calculating psychic that carefully probed his thoughts.

171

James grew silent. He realized in that moment he tipped Li's hand. It was a strategical blunder and he regretted it.

"Then it is as I feared… I am not alone!" Cyrus realized.

"Since we are connected, I wonder what it is that makes you so cruel. Is it the power?" James cryptically put to him. "I suppose I should probe around while I'm here, find out what makes the enemy tick."

"I can do the same to your mind," Cyrus threatened, "I can use the information you know about the military to track your movements and crack computer codes. I can learn your name, where you live, your relatives, and friends, anything I want to know about you, and then use it against you."

"I can't let you do that, old boy," James said as he tried to resist the intrusion of the other psychic.

"Who is going to stop me… old boy? You?" Cyrus told him. "You are pathetically weak compared to me," the rogue said as he pushed away James' poor attempt at resistance. The general tried to fight back but could not stop the more powerful psychic from invading his memories. "… and you call yourself a soldier? You're pathetic! You know nothing about real power…" Cyrus said as he pushed deeper into James' mind.

Sweat broke out all over the general's body as he tossed and turned in his bed. He could not break free to wake up or open his eyes. Cyrus held him, a prisoner inside his mind, while the dastardly fiend probed his memories.

"Li…" James whispered. "Li… help me…"

Just when he feared the battle lost, a powerful presence entered the psychic landscape, his presence so strong, that Cyrus assault on James suddenly halted.

"That's enough, Cyrus," the calm voice said. "Leave him alone. Go back to your mind. If I find you trying to invade his mind again, you will not like what I can do in retaliation."

"You!" Cyrus angrily linked as his frustration mounted. "So there *are* more of us. Where are you…"

"Never mind, go away, and don't come back here or you will regret it," the quiet yet powerful voice pressed hard on Cyrus. The warped individual slipped away from James' mind and started to place a powerful block to keep Li from following.

All at once, James felt a great weight lift from his mind. He took in a deep breath, relieved of the pressure.

"Master Li?" he asked.

"Yes," Li replied with his kind voice.

"I'm… I'm sorry… this all my fault. If I hadn't antagonized him…"

"Please don't blame yourself for anything," Li reassured him.

"How did you sense my call?" James wondered.

"We need to discuss a few issues about being a psychic, some of these are very important. The team from America will arrive in two days. Meanwhile, I want you to practice a special technique for me. We call it 'blocking technique.' We use it to keep other psychics from incidentally intruding into our thoughts. Are you ready for a lesson?"

"Just a moment," James linked to him. "You said you are coming to Australia?"

"Yes, in two days," Li informed him.

"But, Penelope and I..." James objected.

"Don't worry. We'll set up a temporary quarters outside your home. The only thing we'll need is some dirt and a little water to start," Li told him.

"You can have as much dirt and water as you like, Li," James told him. "It is the least I can do for you. You don't have to sleep in tents. Are you certain..."

"I appreciate your offer, general. Trust me, that is all we shall need. You'll be joining us in our desert campaign. You know this country far better than we do. We'll need your expertise if we are to defeat this madman. Agreed?" Li requested.

"Agreed! I look forward to meeting you at last," the general told him.

"First thing first, let us discuss blocking technique," Li continued.

"Very well, how do I start?" James wondered.

"You must think of something very strong and solid, so impenetrable, you cannot see what is on the other side..."

A few minutes later, James Pollack sat upright in his bed. Sweat covered his large frame and he breathed heavily. Penelope took in a deep sigh of relief that he finally opened his eyes. He glanced over at his wife and took her hand.

"James? What is it?" she asked.

"I can certainly understand how a woman feels when she's being trapped by a man," he said to her. He reached over and grabbed a tissue to mop his damp forehead.

"Trapped?" she asked, alarmed. "Are you alright? What happened?"

"That chap in the desert, tried to assault me in my sleep. Thank goodness Li stepped in," he explained.

"Master Li?" Penelope questioned.

He shot his wife a glance.

"So you acknowledge he's a master level psychic do you?" he commented.

A smile crossed her lips.

"Ok, I admit it," she stated. "He has tremendous power, and he saved my husband's life. But what about that desert madman, you mentioned, James? What did he try to do to you?"

James ran his fingers through his moist gray hair. He took in a deep breath while he struggled to find the right words that would not upset his wife.

"He probed my mind," he told her. "I felt completely helpless under his attack until Li stopped him, thank goodness," he said as he patted the dampness with a tissue. "Before Li left my mind, he taught me how to block other psychics or any other unwanted thought intrusion. He's such a decent fellow that Li," James added.

"Darling, I… I wish I knew…" Penelope offered.

She could not comprehend what James must have felt only minutes ago, trying to sympathize yet still feeling the strange and newness of his being psychic.

"Sorry to interrupt, Penelope, but we're having company," he said.

"Company?" she asked.

"Li and his team are coming to Adelaide," he added.

"Here? To our house," she said as she nearly jumped out the bed. "But I have to clean! How much time do I have?"

"Two days," he reluctantly finished.

"Two Days!" she yelled. "Oh, James! I'll have to hire help. I mean really, that's not fair!"

"Penny, they're bringing their own bivouac with them," he told her.

"Well… that's different," she muttered. "But what will the neighbors say when they see all those tents?"

"Trust me, my dear," James said as he relaxed, "they won't see a thing."

CHAPTER TWENTY-SEVEN

MACHINATIONS

A PROUD INSTRUCTOR STOOD AT the front of her class and cast a wary eye on her anxious students. They sensed her unease as she hardly spoke a word this morning since class started. She had to leave them for an unknown period of time. She decided to keep her message simple, to the point, and truthful, the same way she taught.

"Class! Attention, please! I have an announcement," Su Lin said as she addressed her pupils. "I will be absent from this classroom for an undetermined length of time. I do not know when I will return... (or if, I will return)," she privately added. "Star Wind will fill in as your instructor."

"Aw," the class protested. "Do you have to go?" a few asked.

"My trip may only last a week or it could stretch into a month," she told them. "I do not know the exact date of my return."

An older student put her hand up. Su Lin recognized the student as one of her favorites. Her mother worked at the mansion on Running Elk's staff. Her father worked on Zinian's crew. They lived in a big beautiful 3-story Victorian-style home one block north of Main Street.

"Missy," Su Lin called on her.

The shy adolescent wore a white blouse with a decorative yellow and black pattern that matched her black jeans and yellow shoes. She tossed her long straight dark hair as she stood up and politely addressed her teacher. Many female students designed their own clothes. They brought their sketches to Su Lin and she would manufacture them at home with their fusor. She could not tell her students how she accomplished this. However, every Native American in the village had grown to accept this quirky nature of the psychics. How else could they magically produce so much food for the village with no delivery trucks and no gardens? The televisions in their homes had no manufacturing

175

marks on them. Nothing in their homes did. Still, the psychics provided anything the Comanche's desired, including a sacred campground to practice their ancient arts. Every man, woman, and child in the village owed their allegiance to this strange but wonderful group. The children especially loved their teacher, Su Lin.

As she stood before her mixed class of different ages, her mind scanned them to find good, honest, hard-working people, content with this ongoing relationship. However, when the young woman stood up, Su Lin noticed the student's full figure and realized that the young girl had started to blossom into her adult female form. One older boy, Steven, looked at her with dreamy eyes.

"I'd better speak with her mother," Su Lin thought before she continued.

"Don't take this the wrong way, we like Star Wind," Missy said as she spoke for some of her friends. "She's very nice. But, we learn things faster when you are here. Who will teach us music, Spanish, or biology? Star Wind is capable, but she doesn't know the things you do. Why did you say that you don't know when you will be back? Are you leaving Rollo?"

Su Lin knew she could not lie to Missy. Her Native American student's spoiled her with the speed they learned. The young woman would see right through her, though she was not psychic. Su Lin tried to use words that would not frighten the younger children in her class, yet would communicate her trust in the older students, such as Missy, to understand the meaning in them.

"I said that because, I am going on a mission with Master Li... a very important mission," Su Lin began.

The entire classroom immediately hushed and focused on her face. The very mention of Master Li's name brought a feeling of awe into the room. Every person in the village had seen Master Li do amazing things. When he went for walks, the young children constantly bugged him to do something amazing. He usually complied when he implanted a mutual vision in their minds. The psychic group had left Rollo before this occasion to address issues outside the village. They knew that a mission with Master Li could mean anything!

"These assignments we accept to benefit others can be dangerous," Su Lin continued. "However, we have dedicated our lives to help humanity in times of crisis. If we do not intervene in this instance, many innocent people will die. Rollo is kept a secret from the world for a reason. They would not understand us the way your people have accepted us. We will go on this mission and secretly assist those in need, using ways they cannot see or detect... that is our way."

"I'm afraid for you," the student said as her eyes began to fill up with tears.

"Please don't be overly concerned, Missy," Su Lin said and moved closer. She reached down and took the young woman by both hands. "Master Li will be with us," she spoke quietly and directed her comment to Missy. She addressed the rest of the class. "How can I be afraid when Master Li is by my side?"

"Master Li! Yeah!" the younger children cried out in joy. "He will save us!" The teenagers smiled at this naïveté. Although, even they realized that Su Lin's life could be in danger and grew concerned. The children of Rollo loved and respected Su Lin, even the grown-ups. She taught all of them.

Missy sat down. She liked Master Li, as did all of the students. Yet, she feared for her teacher's life, a woman to whom she had grown attached after the last year and a half since the school officially opened. Su Lin crouched down to her level.

"Missy, it is true that life is full of danger," she told the bright girl, "some paths take us into more danger than others do. However, I am willing to take that risk if it means ridding the world of a threat. Perhaps my sacrifice will not be in vain. You may not understand this now, but one day, this principle of sacrifice will be clearer to you. I promise."

Su Lin smiled as she wiped away the tears that started to drip down the young woman's face. Missy reciprocated with a smile. The two young women laughed and hugged.

In a deep, dark, cavernous space whose air felt strangely tepid, three men stood before a large apparatus that resembled an angular box kite wrapped around a long stretched-out oval with protruding fins. Once the back end of this aircraft had a main engine compartment, until this trio altered and changed their configuration. They changed the exhaust ducts, too. After they completed alterations on the main flyer, Villi and his crew built two smaller versions of this same flying apparatus. Since late last summer when they completed the first altered version of the large flyer, Villi started plans to make smaller versions with improved propulsion. He did not realize he would give away those scaled down aircraft away in the fall, just before the headquarters building at the end of Main Street opened ahead of schedule in late October. He gave one flyer to Sir Charles Bickford and the other to Tahir Wadi. The one he gave to the Egyptian had the capacity to go under water, a quality that only Tahir's flyer had. Recently, just after the special WPO banquet, he awarded a third aircraft to General Liong.

All three lightweight, yet extremely durable aircraft, and the large one in the hanger bay, could fly through the atmosphere completely invisible with no tail emissions as they circumnavigated the globe. The new stealth system no longer required the use of any psychic bubble, although Villi suspected that with the bubble in place around the flyer, the aircraft flew even faster. However, the strain of having to maintain a psychic bubble over a long duration was no longer necessary. While his ships created some turbulence in the atmosphere, it was virtually impossible to trace their path with the ship's stealth system in place.

The new engines Villi created for the larger aircraft were even more complex than the smaller versions. Villi knew he had to make this flyer faster and more powerful than the other versions, since they often had to carry equipment as well as passengers. He also wanted to improve over "the previous year's" technology. The transportation head reached out with his mind and turned the engines on. If he increased their revolutions to flight speed, he could create hurricane force winds inside the hanger. The read out stated the engines operated in optimal condition.

"At least we know they run well in the hanger," Villi observed.

"You did it, sir," Victor said with a broad smile. "This new system will give you all the lift and control you need. Better yet, it burns no fuel. Congratulations."

"Yeah," Edward added, "me too."

Villi put his big arms around the two young men's shoulders as he stood between them. He allowed a certain level of pride that he not only trained these two trouble teens, but that they stayed with him out of loyalty for the past two and a half years. Whatever the WPO carved out for its future, Villi felt that he could not deny the presence of Victor and Edward in that vision, if they chose to remain – at some point he would approach the council and request they offer Cecilia's serum to certain individuals such as Running Elk, Star Wind, perhaps Zhiwei's staff, the non-psychic wives, and his two helpers. Villi also knew he was not alone in the WPO membership with those feelings. He looked around his shop.

"This is a far cry from my days as a car mechanic," he sighed aloud.

"I thought you worked in a factory?" Edward questioned.

"Yeah, you told us you worked on an assembly line," Victor added.

"I did, but sometimes I had to work on cars, too," he told them.

"Was that before you were a cop?" Edward asked.

Villi nodded, "Uh, huh. My hands were black with grease every day. I was very young and very naïve. But that hard work helped me prepare for being an officer."

"We don't even use grease, Villi," Victor spoke up.

"No," Villi smiled, "we work in a world that does not require grease... to build one of these," he said as he indicated the big odd airship.

"She's a beaut!" Edward commented.

"She sure is," Victor echoed. "Swift, silent, and slick. No exhaust comin' out of this baby!"

Villi's new engine design did not rely on combustion for acceleration. The magnetic propulsion system used a shielded system that did not generate heat. The powerful magnets inside the ship spun within a superconducting field. In turn, they operated blades that drew air in the front and blew it out the back or down to provide thrust, lift, or acceleration. The energy to drive the system came from modified versions of Chou's power cubes – the little black boxes that contained highly reactive isotopes. As the particles within slowly decayed over the years, the box converted their energy to usable power on demand.

Since the aircraft was four times in size over the smaller "flyer" versions, the engines on the large aircraft put out over four times as much thrust. Villi had never tested these new engines at any speed other than thirty percent, which propelled the craft to Mach 3. Only time kept him from testing the engines at higher speeds. He was not worried about the structural integrity of the aircraft. The fusor-created lightweight parts were invulnerable to any buffeting from the atmosphere. He worried more about the stress demands on the engines at extremely high rates of speed.

"No atmospheric aircraft on the planet is faster," Edward bragged aloud.

"I'm curious about one thing," Victor mentioned. "You told us that when you traveled around in the general's jet it took less time when you surrounded the jet with that thing you create…"

"Psychic bubble," Villi inserted.

"…yeah, that," Victor continued. "What would happen if you used it on this aircraft? Wouldn't it go even faster?"

In all of his zeal to make this the fastest, most stealthful flyer in the world, his goal was to eliminate the need for a psychic bubble. However, Victor pointed out the obvious. With the bubble in place, perhaps the aircraft could go even faster when the psychic shield of energy eliminated most atmospheric resistance.

"Yes, I see," Villi thought to him. "There'd certainly be less resistance."

"We should make a test run," Edward advised.

Villi decided he would mention that to Tahir, General Liong, and Sir Charles at some point in the future. The invited guests left with their passengers earlier this morning. Tahir and Seel returned Salla and Filla to Africa. Then they flew Sarah and Milo to their respective countries. Sir Charles took Camille home before he dropped off Maria and Jonathan. He and William flew to England after that. Madam and General Liong had the longest flight. First they flew Kiran to India and then Leni home to Russia before they returned to China. When Victor brought up the possibility, he started to make his own calculations.

"... we could go... possibly up to Mach 10 (11,840 kph) without putting excessive strain on the engines," Villi muttered. "Yeah, maybe you're right, Edward. Perhaps the bubble would help us go faster."

"You'd have to retract the wings, of course," Victor suggested, "streamline the fuselage."

"Let's try it!" Edward urged.

"Sorry, fellahs," Villi told them. "We don't have time to run flight tests today. Master Li wants the team ready to depart in the next twenty-four hours."

"Where are you off to this time?" Victor asked.

"Australia," Villi told them. "I can't stay to help you prepare the aircraft. I need to help team members prepare. Can you prep the craft for an early launch?"

"Sure... yeah," they chimed in.

"Thanks," Villi said as he turned toward his office.

"Did you hear what he said?" Edward whispered. "Mach 10!"

"I wish I was onboard when they reached that speed," Victor said as he watched Villi leave the hanger deck. "She'll be sleek..."

"Like a bullet..." Edward muttered.

Chou headed across Rollo to the south side. Zinian claimed to have created some special devices that shrunk their living quarters into an incredibly small space. Chou made compact designs prior to this. Last spring, he sent a whole house full of furniture to Germany inside a box about a meter square with a special fusor packed inside another small box. It was the first time someone ignited a remote fusor outside Rollo. Master Li had to cancel the energy wave the device created when Villi turned it on for the first time. However, Chou had never seen anything that compared to the designs Zinian created.

He left his lab and went to Zinian's construction headquarters on the south end of the village, where Zinian kept his machines, tools, and the largest fusor Chou ever created. Zinian needed an exceptionally large fusor to make the big parts necessary for the constructed Chou's lab, Villi's hanger, the parts for all the housing construction in the village, and the largest parts of all which he created as the supports for the WPO headquarters. Chou expected Zinian had something the size of a car. He wondered how he would put his skimmers in the cargo hold if Zinian's temporary quarters took up too much space.

"What's up?" Chou wondered when he showed up.

"I wanted you to see the demonstration," Zinian said.

He held out a flat stiff piece of paper which had a small blue port in one corner. He took a small device that injected some liquid. Almost instantly, a house in miniature sprang from the object and grew before their eyes in seconds.

"How is that possible?" Chou asked.

He no longer needed the eyes glasses he wore for corrective vision when Master Li found him two and a half years ago. However, the nerd he still was, he carried a special set of glasses on his head. He pulled them off his forehead and flipped down a magnification visor that allowed him to see the thousands of collapsed tunnels which rapidly expanded as the fluid spread through the fabric.

"How does that (he gestured toward another seemingly flat piece of white paper) become that?" he wondered as Zinian's flat paper rapidly formed the model.

Zinian used a different construction and inflation method than the one Chou used to create the furniture from compact forms.

"Once I inject this chemical formula it interacts with the dry substance and…" Zinian pointed out. "Whoosh! Nothing can stop it. The mixture will create its own channels and help form rigid walls… forget pumps."

"Why didn't I think of that?" Chou mumbled.

"You think I did?" Zinian shot back.

"Where did you find it?" Chou wondered.

"Beit (bee-it)," Zinian told him.

"I thought Ziddis…"

"Not for chemistry…" Zinian informed Chou. "I went to Beit for the wood formulas when we made the mahogany used throughout the mansion… that wood will last forever by the way. Everyone thought you made the dining room table and the staircase," he said as he shook his head. "I don't mind, Chou. We share everything here. I have no ego to bruise. I only know that the nature-oriented psychics of Beit inspire me far more than techno-oriented creatures of Ziddis. Furry creatures are actually fun to be around."

Chou looked at his friend's model with both admiration and envy.

"I should have spoken up… about the table, I mean," Chou muttered.

"Why?" Zinian shot back. "From the very start, you've been the best friend I've ever had… well, you and Zhiwei. In my mind, it simply doesn't matter. Oh, I forgot to point out…"

"What?" Chou wondered.

"Furniture… comes built in, including things like sheets and towels. Took me a long time to make the sheets soft. In the first batch, they were too scratchy for comfort. The chairs are fused to the floor, but with a little wiggle, they break free and you can move them around."

Chou stared with amazement at the innovation. Zinian really surprised him.

"Thanks for the demonstration, Zinian," he told his best friend. "I can see you won't need my expertise any longer. Too many worlds, too little time to explore these days," Chou commented as he shook his head and walked back to his lab. "We must mind share... one of these days."

"See you soon," Zinian added as he resumed his work on the inflatable house.

Zhiwei and Michael stood outside the security chief's building, across the street from the schoolhouse. Zhiwei not only monitored all security related activity outside of Rollo, but he monitored its citizens, too. With his latest advanced security-oriented computers, and with the help of Selena and Jennifer, they monitored the world in general by utilizing a vast network of communication systems that he tapped via sophisticated devices provided to him by Chou and planted inside most of the world's top government security systems – USA, Russia, China, India, Israel, Germany, France, England, Saudi Arabia, Japan... and several others. He monitored the internal workings of many governments.

Yet, the WPO seemed somewhat of an enigma to Zhiwei. He wanted to invent a device that would replace the cumbersome black cards the psychics constantly dropped, lost, or left behind. Since last summer, Chou had to replace six of the cards, two in Egypt after the affair with Seel and Tahir when they battled the Somali pirates. Zhiwei currently worked on a project for a different type of device that could be used for motion detection, analysis, and communication. He asked Michael to stop by his security building to discuss his new ideas. He stood on the sidewalk in front of the entrance.

"Why are we standing out here?" Michael wondered when he walked up.

"I thought I'd save you some time before you meet with Han," Zhiwei told him.

"Let's hear your pitch," Michael stated.

"I'd like to replace the cards that we currently use to communicate," Zhiwei suggested. "Perhaps a ring similar to one Chou uses with Alexander (the name of Chou's computer) or something we could wear on the wrist," he proposed to Michael, "like a bracelet. Here, I came up with an idea..." he said and demonstrated with a hand-held projector.

Zhiwei held out his arm and the device in his hand projected a three-dimensional image onto his wrist, a gold band that stretched around his arm about three centimeters wide. As the projection continued, a three-dimensional hand came into view and touched the band. It projected its own expandable screen that collapsed at a touch. Michael nodded his approval as he watched Zhiwei's demonstration.

"It's called a SECO bracelet, based on an idea I saw on the world of Tinni, where the psychics were persecuted after they revealed their power to the populous. The few psychics that survived the persecutions live inside invisible pockets of isolation. Eventually, they found a way to communicate with each other and used these special wrist bracelets that responded to psychic energy. They also render the wearer invisible. Their military world found a way to recognize emerging psychics at birth and kill them. Only eighteen psychics survive on a planet of six hundred million beings. They constantly struggle to find any new psychics before their governments do. It's the saddest psychic world in the collective…"

"I've heard of them," Michael responded. "What does the SECO stand for?"

"Secure Exterior Concealment Oscillator, which deals with how the bracelets operate to maintain a psychic's stealth," Zhiwei explained. "The bracelets set up a field, similar to a psychic bubble, which surrounds the person and can be manipulated. The bracelets don't require a power source as they channel psychic energy directly from the surrounding environment. Anyway, I thought we could use these bracelets instead of the cards. Their signal is stronger and we would never misplace or lose them."

"I like the idea," Michael told him. "But, if you are going to fabricate these new devices, you must have them ready by tomorrow," he reminded him.

"I doubt this project will be ready by then," Zhiwei admitted. "I'll need to do more research before I can present a detailed analysis before the board for review. It could take months… or even years."

"If you need any help, let me know," Michael told him.

"I sense trouble," Zhiwei linked as he stared into Michael's eyes.

The tall young man shook his head but did not reply.

"Between you and Villi?" Zhiwei wondered as Michael blocked his thoughts.

"No… well… yes and no," Michael linked back and hesitated. "It was strange, Zhiwei. When Cecilia and I went home last night, it was if we were back in Paris," he told his friend.

Zhiwei raised his eyebrows.

"You're complaining?" he put to his friend.

"No," Michael smiled. "Only, this morning she acted just the opposite, as if I had violated her. She was actually mad at me… for the first time in… I can't recall."

"Hmmm," Zhiwei pondered.

"Ever since we've been psychic, I've known everything about Cecilia. She never kept anything from me," Michael explained. "But this morning, she was downright frosty, I tell you… and completely blocked."

"That is strange," Zhiwei concurred.

"I must go and meet with Han…"

"What did Villi say when you mind-shared with him?"

"That's just it!" Michael said, surprised Zhiwei guessed. "Villi had the same story… said last night he and Su Lin performed the tango and this morning she was cold as ice. He said she acted real strange and it put him in a foul mood. Said he didn't want to mind-share and wished me good luck."

"He said that?"

"Yeah! To me! His best friend!"

"Huh! I don't know who I'd turn to if either Zinian or Chou did not wish to mind share…"

"Sorry, can't help you there. Besides, you should know better. We aren't compatible. You guys like to play as comic book heroes, while Villi and I…"

"You and Villi clash like a waves against rocks," Zhiwei cut in. "I never saw such mental interaction. Still, I'd say you two were about as close as two friends can be," he added with a half-grin. Yet, Michael seemed melancholy.

"Well… gotta go," Michael linked as the two men departed.

Zhiwei watched his friend walk away before he spun around and headed into what can only be described as Rollo's most secure building – his conglomeration of computers, scanners, and other necessities to perform his duty as head of security. As the computer scanned his body for entry, he thought of admonishing Villi for rebuffing his friend in time of need. However, Zhiwei would never interfere between two friends, two men he had known since they started this complex endeavor.

The longer the group remained in Rollo to start their community, the more they came to rely on mind sharing as an essential outlet to maintain their mental health as psychics. Living in a psychic village made everyone acutely aware of what the other psychic members thought, felt, and dreamt. It was impossible to avoid. If not for blocking technique, they might have driven each other mad during that first year.

On the other hand, mind sharing helped them cope with isolation and allowed them to express thoughts and feelings in ways that differed from those exchanged between spouses. Friends came to rely on friends in time of emotional need for this form of mental release, as if they went for a bike ride, a jog, or climbed a mountain together. Yet, before he could scold Villi on what he considered as a breach of psychic etiquette, Zhiwei looked down at his special black card and noticed their resident pilot busy in the hanger complex. He realized Villi must have preparation for the trip as his primary goal today.

"I need to stay focused on Australia," he thought as he headed inside. "I'll let Michael and Villi work out their own problems."

Michael Tyler brooded over his wife's reaction only momentarily. As he walked up Main Street toward the manor house, he reached out to Han and made a link. He had his priorities, too – the safety and welfare of the people he knew as his closest friends.

"You and I need to discuss strategy…"

"Want to mind share? I heard about Villi…"

Han and Michael were compatible and had mind shared in the past. It was easier for Han to mind share with Michael than with Master Li, whose level of power could overwhelm most psychics during any level of interaction.

"Some other time," Michael put to him. "Right now I want your opinion of how we should approach Cyrus and his band of troublemakers."

All at once, a powerful wave of energy passed through Rollo. The psychics paused to listen.

"I want all local members to relax and mind-share," Master Li announced. "It is more important we go to Australia as a team than a group of individual experts. Stop what you are doing and go into some needed down time. That is an order… or shall we say… a needed request."

Michael stopped on the sidewalk in front of his house. Since Master Li had spoken, and he never disobeyed his mentor, he had only one destination in mind.

CHAPTER TWENTY-EIGHT

ODE TO MIND SHARE

THE POINT OF HIS RAPIER penetrated the cloth and nearly sliced his opponent's rib meat from its bone. He knew the man could easily repair the scratch he left behind. Therefore, he did not hesitate to proceed. If his opponent sensed any uncertainty on his part, he was doomed. He quickly thrust again.

"Touché," Villi said as he dodged right and the foil's point ripped through his shirt. He twisted around and made a downward thrust. The point of his sword nearly skewered Michael right through his left thigh.

Michael countered by leaping back and swung his foil around to block Villi's next move. The two long thin blades made a clang sound as they clashed together from such strong opponents.

"You know Cable's counter?" Villi questioned.

"Of course!" Michael said with a slight grin as he backed away.

"See if you can counter this!"

Villi started to his left while he swung down his right arm, left to right. He quickly reversed action by making a rapid downward step with his left foot and pushed off. As he flew to his right, he reversed his foil and came at Michael's neck.

Michael did not bother to move his arm. He lifted his foil straight up from his waist in time to deflect Villi's brilliant move. He dropped down, rolled and swung up toward Villi's groin. Villi could not counter in time. The point headed straight up and would run him through like an animal on a spit. He flipped forward and kicked down. He made a precise strike on the tip of the blade with his foot, but it cost him his balance. He tumbled forward while Michael brought his blade around and headed for Villi with his rapier like a battering ram, aimed straight for his chest. Villi could not move his foil to counter in time.

Instead, he rolled to his left, only to feel Michael's blade pierce his clothing again. This time, however, Michael managed to make a minor flesh wound along Villi's opposite chest wall. Villi winced as pain shot through his skin. But he was far from finished. Michael wasted too much energy and left his other side open. Villi raised his right arm and thrust home.

At the last second, Michael realized his error, he could only look his friend in the face as the point of the blade entered his heart.

"You have bested me... villain," he uttered as he drew his last breath.

The scene around the two men dissolved as they laughed and hugged.

"I believe that is 58 wins to my... 59!" Villi declared with a grin as he pulled back from his friend.

"You won't be so lucky next time," Michael promised, his body starting to fade.

Villi pulled his fencing foil straight up to his face in a salute and faded.

Sweat poured off their real bodies as they withdrew into the privacy of their homes located across the street.

"We need to do that more often," Michael linked as he opened his eyes to the reality of his living room.

Villi took in a deep breath and sighed. They had mentally fenced on previous occasions but never for such a long match. This one lasted for nearly an hour. Both men were exhausted mentally and physically.

"No sex tonight," Michael chuckled. "I'm beat."

"Speak for yourself," Villi countered. "When Su Lin wants sex, no man can refuse her, least of all her husband." He took a few deep breaths and wiped some of the sweat off his face. "However... when I explain our match, I'm certain she'll understand..."

"Oh, of course she will," Michael linked back.

This time the two men chuckled. Su Lin had a very forceful personality when she wanted her way. For that matter, so did Cecilia.

Every psychic in Rollo heard Master Li's announcement and complied. With her clinic time done, Cecilia closed her doors and went to her examination table. Her mind traveled across the park and made a polite knock on her friend's mental threshold.

"Finished for the day?" she asked of her best friend.

"I could stand a little competition," Su Lin replied.

She settled into the chair behind her desk which reclined. She closed her eyes and the two women stood before Devil's Tower in Wyoming.

"Race you to the top?" Cecilia offered.

"Loser has to make dinner... for four," Su Lin bet.

Cecilia did not bother to reply. She took off for one of the great six sided stones lying on its side. She leapt up, walked along its length, and then ran for the sheer wall of rock that rose above the Wyoming plain.

Su Lin ran all out. She used one of the stones as a launching platform and flew through the air until she landed on the side of the monument.

"No fair using power!" Cecilia cried foul.

Su Lin laughed and began to scale the beast with only her bare hands and her feet. About half way up, she managed to kick off her shoes and go the rest of the way to the top. As she struggled up the last hundred meters or so, the panting, sweaty dark haired young woman breathed a sigh of accomplishment, knowing she had bested her friend.

"Took you long enough," a voice said as a hand came down on her shoulder.

Her head jerked around to see Cecilia standing behind her.

"You cheated!" Su Lin declared as she spun around.

Yet when she beheld Cecilia, she could see the young shorter blonde-haired woman had bruises, scratches and torn hands bleeding at the fingertips. Cecilia did it the hard way alright.

"I'm sorry... that must hurt," Su Lin relented.

"Don't worry about it... chef," Cecilia said with a grin.

The two women embraced as Devil Tower turned into a swirl of light and color.

"This way," Chou's voice echoed along the dark and damp cramped corridor. The air had a musty stale odor of trapped moist air under tons of rock.

He and Zinian had a long way to crawl to reach the burial chamber. This air vent led down at a steep angle. One slip and a person could slide to his death. When the two finally reached the end, they came out at a place that had a large dark space on the other side. Zinian pointed and spoke aloud.

"What is that... that... that... that... that?" Zinian's voice echoed.

"The burial chamber... chamber... chamber... chamber..." Chou's voice whispered.

He indicated the assembly on Zinian's waist. Zinian had a tool belt on that also had a long apparatus attached to his back. He took the mechanical device off and put it together. Even with the air being cooler here, the long hike down the shaft took its toll physically. He held up the metallic object and pressed the middle. It expanded until it jabbed into the sides of the shaft. He handed Chou one of the rope seats while he took the other.

"It's secure... secure... secure... secure..."

"Got it... it... it... it... it..."

"You go first... first... first... first..." Zinian offered.

"Oh, thanks… thanks… thanks… thanks," Chou replied with a smile.

He reached into his belt and pulled out a small object. He flicked open the top and a brilliant white light lit up the entire room. For a moment, neither man could see a thing because the bright light was too close to them. Chou dropped it and it fell a long way until it made a huge "thunk" sound on the stone floor below and echoed. They could now see everything inside the gigantic vault.

"Whoa!" Zinian declared. "Nice shiny metal… looks like iron or steel."

Below them they could see two large muscular arms that reached up and held a huge object over its head. From this perspective, they could not make out the face, but both men knew it was the god, Ku, the most powerful being that ever lived on planet Ulip. Similar to humans in physical stature but nearly ten times their size, these ancient creatures had died out three thousand years ago. This tomb had never been opened. They were the first to enter the chamber since it was sealed.

"Good god!" Chou declared as he looked at a scanner in his hand. "The whole thing is made out of platinum!"

"Platinum… platinum… platinum… platinum!" Zinian's shout echoed. "Come on… let's get down there!"

Chou started his seat and it slowly moved down. Zinian followed behind him with his seat moving just as slow. As they dropped they could see that the statue must have represented one of the Ussla men that lived on the planet and were no longer around. It was completely detailed right down to the texture of the skin… and nude!

"Well," Zinian sighed. "We know the male of the species resembles us," he said as he averted his eyes. "I wonder if they have a platinum statue of a large nude woman," he quipped.

Chou laughed but when he did, a loud growl filled the air around them. It was so loud, the vibration shook the air. He tried to stop his seat and fumbled with the controls as he continued to descend. Zinian was frozen with fear. His eyes searched for the sound. At one far end of the incredibly large space, a pair of eyes stared at them out of the darkness.

"Fools!" a voice cried out. "Stupid humans… bungling in where they do not belong. You disturb the chamber of the gods… now you must pay with your lives!"

A gigantic man who stood nearly six or seven meters in height and who perfectly resembled the statue, started across the room toward them. He held a club like weapon in his hand, wore armor, and moved very quickly.

"Chou! We've got to get the hell out of here!" Zinian declared.

"Ha, ha, ha, ha!" the Ussla man shouted.

"I thought you were extinct," Chou stated. For a moment, he forgot his life was in danger.

"As you can see, I am not... but soon, you will be!"

Chou tried to make their seats rise, but the ascent would be too slow. Not fast enough to avoid the grasp of the man who advanced on them so quickly.

"Chou!" Zinian yelled and grabbed the back of Chou's collar.

The two men took off at a run for the back of the giant statue.

"Zhiwei!" they heard a voice intrude. "Zhiwei!"

The Ussla man stopped and transformed into Zhiwei.

"What?" he replied.

"Would you like to join us for dinner?" the feminine voice wondered.

"Chou and Zinian, too?"

"Of course!"

The temple burial chamber melted around them. The men rose from their perspective residences and ventured out toward Su Lin and Villi's house.

"This way!" Li called to her. "Courage."

Running Elk ran along the top edge of a cliff. The waterfall was not far away. She ran up to where Master Li stood. She was not afraid. Her colorful suit flapped in the breeze. He reached over and took her hand. The two took off running and jumped over the edge. Down they fell. They let go their hands and separated. Running Elk held out her arms and stretched out her legs. The flaps caught the air. She soared out over the valley, a human glider. Off to her left, she saw Master Li in his yellow suit with the green dragon. He seemed so powerful, so masterful, so invigorated with energy.

Before she could say how much she adored him, he nodded to the forest floor rising below them. The ride, all too brief, would soon be over. She nodded back. She reached up for the cord on her chest and pulled it. The chute shot out from the back and pulled hard on her jump suit and body. The drag slowed her descent until she floated to the grass that flowed along the river that formed from the base of the waterfall. She saw Li land on the other side.

"We must return!" he called to her.

She knew what he meant. The vision dissolved. She sat at her table inside the kitchen nook, surrounded by her cook books.

"Su Lin wants us for dinner..." he linked to her.

"Better be good..."

"No judging... just bring some wine..."

"What about the alcohol?" she questioned, "and Michael?"

"On this occasion, he's ok with it."

Han stuck his hand in a big pile of green goo.

"What is this stuff?" he asked.

"Lubricant," the big Vstl told him. "That 'stuff' as you call it allows the trees to form tight conduits. If they did not have that 'stuff' the friction would cause them to burst into flames. That would not be good for a city made almost entirely of plant material."

"No," Han replied with a smile, "That would not be good."

The vstl enjoyed the facial reactions that Han so frequently displayed. Vstls had no such reactions. Their faces did not communicate so much information as when humans smiled or frowned.

"I'm so glad I could see you at last, Han," he linked. "I think this shell is better for all of us. So much of your communication is silent."

"Don't I resemble the land dwellers?" Han replied.

"No... they did not look or sound or even thought like humans," the vstl linked. "They were crude, and ugly, and very unpleasant. They did not have art or music or tell stories like you do."

"Not all humans are like me..."

"No, that is true," the vstl replied as he saw it in Han's mind. "Therefore I am glad we have you for this... what did you call it?"

"Mind sharing," Han said.

"Yes, the use of imagination to create artificial landscapes of the mind and then play in them..."

"That is one way of putting it..." Han countered. "Back on Earth, my fellow psychics do this for relaxation."

"I found our mind sharing... very exhausting... since this was a first between our species, I shall inform the other vstls of this... oh, I believe your presence is requested," the vstl informed Han.

Han paused. He did not sense anything. All at once, his voice requested he break contact. Master Li requested his presence.

"How did you know that?" he questioned the vstl.

"Good bye, Han," the vstl said. "I will take care of your shell until you return... and, bon appetite."

"Bon..." Han started to question when his voice pulled him out and he opened his eyes. He looked up at his bedroom ceiling and took in a deep breath.

"Su Lin invited us for dinner," Li linked to him. "Come along, the others are waiting..."

As Han started out of his bedroom, he wondered about the mental power of the vstl and how they may have underestimated them. They were the ones who located planet Earth after Master Li was born. They were the first species to make contact, other than the voices at Galactic Central, when the IPC first probed human brains during those early days when the first conduits appeared in the middle of the Twentieth Century. They would have been the first planet to make contact, but Michael Tyler felt reluctant to perform planetary travel and settled for his own personal mental advancement instead.

"Perhaps there is more to this mind sharing than we first considered," Han thought as he made his way down the curving staircase.

Ahead on the right side of Main Street, from his perspective, he could sense the gathering of psychic minds abuzz with their latest mental adventures. He smiled as he felt he had little to offer. Members seldom chose Han to mind share. However, on this day, when he walked through the front door and the group turned to greet him, they only wanted to hear about Han's trip to Uthx and his first mind share using a shell on another planet.

"What was it like?" the group eagerly wanted to know.

"Better than I could have imagined... on my own," he said in return and began to explain.

Han sat down to a marvelous meal with his friends.

CHAPTER TWENTY-NINE

FAST FLIGHT

AT 3 A.M., MASTER LI abruptly woke and used his mind to travel through the halls of the great manor house until he stood before the large grandfather clock in the hallway outside the library. He detested the constant ticking inside his favorite tomb of solitude. He also wanted the antique device, which he brought back through time, as far from his bedroom as possible. He wanted his bedroom a dark and quiet place, something he never had the entire time he lived in China. Star Wind placed the large stately clock across from the entrance to the library. It told the date, time, even the phases of the moon. Li's psychic body looked upon its delicately carved golden face and noted the time.

"Early," he thought as his comparatively tiny figure rose from his gargantuan four-poster canopy bed, "yet not too early for the world down under. With the time change between here and Australia," he reasoned, "we must acclimate to the new time zone. I'll notify the team to start preparations."

He reached out with his mind to find his favorite pupil, that perpetually youthful man who gave him the label Master Li, Michael Tyler, as he lay in bed with his wife, Cecilia. He found Michael in a shared dream state where he paddled a type of two man kayak with Cecilia tucked in behind him. For a moment, Li tagged along. He watched as Michael and Cecilia worked together and navigated a river's rapids. Psychic dreams could seem extremely realistic, including the sensation of being wet or buffeted. The two psychics laughed as they approached a difficult drop and knew which way to turn the bow of the kayak in order to avoid total submersion.

"To the right!" Cecilia called out.

"Thanks. I see it!" Michael answered.

The deep bluish water spilled over the round rocks and turned into dangerous white water. The pair worked in unison like two ballet dancers in harmony with nature, their prime physical bodies moved with precision. The kayak dipped down and twisted in a sharp decline, following the tortuous path until it shot out through the foamy white water onto the smooth glassy surface of the river. Cecilia leaned forward as Michael leaned back and the pair kissed. After yesterday's cool start, both psychics needed this emotional bonding.

Li hated to interrupt this perfect moment.

"Sorry to disturb you, Michael," Li broke in. "I realize you haven't had much sleep. Nevertheless, we should begin departure procedures right away. Wake the team and go through your checklist," he requested.

"Yes, Master Li," Michael quickly responded.

Michael dismissed the kayak and countryside, which quickly faded from view as the reality of his bedroom returned. He rolled over to Cecilia first, kissed her softly on the mouth, and roused her before he called on the others.

"Master Li wants us up," he said to her mind.

"So soon?" she cooed back, "I enjoyed that dream with you," she added as she stretched.

The couple often shared their dreams. Unlike the worlds of Galactic Central, the world of the dream mind was only limited by imagination, similar to mind sharing, but not as intense. Once they learned to share dreams, Michael and Cecilia explored one another's psyche and debunked any anomalies that plague other minds, such as petty jealousies, sexual deviancy, remorse, guilt, phobias, manias, and dark thoughts. At the end of two and a half years, no couple on the planet had worked out the "kinks" in their minds the way the Beaton-Tyler's had. Michael wanted to press her about yesterday morning's cool reception. Still, she seemed buoyant today and he did not wish to retest the cool water from yesterday.

"You are the perfect pilot," she cooed as she briefly snuggled her husband.

"Don't tell Villi," he linked back. "He'll be jealous."

"I believe they know us better than that," she said referring to their best friends, Villi and Su Lin who lived across the street.

"Time to shower," Michael reminded as he pushed away.

Knowing Cecilia's penchant for taking long showers, Zinian installed two separate showers for their master bedroom when he built their house. Michael and Cecilia, as well as anyone in Rollo, could use as much water as they pleased since the house's sanitation system automatically recycled every ounce of water they used and returned the changed effluence to a specially lined ceramic tank. The filtered waste products returned to the fusor, which recycled them into their elemental form. Nothing in Rollo was ever wasted, not human biological secretions, food scraps, or any other kind of waste.

When Master Li mentally visited the other side of the street to wake more members of the team, he had to make a hasty exit from Villi and Su Lin's amorous dream. He found the naked couple lying in the green grass next to a hidden tropical lagoon. Su Lin let out a yelp when she sensed Master Li's presence.

"Out!" the couple yelled as Master Li quickly withdrew.

"That'll teach him to poke around where he's not wanted," Su Lin laughed in reply. Even Villi found Master Li's sudden embarrassment amusing.

While Michael and Cecilia, or even the other couples had a healthy sex lives, Villi and Su Lin bordered on the pornographic. They could never get enough of each other. Their love, from the very start of their relationship, could only be described with one word – passion.

Master Li woke Zinian and Zhiwei from their dreams. They explained the situation to their Native American mates and bid them adieu after they prepared to disembark for the overseas journey.

Chou and Star Wind, while officially married for only four months, endeavored to cope with Star Wind's newly "developed" psychic ability. Although Master Li could not detect a fully-formed conduit inside her brain, he did find a different anomaly that he called "a bridge between Running Elk and us." Star Wind could exchange thoughts with most psychics, and with some effort on Chou's part, the couple also shared dreams on occasion. After Master Li's middle-of-the-night intrusion, Star Wind prepared Chou's breakfast while he showered.

"Why depart at this hour?" she linked to him from the kitchen.

"Time difference," he linked back as he toweled off. "We'll have to take that into consideration when we speak via our cards."

Villi made his way toward the hanger before the rest of team and called out to his assistants on his way. By early February of 2019, the two young men, Victor and Edward, his "hanger crew," grew accustomed to having their boss directly address their mind. The young men rose and headed out to the aircraft while they rubbed sleep from their eyes and yawned. They stood by the aircraft and the hanger deck controls should Villi need them during takeoff.

The entire group and a smattering of guests quickly assembled inside the hanger by 3:30 am, Han and Master Li were the last to join them. They flew up out of the darkness on one of the recently constructed hovercraft with a floating cart behind them, piled high with four large pieces of luggage. Master Li floated the objects into the aircraft's cargo hull on top of the other devices and luggage that the rest of team had already stored. The group moved to the side when the ship produced a ramp from its side that descended to the flight deck. The team boarded the sleek oval shaped fuselage and took their seats inside the craft while Villi went forward into the clear bubble cockpit, took his seat, and started his control panel.

"Activate all systems," he calmly spoke as he took the main pilot's seat.

"All systems activated," the computer responded. "Compensating takeoff thrust controls for additional weight," it spoke in Russian.

"I thought I placed our passengers and their luggage into the calculations," he speculated.

"Additional devices in cargo hold have high density and increased weight," the panel informed him, "accessing additional energy calculations for Australian destination."

A large arm swung out of the wall across the deck from the aircraft and intersected a place near the aft section. Victor and Edward, who by this time had retreated to the control room, looked out the large window confused as to why the ship needed extra energy modules.

"What's wrong?" Victor questioned.

"Additional weight," Villi linked to their minds. "The computer is trying to compensate with additional power storage should our energy cells expire due to the long trip."

They waved back that they understood.

"I forgot… Zinian and Chou brought some things over to the hanger last night and loaded them into the flyer," Edward told him. "I should have mentioned it. The objects seemed small compared to the luggage…"

"…small but very dense," Villi told him when he scanned the cargo bay. "They added a significant amount of weight."

The fusor on the lower level sparked and began to spew out numerous small energy blocks according to the specifications. A robotic arm snatched the freshly made devices and placed them into a supply transport elevator which brought them up inside the utility arm. These new power cubes slid into position on standby mode in case they were needed. Villi and his crew inside the control tower watched as the arm fed them into position.

"Everyone aboard?" Master Li asked, although he knew the answer without question.

The ramp disappeared and remolded with the side of the ship. The door seamlessly sealed shut. The seats automatically strapped the team members into their seats.

"With the new propulsion system, there is no need to use your energy on this trip," Villi informed his fellow psychics. "We have stealth technology, so no bubble is really necessary at all. However, Victor suggested that with the bubble around us, we could go much faster. I thought we'd test our maximum speed limit. Master Li, would you mind forming a psychic bubble around the flyer for the duration of the trip?" Villi requested.

"I'll tap into your superconductors," Li informed him, "to amplify my bubble."

Villi turned on the magnetic drive and waited for Master Li to link with the device. Li's great power surged into the circuits, which threatened to destroy the drive mechanism. Surge alarms went off. Poor Villi nearly jumped out of his seat as he scrambled to find the problem.

"Sorry, Villi," Li apologized and backed off his energy flow to a trickle.

Villi breathed a sigh of relief when the indicators returned to normal. With the psychic bubble wrapped around them, the aircraft instantly disappeared to the assistants. This aspect of takeoff never grew old to them. They slapped each other's hands and watched a nearby screen that superimposed the image of the flyer on the scene in front of them.

Villi's flight control board changed from yellow to green.

"All systems ready for takeoff," the computer told him.

"Maneuvering jets into position," Villi linked back. "Hover Z axis to ten meters. Bow angle up thirty degrees."

The strange aircraft – a combination of the sleek and boxy – gently lifted off the ground, changed its attitude, and pointed its nose at an upward angle for takeoff position.

"Hanger exhaust ports at maximum," Victor indicated. "Blast shield up."

"Magnet drive to achieve thirty percent output in one minute. Inertia dampeners on," Villi ordered. "Forward thrust in five… four… three… two…" he announced.

Unlike an ordinary jet aircraft that had to build up speed as it used the length of a long runway, Vill's aircraft shot from the hanger into the air like some arrow that instantly took flight. The boxy craft banked to the left and rose higher as the computer followed the encoded flight plan.

"Fold wings prior to Mach 3," he ordered.

"Folding wings… Mach 3 in twenty seconds," the computer informed him.

"Maintain Mach 3 for one minute and gradually increase thrust to sixty percent. Sixty degrees total on the bow plane," he ordered.

The wings folded back into the fuselage and made the aircraft one slick oval shaped craft with only moderate side and tail flaring wings. In a smooth transition, the computer applied much greater thrust. Suddenly, the aircraft shot up high into the troposphere.

"Mach 3…" the computer chimed. "Approaching Mach 4… Mach 5… now at Mach 6," the computer read aloud.

Villi reached up to activate the fuselage opacity control. The entire top of the fuselage turned clear and allowed the passengers a view of the night sky without any lights or clouds to obscure the view. As an added bonus, Villi activated a sensor that made Galactic Central's galaxy location sparkle.

"Now that's what I call in-flight entertainment," Chou sighed.

The team leaned back into their seats and took in the magnificent view. With no atmospheric interference, the universe opened up before them. A billion times a billion stars positively dusted the black sky above them. For a few minutes, Villi allowed the passengers a view of this sight until he turned the attitude of the aircraft toward their new destination, which would not afford a very good overhead point of view.

"Sorry, but we'll be increasing our speed even faster soon," he informed them.

"Awwww!" the members cried when the ceiling turned opaque.

"Maximum thrust," Villi ordered. "Master Li, hopefully this is the moment when I thought your help will change our velocity." Villi purposely silenced the computer's voice. He glanced down at the speed. The engines no longer had to work as hard and their air speed increased significantly. "We are officially the fastest object to fly through Earth's atmosphere," Villi informed them.

"What is our speed?" Zhiwei asked out of curiosity.

"Without Master Li, the most I could achieve was between Mach 7 and 8. But with his help, we are currently flying at Mach 10," Villi answered.

"Too fast for a jet aircraft, but not a spacecraft on re-entry," Zhiwei observed, "or a nuclear warhead."

"Why did you say that?" Master Li interjected.

"We might be spotted on the new multispectral satellite surveillance systems that NATO launched two days ago," Zhiwei linked to Master Li. "They're not supposed to activate the system for several weeks until they work out the software issues, but I understand the scanners are in working order. Should they run a set up scan over the Pacific…"

"You didn't inform me about this development," Master Li countered.

"It only just occurred to me, Master Li," Zhiwei apologized. "Sorry."

"I don't believe they'll understand what they see even if they do spot us," Villi linked back and dismissed the concern. "We'll appear as an atmospheric phenomenon, Zhiwei. Don't you think?"

"If that is what you believe," Zhiwei stated. "As head of security, it's my job to worry about such things."

Master Li glanced over at Han. The strategist simply shrugged the matter off.

"I don't believe the Allied Forces Security Network has that scanning capacity yet," Han linked.

"Let's hope not," Li said as he leaned back and closed his eyes.

Villi informed them that the trip would take less than two hours. Since they flew back through multiple time zones, ordinarily they would go backward in time. However, they also crossed the International Dateline.

"Which means we'll arrive the night after we left," Michael noted.

"Yes, but at our current speed..." Han started to calculate.

"You forget we had to slowly increase our speed to reach Mach 10 and we'll have to slow down long before we land," Villi informed him. "At any rate, you can eat now or take a nap if you choose."

"I'm famished," Su Lin spoke up and rose from her seat.

"I'll help," Cecilia added and joined her friend in the galley.

After everyone ate some light breakfast, the team decided to rest, including stalwarts like Han, seeing as Master Li had sole control over the psychic bubble. Li did not fear entering a meditative state this time. He knew that Galactic Central had nothing planned for him since he checked with the director before embarking on this journey. Even Villi briefly napped until the aircraft came within sight of New Zealand, when he instructed the computer to wake him.

"Entering New Zealand airspace," he heard on waking.

"Apply reverse night vision on the cockpit window," he said when he noticed the local time in Adelaide.

Miraculously, the outside turned to daylight and appeared in natural color although the stars turned into black points in the blue sky. Villi saw everything below him as if he were landing during the day. After several minutes passed and he checked some local news channels to monitor for any "odd" occurrences that may have happened during their flight, he began his approach.

"Begin approach landing with flight vectors as we near the given coordinates," he linked with the computer's psychic interface. "Start air braking maneuvers. Put up destination and calculate altitude adjustments. Open wings for additional brakes and maneuvering when we drop below Mach 2."

"Acknowledged," the computer complied.

The exact location of James Pollack's residence came up on the screen, just outside of Adelaide. The computer then drew a line of descent through a three-dimensional map that showed the remaining flight path and estimated the time until touchdown.

Not long after that, Villi woke the team from their brief self-induced slumber, although Master Li simply changed over from his meditative state.

Han woke up the very second Master Li altered his status and the two men began to immediately discuss Cyrus' profile. Michael started his take-charge role and launched into a series of orders, more in the form of requests.

"Zhiwei, would you prepare a secure perimeter once we land?" Michael reminded. "Zinian, please review your checklist," he linked next. "We'll need that structure up first thing. Do you require assistance?" he asked. Zinian simply shook his head in reply and jerked a thumb toward Chou. "Su Lin do you have..." Michael began.

"I've decided to help Zinian complete set up," she linked to Michael. "I'm certain he and Chou packed a fusor in there. I'll be responsible for its setup."

"I'm helping her," Cecilia chimed in as the women exchanged glances.

Su Lin rose and went to Cecilia's side. The two young women erected a block around them that even Master Li found difficult to penetrate.

"Chou, you have some additional equipment..." Michael mentioned.

"I'm on it, after I help Zinian, Michael," Chou quickly replied.

"The team is ready, Master Li," Michael reported.

"I'd like everyone to spring into action once we are down and Zhiwei pronounces the perimeter safe," Li told them before he resumed his private interaction with Han.

The aircraft quickly streaked down through the atmosphere toward its destination. However, once he saw the topography of the ground around Pollack's property, Villi realized he would have to stop forward progress in the air and perform a vertical landing. The general surrounded part of his property's periphery with a "shrub" tree that resembled Italian Cypress in height and coverage. This helped him isolate the grounds of his estate from his neighbor's property.

"Seatbelts," Villi instinctively linked as he started to switch from main engines to maneuvering thrusters.

The craft's occupants could not feel the tremendous changes of force as Villi slowed their velocity from Mach 2 to zero in less than two minutes, thanks to his inertia dampeners. The wings gradually emerged from the sides of the great flyer when their speed dropped below Mach 2.

"Cut main forward velocity engines," he linked to the control panel. "Change over to thruster controls. Come to a dead stop at three hundred meters over final destination. Prepare for vertical landing."

"Computing changes," the computer complied.

Villi lowered the landing gear while the aircraft hovered in the air. He noticed the general's house off to his left as he slowly descended onto a desert-like space with sparse vegetation. The open area seemed especially convenient with its proximity to the house while hidden inside the rim of trees. Unfortunately, the thrusters agitated a large dust cloud around the descending aircraft. Despite a lack of invisibility, Villi gently set the craft on the ground and shut off all engines.

"External fans to dissipate excessive dust," he ordered as the fans inside the thrusters began to blow in several directions above the aircraft to clear the air. "We are on the ground, Master Li," Villi notified him. He kept the control panel activated in case Li wanted to maintain the aircraft's stealth system.

Zhiwei immediately scanned the surrounding houses and lots. He tried to sense if any neighbor saw the dust kicked up by the landing. He also checked for any animals, such as barking dogs alerted by the noise.

"Perimeter is safe," Zhiwei declared.

Master Li dropped the protective bubble around the aircraft, although Villi's stealth system kept them invisible to the naked eye.

"You can shut down your stealth system, Villi, as soon as Zhiwei sets up his perimeter system," Li ordered. "Michael?"

Li deferred the rest of the decisions or "orders" to Michael as team leader. Meanwhile, Michael sought out James and Penelope Pollack inside the house and notified them of the group's arrival.

"They're wide awake," Michael told them, "and expecting us. I believe we should start set up while a contingency group meet the general. Chou has offered to help Zinian unload and construct our new residence. Cecilia and Su Lin will help turn on a fusor. We'll need you to block the initial wave blast, Master Li, when it turns on for the first time. Zhiwei, I'd like you to set up your security devices as soon as you can. Villi will secure the aircraft and make it ready for immediate departure should the need arise. That's about it. Master Li?"

Master Li struggled to his feet while he addressed the group.

"I want any available members of the team to accompany me," Li suggested. "We should formally meet and introduce our group to Major General James Montgomery Pollack and his wife, Lady Penelope Fitzhugh Hawkins Pollack. Michael, I'd like you to especially come along."

"Yes, Master Li," he answered.

"Let's recharge," Li advised. "We don't know what awaits us or when we'll suddenly need to use psychic energy."

Master Li regained his physical stature when he pulled psychic energy from the Pollack's neighbors. The rest of the team followed his example.

"General," Zhiwei quickly linked when he noticed the general's hand going for a switch, "do not engage the flood lights to your property," he advised. "We have adequate light sources and do not wish to attract unwarranted attention. Master Li and some others in our delegation are on their way to greet you," he linked.

"Uh, thank you… Zhiwei, is it?" the general linked back.

"Yes, sir," Zhiwei answered, "and thank you for complying, sir."

The backdoor to the house opened and the elderly couple stood in their doorway to greet the group as Li and the others crossed the yard. The first thing that struck the general was the small and seemingly frail condition of the group's leader, Master Li. He could not imagine how such an insignificant person should possess such unlimited power and prestige.

As Master Li approached, the general bowed using a hand to signal his wife to do the same. Master Li smiled but immediately intervened.

"Tut, tut," Li said in response to their show of courtesy. "None of that," he told them. "We can dispense with treating me like some royal personage. I'm just one of the team," he continued. "May I present Michael Tyler," Li began. "Michael currently holds the position as head of the World Psychic Organization."

"Now this is a fellow I can respect!" the general thought when he regarded Michael's size and stature. He did not realize his thoughts echoed throughout the group.

Michael nearly blushed with humility when the general stepped forward to shake his hand. He nervously glanced over at Master Li who quickly hand signaled, "shake his hand." Michael shook the general's hand but did not admonish the general on psychic social etiquette or protocol. He assumed that Master Li or Han would assist the general later.

"This is our master strategist, Han Su Yeng," Li next introduced.

"Han," the general said and shook his hand.

James was anxious to find out what Han thought of Cyrus. However, before he could speak up, Li distracted him with further introductions in no particular order. He remotely linked the general with Zinian, Zhiwei, and Chou who were busy with equipment. He also introduced Cecilia and Su Lin as they unpacked the fusor.

"This is our pilot and head of transportation, Villi," Li finally said as the tall Russian walked over to them.

"My pleasure," the general said as he took Villi's hand and gave him the same appraisal he gave Michael about being a fine specimen of manliness. Villi beamed over at Michael who smiled and shook his head at his proud friend.

"I can't begin to tell you what an honor it is to finally meet you at last," the general said as he addressed the group, though his mind still broadcast doubts about "the little old man."

"The great Master Li!" Penelope suddenly declared. "We are so honored by your presence."

She rushed over to Master Li and uncharacteristically put her arms around him with a familial hug. Unlike the skeptical general, Penelope gushed over

Master Li. She did not know why, but she could not take her eyes off of him. The attention she lavished embarrassed Li somewhat. The citizen's of Rollo treated him with more respectful formality as a leader and less with celebrity status.

"Please, come in and sit down," she offered.

"Yes, Penelope made a fresh pot of tea," the general said aloud as a courtesy for his wife. "I sensed you coming."

At that moment, Han and Li exchanged glances.

James directed the group into the living room and after a series of pleasant verbal exchanges on Penelope's behalf, the group settled down to business. They opened their minds and quickly became acquainted with each other in short order. Master Li sensed Su Lin about to activate the fusor. He quickly placed a psychic bubble around the immediate area and prevented the initial blast from being detected by the local government.

The excited general peppered the group with several questions, each one answered with all expediency. He leaned to one side and looked out a side window in his home at the large sleek yet boxy aircraft the group traveled in to Australia. From his angle, he could not see Zinian's house going up.

"That is an aircraft?" he questioned.

"Yes sir," Villi replied.

"You left yesterday?" he continued.

"Two hours ago," Villi chimed in.

"Two? Must fly fast," the general commented as he continued to glance over Villi's shoulder at the aircraft.

"At our top speed, we cruised near Mach 10," Villi told him.

The general whistled and tried to keep his comments aloud for his wife's sake. The whole time they spoke, however, Penelope's head went back and forth as she followed them, for the general tried to implant the linked part of the conversation into her mind.

"Weapons?" he wondered.

"Forbidden by our charter," Villi calmly replied.

"Full of other gadgets from the future, no doubt… hush, hush… top secret stuff, eh?" the general quietly wondered.

Villi chuckled.

"…with a fine strapping lad at the controls, too," the general thought.

This time Villi laughed before he glanced over at Michael with his sober expression.

"You will find it difficult to withhold information in a psychic community," Michael pointed out to the general.

General Pollack smiled somewhat sheepishly at that, when he realized what Michael implied, that he had unintentionally broadcast some personal thoughts. He enjoyed having other psychics around to share his open feelings, though he barely knew enough about blocking to keep the flow of information on a formal level.

"I'm neglecting our guests!" Penelope suddenly spoke up and rushed to the kitchen.

She returned shortly thereafter with a pot of green tea, as the general indicated was Li's preference. She also offered the visitors some of her home baked cookies. Cecilia and Su Lin walked in at that moment, having finished their house assignment. Cecilia reached down and picked up a cookie from the plate as if she were famished.

"Mmm," Cecilia spoke up, "they're very good."

Su Lin made one float off the plate and over to her hands.

Penelope gasped when she saw that happen.

Su Lin started to apologize when James spoke up.

"She has very good control. Don't you agree, dear?" he put to his wife.

Penelope nodded her head up and down, but did not know what to say after that. In fact, hardly anyone spoke. Cecilia looked around at the silent group. The meeting seemed awkward as the youthful group and the older couple seemingly had little in common. The general made several attempts at small talk before the room fell into silence.

Only ten minutes after they arrived, Su Lin caught sight of Penelope stifling a yawn. At that moment, Chou openly reported to Michael that he and Zinian had completed the temporary quarters outside. Zhiwei also established holo-emitters around the perimeter along with other security devices to warn them of any immediate intruders.

"I believe it is time the team should retire to our residence," Li mentioned to his hosts.

"You have a place to stay?" the general asked.

"Our friends set up a… bivouac, I believe you call it," Han replied.

Zhiwei, Zinian, and Chou entered the general's living and formally met the general and his wife. However, the men sensed Penelope's fatigue as did the others in the room. Li hand signaled to Michael and the rest of the team that they should make a polite excuse to leave.

"You must excuse me, I'm rather tired from the trip," Michael said aloud.

"Oh?" Penelope replied and stood up as if on cue.

When she stood, the entire group rose out of respect. One by one, the team thanked Penelope and the general for their hospitality before the Rollo group exited the house. Rather than shake his hand, Master Li bowed to the general and his wife before he withdrew. Li strode from the house with this entourage in front of him. Outside, on the opposite end of the property, a tall structure stood next to the jet, larger than the general's residence, which now paled in comparison.

"Good heavens!" Michael exclaimed. "Where did that come from?"

"Those are our quarters," Zinian said and winked.

"How did you manage that?" Villi wondered as he and Michael were inside the general's house when Chou helped Zinian erect his wonder building.

"By compacting atoms and removing all foreign bodies between spaces, I could layer flat lattices that would expand into cylindrical shapes when activated by the interaction between..." Zinian started to rattle.

"Forget it!" the whole group responded.

Zinian shrugged and grinned as they crossed the open space to the narrow yet tall three-story building. The group stopped before the front door, which Zinian opened with his mind. He led them into an efficiently designed space, with white basic walls and a floor covered with something that resembled carpet underfoot. While the sidewalls had windows, they held no adornments or color. The windows had no curtains but did have some sort of clear substance that served the same purpose as glass. The living room and other rooms had furniture, though Zinian purposely colored them gray for contrast. He held up his hands to gain their attention and then cleared his throat before he linked.

"Chou and I tried to keep the design simple and basic, to fit everything into a small package that we could easily open, set up, and destroy if necessary," he explained as he gestured to a staircase along one wall. "The upper floors have five bedrooms complete with basic furniture, mattresses, and linen," Zinian pointed out. "The chairs and some of the movable furniture are slightly affixed to the floor. Just give it a swift pull to break the bonds at the bottom, but not too hard or you'll rip the chairs apart. Naturally, the married couples will share bedrooms. Unfortunately, each floor has only one bathroom, three in all. Sorry, but I had to squeeze them in as it was, with the plumbing being so difficult to flatten. We'll have to share those," he apologized. "Thanks to Su Lin and Cecilia, we've activated the fusor and used it to fill the water tanks. This floor has two bedrooms, one for Han and one for Master Li." He stepped further into the main room. "The downstairs bathroom is over there. The kitchen is behind me," he gestured, "complete with the aforementioned fusor. We had to box that separately, just as we have on other remote missions. We couldn't flatten that!" Zinian declared and laughed at his own joke, which no one else found amusing. "This area can be used as a meeting room, in case we need one," he said. "All the comforts of home away from home," he added.

"It's definitely... big," Michael stated as he looked around.

"Well, I like it!" Villi declared, amazed with the space.

"I think you did a great job, Zinian!" Han added.

"This is unbelievable," Zhiwei put in as he ran his hand down the wall.

"Nicely done, Zinian," Master Li said. "You and Chou did admirably well."

Zinian had transferred their luggage from the aircraft once the "house" expanded. However, he left the luggage in the hall upstairs, while he placed Master Li and Han's luggage in their bedrooms. The group fanned out to claim a bedroom and unpack their personal gear. Master Li headed toward the kitchen and gestured for Zhiwei to join him.

"Just a moment Zhiwei, I need your report," Li requested.

While the two men sat together at the kitchen table, they munched on some fusor created items. Zhiwei pulled out his special security black card and laid it down face up on the kitchen table. After the card expanded, a three-dimensional map of Adelaide appeared on the table between them with General Pollack's house as the center.

"The immediate area is clear of any people or animal life that could intrude into our privacy," Zhiwei gestured around the realistic layout. "The trees help to provide a natural wind break and assist with cover, though the holo-emitters will camouflage the structure and the aircraft. Fortunately for us, the general's family had enough money to purchase a large tract of land here. He lives at the end of a long private drive near the top of this hill. No neighbors have a direct sightline to this part of the property. I have perimeter-warning sensors planted should anyone approach by car or foot. If someone should fly directly in, the sensor on the top of the structure will give us about ten minutes warning at least."

"Very good, Zhiwei," Li told him.

Villi entered the kitchen and stood by the large window. He gazed out at the distant city of Adelaide and wondered about their target, as did Han, who entered the kitchen right after him, both men intended to prepare a light snack with the fusor.

Zhiwei touched the three-dimensional map with three fingers and the screen collapsed to credit card size before he slipped the black card into his shirt pocket. Master Li glanced over at Villi near the window. He sensed the young man troubled over their presence in Australia.

"Villi?" Li queried him.

"He's out there… isn't he," Villi quietly linked.

"Yes, Villi. Can you tell me about the aircraft," Li insisted.

"The aircraft is secure, Master Li," Villi linked in response to Li's request. "No problems with the superconducting drive on the trip over. The engines are in excellent shape and performed without a flaw. We have enough energy to fly around the world several times and back with a reserve. The computer indicates we left no atmospheric trace behind us, not even a wake. If NATO has a special satellite, it would need to read directly off our fuselage, which I find highly unlikely."

Zhiwei harrumphed as he walked out of the kitchen.

"Excellent," Li linked and thanked Villi for the safe flight.

However, Li sensed the same unease that Villi expressed in several team members. He linked to the entire group.

"I want everyone to employ blocking technique tonight," he instructed. "No shared dreams or shared thoughts except for close communication. I don't want Cyrus to know we've landed in his back yard. The last thing we want to do is tip him off to our presence or our numbers. Han is hoping that surprise will work in our favor," he informed them.

Han finished his snack and headed to his room where he unpacked his luggage minutes before.

"I'm going to retire," he linked over his shoulder to Li.

Upstairs, Michael unpacked their bags and put away their things while Cecilia finished her shower. He tried the bed and found it surprisingly comfortable though slightly cramped for his size. He kicked off his shoes, lay back on the bed, and stared up at the plain white ceiling. He closed his eyes and wondered if he could fall asleep.

"I wonder why Cecilia has been so... so standoffish lately," he pondered as he drifted off. "I swear I thought she was in pain when we headed to the hanger this morning..." Yet, he never questioned his wife later as she seemed bright and cheerful in private, even took his hand when they walked back from the general's house.

"Blast!" everyone heard on the second level. The shower automatically cut Cecilia off at two minutes. "Zinian!" Cecilia called out. "Turn this back on!" she yelled with her mind as shampoo bubbles dripped down her face.

This time the whole house laughed at Cecilia's predicament. However, Zinian had to remind her that everyone was limited in water use due to the tank size.

"You've two minutes more and that's it!" he told her and mentally reset the shower's timer.

No one could recall her ever moving as fast in the shower.

In his bedroom, Master Li poured over a scroll of ancient text that he brought along in one of his bags while he blocked out any interference around him. Once he sensed the group at rest, he put his scroll away and settled into the bed that Zinian made especially for him. Despite his attempts at rest this evening, problems plagued his mind. No matter how comforting the bed felt to his old bones, it was the presence of evil – so close and so intruding – that kept the elder psychic from falling into a deep or more restful sleep.

He decided he had to act on his fears. He reached across the universe in search of guidance and expertise. His ethereal body, which could defy the dimensions of time and space, appeared on Artane, looking for answers.

"Ah, Yuii... glad to see you are awake and unoccupied... I could use some advice."

CHAPTER THIRTY

AT ALL COSTS

THE FOLLOWING MORNING, THE GENERAL rose at his usual time of 5 a.m. along with Penelope. They followed their time-honored routine. She went to make coffee while he showered and dressed. They exchanged places in the bathroom while he set the table and she showered. After she dressed, the couple ate a light breakfast before they crept to the back door and peered across their side yard toward the large vacant area.

"Good lord! Will you look at that!" the general declared. He invited his wife to peek around the door.

"What? I don't see anything," Penelope said as she gazed at the empty spot.

"You mean to say, you don't see a huge monstrous building in our side yard?" he asked her. "Granted, a rather strange field surrounds the object…"

"Huge?" she questioned. "How big is huge?"

"Gargantuan," he replied as he moved back into the kitchen.

"Gargantuan?" she echoed. She tilted her head and squinted her eyes as if that would help.

"Chou is a man of his word. He informed me last night that he had devices which made Rollo invisible," James told her. "He must have portable ones that cover up their… my word, Penny, they put up an apartment house out there!"

"In our yard?" she questioned. Unable to picture anything, she closed the door and turned toward her husband. "Finish your coffee, dear," she indicated as she resumed her seat.

James chuckled over the absurdity of what he saw.

"I can only imagine that Han's description of the WPO headquarters in Rollo is understated," he said to her.

As James returned to his coffee on the kitchen table, Master Li's voice came to him.

"I know you can see us. Come to our dwelling, general," he requested. "Bring Penelope. Han and I must speak with you this morning."

"Up already?" James asked.

"This is actually the end of our day," Li relayed back. "We've had to make some adjustments. I've been awake for hours."

"Right," James replied. "Be there in a jiffy."

"What is it?" Penelope asked. She saw his face lose focus and knew he had some kind of internal conversation.

"Master Li invited us out to their building," he told her.

"Oh, good!" she declared. "I'm dying to see what a gargantuan looks like!"

The couple left the house and walked in the direction of the aircraft and crew quarters, both Penelope and the general felt intensely curious about what they would find. When the general arrived at the exterior edge of the field, he was afraid to step into the projection, although he could see the temporary structure on the other side. He held out his arm to stop Penelope.

"I'm not sure if we should go further..." he began.

"Simply step through, sir," he heard Zhiwei's voice. "I've programmed the security field to recognize you and Penelope, though she will not see the holo-field as you do. Once you pass the barrier, walk up to the front entrance. The door will open for you."

"Wait a minute," James cautioned.

He stepped through the field and disappeared. Penelope took in a sharp breath. It alarmed her even more when an arm stuck out of nowhere, grabbed her wrist, and pulled her through. At once, the sight of the building and the aircraft clearly became visible as if someone lifted a great veil to reveal a new object beneath. Penelope gasped when she stepped through the field and everything popped into view at once. She felt dizzy and grabbed James' arm for support.

"You were right... it's unbelievable," she said as she swallowed hard while she cautiously moved closer. "That's no illusion. It looks solid."

She did not know which way to look. Her head turned back and forth as she looked over at the strange aircraft and back to building while they walked nearer to the building. Finally, the couple arrived at the front door and it magically opened for them. Stepping inside, they could not believe the size of the interior structure. Penelope ran her hand over the walls to feel the texture of the material.

"This is amazing stuff," she said. "Every being on earth would have shelter... a place to call home," she unselfishly thought.

"Unfortunately," Li interrupted her thoughts, "that is not possible. We cannot share this technology with humanity due to the dangers we discussed with your husband," Li reminded Penelope.

"Yes, I recall," the general relented, "introduce a high level of technology too quickly and it will eventually lead to self-destructive tendencies... pity," he thought.

The general and Penelope walked through the center of the house to the kitchen where Li, Han, Michael, and Zhiwei sat at the kitchen table. Chou brought out some kind of device – a long black rod that he bent in five places. He attached the free end to form a frame which he placed on the table. He placed a small black cube at one corner of the frame. Finally, he reached into his pocket and pulled out a remote control. The moment he turned the device on, a three-dimensional rendition of the planet Earth with amazing detail appeared to float before them over the frame. The realism impressed everyone.

"Wow!" Michael declared. "I've never seen that!"

"It's so real," Zhiwei added.

Even Han seemed impressed with the new device Chou introduced to them. The group could see clouds in motion as the planet slowly rotated. The detail and minutia were beyond any previous projection Chou created. James bravely stepped forward, pushed his hand into the Pacific Ocean, and pulled it back out, as he expected it to be wet.

"That is the most realistic projection I've ever seen," he said.

"Thank you," Chou said, almost blushing from the accolades.

He moved around the globe and stood next to the general.

"You had the right idea, just not the right motion. May I?" he asked and the general moved back.

Using his hands, Chou reached into the image and pulled the continent of Australia out, so that the globe shifted and brought the single country up to eye level, wrapped in three dimensions the image followed the curvature of the planet, though less noticeable at this magnification. Chou made the outline of a box in the air with his fingers around a part of the landmass. Again, he reached in and pulled this area into a larger view so that the image zoomed inward. The detailed map of Adelaide that followed startled the general. They could see ships in the bay, cars that moved on streets, and aircraft taking off from the local airport.

"This is in real time?" the general questioned.

"No," Chou told him in a link. "We don't have that capacity... yet," he added as he glanced over at his friends. "This is an extrapolation which the computer compiled from data and put together based on a series of satellite photographs and time schedules it obtained from local computers. To see this in real time from space, we would need to launch our own satellites, which we have planned at a later date. Still, I can give you a very close approximation of the terrain in any location and represent it here as a tangible three-dimensional image."

"What our mobile division could do with this," James uttered.

"Can you pinpoint the area where you believe Cyrus has his army," Li asked.

James mimicked Chou's motions. First he pushed the image back away from Adelaide, moved the map, and then enlarged an area of Western Australia. He drew a circle in the air, which stayed for a minute before it began to fade.

"Somewhere in this region I imagine, judging from the note," James told them, "which I...well, I'm sorry to say that I..."

"...destroyed," Han finished. "The note no longer matters, James," Han reassured him. "We have its exact contents from the memory in your mind."

"You are a clever bunch," James replied.

Han studied the general for a moment. Being this close and the general not yet trained in completely blocking his thoughts, Han could search the general's military information. Finally, after nearly a minute in uncomfortable silence, Han turned away and took on an introspective facial affect as he stared unfocused at nothing. Everyone watched as Han calculated their mission.

"What's our approach?" Li finally asked him.

James started to offer his expertise when he noticed the room's attention shifted to Han.

"This Cyrus is a clever man," Han pointed out. He pulled a laser pointer from his pocket, which he clipped to the end of his finger. "After studying the terrain and the movements of the Australian Army along with its Air Force, I can safely conclude I have his whereabouts within a few kilometers," Han told them.

"That's amazing!" the general uttered.

"The terrain in this part of the desert has a few washouts, small valleys created many thousands of years ago when the western part of the continent held more moisture than it does today. He's probably in one of three areas. The first one is probably too close, so he'll choose the second further to the west. This particular valley represents an ideal area just outside the Air Force routine fly zone," Han pointed out.

"That's top secret!" the general declared.

"Not any longer," Zhiwei broke in, "and if Han knows it, you can bet Cyrus knows it, too," he informed the general.

"Did I give that information away to Cyrus?" he question.

"I don't think so," Han continued. "He probably obtained that information long before he encountered your thoughts. Remember, he didn't know you existed until recently. I would say he entered one of your military bases and bypassed its security. In his clumsiness, he may have injured some of your sentries. Check local infirmaries for any unexplained brain injury admissions in the past month. Also, if you have any missing equipment or supplies you can bet Cyrus had something to do with it. Now, if you will please allow me to continue," he said as he moved back to the floating image. "Notice how these natural formations protect his west and east flanks," he said as he moved a red arrow around. "More than likely, he would place a large contingent of men on the south end because he would know the flatness of the terrain lent itself to barracks, and a possible area to place drainage ditches, I believe called latrines. With this hilly terrain, we cannot easily approach from the north without being spotted when we crest these hills. That leaves the southeast, the most likely route of approach for staging our operation," he indicated. "If we try to create a diversion here (he pointed to the north), he'll anticipate that move and spring the trap he probably has here (he pointed to the southeast), as he realizes this is his one weak spot, so he's certain to have fortified his forces here," Han said as he showed them an area along the only visible clear path to the valley.

"How do you know this?" James questioned.

James felt the attention in the room shift to him, although he still stared at Han. The twenty-eight-year-old Chinese man half-smiled in response to James' question. Michael stepped up to explain.

"Han studies our targets extensively, James," Michael explained. "He has degrees in psychology, mathematics, physics, and statistical probability. Without boasting over my friend's accomplishments, Han is probably the greatest living expert in strategy. He knows more about Cyrus than the people closest to him," Michael stated. "If he believes that Cyrus has placed a trap here," Michael pointed, "then he is probably correct. Han?"

"If you will allow me, sir," Han requested.

James seemed a little embarrassed. His proud posture shrank when he realized that his years of military prowess did not apply in areas such as this. He shrugged and gestured toward Han.

"Please continue," he linked.

"Don't feel as if your experience isn't needed, general," Han pointed out, sensing the general's injured pride. "It is. However in this instance, the addition of having a rogue psychic at the core of this incident is presently outside your realm. However, you were right to question, general," Han told him.

"Thank you, Han," the general quietly replied. Penelope moved in closer to him.

"Let me help you see our course of action," Han addressed him. "Stealth will account for some of our initial success in mounting an offensive, as well as surprise in our approach," he pointed out. "However, we will need air support as well as a ground force to take out motion sensors that he probably placed here, here, and here," Han gestured. "I would suspect Cyrus also placed rotating sentries here and here," he pointed, "as well as land mines here, here, here and here," he continued to indicate places on the floating map. "In addition to being a classic paranoid, he is quite ruthless and has no qualms over killing innocent victims should they stray over his traps. We need to deactivate those landmines no matter what happens," he said as he glanced over at Li.

Master Li made a quick silent link. When the general saw this, he realized that the psychic team operated on a level beyond any he had ever considered possible. He knew that their level of communication and understanding surpassed anything ordinary people could comprehend. He listened carefully as Han continued to describe their strategy while Penelope supportively clung to his side.

"He'll have his own tent on the north side with an elite guard surrounding this position since he considers himself a distinct individual and in an elevated status above those around him," Han pointed out as he described Cyrus' psychological profile. "Though he rules by fear, he is still fearful of attack. I would say, taking his paranoia into account, his mind is also a mixture of schizophrenia with wild mood swings, possibly bi-polar. He also suffers from severe sociopathology. To instill a high level of fear in his men, he has probably sacrificed half a dozen soldiers as examples. He can't afford any more than that. Remember, his magic number is 200, which he needs to achieve his energy goal. Hence, he probably took slightly more than that number with him into the desert, knowing he would make sacrifices. While he suffers from mental illness, he is far from being an imbecile. He knows that his plan requires a certain level of psychic energy... and he calculated that 200 is the number which will precisely allow his plan to happen."

When Han stated the last part, even Michael seemed puzzled.

"Excuse me," Michael spoke up. "Has something been decided here I am not privy to?"

"Yeah," Zhiwei spoke up, "I don't get it. What level of psychic energy?"

"Sorry, gentlemen," Master Li broke in. "Han privately conferred with me last night and we worked out some figures. Han?"

Han pushed back the image on the globe until the entire planet was visible again.

"Computer," Han addressed the globe's controller, "insert the current orbit of the International Space Station, compute its probable location," he requested.

An object appeared as a flashing yellow dot.

"Enlarge object to three times its current relational size to the planet," Han ordered.

The floating dot enlarged into a tiny model of the International Space Station. It slowly moved across the African continent and headed for the Indian Ocean.

"Hypothetical," Han said aloud. "Place current position directly overhead relative to the surface and rotate the planet until the space station is at 238 degrees latitude, 14 degrees longitude with 22 degrees of Zenith," Han said. "Use a light ray source from this ground point," he added and touched his finger on a point west of Warburton.

"What good will that do?" Villi asked.

As the planet began to rotate and the space station changed its position in orbit, the turned angle caught the ray of energy from the surface and made a visible beam of light that reflected off at an angle away from the globe into space. The men and women gathered around the globe suddenly hissed in response to what they saw. They knew that Han discovered the secret to how Cyrus would move the asteroid.

"So that's how he's going to do it," Cecilia said as she watched from across the room. "He's going to bounce psychic energy off the solar panels of the space station. The power in those panels will amplify the signal."

"Brilliant, I'd say," Su Lin added when she joined the gathering.

"More like diabolical," James put in. "Ok, so he's using the solar panels on the space station to bounce and boost his signal. But why does he need 200 men?"

Master Li stood up and walked over to the globe next to Han.

"First, we went to Galactic Central with our hypothetical," he explained. "No one had an answer. They directed me to Artane. I personally spoke with Yuii last night. We poured over study after study related to sending psychic energy through space. It seems our Cyrus is a natural when it comes to calculating the amount of energy required to boost his signal."

"Or someone is," Han interrupted.

Master Li nodded and acknowledged Han.

"Or someone is," he corrected. "With 200 men in a tight formation around him, he can simultaneously drain the energy from his men and focus a beam on the mirrored surface of the space station's solar arrays. Using the energy in the solar array to help boost his signal, the panels will amplify the beam with enough intensity to project a narrow hole through space. The burst is powerful enough to nudge the asteroid by 0.00038 degrees. Han and I are not certain of the exact time, but we assume he must perform this maneuver within the next thirty-six hours. That window of opportunity is rapidly closing. The result will slightly alter the asteroid's path and speed. This will place the asteroid into a closer orbit with Earth so that the combination of the sun, earth and the moon's gravitational pulls will change its trajectory into a precise collision course with the planet."

Master Li and Han exchanged looks. The older psychic nodded his head to the younger one as if he acknowledged some debate that took place earlier. Master Li went on to address the gathering.

As to the precise calculation," he continued. "Han figures he could not do this on his own. He must have discovered the presence of the asteroid and then located an expert who made the calculation for him," Li explained.

Satisfied with Li's explanation, Han put his pointer away. He glanced over at Li. Master Li hand signaled Han to relate the final fact.

"Last night," Han informed them. "Master Li decided to enter Cyrus' mind in his sleep. He avoided any intrusion into his dreams and made a quick scan of his thoughts. Master Li withdrew after he scanned his mind for less than a few seconds. We don't believe Cyrus detected the mind tap. Otherwise, he would have instantly blocked Master Li if he tried an attack while Cyrus was awake."

"Way to go Master Li!" Villi stated.

"If you thought the first part of his plan was diabolical," Han continued, "the next part is even more extraordinary," he told them. "He plans to alert the local astronomy society on the location of the asteroid. Once they make the calculations, the news will spread and the world will go into a panic. On its altered trajectory, the asteroid should impact the ocean between China and Japan. The result may probably destroy most of Japan, South Korea, and the eastern seaboard of China, including Beijing, although its capital is relatively far enough inland to escape total destruction. In reality, he doesn't really want the government to completely collapse. Instead, he secretly plans to abandon his temporary army, travel to China, and convince their Defense Department to fire a nuclear bomb at the asteroid in an attempt to destroy it. The United States will object to this approach, of course. Despite their protest, they will be unable to stop the Chinese, as Cyrus figures, because China will have the backing of South Korea and Japan. However, instead of firing on the asteroid, Cyrus intends to divert the nuke to fall on America and start World War III. Before America can properly retaliate, the asteroid would hit and destroy much of China's defensive systems," Han told them. "Then, believe it or not, he plans to take over and control whatever remains… this is what he thinks…"

"... he thinks that he is only one of three such psychic men in the world," Li finished.

At that moment, Master Li spread the vision of what would really happen: a powerful nuclear weapon igniting over America and the asteroid striking the planet shortly afterward, which causes mass destruction on both sides of the planet. As the room watched with horror, Master Li forced the computer to project the devastation onto the globe exactly as Cyrus envisioned it.

"This madman must be stopped at all costs," the general whispered as he felt Penelope tightly squeeze his hand.

"Yes, sir ...at all costs," Han echoed.

CHAPTER THIRTY-ONE

BLINDSIDED

SALLY FINLEY WALKED UP THE busy hallway with a stack of papers in her hand. As she passed a window, the outside called to her, as a siren calls to a sailor, the song impossible to ignore. She noticed that the overcast morning's cloud-cover had lifted and left a clear blue sky overhead. By the time she arrived back at her desk, she pulled up the weather report on her computer screen – a balmy 27.7 C degrees (eighty-two degrees Fahrenheit) outside with a moderate dew point – a perfect day.

"It's much too nice to eat inside," she thought. She picked up the phone and called her friend, Miriam, who worked on the other side of the building.

Sally and Miriam met during their orientation day eight years ago and remained friends since that time. When these two clerks from the Brisbane Government Office Building took their lunch together, weather permitting, they usually went to the park across the street. Both loved the warm fresh air and the break from the stuffy offices they occupied year round. When the Australian summer returned, the two friends could not wait to resume their outside excursions. Sally Finley called her friend, Miriam, to convince her that the park would be perfect for today's lunch.

"Look out the window," Sally said to her friend, "the vendor's are out today... fresh sandwiches. I can hardly wait!"

"I get the picture," Miriam said. "It's 11:43," she said as she glanced up at the clock. "I'll meet you by the elevator in ten minutes. Remember not to punch and we can take longer than 30 minutes," she giggled.

The two women met up at the elevator as agreed, eager to exit the building and make their way over to the large centrally located park area, with its trees, a large fountain, also plenty of benches and tables for city workers to take their noon breaks. On nice days like this, the park bustled with workers on break, street musicians, mothers downtown shopping with their pre-school children, and tourists milling about. Office buildings and shops surrounded the park on three sides, with the government building in the middle at one end. The street vendors hawked their wares, flavorful smoke rose from their grills, which spread fresh smells of cooked fish, burgers, or even sausages. Some vendors carried a variety of cold beverages, salads, fresh fruit, ice cream, chips, and other treats, too.

The two women hustled to stand in the queue of their favorite stand. They adored the brash young man with long blonde hair that liked to flirt as he sold bratwurst sausages, hamburgers, shrimp, and other grilled delights.

As the clock ticked down to twelve noon, the two women talked in line while they waited their turn to order. The sizzle, smoke, and smell of the grill were just a few feet away and beckoned.

"...and demanded extra hours without scale! Can you imagine?" Miriam said as she shook her head.

"I can't believe your boss sent out a memo like that right before the holidays. Who does he think he is?" Sally replied to her friend as they shared office gossip.

"At least I don't' work in the D.A.'s office," Miriam said. "I heard from Mary Winters that..."

From the distance, the municipal whistle blew, which signaled to all present that the official time of twelve o'clock arrived. In that instant, a terrible fate descended on the lovely serene setting.

"BOOM!"

A gigantic explosion ripped through the peaceful park. Pieces of flying debris, concrete, steel, and glass, shot through the woman's soft flesh, and tore them into pieces. What would be left of the two friends, or anyone else in the park, would be unrecognizable to their relatives, since they were in such close proximity to ground zero.

The Brisbane government office building blew into smithereens. The blast rocked the entire downtown with earth-shaking magnitude and sent out an enormous shockwave that destroyed everything in its wake! Great chunks of the government office building turned into lethal projectiles that flew outward in a thousand directions. Chunks of concrete, steel, and glass rained death and destruction on the people in the square. Screams of pain and anguish cried out as the explosion tossed torn, bleeding bodies flailing through the air. Pieces of their soft flesh landed everywhere amidst the rubble. Over a thousand employees inside the GOB instantly met their fate. In just a few seconds, what had once been a building of twenty stories turned into a heap of twisted steel and smoldering chunks of debris.

Sally and Miriam never knew what hit them. In less than a second, their world ended as this despicable terrorist act added their lives to a statistic of history. The casualty figures from this day would be the highest ever recorded for a single terrorist event in Australia.

Within minutes of deciphering what happened, news organizations turned their cameras on the gruesome scene while talking heads spewed as many facts as they could find or speculate. Television news quickly spread around the world with its electronic eyes coldly scanning the scene to fulfill some ghastly audience fascination with the morbid.

"Perhaps as many as two or three thousand are presumed dead when the Brisbane Government Office Building exploded at noon today," the television announcer broke into television broadcasts across Australia. "It is presumed that a bomb destroyed the building, located right in the heart of the city, making it ground zero. The blast leveled the twenty-story structure to the ground in seconds," the news anchor on the television said. "Fire has spread to other nearby buildings. Debris has blocked access by the Fire Department. The blast tore through the city center park, crowded with midday shoppers. We are not certain at this moment what caused the explosion. Government officials informed news organizations that despite the size and intensity of the blast, a nuclear device did not cause the explosion. In Canberra, the Prime Minister called for a state of emergency. All military forces are on alert..."

The temporary house in the general's side yard buzzed with conversation that morning, once Master Li dismissed the early meeting to enjoy breakfast with their hosts. James and Penelope eagerly added their voices to the youthful Rollo group around the kitchen table, intrigued by their keen intellect, exuberance, and unending vitality. Master Li rubbed his hands together and smiled.

"Let's have a hearty breakfast to start this day," he said as he signaled to the men and women standing around.

"James and I have had our breakfast," Penelope spoke up. She did not wish to put out anyone having to cook. "Besides, the table isn't large enough," she thought as she glanced about the room at the nine psychics plus the two of them, "...and you've no stove! How will you cook a meal?"

"If you'll allow us," Zinian said as he walked up to the table.

When he stood at one end, the other psychics backed away. Following their lead, the general and Penelope complied, too. Chou grabbed the other end. The two men literally pulled the tabletop further apart and added an additional two meters in length.

"Oh... that's handy," Penelope observed and then mentally quipped, "Does it come in colors?"

Zinian smiled, went to a panel in the wall, and brought out what resembled a flat stick. In a series of quick moves, it turned into a chair. He touched a pad on the side and the seat cushion inflated. He proceeded to add more chairs until each person had a seat. Everything the psychics did left Penelope in awe of them.

"I could make a fortune marketing those things," she thought, when James put his hand on her arm and shook his head.

"They can hear what you are thinking," he cautioned.

"Well, not being psychic, I'm going to have a difficult time keeping my opinions private, dear," she told him.

"Don't worry, Penelope," Cecilia spoke up. "We're an open society. We like to hear what other people think. Don't hold back on our account."

Meanwhile, Su Lin stepped up to the fusor. More than any of the Rollo psychics, she had the most experience using the fusor as a food producer. She and Villi often threw parties and invited their friends as guests to their soirée. After all, when she lived in China, Su Lin not only studied education, she studied the culinary arts and intended one day to open a restaurant as well as work a teaching position. She used the fusor more extensively than anyone did in Rollo with only Running Elk being the exception.

"Full pie pan of Quiche Lorraine," she started to list.

"Oh, I love quiche," Penelope cut in. "What is that, a microwave oven?" As Penelope watched, she saw a completely baked item materialize out of the air onto a preparation staging area inside the fusor. "What the devil?" she questioned. She stood up, moved over to the fusor, and started to reach inside.

Su Lin grabbed her hand.

"Unless you want the atoms in your hand scrambled, I would not recommend anyone reach into a fusor's atomic stasis field," she advised. "The internal mechanism will push the item out to you," she indicated.

As Penelope watched, the quiche slid out from the front of the fusor, piping hot, and in a perfectly baked condition. Skeptical, she touched the pie and smelled it at the same time.

"Seems like the genuine article," she noted. "James? Have you seen one of these?"

"No," he said as he came over and stood next to her. "How does it work?" he asked.

"I only know the simple version," Su Lin explained, "this takes the atoms of one substance – in this case we have a funnel with a variety of granules in a feed shoot – and breaks them down into basic elements such as oxygen, hydrogen, carbon, nitrogen, and so on. Then it rearranges those atoms into specific molecules and rapidly compiles them until it builds a lattice of that substance, only it does so at extremely rapid rates of speed. It can duplicate the exact molecules of any substance."

"Any substance, as in any living thing, such as duplicating one of us?" the general's wife conjectured. She turned to others in the room as she sought an answer on their faces. Chou stepped forward.

"Not exactly," he cut in. "I invented the Earth's version of the fusor to make building materials initially. A device called a reader, allows the fusor to duplicate anything made of cellular DNA. They can also create some electronic devices, if I have the proper code. While we generally re-create animal flesh and living plants for meals, the idea was not to replicate people," Chou told them. He glanced over at Master Li. "That's part of our ethical code of behavior found in our charter and why we have each new candidate sign the Psychic Pledge," he told her. "Introducing alien technology among ordinary people could result in disastrous consequences."

Penelope leaned over and stared intently inside the black box. This portable version was Chou's latest – smaller, more compact, easy to set up and break down.

"So you are not creating goose-stepping armies tucked away in some warehouse waiting for the right time to strike?" she wondered aloud and glanced about the room.

For a second, activity in the kitchen came to screeching halt. Even Master Li stared at the aging woman until they all read the sarcasm in her mind and burst out laughing when they realized she made a joke.

"You'll fit right in with this crowd," Cecilia quipped as she gave her a hug.

Penelope nodded back and took her seat next to the general.

Su Lin resumed her magic with the fusor. She made pots of fresh-brewed coffee and tea, followed by fresh-squeezed orange juice, pancakes, frosted sweet rolls, glazed cake donuts, pitchers of maple syrup, freshly churned butter, fried eggs, scrambled eggs, rice cakes, smoked fish, steamed vegetables, fresh tomato slices, buttermilk biscuits, cheese omelets, fruit and cheese-filled crepes suzette, raw whole milk, raw cream, raw sugar, organic orange blossom honey, a variety of fresh fruit, apple-wood smoked bacon, and thick fried link sausages.

Penelope saw the tremendous amount of food spread out on the table. While everyone feasted on what he or she wanted, Penelope merely sipped a cup of tea and munched on a piece of toast sweetened with a drizzle of honey.

"All this food going to waste," she thought, "when the world has so many mouths to feed. This machine could end world hunger," she thought as she watched the young people stuff their faces while they discussed various aspects of Australian life with James. Only one person in the room heard her thoughts.

"They do what?" Villi wondered at the general's comment.

"... they run toward these tall goal posts," James said as he described Australian rugby, "*if* they don't get tackled on the way, and..."

"We can't do that, Penelope," Master Li interrupted.

"What's that?" James said. He stopped speaking as he turned toward his wife.

"She wants to use the fusor to end world hunger," Li explained. "I told her, we could not do that. We cannot share any of our technology with them..." Li said and indicated the outside. "Didn't you understand that principle? They won't use the fusor to end hunger," he tried to further explain.

"They won't?" she questioned. Her eyes rose up from staring at the mounds of food on the table and met his. "Why not? Why can't we help the poorest people of Africa or Asia or South America with this device?"

Li rose from his seat and crossed the room. A saddening silence fell over the joyful conversation as Li pressed home his point to the wife of the newest WPO member. While James readily understood the concept, Penelope still could not grasp its simplicity.

"My dear, Penny," Li began as he moved into the seat next her just vacated by Cecilia. "The leaders of Africa, Asia, or whatever impoverish nation you chose, no matter how many of their people died of starvation, would not use the fusor for food."

"They wouldn't?" she stared at Li with wide eyes.

"Unfortunately, no," Li spoke quietly. "They would create weapons, terrible weapons in a lust for power, weapons that would challenge the established powers in Europe, America, Russia, and China," Li said. He made a gesture in the air and showed a private visual that appeared in her mind at the same time. "A great war would break out. Soon either the Russians or the Chinese would steal the fusor technology," Li voice rose dramatically. "They would make more powerful weapons than the Africans did. When the American spy network managed to steal the technology – and who would stop them – they would create armies of men, and weapons that strike down from space. The grab for power would escalate, until mankind strangled itself around the neck..." Li's voice faded until he spoke quietly. "...and all because someone had the good intentions of using this device for the benefit of mankind in a world full of corruptible people."

Master Li's words brought tears to Penelope eyes when Li swiftly and gently reached around her shoulders. He patted her back and held her as James looked on with sympathy. Li knew he had to impress on her the seriousness of the WPO's commitment to its principles.

"Penelope, the fusor is not the only technology we have that is marvelous," Li continued. "When you come to Rollo, you will see many wonderful things. However, technology is not the answer to the world's problems, and we are not here to rely on such devices to resolve our problems. We have personally come from half-way around the globe to stop a madman from destroying others," he spoke aloud. "The time for action is at hand," Li said.

Master Li reached out and absorbed power. James felt his power surge and spread through the room. Even Penelope sensed a great change come over the seemingly frail old man. He seemed to grow in stature.

"Su Lin, clear the table," he ordered. "Zhiwei, monitor our current security status and clear us for take-off. Han prepare our plan of attack and brief the general. Be certain our maps are current. Cecilia, stand by with your remedies and injury repair kits in case we go into battle. Chou, prepare your special transportation devices. Zinian, you help him. Villi, prepare the aircraft for liftoff at a moment's notice. Michael, coordinate the entire effort, check with each member on their preparedness, and then go over our equipment status. We leave at noon for the desert with General Pollack," Li instructed. He stood up next to Penelope.

Penelope gazed up into Master Li's eyes. At that moment, even a non-psychic person understood the power and command he had over everyone.

"I'm rather naïve I suppose. I thought I could end world hunger," she said as she wiped a tear from her eye. "I'm just a silly old…"

"Nothing of the kind," Li said and dismissed her self-effacing comment. "We all want to end world hunger, poverty, disease, graft, avarice, ignorance… the list goes on and on. We will do what we can to eradicate those things over time, Pen," Li said softly to her, "in our own quiet and unobtrusive way. Meanwhile, James needs to dress for combat and make ready for our assault. I would like you to help him prepare. Can you do that for us?"

Penelope brightened and stood up, ready to do her part. She actually stood taller than Master Li.

"He'll be packed and ready by noon," she promised as she held out her hand and Master Li shook it. "I want to be a good member of the WPO," she said to him. "I'm a proud member of every club I ever joined," she told him, standing tall. She saluted Li.

Master Li smiled and returned her salute. Penelope headed over to her husband. He gulped down the last of his coffee. She glanced over at Su Lin just as the young woman made everything fly off the table and squeeze back down into the back of the fusor that seemed to instantly gobble every particle right up. The "sand" pile above the fusor (its fine grains actually made up of a variety of inorganic substances, such as ordinary sand, chalk, shale and coal) grew in size.

224

"You mean…" Penelope started, when Su Lin broke in on her thought.

"We may produce a variety of materials in abundance from the fusor, but nothing is ever wasted. We recycle everything," Su Lin said as she squeezed the last bit of their huge breakfast feast into the open recycle chute, where it promptly converted back into the easily-transportable compact tiny granules. "Every atom returns to its dormant state until needed."

"But what about the food we ate…"

"That food is quite real and is being digested by the body as we speak," Su Lin finished. "In fact, the food is quite pure, based on DNA samples taken from a variety of wild or organic samples without any bacteria, viruses, parasites, processing chemicals, pesticides, or preservatives," she added, "wholesome and natural, as nature originally intended, only in this case, we bypassed the growing process." Su Lin smiled as she mentally lifted and dumped a pitcher of milk into the fusor's back. "Villi, Han, Chou, and Michael traveled all over the world and collected thousands of samples. We can make practically any dish or substance including some formulas that humankind will never know."

"I have much to learn I see," Penelope realized. James waved at her to follow him back to the house. As they walked away, the couple talked over what they had seen.

"Amazing…" she sighed.

"I'm grateful you finally understand, Pen," he said as he placed his arm around her shoulder while they walked.

Over the hours that followed, the Rollo team and the general scrambled to make their preparations. Penelope brought the general's gear to the back step while he changed into his uniform. Zhiwei brought out a number of security devices. Cecilia went over a list of supplies she brought. Su Lin made survival rations for the desert in case they were needed.

Zinian assisted Chou with a new hover device that he created for the desert. The two men had stored them in the aircraft's cargo hold prior to takeoff. They, and not the inflatable house, added the "bulk" due to their drive mechanisms. More than any item, these "skimmers" added most of the extra weight which the flight computer had to compensate. Han formulated and refined his plans, while Villi went over the aircraft and decided how sand might affect the air intake ports which could affect certain moving parts inside the superconductors. Under Chou's advisement, he installed filters over the air intakes and tested their efficiency with the computer. Michael checked on everyone's progress, to see if he or she needed assistance, and how soon they would be ready.

Master Li sat in the middle of the living room and calmly read over the scroll he studied last night. He did not wish to disturb anyone during his or her preparations. Han sat at the kitchen table reviewing strategy maps while Master Li carefully read the rune-like hieroglyphics. Suddenly he stopped, gasped in some air, and clutched his chest as if he were in the middle of a heart attack. A terrible feeling passed through them. Li nearly fell over onto the floor. The others in the house felt it, too.

"Han!" Master Li cried out. "What time is it?"

"Twelve noon," Han replied as he walked out the kitchen. "Would you mind telling me what the hell that was?"

"James!" Penelope's voice shrieked from an open window.

Upon hearing her voice, Master Li sprinted out of the temporary house and ran across the yard for the back door of the general's house. The other psychics sensed the urgency and followed. Running up on his right flank, Li sensed Villi running faster. He also felt Michael and the others on his heels. Zhiwei came out of nowhere on his left. All of three of them reached the door at the same time with Master Li in the lead. Just as Li's mind touched the doorknob to open it, a great thundering rumble shook the ground around them. The group stopped and turned around. In that moment, they could see a great wave of energy pass through the ground.

"What is going on?" Han wondered from the back of the group.

"Something terrible just happened, I fear," Master Li said.

Their minds instinctively linked as one. Master Li mustered his strength and sent out his ethereal body over the countryside. He flew across Australia toward the location of the misery they felt. Coming up over a rise, they witnessed smoke rising from the center of a large Australian city. Li moved closer and zoomed down into the heart of the city. To their horror, they witnessed first-hand the events that took place in Brisbane only seconds ago. When Master Li came across a baby carriage toppled over in the rubble, Cecilia begged him to stop the flow of shocking images.

"Master Li," she whispered to his mind, "please... withdraw... I can't take this."

The flow of images stopped. The group glanced around at each other while they regained their vision. Master Li shook with anger as he tried to reach out with his hand and open the door. He struggled to grasp the doorknob. This incident clearly un-nerved the great man.

"Silly damn thing," he spoke aloud, unable to muster the energy in his hand.

"Allow me, sir," Michael said as he reached around and turned the knob.

"I'm sorry, group," Li apologized at once. "I must be growing feeble!"

Before anyone could protest, Li pushed the door open with his mind and swiftly moved into the couple's living room, followed by the others. They discovered Penelope sitting before the television. She had on a live broadcast from Brisbane. The station quickly switched over to an anchor in the studio trying to address the public and the news team coordinated the spontaneous broadcast. A "live" reporter in the field – in the park at the time to present an on air weather segment – was a friend of the anchor and presumably dead. The anchor struggled to speak as the shaky images from the scene began to filter in. Penelope had the same reaction to the tragedy.

"I can't believe it," she said, deeply moved as the television showed the images of downtown Brisbane on fire. Tears slid down her cheeks. She had many friends in Brisbane.

The first ghastly images from the scene started coming in. She could not take the sound of the description and turned it down. The psychic group watched in silence as Penelope buried her head in her hands and wept. The live image went to the corner of the screen and a man's head filled the center portion. Penelope glanced up when she saw the new image.

"The prime minister," she whispered, as she sensed the others gather around. She turned up the sound.

"…declaring a national state of emergency…" he droned on while he read from a prepared text. "…full military alert…"

"Is it war?" James wondered as he hurried to her side. He partially sensed what Penelope saw when he reached out to her mind. Seeing Penelope in such an emotional state, he sat beside her and placed his arm around her as the Prime Minister droned on about what the government would do next.

"Not war," Han's voice cut in as he linked with everyone including Penelope. They turned to look his way. "It's him," he told them. "Cyrus is behind this. He doesn't want the military coming into the desert. He's starting his assault on humanity today, this minute. This was the smart thing to do. He wants to spread chaos, divide forces, and divert attention away from his activities. He's taking the battle to us, I'm afraid," he pointed out. "He's struck the first blow."

"Oh, my," General Pollack said as he realized the truth of Han's words. "This is my fault," he said, resigned. "I waited too long to act. I should have confronted the blighter a week ago…"

"Had you gone out to his campground, unprepared, on your own," Li explained, "Cyrus could easily have eliminated you as a threat, general. You were right to wait for our arrival."

"You could not have stopped this," Han further explained. "Cyrus planned this attack weeks ago as part of his overall strategy, only somehow we missed it," he said instead of blaming Li. "He not only robbed one of your bases of basic military equipment, he took weapons, too… very powerful ones from the devastation. When the investigators finish, they will find the latest weaponry at the heart of this massive explosion."

"Small wonder General Sanders tried to cover it up," General Pollack muttered.

Han shook his head and continued. "Cyrus sent a trained demolition team to Brisbane. They must have worked on the building during the night. They set charges in places that were intended to do the most damage, to blow the building outward into the square," Han pointed out. "However, that is not the worst news. This is only the first shot fired. I have no doubt they are already moving teams to strike other targets," Han said as his eyes scanned the room. "The next time he strikes, it won't be one target; it will be two or three simultaneously." He paused to look at the general for a moment. "I fear we shall have to split up. The military will definitely call the general to action."

"Our purposes will not be that distant," Master Li interjected. "Some of us possessed with needed military tactics will have to find their own way," he said as he glanced at the general. "The rest of us will go after this madman, not tomorrow, not tonight, now, this minute. Villi prepare the aircraft for takeoff. Team, prepare for immediate departure."

"But Master Li," James protested as he stood. "What will you have me do?" he asked.

"As Han stated, the army will contact you. They are probably scrambling to come up with a plan at this moment," Li told him. "You must go after these strike teams before they do more damage to Australia....and James, you have an advantage..." he winked and tapped his skull.

Every psychic glanced over at a portion of the wall. They could sense a sudden rush of electrical energy. No one in Rollo had a wall phone or had ever seen one. Not many in the public had them. This was one of the perks the military gave to the general.

At that second, the wall phone began to flash and ring, indicating a call coming through. Master Li signaled his troop. The nine-member group moved through the kitchen and out the backdoor of the general's house. They headed straight for the aircraft.

"With any luck, perhaps our timing will still be a surprise," Li commented to Han as they sprinted side by side.

"Let's hope so," Han retorted.

CHAPTER THIRTY-TWO

ON THE RUN

"WAIT A MINUTE, YOU IDIOT! Cyrus said to stay at this location and observe!" Ned yelled back over his shoulder to the other men as they started to retreat.

"Yeah… and Girard told us to get the hell outta here!" Rupert responded with a harsh whisper. "Who ya gonna believe? Girard looks out for us. Only an idiot would stay… now come on! Get into the truck with the rest of us. The other team is already headed out of the harbor."

"Ned, they'll cut off the city an' surround the place with troops," Simon advised. "This place will be crawlin' with all kinds of government creeps lookin for the bombers. If we don't start out now, they'll trace our footsteps. We must get away from the city," he added.

Ned backed away from their vantage point and moved with the others to the waiting truck. Cyrus ordered them to stop at this location and watch the blast occur to make certain it exploded on time. Yet, Girard, who had trained and organized the strike teams, knew a great deal more about military tactics than Cyrus did. He overheard what Cyrus requested and countermanded his order afterward. Simon understood his reasons and intended to follow Girard's advice. Therefore, Ned decided to listen to Simon's counsel since he trusted him. Plus, Cyrus would not punish them if they carried out a string of successful attacks. The only way they could do that would be to move on to the next target.

"I hope you know what you're doin," Ned said to Rupert as he hopped into back of the truck.

"I ain't listenin to that freak's advice… stay here, like I bloody well want to get caught!" Rupert hissed. "I say we join the other team on the island. Besides, we ain't supposed to split up till tomorrah night. Now, let's get outta here!" he signaled the driver when he saw Simon and Ned jump into the back. He swung into the passenger seat and slammed the door shut.

The truck tore away from its parking spot, twisted up the road and back onto the main road heading east and north before the driver, young Vince Wesley, shoved his foot to the floor and pushed the truck as fast as he could along the highway. For over an hour, they drove north and managed to put further ground between them and Brisbane. Vince made good time, passing up most cars northbound while Rupert watched for highway patrols. Rupert glanced down at his watch.

"Any second now," he muttered.

All at once the ground shook around them and the sky lit up with a giant fireball that punched a hole into the blue sky. From the back of the covered truck, the men had no vantage point to see their handiwork. Rupert, in the front seat, looked into one of the truck's big side mirrors and watched as something akin to an expanding mushroom cloud rose over the city.

"Good lord..." he whispered under his breath.

"Did you see that?" Vince asked Rupert. "The blast, I mean..." he commented after he saw the initial fireball in the mirror. The young man gripped the truck's steering wheel so tight, his knuckles turned white. He kept his concentration on the road, afraid to look back.

"I'm right next to ya," Rupert said as he wiped the sweat off his face. "Yeah... I see it... we gotta move onto the next target, just like Girard said to... stay and watch what the military does, Cyrus tells us," he muttered, "that man's balmy!"

"Do we radio in?" Vince asked.

"Are you nuts?" Rupert practically yelled at him, "and bring the military right down on our position? They'll be monitorin' all communications! You want to give away our position?"

"Jus shut up and keep drivin," Ned told Vince through the window, "... and don't stop till we get to the rendezvous."

Simon stuck his face in the back window.

"Hey! Do you remember where the meetin' place is?" he yelled.

"Get your head back in there!" Rupert said as he shoved his hand against the young man's head. "Of course we know where it is... dat's where were headin, ain't we?" he yelled back. He glanced over at Vince to make certain. Vince nodded back to him. Rupert straightened around in his seat.

"Ya takes a right up there before we get to Gympie, Vince," Ned pointed out as he gestured through the back window. However, the other two men ignored him.

"Them charges flattened dat building... didn't they?" Vince commented.

"I said shat up and keep drivin," Rupert told him.

"You ain't no officer," Vince grumbled back.

"…an you ain't no freakin chauffeur," Rupert told him. "Jus hurry up and go as quick as you can," he said. "Forget about what happened. It's done and over with," he said. "We got other things to think about now."

The men lapsed into silence as Vince pushed the truck as quick as he could down the road to head for the coastal spot.

"Now how did those psychics know that damn wall phone would ring?" the general said to his wife.

"How do they know anything?" the wife said.

"Answer it!" the general urged.

Penelope touched an area on the wall and an image of the general's boss, General George Sanders, appeared. He had a stern expression on his face with a deep furrowed brow on his forehead as his eyes swept the room for the general.

"Penelope?" his commanding voice sounded.

"Yes, general," she responded.

"I must speak with James, at once! We have a national emergency on our hands!" he spoke forcefully.

Penelope moved to one side. James Montgomery Pollack never shirked from battle, quite the opposite. He stepped into view so that Sanders could see him.

"I am here, sir," the general declared.

"We have a situation, James," the general began.

"We caught some of it on the news, sir," James said and reached for Penelope's hand.

"Right now we need every man we can move into position. We don't know if other attacks may follow," General Sanders spoke, his voice clearly moved by the day's events. "I've sent a harrier to your position. It should arrive soon. Put out a marker, James. Then report to Melbourne's HQ at once and pick up your orders there, general," he told him.

"Yes, sir," General Pollack saluted.

"Call me with an update as soon as possible. Sanders out," the general said before his picture disappeared and the screen returned to the color of the wall.

James turned to Penelope. "I know what you're thinking, remember?" he said as he embraced his wife.

"I must learn to keep my thoughts vague," she whispered just before their lips touched.

"Either that or keep them lovingly about me," he linked to her mind.

The two embraced and kissed before James headed to grab his emergency flight suit.

"That you'll always have," she thought as she watched him go.

Within a matter of minutes, a harrier jet approached from the east and landed in the precise location where James placed the marker in his yard.

"Why didn't you put the marker over there?" the pilot yelled. "You have all that space," he pointed to the part of the general's property where the psychic's house sat, though the pilot could not see it.

"Oh, I, uh... I just planted new grass seed there... come on, let's go, captain," the general said as he put on his helmet.

"Yes, sir," the captain responded.

Penelope stood just inside the backdoor and watched while the jet aircraft lifted vertically off the ground and then whisk her husband away.

"Please be careful darling," she thought to him.

"I will," he told her as the jet took him out of range. "I love..."

When his thought suddenly ceased, Penelope took in a quick breath. For a second she thought she might never see him again.

Outside Brisbane, another scenario took place, as terrorist bombers led by a contingent of men hand-picked by Girard, fled the first target city by way of the Brisbane River, heading past Fisherman Islands and out to sea.

"How much longer?" an unshaven man grunted from below. "I'm getting cramped!"

"Keep still..." the pilot said as he steered the boat out of the harbor. "Girard told us we must clear the harbor patrols. When that bomb goes off, no one must suspect we are fleein' the scene. We need to fit in with the rest of the boat traffic headin' out this mornin'. We'll simply be regarded as tourists, like everyone else. Wave, Jerry," the man named Stanley said and poked his friend in the side.

The border patrol boat passed them, going in the opposite direction. Stan and Jerome, known as "Jerry," had their fishing gear out on the aft deck as they made a long slow turn past the mouth of the river and began to move north. They casually lifted their hands when the patrol boat passed them. The authorities could not see the six members of the demolition crew as they crammed inside a small room below deck. Stan knew that if he pushed the boat up to full speed, it would attract attention. He studied the pattern of fishing boats that navigated this corridor for two days before they killed the owner of the boat yesterday and took the watercraft up the river into the heart of Brisbane.

The demolition group trained on this mission with Girard for two weeks. They prepared for this particular operation from the very beginning once Cyrus pointed out his plan to spread chaos throughout Australia.

Master Li did not detect the plan inside Cyrus mind, because Cyrus purposely kept the information out of his own head. He concentrated on the one scenario he knew the intruder would find. He laid out his "diversion" plans on paper and then handed over the project to Girard. Cyrus told him to "work out a plan to our advantage." Girard – who had previous military experience – did just that. Once Cyrus explained what he wanted, Girard planned a series of attacks that would cripple the nation and send the population into a panic.

"We can hardly breathe down here!" one of the men complained. "Open the bloomin front hatch at least," the same man cried from below.

"Jerry..." Stan said as he turned to the younger man behind him.

"My name is Jerome," the youth protested.

"Your name will be shark bait if you don't open that front hatch," Stan barked at him. "I'll send you below to explain why you didn't open it!"

Jerry sat up and locked off his fishing pole. He inched his way around the outside edge of the boat on the narrow walkway to the front. He reached over to open the outside latch and knocked on the top. Underneath, hands scrambled with inner locking seal. He could hear the men argue over who was in the better position to unlock the seal. Even with the wind blowing, Jerome could smell the sweat and body odor that leaked out of the opening when he braced the hatch into the open position. He heard a few men cough and take in deep breaths of air.

"That's more like it!" one said.

Jerry glanced back over his shoulder. The patrol boat that passed them moments ago, moved south toward the horizon. As soon as it cleared their view, he resumed his previous spot next to his fishing line.

Stan opened up the door below which allowed more fresh air to circulate.

"Sorry, mates," he said to them.

"'bout bloody time!" one of them shot back.

For nearly an hour, the sun beat down on the boat as they gradually chugged their way north away from the mouth of the Brisbane River, past the airport to the open sea. Once at sea, Stan knew they had an appointment to keep. Girard instructed the men to meet up after the crews split and went in different directions. That way, if the authorities caught on to one team, the other team would get away and finish the objective.

Stan had to be at the rendezvous point in four hours. As he pushed on the handle, the boat's bow lifted up out of the water and briskly cut through the ocean waves that pounded the hull while he turned his heading due north. Soon, he had Moreton Island off his starboard side with Bribie Island coming up off the port.

He glanced down at his wristwatch and then over at Jerome. The youth looked back at him, sweating, despite the fair weather and wind on his face. Though just a few "clicks" from shore, they could barely make out the coastline of Australia that ran past on their port side. As with any timepiece, staring at the second hand as it moved around the clock face usually slowed time. In this case, Jerry had a digital watch that slowly counted down to zero, which he set when Stan started the timer on the bomb.

"I wonder what it will be like… in that square, I mean, when the explosion goes off," Jerry wondered.

"Jerry… er, Jerome, you wouldn't want to be there," Stan replied. "Do you realize how much explosive we set last night? We placed charges all over that building. The shock wave within a block of that place will knock you clean off your feet," he said as he glanced down at his watch.

He had not counted on the last patrol boat being so late. When they timed their movements, the patrol was supposed to pass by nearly a half hour ago. He had to shorten the distance between the boat and their meeting place as quickly as he could. He shoved the speed controls all the way forward.

"Hey!" they heard from below. "What happened? I didn't hear no blast!" one man said.

"Shut up!" Stan said. "Your watch never did work right… two minutes," he told the man below.

The boat continued to slice through the water as they quicken their pace north, while each second moved them further away. Stan nodded his head toward the younger man.

"Must be almost time. How much left?" he asked.

Jerome held up his digital timer and counted the remaining seconds.

"Six… five… four… three…"

The men from below pushed out of the doors and walked onto the aft deck. Stan tied off the boat's wheel. He wanted to see the results of the demolition, too. He glanced up in time to see a great flash on the horizon to the southwest. The cigarette in his mouth dropped from his lips onto the boat deck. The group of men watched with strange fascination as the shockwave travelled across the surface of the water toward them, visible as it spread out from Brisbane.

"Boom!" the loud sound struck the boat with a slap and shook them.

The sound nearly deafened Stan's ears.

"Good lord!" Jerry said as he moved toward the side to get a better view. "I ain't never seen nuthin like that!" he said as his mouth hung open.

"The team packed the whole ventilation system with them weapons, thanks to the Australian army," Stan said as he cleared his throat. "What did you expect?"

The men watched in silence, dumbfounded at the enormity of what they did. A giant fireball spread upward into the sky over Brisbane for a moment. A huge cloud of fire and debris rose into the atmosphere which resembled an atomic bomb's mushroom cloud.

"Nobody could live through that!" Jerry commented.

Stan pulled out his map. He had to start making his turn toward the coastline once the boat passed Skirmish Point. He could turn inland and parallel the coast the rest of the way, passing Maroochydore, a moderate city coming up on their portside. They still had a long way to go.

"You boys better get back below. I'll keep the doors open. Just stay out of sight," Stan recommended, "in case we come across any coast guard cutters."

He took out another cigarette and lit it. His hand shook as he moved the lighter closer to his face.

"I'm glad that's over," he said as he took a puff.

"God help us…" Jerry commented.

"This will most certainly go down as the most despicable terrorist act in Australian history," Stan added.

"They'll come after us for sure," Jerry said as he turned around and looked at Stan.

"Don't count out Cyrus," Stan said and pushed the hair back off his moist forehead with a trembling hand. He reached down and held it steady with his other hand and hoped Jerry did not notice. "You've seen what he can do. That man is capable of anything. As far as he is concerned, this is just the first shot in our war against… them."

Jerry resumed his seat on the stern and pretended to fish. Yet, his eyes intently watched the column of black smoke as it rose over the city of Brisbane. He knew that after that moment, he had no future. Once they set off those charges, the people of Australia would never rest until they brought the men responsible to justice.

Stan felt nearly the same way. He realized he had committed to something that seemed to be spinning out of control. Only fate knew what lay in store for him.

"Can we relax yet?" Jerry asked.

"I won't be able to breathe easy until we pass Noosa Heads and come within sight of Rainbow Beach," Stan told him as he turned the boat's wheel toward shore. "Then it's on to Fraser Island for the night and our next target, Maryborough while the other team hits, Bundaberg. Even if the country's on military alert, they won't be expectin us there," he said, his face grim. "By the time we finish, they'll think we're at war… and they'd be right to think it."

CHAPTER THIRTY-THREE

A LONG DAY'S JOURNEY

MASTER LI STOOD WITH MICHAEL, Cecilia, Su Lin, and Han outside the temporary bivouac they had erected. He wondered if it was only for the one night. It seemed an incredible waste of time and effort. He had not scanned his mind, but he was certain Zinian spent hours on Beit and even more hours at his construction site working on its construction. With all the hours he spent away from home, Li wondered how his marriage was holding up. When Zinian saw Li staring up at the building, he walked over and stood next to him.

"Are we going to leave this building behind?" Li put to him.

"It should last for… about four days," he linked back.

"Why four days?" This caught Master Li by surprise.

"The next scheduled forecast for rain," Zinian informed him. "The whole thing will turn into a big puddle of goo and wash away in the next storm."

Li glanced over at Zinian.

"What if it had rained last night?" Li wondered.

"Then we would have run for cover," Zinian said with a blank stare.

Villi burst out laughing but Zhiwei didn't think it was as funny. He was on the third floor with Chou. Zinian shrugged his shoulders but Zhiwei gave Chou a stern expression as the young technologist walked up.

"I didn't know!" Chou linked. "Anyway, the next part is ready, Master Li."

"Is this the transportation after we land?" Li asked Chou.

The scientist nodded and gestured for the group to follow him to the cargo hold. The short statured man with ruffled dark hair seemed to relish the spotlight as he linked with the group including Villi.

"I need to tell you a few things about the floating platforms," he started to explain. "First, I had to travel to Ziddis for this one…"

"Where else?" Cecilia commented.

Everyone knew how much Chou loved to visit Ziddis.

"…Unlike the hover cars we use around Rollo," he continued unabated, "these vehicles had to be especially rugged to travel over open terrain. I took into account the heat, sand, water, and brush. They also had to be more powerful if we were to transport cargo and people. It took me hours to understand how they worked. I had to sit through seven technical lectures before I could gain a private audience with a level five manager."

"I'm sure they twisted your arm," his tall friend Zinian commented next to him.

Everyone in the group chuckled, because they knew how Chou often sought to raise his level of acceptance on Ziddis. Five was the highest level he ever contacted. The Ziddis technocrats above that level regarded Earth as primitive.

"When I asked about short travel missions across desert-like conditions, and our need to have separate independent devices, they wanted more information. So, I explained Earth's gravity, our atmosphere, conditions on the ground, and so on. Again, they referred me to Techno-World's museum, my usual stopping off place," he explained as he passed along his latest memory of Ziddis to their minds. "I modified one of their designs and came up with a device I call the skimmer."

Chou sent them a mental image of a platform just over a meter square with a side bar around its periphery and a control panel attached to a shaft along one side. In his mind, he stepped up to the platform which rested on the ground. One portion of the side bar opened, which allowed him access inside. He placed his hands on the sides of the control panel, which responded to his touch.

"Unlike the hovers in Rollo, this control panel is made for the psychic mind," he demonstrated. "The device interacts with your thoughts. However, like the Rollo hovers, they cannot fly through the air like a plane. If you happen to approach a cliff where the drop off is steep or straight down, an automated stop system will keep you from careening out over the edge. Oh, one last thing, if they fail due to gun fire or an explosion, move away from the platform quickly. They self-destruct and not by dissolving either."

The whole team moaned.

"Go ahead and show them the one you set up," Master Li insisted.

Chou lowered the cargo ramp and manually rolled one of the heavy platforms that he put on a cart with wheels. He stepped up and the rail slid open for him. He grasped the handles and the control panel instantly sprang to life.

"Sensing Chou," it said, "interfacing."

"Don't worry," Chou added, "this model doesn't require a drop of blood. I programmed them to accept any WPO member. But someone like Penelope could not ride one of these unless she stood behind the general."

A seat automatically came up out of the platform and snugly cupped around his behind. The control panel tilted down to face him.

"That seems personal," Cecilia quipped in regards to the seat.

Michael smiled when he thought of his wife's behind.

"Oh, I don't know…" he started. "I'd like to see your bum in that tight…"

Su Lin nudged him.

"Pay attention," she directed.

"You can stand or sit," Chou told them. "It doesn't matter. Both ways are comfortable as far as I'm concerned. Let me demonstrate."

Chou barely moved his hands and body when the platform rose up off the carrier and hovered in place about half a meter above the surface, slightly higher off the ground than the Rollo hover devices. It easily turned under his touch and the scientist went straight for Penelope's flower garden. She had three large boulders of different sizes. Chou's device arched its front over the boulders while it kept the seat perfectly level. The platform continued forward, and gradually dropped down the other side of the boulders. He headed for a set of stairs on the hillside. The platform easily slid down them. He backed up the stairs in reverse. Chou steered for the fishpond and purposely stopped the platform right in the middle of the water without sinking or disturbing the water underneath, a feature not available on the Rollo hovers.

"I can position the skimmer here all day and not worry about going into the water," he said as he jumped up and down. "We can cross rivers, lakes, streams or ponds without worry about going down… unless you run out of power. Even though they use a lot of power," he said as he looked down, "a lot of power, you've got two back-up power supplies to the main power brick, good for about 280 kilometers of hard travel from the main brick, an additional seventy clicks from each secondary backup brick. I had to invent a new form of energy storage. They actually use more power than Villi's aircraft. Anyway, that should be enough to reach the encampment from the landing site and return with lots of room to spare. Stranded, we could nearly ride back to Adelaide if we had to on these. We could certainly make it to Warburton. I brought nine platforms. It will take about twenty minutes or less after we land to set up all nine of them with a little help."

"How fast can they travel?" Villi wondered.

"Fast," Chou replied, meaning a person could travel faster than was probably recommended.

Chou floated back to the group. Michael walked over to the edge of the skimmer and dropped down. He started to wav his hand underneath.

"Won't it get hung up on some big bush?" he wondered.

Chou leapt off the skimmer in a surprisingly quick move. He grabbed Michael and pulled him back before Michael could put his hand in the space.

"Not recommended," Chou firmly linked. "This is the first time I've tried to create a sophisticated anti-gravity field outside the Rollo hovers, which can only bear a small amount of weight by comparison to these hefty vehicles that can carry up to four tons," he informed Michael. "I would not suggest you put your hand under one of these," he warned. "Like the fusor, I had to create a special shield to keep the radiation from penetrating through to the rider on the platform. While short exposure underneath will not harm a human or an animal," he said. "Long-term exposure will kill you."

Michael stared down at the device with concerns for the environment.

"Oh, the environment is quite safe," Chou pointed out, "if we keep from putting our feet or hands under one of these for longer than five minutes, they're safe," he concluded. "Just don't hover over a fox hole or a snake for very long. It will fry them."

"Now if they only served tea, they'd be perfect," Han thought.

"I did include an emergency supply of water for survival purposes," Chou put in. "I stocked each flyer with the special food packets that Su Lin created. Each carrier contains six liters of water. If rationed and if you traveled by night, you could last three or four days in the desert. I couldn't fit any more food or water because of space, not because of weight," Chou added. "The sides have special pouches that contain other essentials – a backpack, a temporary shelter that can be set up multiple times, and a communications card, should the flyers completely fail and we must walk."

"Assuming the thing doesn't self-destruct if damaged and kill us!" Han added.

"Thank you, Chou," Master Li said. "A very good demonstration…"

"Master Li," Zhiwei interrupted, "A harrier jet is approaching our position."

For a moment, Master Li closed his eyes. The aircraft moved in above them before it floated down into the yard near a yellow smoking rod. General Pollack ran out and gave the invisible group a quick wave before he ascended into the cockpit, donned a helmet, and then took off. He left Penelope standing in the doorway, waving goodbye. She could not see Master Li and his group. She returned to the house. Li turned his attention back to the team.

"Anything else before we leave?" he requested.

"I want each person to take one of these," Cecilia said as she stepped forward. "Open," she requested. She made her husband the first guinea pig.

"What is it?" he asked as she placed the tiny white square under his tongue.

"This will diminish our need for water, but only for the next 48 hours," she added. "You can drink any amount you like," she told them. "However, you can survive on less than 200cc of water during 24 hours and still maintain normal fluid balance including kidney function, normally an impossibility," she concluded.

After she placed one under each tongue, Cecilia turned to Master Li. He raised his arms and refused to take one.

"Time to go," he said and waved to them. "Villi prepare for liftoff."

Within a few minutes, the crew sat in their seat with their safety belts strapped on. Villi employed maneuvering thrusters once the stealth controls enveloped the aircraft in an area of influence. The moment they cleared the general's yard, Villi changed to the powerful rear thrusters and headed off across the Australian continent in pursuit of a rogue psychic and his army.

"Master Li," Han privately linked. "You should be aware that the population is sparse out here at best," he said. "We may have difficulty recharging our psychic energy levels."

Li closed his eyes and sent out his psychic feelings. He roamed for a time over the nearby countryside. Han correctly pointed out that beyond Adelaide, the group had very little psychic energy to draw upon, not enough to thwart a two hundred person army should Cyrus set his men against them.

"I want each member of this group to absorb as much psychic energy as we can muster," he said as the aircraft silently and invisibly flew over the city while it headed north and west. "I would keep the altitude as low as possible and watch your speed, Villi. Han will give you the precise location of the landing site that he and Michael chose," Li advised, "We don't wish to tip our hand to Cyrus."

"Acknowledged, Master Li," Villi linked.

He trimmed the aircraft's altitude and brought his compass bearing toward the north. Two hand controls rose up out of the panel and bent back toward him. He took one in each hand and dropped all computer controls over the aircraft. Villi decided to fly his "baby" manually. While those in the cabin could not directly see through the front of the clear cockpit, the sight this time might have sickened them. Villi slid between buildings, trees, and other obstructions as he slowly poured on speed and kept the aircraft only three hundred meters off the ground. Ordinarily, he might have left a huge wake behind him. Since, he slowed his speed considerably, the stealth controls helped to dissipate any vortex from the aircraft. His boxy wings gave him complete control of all three axes.

Master Li leaned back in his comfortable leather chair and tried to relax, unaware that another psychic could sense his powerful presence on the continent.

CHAPTER THIRTY-FOUR

A SENSE OF URGENCY

"GIRARD! GET IN HERE!" a loud voice intruded into big man's dreams.

The aging rugged man heard his name called, yet he knew from its immediacy, the words traveled only to his mind. He slowly stirred from his bed and pushed the nude woman lying on his bare muscular chest away. He stretched his large naked fit frame and yawned. He flexed an arm and noticed that since they started training, he was in the best shape he had been since he was in the military years ago. He stood up and walked over to the mirror. His pecs stood out. His abs rippled down his front. His shoulders seemed wider and his arms curved with bulging biceps. He was all man and a big one at that.

"...didn't hurt my prowess either," he noted as he considered last night with Cyrus' latest acquisition.

He liked the young dark-haired girl, and oddly enough, she preferred him to the rest of the men. Girard thought he would keep her in his tent as his sole possession... for a while at least. As he pulled on a heavy jacket, he glanced over at the girl.

"If we ever leave this place," he thought as he prepared to leave the tent, "I could take her with me."

He stepped up to the flap that acted as a door to his large tent. He knew the night guard on duty outside his tent did not hear Cyrus' private call. Cyrus communicated directly into Girard's mind. The moment he threw back the flap, the guard reacted, startled.

"Sir!" the man said as he stood to attention.

"At ease," Girard told him. "Rather cold tonight," he commented, seeing his breath.

"Yes, sir," the man responded.

Girard could see by the man's blanched hands and purplish-white lips that despite his condition, he would not complain, yet was very near frostbite.

"Go back to your tent at once," Girard ordered out of consideration. "I no longer need a guard tonight," he told the man. "Send the relief at dawn when the air starts to warm," he told him.

"Sir? My post… I shouldn't… I mean, I'm sorry, sir…" the man stammered, concerned about repercussions.

"Don't worry soldier," Girard told him. "I'll take care of that. Go get something warm to eat and drink before you settle in. Then catch some needed rest. That's an order. Understood?"

"Yes, sir," the grateful man replied and headed off to the northern part of the center quarters where Girard kept his elite force.

The center part of the men's quarters had finally grown to 204 men in the last few days. The extra four were part of that overflow Han predicted Cyrus would use as examples. He didn't need to do that any longer. The men were convinced of his invincibility and power. Lately, however, the men seemed disheartened. They questioned their purpose to train and itched for some kind of action.

Girard wondered how the men's morale would recover once he sent his crack demolitions teams to the eastern seaboard. He pulled them from Company A. He missed a few of them already, especially Stan, as he had been one of the most helpful and obedient men he recruited, a born platoon leader. He wondered how or if they pulled off their mission, or if the authorities caught them and foiled the plot. Cyrus had yet to inform him of the team's progress. In fact, Cyrus would not speak to anyone, even refusing to meet with him for the past twenty-four hours.

Girard glanced up at the fading stars overhead as he stood outside his tent. With no lights out in the desert, he could see a multitude of stars twinkling in the clear sky overhead.

"Perhaps Cyrus has news of the team," he thought. "But we won't know until ten o'clock. That's when we set the time for the blast."

He looked down at his watch and wondered if the strike teams had carried out their mission in Brisbane. If all went as planned, they would have planted the explosives and started out on their separate paths. He hoped they had enough sense to "get the hell out of there." At least, that is what *he* advised, despite Cyrus' direction.

"5 a.m.," he noted. "Can't a guy get some sleep!" he wondered as he rubbed his face and trudged up the steep hill.

Girard hated these early morning calls. He pondered the mental health of the troop's leader, Cyrus, or if he had slept with these visions lately that woke him in the middle of the night. When he walked up to Cyrus' large tent, the two men guarding the outside were nearly frozen and half-asleep. He dismissed them for fresh replacements and told them to take their time before they sent two fresh guards.

"Sir... the leader..." one protested.

"I'll be inside," he said before he dismissed them. "Cyrus will be safe."

When he walked through the meeting area to the bedroom part, he found Cyrus awake, bent over a large center table. The canvas door to Cyrus bedroom stood open with a faint light coming out. For a moment, he questioned the status of the nude woman on his bed, with her limp arm draped over the side. He thought he might have to dispose of another body. Then he saw her move and breathed a sigh of relief. He turned his attention to the slender pale figure staring at the bluish hue in front of him.

Cyrus drew his heavy long coat up around his shoulders. Although daytime temperatures in the desert could climb over 100 degrees, the air in the dead of night grew cold, often plunging to near freezing. Cyrus stood over a table covered with maps, the only light came from a thin laptop computer.

As Girard approached, he saw the screen displayed a stretched out version of the planet, with a series of wavy lines from one side to the other. Girard noticed that Cyrus paid particular attention to the throbbing light position on the screen.

"These are orbits," Cyrus stated as he answered the question in Girard's mind. "They follow the path of an object in space that circumnavigates the globe several times a day."

"You mean the space station," Girard observed.

"So!" Cyrus glanced up at Girard. "You aren't a complete idiot."

"I thought you read my mind," Girard replied. "You know my history."

"Yes, you were in the military... dishonorably discharged... they didn't pin that murder on you... friendly fire, they termed it, to avoid a lawsuit," Cyrus sarcastically said as he made Girard grind his teeth. "I believe you ran a syndicate inside the prison after your next murder. Some self control problems... but, yes... you'd need some intelligence to run a numbers game," he snidely remarked while he kept his eyes on the screen.

Cyrus stared at the screen and mumbled incoherently. Girard cleared his throat, a bit impatient as to why Cyrus roused him so early in the morning.

"You wanted me, sir?" Girard asked while he held back any display of temper.

"I used the codes from General Sander's mind to break into the satellite feed," Cyrus began. "This is the current location of the station," he pointed to Africa. "Soon, it will fly directly over our position. When that happens, I will use it to our advantage," he spoke so quietly that Girard could hardly hear him. He finally turned his face toward Girard. "We have a problem. I need your help. A meddlesome Chinese man has arrived in Australia. I can feel his power."

"Is he responsible for troubling your dreams?" Girard asked.

"You figured that out, too, eh?" Cyrus noted. "Yes, he is the one. We must be ready for him. He's brought a team of experts and hopes to defeat me. But as with any plan of battle, we will outflank him and counter his surprise. Right?"

"If you say so," Girard carefully responded. "You haven't told me if the strike force has accomplished its mission. I'm worried..."

"You? Worry?" Cyrus spit at him. He started to laugh and noticed how it wounded his second in command. "I don't believe it. You really do care for these men, don't you?"

Girard knew better than to challenge Cyrus, well aware of the man's power. He kept his mouth shut and lowered his eyes. Cyrus probed his mind.

"You want to know about the mission you planned to divert the military, is that it?" the pale young man asked.

He seemed so meek and so small compared to the much larger, beefier Girard. His lack of size did not fool Girard. He knew Cyrus to be a formidable foe with his secret power.

"Your strike team was more successful than we originally thought," Cyrus told him, grinning. "I remotely disabled the building security so they could gain entry during the night. They've already planted the charges and started the timer. The men are on their way to the rendezvous point. The blast will go off as planned and the military will most likely react exactly as we anticipate. They'll focus their attention on the east and that distraction should take the Australian psychic with them," he said as he gleefully rubbed his hands together.

"Did you say 'psychic,' sir?" Girard questioned. "You've never used that term before. What does a psychic have to do with this?"

"Haven't I?" Cyrus said. He realized he let out more information than he intended. He brushed his own comments aside. "It no longer matters... I might as well tell you everything, since I will need your advice at times in the future," Cyrus said. He turned toward the woman for a second to check her sleep status before he continued. Girard watched with fascination as the canvas door closed on its own accord.

"I am psychic," Cyrus began. "I have power given to me since birth. That is how I control people. It's no mystery to those of my kind. You see... I discovered that I am not alone. Another man, a general who lives in Adelaide, has the same ability. He only realized it recently. He is weak," Cyrus spat. "However, he could make trouble for us. Right now, thanks to your demolition team, the Australian Army will divert this active-duty general to Brisbane. That will keep him busy while I deal with these American's. I believe they will come for me… sooner than later… and we must be ready for them."

"Whoa!" Girard said as he backed up. "The American's sent a strike force against us?"

For the first time in months, Cyrus actually detected something akin to fear in Girard's mind, as if going up against an elite American military strike force would be suicide.

"No, Girard," Cyrus tried to explain in simple terms. "These are ordinary people with no special weapons… in fact, they don't believe in weapons. They think they are invulnerable without them, and that is their weakness, which we will exploit!"

"How will we do that? If you don't mind me asking, sir," Girard questioned.

"We surprise them before they have a chance to act," Cyrus told the large man.

He walked up to Girard and put his hand on the big man's arm. Even the touch of Cyrus' small, pale, slender, feminine hands made Girard feel uncomfortable. He tried to ignore his feelings of revulsion and allowed Cyrus to do as he pleased. He tried to think of Cyrus as a masculine woman as that was the only way he could tolerate the man's touch. He shuddered to think about Cyrus' other perversions.

"I have another mission in mind," Cyrus requested, "similar in execution to the one you just accomplished for me on the east coast," he told him. "Once again I will give you the parameters and you will carry out the attack without my knowledge."

"Do you believe we will be that successful?" Girard asked. He needed Cyrus' reassurance.

Cyrus gave him the same expression a father would use to discipline a child – that hard, blank, steely stare that means business. The big man saw it and fell silent. Cyrus gestured toward a map on the table. He put his finger on a spot just southeast of their current location.

"I've studied the terrain here for months," Cyrus continued. "We only have one weak area. I believe they will attack from this location, probably fly here and come across by land. I can feel his energy and will sense when he draws near. That will be their flaw. He gives away their position." He ran his finger from Adelaide to their present position, yet stopped just southeast of the camp. "We must strike them here before they have time to regroup after they land. I know how you like to plan these things out," Cyrus put to him. "I'll merely tell you what to expect. If you tell me the details, he'll search my mind and attempt countermeasures. Therefore, you must say nothing to me.

I will give you the signal. Then, you must act. Is that understood?" Cyrus added the last comment directly into his mind.

"Your orders could not be clearer, sir," Girard answered.

"Oh, and Girard," Cyrus added. "We need to rouse the men and work up their emotions," he told them. "Say whatever you like to rile the troops – tell them that these weird people tortured others – but instill anger. That emotion confuses these Americans. For example…"

He moved closer to Girard and ran his hand down the front of the big man's body until it stopped above his waist. He glanced up and noticed Girard had his eyes closed with a grimace on his face. Cyrus laughed and walked away.

"See? I know what makes you angry," he said as he stood next to the table and then slammed his fist down. "Now go out and make them angry… tell the men anything you want, but do it!" he demanded.

"I will do as you say," the big man replied. He saluted and left the tent.

Outside, in the brisk chilled air, he stared up at the fading night. The light that shown from inside the tent went out. That meant Cyrus returned to bed and he could freely think without the "perv" eavesdropping on his mind. He thought about what Cyrus revealed to him just now and why it had instilled fear inside him from the moment he met the little pipsqueak.

"Psychic… I should have guessed from the start," he thought. "Cyrus is using his… psychic power on us. He must represent a new kind of human evolution in our species. That is why he fears these others. It also means their kind might be more widespread and organized than Cyrus considered. Their kind could change the whole world and be very profitable for someone… especially if the right people found out," he considered. "I believe this information is more valuable than anything Cyrus could promise me," he thought as he walked toward his tent. "So intense anger shuts them out of the mind… I'll remember that… Cyrus!"

He stopped outside his tent and considered what value he could place on this new information – how he could turn over Cyrus *and* the American's to the Australian authorities while he cashed in on the prospect. He could write his own ticket.

"They'd pay me a fortune," he thought.

As Girard walked to his tent, he formulated a plan.

"The timing's got to be just right," he thought.

The moment Girard entered his tent, he could see the young woman spread out on his bed. She looked so vulnerable, so weak, so open to his masculine power. He liked her like that, submissive, willing to do whatever he wanted. It played with his imagination. He also liked the idea that she did not care how many times he brutalized her. She seemed to like it when he did

247

and wanted it that way. He noticed she was awake. Although he previously thought he would take her with him, this new plan he formulated left her out of his future. She was a tramp. He could have dozens just like her, any time he wanted one.

"Too bad," he thought as he approached the bed. She smiled up at him. Before she could speak, he grabbed her things. "Get out!" he growled as he tossed her clothes into her face. "Bunk with Lissen. I can't have you around as a distraction."

She struggled to put her clothes on as she ran from his tent. The moment she left, Girard sat at his table and started to write down his plans.

"So, Cyrus wants a surprise," he thought as he pulled out his area map. "Cyrus is gonna get a surprise."

CHAPTER THIRTY-FIVE

APPROACH WITH STEALTH

"EVERYONE NEEDS TO STAY IN their seats. This might be a bumpy ride for a while," Villi warned from the cockpit. "I'm flying at low altitude, which means I have to slow my speed and dodge the occasional obstruction. Australia has these... stone hills that rise up out of nowhere. Mostly, the terrain is just flat."

Master Li turned his head toward the back of the cabin, his soft snowy white hair hung down over his wrinkled kind face. He pulled his hair back from his face and ran his bony fingers through his mane as he addressed the group.

"Do you recall the meditative exercises we practiced?" Li asked. "This is the perfect time to employ those methods and preserve our psychic energy."

Most in the group nodded or replied mentally.

"We should heed Villi's advice and remain buckled in for the remainder of the trip," he recommended. "Han suggests that since we are crossing a large area with few people around, we conserve psychic energy, just as we did when we crossed the ocean. We'll need it to interact with the skimmers and other purposes. Enter your meditative states. Villi will fly the aircraft in stealth mode," he stated.

Master Li and the others leaned back into their seats and tried to attain a state of meditation. Within moments, everyone onboard the aircraft fell into a trance-like state except Villi.

For a few minutes, Master Li stared out the window at the blur of scenery as it streaked past. He found it difficult to concentrate on entering a meditative state. He wondered if Cyrus would try to place terrible images in their minds, such as ferocious lions or dust tornados, as a defensive move. This would be the first time in their brief history that pitted psychic against psychic in a head on battle. The Rollo, and the entire WPO membership for that matter, consisted mostly of pacifists with perhaps Villi being the one exception.

"Would they be capable of fighting like soldiers?" he questioned.

Master Li confronted the last fully developed rogue psychic alone – his first cousin, walled up inside a mental hospital in northern China. He prepared for that battle by absorbing as much psychic energy as he could. They were surrounded by people in a heavily populated area. The man turned out to be such a formidable foe, Master Li felt compelled at the time to match violence with violence and used his incredible power to destroy the other psychic, a mistake that he regretted much later. The memory of that day sent a chill through his body. What would he do if Cyrus used similar techniques on them? Would confronting a powerful rogue psychic provoke another violent reaction in him? Conflict tormented his mind.

"I am a man of peace," he thought. "How could I choose such a resolution?"

The results of that day often bothered the great Master Li, though he never shared those thoughts with anyone, not Michael or Han or even Running Elk. Yet, the voices of Galactic Central knew how Li felt and sympathized with his plight.

"You had every right to respond the way you did for survival," the director once tried to comfort and reason with him.

"Small comfort for the man who incurred my wrath," Li responded.

Gradually, fatigue pulled him down. He had denied himself sleep for so many days, his body demanded rest. He closed his eyes and did not meditate. He fell into deep, deep sleep.

For the next hour, Villi fought the controls of the aircraft as he increased the inertia dampeners to maximum and slowed his speed even further to avoid any unintended accidents. Unlike a plane made of aluminum, this aircraft could withstand a direct impact with a stone cliff... if the inertia dampeners provided maximum deceleration and protected the occupants from absorbing the kinetic energy. The sudden slam into a wall of rock might do more damage to the mountain than the aircraft. Still, such an abrupt halt had never been tried and its impact on the passengers could not be predicted without further testing, something Villi did not have time to accomplish.

"Analysis of flight intent complete," his panel squawked.

"What?" Villi asked.

"You may fly in auto mode if you desire," it told him.

"Don't send us tumbling over the landscape," Villi said to it.

He found his eyelids heavy. He closed his eyes intending only to rest for a few minutes. The next thing he knew, the control panel alerted him awake.

"Approaching destination," it said.

"I must have fallen asleep," he said as he sat up and looked over the aircraft's sensors.

Villi turned off the automatic controls and took over manual flight.

"Warning," a voice stated, "large outcrop of rock approaching intercept vector at your current altitude."

Villi looked up in time to see a wall of orange rock coming straight at them. He turned to avoid the outcrop. The sudden flip and turn defied the inertia dampeners. It threw everyone over to the side. The rough ride roused Li from his stupor.

"What was that?" Li asked as Villi's turn buffeted him.

Yet, Villi found that even after he missed the large rock formation, he had trouble with the aircraft. The whole body of the aircraft shook as if it were coming apart. A strong vibration shuddered through its entire hull.

"What wrong?" Michael asked as everyone in the cabin shook from the vibration.

"I don't know," Villi replied via a link. "Feels like I'm fighting a head wind or something. Did I miss a weather report? We aren't flying into inclement weather, are we Master Li?"

"Who's to say we aren't?" Li told him.

He wondered if the attack had started. Cyrus may have put an illusion into their minds so they felt the experience of turbulence in an effort to thwart Villi's skills as a pilot. The group could feel the aircraft slow down and the landing gear doors open beneath them as the computer employed the wheels.

"Coming up on the touchdown point," it informed them.

All at once, Master Li discovered he had trouble breathing. His forehead broke out in a sweat. He could not sit up.

"Master Li, are you ok?" Han asked.

"Why do you ask that?" Master Li inquired, catching his breath.

"I can't explain it, Master Li," Han linked as he tried to express his emotions. "I don't feel well. I feel weak as if I had no energy."

Villi looked down at his control panel. The indicators started to turn orange. Not one or two, but all of them started to fluctuate and change.

"Try to concentrate on landing the aircraft," he thought.

Just as he started to set the aircraft down, he could no longer sense Master Li, as if he had vanished.

"Not again!" he moaned. Master Li ditched Villi during their flight to London nine months ago. One of the original designers of Galactic Central opened a temporary rift in the fabric of space and snatched Li from Earth. "What do they want now? Isn't this bad timing on their part?"

Just then, he realized that it was not just Master Li whose psychic signature grew faint. The rest of their team began to vanish, too. Villi started to panic when he could no longer link with Su Lin. The computer immediately set the aircraft into a landing position. Villi's whole panel turned bright yellow – the disconnect signal.

"Stealth controls off," it chimed.

"I didn't order that!" Villi cried and tried to change it.

"Auto landing procedure engaged," the computer continued.

"Hey!" Villi yelled and slammed his fists down on the control panel.

"Master Li!" Han cried out. The strategist yanked off his seatbelt and tried to be near Li's side. Han fell to the floor.

The rest of the team started to rise but found they had no energy, no vitality, and curiously no desire. Li sat very still with his eyes closed. Drenched in sweat, his white hair matted to his forehead, the master level psychic sat very still. Han pulled his body up. His fingers trembled as he leaned Master Li's seat back.

"Go through the checklist," a weak voice whispered. It was Cecilia. "Breath and heart rate, Han," she tried to point out.

"What's going on?" Li sputtered as he tried to come alive.

"Well, we know he has a pulse," Chou whispered.

Han stood up. He felt dizzy. He staggered over to the galley and filled up a glass with cool water. He brought it over to Master Li who took a tiny sip. Color slowly returned to his face.

"Feel any better?" Han asked with a worried expression.

"I'll tell you in a moment," Li uttered as he spoke through parched lips.

The elderly man weakly grasped the half-filled glass and took a long draft before he eventually handed the empty glass back to Han.

Just then, the aircraft jostled when the wheels of the aircraft touched down on the road. Han had the presence of mind to glance out the window and saw the ground coming up. He fell backward into his seat and grabbed the sides of his chair. The computer set the craft down so hard, it jerked everyone around. Villi came up out of his pilot's seat and headed back into the cabin.

"Is everyone ok?" he wondered. "I don't know what's going on!"

"We'd be better if you'd land this thing a little softer next time," Zinian quipped. It was the last thing he said before his eyes rolled back.

Villi did not respond. He suddenly had a difficult time trying to stand up. He looked around at his friend's faces and noticed anguish and distress. He could not sense energy or thoughts from anyone. After two and a half years, the silence was deafening.

"Master Li," Villi addressed him. "What is wrong with me?"

"I wish I knew…" Li began and his eyes when toward the door. He tried to point toward the door. "The door…" he struggled to speak.

"Air… you want some air?" Villi thought. He didn't know. For the first time in his life, he did not know what Li meant by a gesture without a thought between them.

Villi turned toward the door and touched the control. The door opened and the steps lowered.

"Noooooo!" Master Li weakly protested.

However, Li's warning came too late. A second later, the team watched with horror as a loud sound went off and Villi's body crashed into the opposite wall as if knocked away from the doorway by an explosion. A bright light flashed and the whole team blacked out.

CHAPTER THIRTY-SIX

AN OLD FEELING

TWO HOURS AFTER HE DEPARTED Adelaide, General Pollack touched down at the base outside Melbourne. He did not bother to wait for a staff car. He borrowed a jeep from the ground staff and drove straight to General Wallace's offices, only to find his commander's offices strangely absent. He exited those rooms and backtracked to the main staff offices.

"Private!" he barked to one of men on guard duty. "Where can I find..."

"General Pollack?" the man questioned. "The colonel wanted me to direct you to him right away," he said and pointed up a hall. "I must have missed you on the way in... sir."

The general did not wish to admit he bypassed the lobby.

"Uh... yes, carry on," he muttered and headed up the hall in the direction indicated.

He found General Sander's people in charge of a hastily constructed, make-shift command center. Sander's lackey, Colonel Evans, sat at a desk with a headset on, speaking into a microphone while he watched six screens in front of him. Some of the images were from live satellite feeds, while other video came in from live cameras in the field. Evans and the two men who flanked him had large desktop computers in front of them. They constantly typed or spoke orders, updates, and messages into the devices.

"What's going on?" the general asked.

Colonel Evans did not answer the general. Instead, he pointed to the largest screen on the wall divided into four distinct pictures, each one showed a satellite photograph taken before and after the attack. Evans spoke into his mic again. He spoke so softly that the general could not hear him.

"Is this all that we know?" General Pollack asked.

Col. Evans finally went to the printer and took the fresh page as it spit out. He handed it over to the general and didn't bother to salute his superior officer.

"General Sanders wants you in the field at once, general," Colonel Evans relayed to him. "Here are you orders, sir," he told him. "He wants a perimeter set up around the city. The Prime Minister authorized the general to take over control of the city temporarily while they shut down any possible escape routes. All traffic has been re-routed. General Aden is headed to protect the government in Canberra. Intelligence believes other attacks may follow."

"For once I agree with the analysts!" the major general thought.

He started to look down at the paper when the colonel continued.

"General Sanders has four task forces scouring the area for the culprits," the colonel continued, "on the river, at the waterfront, in the city, and in the air. The general is overseeing the effort from a helicopter. The prime minister is on his way to the survey the scene along with members of the cabinet," Evans informed him.

"Have they located the perpetrators?" the general asked.

"Not yet," Colonel Evans told him, "though we're following several leads."

General Pollack finally glanced down at the orders in his hand.

"What?" he objected. "I'm to take a land-based column and establish a perimeter across the north," he said as he read them over. "What is that supposed to accomplish?" he asked.

"The general feels this will cut off any escape route out of the city," the colonel answered.

"Cut off... doesn't he bloody well know that they've left town by now!" the general declared. "They're probably on their way to Sydney," he conjectured. "I hardly expect they've gone to the north!"

"We've taken that contingency into account," the colonel responded. "Lt. General Lehman is taking the south end of Brisbane. He's there now. We've also beefed up shore patrols. The police are stopping traffic on the highways in and out of principle cities," he went on. "The prime minister is ready to declare martial law if necessary. That is what we are recommending."

General Pollack stared at the colonel for a second.

"Martial Law?" he responded. "That's a bit drastic, don't you think. The American's did not suspend their constitution when the terrorists attacked New York. I don't believe we should either. I'll make my own recommendation to the prime minister," he said.

"General Sanders is with him now," the colonel told him.

"Where is General Wallace? He's Chief of Staff; he should be..."

"General Wallace, sir," the colonel swallowed hard, "was scheduled to deliver a speech in Brisbane this afternoon…" he hesitated. "We have not been able to contact General Wallace…"

"You mean… he might have been at the…" James speculated.

The colonel nodded.

"Oh, this does change things, doesn't it?" the general said. "Do you have a jet available…" James began, when the colonel cut him off.

"Your pilot is waiting to take you to your company, general," the colonel informed him. "They are en route to the scene."

General Pollack cleared his throat and gritted his teeth.

"Very well, colonel… then I will be on my way," James said as he faced the junior officer.

The colonel, finally catching the hint, stood up and saluted.

"Good luck, General Pollack," Colonel Evans told him. "By the way, sir," he added, "I…" He hesitated to put in his personal feelings. He straightened, "I'm inclined to agree with you… sir!" he said and saluted again.

Major General Pollack knew that General Sanders played him for a chump in this situation and he resented it. He crumpled his orders in his fist as he stormed out and tossed the wad of paper into a waste basket. When he walked from the HQ building, a driver flagged him down. He had a car with a military police escort.

"Sir, they sent me to drive you to the airstrip at once," the private said as he saluted.

"Let's go," the general responded and stepped into the back of the car.

With sirens blaring and lights flashing, the general's car and his escort of military police, streaked toward the base's airstrip. Inside the car, the general quietly considered the implications of what would happen to the corps if General Sanders took over, not just Army command, but became Chief of Staff. If he convinced the Prime Minister to declare martial law, Sanders could enhance his public position at the same time, which had political implications down the road.

"This is a black day for my country," he sighed as he thought of the innocent people, brutalized by the blast, injured or dead, and what this would mean for Australia's future.

A few minutes later, the driver pulled into the airstrip. Shortly thereafter, the Harrier jet lifted vertically once the general returned to the co-pilot's seat.

"How fast can this thing go?" the general asked the pilot.

"My top speed is 1080 kph, sir," he answered.

"Do you have enough fuel?" the general wondered.

"I have a full tank sir," the pilot responded.

"Then fly me to Brisbane at that speed," the general requested.

"Yes, sir!" the pilot answered. "I could push our speed a little faster... it will burn more fuel..."

"Do it," the general advised.

Within twenty minutes, they were passing Sydney airspace and the general had his company of men on a communication link. Colonel William Darling, the officer temporarily in charge, informed him that they were in the process of closing down the north and southbound access to the city. James knew this officer. He was part of General Wallace's staff in Canberra. He also met Bill Darling at Digger's once when General Wallace brought him there. He liked Colonel Darling and trusted him.

"I'm on my way, Bill," James told him. "It will probably take me another thirty minutes or less to arrive. I wish to address all the junior officers the moment I touch down," he ordered. "Call an impromptu staff meeting."

"Yes, sir," the colonel answered.

As the jet approached the freeway, General Pollack could see the long column of vehicles that stretched out along the entire north side of Brisbane. A dark green band of military tanks and trucks literally cut off every north and south bound road. As the jet swung around to land, the city seemed strangely silent. A column of white smoke still rose from the city center in the distance.

Having delivered its package, the Harrier jet lifted back into the sky and flew to the Brisbane airstrip to refuel before he returned to the military headquarters. Three officers in charge of north companies approached in other vehicles to join the colonel and the general: a captain and two lieutenants.

"Does anyone have a map," James asked.

One of the assistants ran over with an electronic pad. James motioned for the men to gather around him.

"I will only explain this once, so listen carefully," he told them. "Captain Hastings, take your column of vehicles into these areas of northern Brisbane. This is a show of force and nothing more. If you encounter traffic on the street, tell people they must stay in their homes until further notice... for their safety."

"Yes, sir," Hastings replied.

"Lieutenant, I want manned checkpoints here, here, here, here and here," he said as he indicated the general roads north out of Brisbane. "Use subordinates to patrol the smaller roads."

"Yes, sir," the man answered.

"Colonel Darling, I want you and your men to block all traffic north or south on Route 1. Take trucks and pick up all the drivers. Tell them to lock their cars and take them to these locations. No shooting if people start to flee on foot. Call in a chopper and run them down. We only want to see ID and reasons why they are in or near Brisbane. All of this will look good to the press and the prime minister. However, I believe the entire effort is futile. This is only an exercise for the public so they believe they are safe."

"Sir, I don't understand," the colonel spoke up.

"Bill," the general said as he lowered his voice, "I've followed your career from the beginning. You know me very well. The way I see it, the men who pulled off this dastardly act probably left town hours ago."

"Where do you think they went, sir?" the captain asked. "They couldn't have flown out. We heard that all flights in and out of Australia for the last 24 hours have been thoroughly screened."

"That's just it," the general stated, "I believe they left by innocuous means. They set these charges and then headed out of city hours ago in a van disguised as a repair service or on a boat disguised as a fishing expedition. They simply blended in with the other traffic. People probably saw them leave the parking garage and thought they were just the air conditioning repairmen."

"It would be impossible to find them. We'd have to search cars up and down the coast," the colonel stated. "We don't have enough men for that," he said.

"Bill, I want you to stay here in Brisbane and follow General Sander's directives. Meanwhile, I'm going to take a contingent of men with me. If Colonel Evans is correct, and General Lehman did cut off the south roads in time, then they've only one avenue for escape, if that is their plan."

"What else would they do?" the captain asked.

"Plant more bombs… cause more damage," the general suspected.

"Yes, but the whole country's on alert," the lieutenant stated. "Sooner or later, someone will spot them."

"People who blend in?" the general challenged. "These are not foreigners… these are fellow countrymen. They look just like you and me."

"How on earth do you know that?" the colonel questioned.

"I have… some top secret information. I also suspected as much," the general replied and started to move away.

"Where are you going?" the colonel asked him.

"I've a hunch where they might be," the general stated, his eyes looked north.

"I don't know if I can cover for you, sir," Colonel Darling told his superior. "General Sanders said that he specifically wanted you to…"

"…Sanders is busy with the prime minister, whom he hopes will declare martial law…" General Pollack let that drop and saw the shock on their faces.

Captain Hastings gritted his teeth. His wife worked for the State Department in Canberra, where the seat of Australian government is located.

He knew her feelings in this regard, that martial law should be the last resort.

"He can't do that..." the captain started to say, when General Pollack put his hand on his arm.

"Easy, Bob," James said with a calm voice. "If things happen the way I believe they will, it may not come to that."

"Sir?" the captain asked.

"Trust me this once," the general pleaded with his officers. "I'll need about six hours. Can you give them to me?"

"Sir, yes, sir," they responded.

"Good," James said, relieved. He glanced around at the lead cars. "I'll need a sergeant and some of your best men, someone good with a knife, used to doing close work. I may have to do some clandestine stuff here," he said.

"You know something about this," Colonel Darling guessed. "Did someone tip you off?"

"Like I said, Bill, I'm acting on a hunch," the general admitted. "Can I trust you men to back me up?"

He held out his hand. The other officers placed their hands on his.

"Good luck, sir," Colonel Darling muttered.

A few minutes later, General Pollack watched as the column of vehicles began to break up. One contingent headed south, while some of the others crossed the highway to make an organized block on the other side. He waited for a sergeant to report on the assemblage of his strike team, when an old familiar face approached him.

"Sergeant Beery!" James grinned. "You're a sight for sore eyes. What the devil are you doing here?" he asked. "I thought you were back in Adelaide?"

"You dinna think I was gonna miss out on any action under my old commander, sir. Did you?" he wondered. "When I overheard those officers as they streamed out of Diggers' I knew what I had to do. I went to the airstrip and had your jet ready in Melbourne. I made certain the pilot would stay at the airstrip for you. When General Sanders caught wind of what I done, 'an Evan's told me Sanders give you orders to get you out of his way... more or less... sir," Berry added with his Scottish accent. "I knew what I had to do... find a way to help ya."

"I wondered why I had a Harrier jet at my disposal," James said as he shook his head.

"I'm still cover'in your backside, sir," Berry said as he saluted. He grinned with a broad toothy smile.

It pleased James to no end that his men should be so loyal to him. He hoped he would not disappoint them, for he had an important ace up his sleeve that he intended to use.

"Assemble our strike team, Beery," he ordered. "We leave at once."

"Beggin' your pardon, sir, I took the liberty..." Berry said and nodded to his right.

James glanced over Beery's shoulder to find a truck of men and a military car waiting along the side of the road.

"Just give us a direction, general," Beery requested.

"North," General Pollack told him, "as fast as these vehicles can safely go. We have some criminals to catch and as far as I can figure, we're about three or four hours behind them."

For a second, he closed his eyes and sent out his senses. Cecilia spoke to him about extending his senses beyond the immediate area. While he could not communicate with a psychic that far away, he could visualize the land over great distances and discern certain details in rapid succession. The move drained a great of energy from him and made James dizzy. For a second, he started to weave. He remembered to pull additional psychic energy to maintain his alertness.

Sgt. Beery curiously watched his old commander for a second, uncertain if he was going to topple over. He did not question what the general did. He believed in Major General Pollack. After all, the general led Berry and his fellow privates out of Afghanistan's mountains without a single casualty.

"We're too late for Caloundra," the general whispered with his eyes still closed. "They're already on their way to... to... to Fraser Island!" he finished and opened his eyes. "Fraser Island?" he questioned and turned to Beery. "Where the hell is Fraser Island?"

"Yes, sir," Beery said as he stepped in close so the other men did not hear them. He lowered his voice. "It's to the north, up by Maryborough, sir," the sergeant explained. "You remember Fraser Island, sir. You took the misses there once, a long time ago... I believe."

"Fraser Island! Yes, of course... good lord, that was a long time ago," James recalled. "You have a great memory, Beery," the general complimented.

"Thank you, sir," the sergeant replied. He tipped his head in closer. "If you beg my pardon, sir, may I ask... what makes you believe we'll find anyone on Fraser Island?" the sergeant wondered.

"Do you remember... Periwinkle?" the general whispered the last part.

The sergeant nodded his reply.

"I brought you back from the Afghanistan campaign," the general began. "You helped me out a jam that day, sergeant, because you trusted my judgment. The same thing is happening today. You must have blind trust me as you did on that day so long ago in Afghanistan," he explained. "I feel that I know the way," the general spoke with conviction. "That's the best way I can explain it."

Berry looked in the general's eyes and saw that same conviction in the old man's face that he saw over thirty years ago. He trusted that face.

"Sir!" the sergeant shouted as he stood up straight. "I understand the orders, sir. We'll get you there!"

He stiffly saluted and headed over to the truck. The moment he approached his men, Beery started barking orders. He held open the back door of the car for the general and saluted as the general approached. James stepped into the back of the military car and the driver sped forward. The sergeant went into the passenger side of the carrier truck and yelled at the driver to "keep up with that car!"

"Where to?" the driver questioned.

"Shut your stinking mouth, corporal!" the sergeant barked. "Is that clear?" he yelled.

"Yes, sir!" he answered and pushed his right foot to the floor.

Chapter Thirty-seven

Dead end

"Last time you looked into my mind... I looked into yours," Cyrus mused as he gazed at a map of southern Australia. "Let's see... you tap into other peoples' psychic energy and absorb it. Well, I sort of knew about that part," he commented.

"Sir?" a young man said when he entered Cyrus tent.

"I'm finished," Cyrus said as he indicated his bed. "Please dispose of that."

The private slung the limp body of another victim over his shoulder like a sack of potatoes and set out to bury her away from their camp. Naturally, he said nothing to Cyrus. He thought it strange that she should have no mark on her body. Unlike the women that Girard shared with his men – they often had bruises or scrapped skin from being thrown on the floor or even rug burns – this woman, and the last one he buried, had no marks at all. He did not question his leader's behavior. He feared Cyrus. They all did. Therefore, the young man followed orders. He took the body without question and left his commander alone in his tent as the pale slender man mumbled over maps and pictures on his laptop computer.

"I suppose I came by this absorption technique naturally," Cyrus continued to speculate and privately chuckled. "You people make me sick. You are all so nice and polite to one another. How boring! Ooo, it's such a big taboo to never borrow energy from another psychic. You consider it an attack," he thought. "What a great idea. You gave me inspiration. When it comes to war, we do what we must to survive. That is the bottom line to war, a question of survival... Mister Li," Cyrus sarcastically spat out and grinned when he did.

He picked up his radio because he did not wish to use his power.

"Girard, I need you," he spoke into the short range instrument.

"Sir?" Girard answered. He wondered why Cyrus did not speak to his mind. He had been training with the men all morning. They were hot and sweaty. Girard had come to love these work outs. He was in the best shape of his life. His muscles were pumped.

"Come to my tent at once," Cyrus ordered. "Tell Lissen to take over."

Girard could not infer any tone from the message. However, he was used to Cyrus disruptions. He glanced over and saw a private heading away from Cyrus' tent with a body slung over the man's shoulder.

"He killed another one," he thought. "I'll have to travel into town tomorrow and find some more women," he said as he called to his second. "Lissen!" Girard cried out.

The eager young man with the shaved head ran up and stood at attention.

"Yes, sir!" he saluted, just as sweaty as his superior.

"Take over," Girard ordered. He nodded his head toward Cyrus' tent as he turned to go.

Lissen understood that Cyrus must have called Girard away. The big man sprinted up the hill to the building large enough to house twenty men. Only one man stayed inside this large air-conditioned space, and no one questioned him or his luxuries.

"Sir!" Girard called out as he entered the cool interior. The air felt refreshing, although Cyrus did provide some fans for the other tents.

Cyrus stood over his table with his portable computer open. Girard watched as the scrawny youth poured over a stream of satellite information. The bed behind him had half of its sheets lying on the floor. Cyrus did not bother to look up when Girard entered.

"First off, I thought I'd let you know of our success," he began.

"You mean?"

"Yes... we fired the first shot across their bow... the enemy is scramblin' to find your team... of course, they won't," Cyrus confidently stated. "Did you send a contingent of men to the location as we discussed earlier?" Cyrus asked. "As you might recall, I did not wish to know any details," he added.

"Yes, sir, I did," Girard confirmed. "However, I must add a note of caution. That position is at least ten minutes away from base camp. That's a long stretch from here without support. They might be spotted."

"I doubt it," Cyrus told him. "I took care of that," he threw out. "The flyovers have ceased, at least for the time being," he added.

"Very good, sir," Girard stated. "May I ask again, why you feel this team will land here? Our base is five kilometers away."

"It is a tactical move on their part," Cyrus explained as he gazed into

Girard's eyes. "I want you to contact those men. If they spot a strangely shaped boxy aircraft that lands…"

"Who is landin'?" the big man questioned.

"As I said earlier, the American will try to stop me with his strike team," Cyrus told his second. He saw the change on Girard's face. "Don't worry. I'll protect your men. Don't I have your best interest at heart?" he asked his second. "What's goin' on outside?"

"Exercise," Girard said.

Cyrus stopped speaking and closed his eyes. He turned, faced away from Girard, and held out his hands as if groping in the dark.

"They're almost here!" he said and quickly spun around. "The aircraft bears down on that position. Call yer men and tell 'em to take up positions at once. Alert 'em to anythin' unusual or strange. Tell 'em to rush in the moment the door to that airplane opens!" Cyrus ordered. "Use stun grenades, that sort of thing, but alive."

"Yes, sir," Girard replied and understood what he meant by alive… bring them back alive. He pulled out his radio and began to speak in a low voice. He gave a few brief orders and put the radio back on his hip. "They're ready," he said.

"Good," Cyrus stated as he moved closer to the big man, which always made Girard feel uncomfortable.

"How much time do they have…" Girard began.

"Not now… I must concentrate… prepare… better get rid of the women," Cyrus ordered. "Have Lissen put the women in a truck, take 'em into the desert and return right away. I want 'em out of the way."

"What about the men…"

"Don't worry… if all goes well, we'll find 'em later. After you get rid of the women, alert the compound! Assemble the entire group at… 1300 hours." He read Girard's mind and added, "Don't worry about the strike team. They'll find their way back here. I promise," he told the big man.

"Yes, sir," Girard answered.

"You have your, orders," Cyrus told him and waved his hand toward the exit.

"Yes, sir," Girard nodded.

He marched from the tent, cupped his hands, and began to bark his orders right away. Cyrus heard the men scramble inside the main tent as most wanted to clean up before any possible "inspection." A few minutes from now, Cyrus would make a grand entrance, certain to cement his position as their leader. He knew a little about placing visions in their minds. Later, he intended to use that devotion when he drained them of psychic energy to blast away at the asteroid. The timing for the action flashed on his computer.

Twenty-four hours from now, he would set his plan in action and change the course of human history. For now, he had to perform a needed celestial adjustment.

"With two hundred men at my disposal, I can fill up with as much psychic energy as I need to carry out my plans," he thought.

Cyrus sat in his tent and meditated for the next several minutes. Slowly and most certainly he gradually absorbed nearly all the psychic energy he could drain from the people aboard the aircraft moving ever closer to his position. As the aircraft grew nearer, his task became all the easier. He never felt like this in his life. His body pulsed with power. He thought he could accomplish anything.

"I am the most powerful psychic in universe," he thought, "even stronger than that Chinaman!"

He opened his eyes and looked into the mirror. He positively glowed with the energy he absorbed. He grinned at the psychic being he saw. He flexed his power the way a weightlifter flexes his or her muscles.

"Girard! Come here!" he called.

When Girard entered the tent, he fearfully stared at Cyrus. The young man floated in the air above his chair. He never saw him do anything like that. While he did not see the glow, he could sense that Cyrus felt supremely confident. Cyrus held out his hand and his long coat floated over to him. Girard never saw him do that either. Something had changed. Something was different about Cyrus. Girard wondered if he could ever challenge these psychics without their knowledge. He lowered his eyes and emptied his mind lest Cyrus hear his mutinous thoughts.

"The men are assembled and ready, sir!" Girard told him.

"Go outside and wait for me," Cyrus replied.

Cyrus flipped his long coat behind him like a cape. He swaggered up to the entrance to his tent. In a few minutes, he would need every ounce of energy the men had in them to perform his deed. The die would be cast and no one could stop him, not even the oriental man whose energy he just drained. He reached out and entered the minds of all two hundred men at the same time, a concept he only attempted in practice a few times over the past week.

He moved up to the double flap and made it part before him. He placed an image into the mind of every man present of a larger, taller, and meaner Cyrus. He stood up on the hill before them, wearing a cape and cowl instead of his long coat, the black garment flowed behind him. He appeared to them as if the devil has risen from hell. This vision struck fear into many of the men's minds. That response pleased Cyrus. The core group, the ones that showed the most loyalty to Girard, raised their fists in the air.

"Cyrus!" they shouted, "Cyrus! Cyrus! Cyrus!"

He held up his hand and moved toward the edge of a platform where he sometimes sat and watched the men exercise. Girard saw this vision, too. Unlike his men, however, he had seen Cyrus only moments before. He knew that Cyrus created this illusion in his mind. He moved over and stood to the right of Cyrus and stared out at the startled faces of his men. He gauged their reaction, watched them, ready to back up whatever his leader said.

"They fear and admire him," he thought. "Perhaps that is best," his thoughts continued, "they might survive his wrath should he fail, whereas, I may not... I must think of some alternatives for my own survival."

Cyrus basked in his own glory and did not sense the thoughts of the man who stood so close to him.

"Men," he called out, "we have struck the first blow. Our enemies tremble before us. They run around confused. Now we start the next phase of our plan. Even as I speak, our strike teams move to attack them again. Observe your leader!" he said as his voice boomed about the canyon.

Even Girard felt compelled to watch Cyrus. His body began to glow. His eyes turned yellow. He raised up his arms and flexed his muscles.

"Aarrgh!" he roared. His body slowly lifted off the ground into the air.

The men watched amazed as Cyrus put the illusion into their minds. Only Girard realized at the last moment that it was a ruse. He could see from this angle the young man's thin shadow on the boards, and the fact Cyrus had not risen at all, the shadow's feet still touched the platform.

"Sir!" a voice broke into Girard's earpiece. He recognized his security detail from the other location. "A strange aircraft just landed near out position..."

Girard pulled up his radio. He changed the frequency on his communicator and turned away from the spectacle.

"This is Girard," he spoke into the mouthpiece.

"Sir?" a voice responded.

"I want your men to surround the aircraft with weapons drawn," he ordered. "Use shock and flash grenades the moment you see any door open. Board the aircraft and bring the passengers back to the base camp... alive."

"But sir, we thought..." the man began to protest.

"Just do as I say. That's a direct order. Got that soldier?" Girard told him.

"Yes, sir!" the voice answered.

"Good. Girard out," he said and signed off.

He turned his attention back to Cyrus. A beam of light shot upward out of Cyrus' body into the afternoon sky. Every man's jaw dropped. Cyrus kept his eyes closed and concentrated. In outer space, one hundred miles above them, a massive machine complex glided silently through outer space over the continent of Australia. Cyrus entered the mind of the station's commander. The man sealed off his section before he activated the controls that changed the attitude of the enormous spaceship. To the surprise of the crew and those monitoring on the planet's surface, the gigantic complex began to rotate.

He sensed that every alarm and every emergency beacon went off aboard the massive space-going vessel. Cyrus reached out and instructed the commander to silence them. The other men and women onboard, instead of responding, lapsed into a coma like state after they cut off NASA's communication simultaneously. In the silence of the floating void, the huge structure began to rotate its attitude, angling its massive solar array panel until it turned one side toward the planet Earth below. Once the station turned on its side, Cyrus could bounce his destructive beacon off its powerful solar array. He would need to wait for his body to recharge and the station's orbit to return to this attitude before he sent the final blow to the asteroid. With the power of the psychics to aid him one more time, he would send his powerful beacon into space. Their energy worked better than any he could pull from the men around him. Inadvertently, the Americans had played into his hand by coming to him. He simply channeled their energy into space.

To keep the station in this position, he needed to eliminate its crew. While he still had the power to affect the craft overhead, he ordered the man in the command position to open an outside valve and vent the interior atmosphere. Cyrus prevented the onboard computer from overriding the emergency airlocks. Within seconds, the space station held the floating dead bodies of five astronauts. As the station moved further away in its orbit, Cyrus power could not reach and affect anything onboard. He released his formation of the energy flow and took in a deep breath. Creating the beacon drained his psychic energy to the point that his illusion began to fade. He quickly turned from the men and entered his tent, calling to Girard at the same time.

"Girard... quick... I need you..." he whispered to his mind.

"Cyrus?" Girard questioned when he saw the pale young man return to his natural form and quickly duck into his tent. "Are you ill?"

"No, you big lummox," Cyrus replied. "Just weak."

"I see," Girard replied as he approached.

Cyrus seemed less of a threat inside the tent now that he had shrunk back to his former self. For a second, Girard realized the pale young man was drained of his power and helpless. For the first time since their initial encounter, Girard saw an opportunity. Cyrus staggered to hold his head up. He leaned against a pole and gasped for air.

"This is it," Girard thought. "If you are going to kill him, now is your chance." He started to make his move. He stretched out his big wide hands.

He could easily break Cyrus' neck in a second, when he heard a great cry coming from behind him.

"Cyrus! Cyrus!" he heard growing louder. "Cyrus! Cyrus! Cyrus!" the men shouted.

Girard pulled up short. If he killed Cyrus, it would mean every man for himself. He could not duplicate anything Cyrus did. Despite his resentment, Cyrus had given him a great deal more than he had when they first met. He had a new truck, bedded many women and had a locker full of money in his tent. Yet he also did some horrible things, too, in front of the company. Two hundred men knew him well, his face, his name, and what he allowed to happen. They could tell the government what they knew, the atrocities, the torture that took place in the camp. He trained the demolitions squad. They could connect him to the bombings. He'd become a wanted criminal. The military would put a price on his head. He'd get life in prison or worse. Despite his plans to the contrary, he did not want that future. Now was not the time to make his move.

He reconsidered murdering their prophet. Instead, he supported the young man up under his armpits and helped him walk back to his bedroom.

"Let me help you," he said as he supported Cyrus toward his bed. Cyrus went limp. Girard reached down and gently lifted the slender lad into his arms. He carried him the rest of the way.

"Thanks," Cyrus said as he leaned his head on Girard's big shoulders.

Girard laid him down and hesitated over his body. He saw how the coat and clothes twisted around his skinny body. Like some protective parent, he stripped the young man of his clothes except his underwear and slid him under the covers, tucking him in.

"Cyrus?" he quietly asked.

"What is it?" Cyrus softly answered; his eyes closed.

"Why don't I just give my men orders to shoot these Americans?" he finally requested. "You don't need them, sir. You are the most powerful psychic on the planet." He could not believe the words that came out of his mouth.

"I can't do that... not yet..." Cyrus gasped as his energy level dropped. "I still need their energy to fire on the asteroid..."

"Asteroid?" Girard wondered as he backed away.

"The one that will change history..." the lad softly muttered.

He glanced over at the computer on the table. He saw on the screen a crude animation Cyrus created that showed the path of an object enter the Earth's atmosphere and strike the East China Sea. While it was not detailed, when the blob struck that part of the map, it flashed in bright yellow: target zone. An energy wave spread outward that covered an enormous area now shaded with gray labeled, "area affected." His eyes widened with the realization what Cyrus intended.

"He's gonna destroy half of Asia!" Girard whispered aloud. He did not realize Cyrus was still awake.

The frail young man managed enough energy to roll over. He opened his eyes and looked up at the big man standing next to the bed. He could not see into Girard's mind. He did not know that Girard just now discovered his plan.

"I know you want to kill them," Cyrus gasped, "the Americans..." he added and fell back, closing his eyes and fading.

His words broke the silence. Girard spun around. Sweat broke out on his forehead. This made up his mind. Cyrus was a madman. He could not let the little pipsqueak carry out his plan and destroy the planet. He was a killer, true, but not in the vein of a Hitler. Girard could not stand by and allow so many innocent people to die. He had to kill Cyrus... right now... this instant. He started for the bed. Yet, when he tried to attack, something held him back. He could not move closer. His arms could not bend closer. As much as he strained, he could not quite grasp the scrawny kid's neck.

Cyrus' eyes fluttered open. He saw Girard's intent. Behind him, he noticed his computer playing out the animation. He realized Girard must have seen and wanted to stop him. He saw how the big man's outstretched arms strained against an invisible force, one he found mysterious. He realized in that instance that psychics must possess some sort of defense mechanism and that probably only another psychic could kill him. Had he known of Master Li's cousin and that history, he would have discovered that the Chinese Army had the same difficulty destroying him... so they locked him up instead.

"You cannot hurt me," Cyrus hoarsely whispered when he saw Girard with his hands extended, "even if you wanted to. We have some sort of built-in defense mechanism. I'm not certain... perhaps shooting one of us is not out of the question. Yet, I understand that even that is difficult. But, the Americans... I need them, Girard... and don't worry. I can keep them in a weakened state once you bring them back here. I can drain their energy and become very powerful... but... about my plan... sorry I didn't tell you sooner... I should have... I only wanted to..."

Cyrus closed his eyes. His head started to droop.

"What?" Girard demanded.

Cyrus struggled to open his eyes. He could barely speak.

"We must succeed, Girard... you and I... we're in it together... to the end. Oh, If you deem these Americans too dangerous to your men or even to me," he uttered, "I leave the decision to you. Go ahead and shoot them the moment they try anything."

Cyrus finally faded at that moment. When he did, Girard noticed the force that held him at bay lessened. Still, he could not strangle the youth. Instead, he pulled out his gun, cocked the trigger, and tried to aim the barrel at Cyrus' head. Yet, he could not aim the barrel at Cyrus. Some force kept pushing the end away to one side or the other. Frustrated, he holstered the weapon and turned toward the exit.

"Perhaps I need to catch him off guard. Cyrus may have read my intention just now. What if I did kill the Americans?" he thought. "With only Cyrus left to kill… sooner or later, I'm sure I could finish him off…"

Girard smiled at Cyrus willingness to give him that decision. He decided he would tolerate Cyrus, if he had to keep him around. He did respect his special power. They would continue their odd but necessary arrangement… for a while longer, at least. However, something about this whole idea bothered him. Why would the American's send an old Chinese man? What good would he be in a fight? What was so special about this old man? Did he know a way to prevent Cyrus from moving the asteroid? He didn't have much time to find the answer, as he could see the speed of the space station on the computer screen.

"I've got to investigate these Americans personally," he thought as he exited the tent and started down the hill. "Lissen!" he yelled. "Bring me a humah!"

He decided to intercept his men at the strategy point and appraise the threat from this strike team before his soldiers brought them into base camp. He quickly gave Lissen orders to take the women from base camp and drop them off in the desert, anywhere away from here. Lissen roared over to him, driving one of the big wide vehicles with dust flying everywhere.

"I'll run the women out…"

"Before you do that," Girard said to him as he jumped into the vehicle. "Have men guard Cyrus' tent but not go inside. Then take the women away from here. I'm runnin' down to check on our guard post southeast of camp. Wait here to hear from me. If I don't check in within thirty minutes, I want you to personally wake Cyrus and inform him of the situation. Understood?"

"Yes, sir!" Lissen said and saluted.

Girard took off at the fastest speed he could as he bounced across the open desert and headed southeast. He worried about his men when they confronted this unusual group from America. He pushed his vehicle and drove like a man possessed across the rough terrain.

CHAPTER THIRTY-EIGHT

PERIWINKLE

SERGEANT BEERY WOULD NEVER SAY it, but he had his doubts about his old commander. Yet, he would never express those doubts aloud. He knew Major General James Montgomery Pollack and his wife Penelope very well, as he should. He served under the general for over three decades. In the twilight of his years, the general repaid Berry's service. General Pollack obtained the desk position for the sergeant at the Diggers' Club. Devoted to military service and never having married, Beery intended to retire from the army in a few years. He dated many women through the years, but he always considered the army his first wife.

In all the years he knew General Pollack, the senior officer never said a harsh word to Henry Beery. Yet when the indigenous man visited and left the secret note, General Pollack bristled, fussed, and behaved with a short manner. Later, he personally apologized to Sgt. Beery about the matter. Berry recalled the humility on the general's face when he told him: "I don't know what I'd do or how I would feel, if I ever walked through that door and did not see your understanding face."

So as Berry pressed forward down the road with this green corporal driver next to him, and the man questioned the general's sanity, he gritted his resolve to follow the officer he grew to trust over all of those years.

"If he wants me to go to Fraser Island," Beery thought, "then we go to Fraser Island, except…"

"What makes you think the general knows what he's doin?" the driver mumbled. His words brought Berry back to reality.

The sergeant eyed the young man next to him and shook his head.

"I don't mean to speak down to you, corporal," Berry responded. "But, you don't know nuthin about that officer up ahead. You wasn't around back

271

then, so you don't know what this man did for us... takin' out a nest of terrorist on his own... he saved the life of every man in our company... and he did it all based on a gut feelin'," Beery recalled. He turned his attention out the window.

"General Pollack did that, sir?" the corporal asked.

"Oh, yes," Beery said as he leaned back in the seat and rubbed his reddish-white mustache. "They dropped us off with the idea we could capture Al-Tamby."

"I heard about Al-Tamby," the driver perked up. "Wasn't he the man who stole the nuclear weapon from Pakistan? I heard General Pollack's mission was top secret. We weren't allowed to openly discuss it."

"That's the one," Beery said. "To the rest of the world, top secret. But inside the Australian Army, General Pollack's mission has become legendary to young recruits. The American command gave the Australian's a green lit to go in with a special squad to find him. The Russians, the Chinese, and the Americans diplomatically had their hands tied. Later we found out the American state department turned to the Australian government for the secret favor. The high command knew it was probably a one way mission. They looked for volunteers and had trouble findin' any. So, Captain Pollack stepped forward and volunteered," Beery said and shook his head.

"Why did he stick his neck out?" the driver asked.

"Love of country... ambition... dedication... who knows why some men do those things," Beery speculated. "At any rate, I went as a second on the strike team. They dropped us in and we were on our own. We found out later that an Indian assassin killed Tamby when he unexpectedly turned south and tried to smuggle the weapon across the border through India. The information the American's had about his location was all wrong. Turned out they followed the wrong band of terrorists with their drones. Tamby was already dead by the time the choppers left us on our own. The Pakistani's recovered the weapon and glossed over the whole thing. Our mission became a sham. They couldn't send anyone back to pick us up as we had no way to contact them and were in Afghanistan illegally. We would have to walk back to Pakistan, over two hundred klicks away. We didn't know that our Australia commander considered us expendable," Beery said. "After walkin through the mountains for three days, we heard the news from a local villager about Tamby. Since we were radio silent, we had no way of sending our position. The men got upset. They argued over what to do and feared local snipers would pick us off, one by one. Cpt. Pollack told us that we were going to survive. When we asked how, he said we were going to walk out of Afghanistan. So we headed due south. We didn't know that a group of terrorist fighters had flanked our position. They followed us for three days. They intended to strike the next day and surprise us. They would have killed us, too."

Beery stopped speaking. He stared at the general's car in front of them, as if he could still see the general's young face thirty years ago.

"What happened?" the driver demanded. Beery straightened and resumed his story.

"That was a tense night," Beery told him. "Some of the men feared we were not going to make it. But the general wouldn't hear of talk like that. He said we was all goin' home. I laughed at the time…" Beery said his voice fading. "Actually, I knew we were goners," he added, "but I wasn't gonna let on!"

The corporal glanced over and saw the sergeant deep in thought.

"Sir," the corporal spoke up. "The general's car is turning," he indicated.

"Follow him," Beery indicated as they left the highway and headed down the off ramp.

Sergeant Beery sat up when the general's car plowed past the stop sign, driving faster than he did on the highway. Before the driver could object, Beery simply gestured toward the road as if to say, "Do what he did!" However, inside Beery began to wonder if the general had gone off the deep end.

"What's he up to?" he thought. "He *is* headin for Fraser Island. The ferry is at the end of this road near Inskip Point," the sergeant told the driver as he recognized the turn off.

For the next twenty minutes, the corporal had difficulty keeping up with the general's car as they hurdled headlong through small towns and hamlets. The general's flags fluttered on his car and no police officer dared pull over the speeding vehicles. The general's driver honked the horn several times and swerved while he ignored stop signs, red lights, and anything that slowed their course, even pedestrians who managed to dive out of the speeding car's path, though the general's car injured no one.

"Beery!" the general's voice broke through on the radio. "We're coming up on the ferry at Inskip Point," he said. "Find out the schedule. If we have to, we'll have someone in HQ call the boat's skipper to make the ferry available for us."

"Aye, sir," Beery responded. He popped open a small device he had in his pocket. In seconds, he entered the network, and pulled up the ferry schedule. "General?" Beery radioed back.

"Yes, Beery, what is it?" James responded.

"The ferry runs every half hour, sir. We should see it either comin' or goin' at this time of day. We shouldn't have to wait for it very long, sir," he told his commander.

The general acknowledged the message. As the two vehicles slowed down and approached the docks, the sun grew low in the sky, near dusk. They did not see any lights in the boathouse. The general also noticed that the dock house on this side held no attendant. They did not see anyone around. James hopped out of his car first. He hand-signaled Beery to sit tight. He cautiously walked forward and pulled out his side pistol before he inspected the boathouse on this side. The men watched anxiously from the vehicles as the general disappeared inside the building.

"Should we be going in there instead of the general?" the driver asked Beery.

"You'd better stay alert and be prepared to follow his orders," Beery reminded him.

The general returned within a matter of seconds. He holstered his weapon as he walked over to the truck.

"No signalman," he said, puzzled by their absence. "I feel something queer is going on here. We should wait here just a few minutes longer," the general said. "Tell the men they can stretch their legs."

While Beery passed the order, Major General Pollack walked down to the docks and sent out his feelings. He was amazed at the way his senses picked up tiny minutia that revealed clues to him. The men that attacked the government building in Brisbane had been here. With his enhanced sight, he looked down at the disturbed soil around his feet. He noted the boot prints. The tire tracks. He followed their movements on the ground. He noticed that a van had stopped… four men got out and waited. One of them made the mistake of laying his automatic rifle on the ground. It left a slight impression.

"They must have driven the van onto the ferry and headed over to…" he thought.

James looked across the water to the opposite side. He remembered Cecilia's lesson. His eyesight stretched out like binoculars. The other shore clearly came into view. James remembered to pull psychic energy from his men before he attempted this.

"They left a sentry on guard," he thought as his eyes searched the opposite shore. "The ferry is unattended… the driver is dead," he realized as he scanned over the vessel. He began to wonder how many men the terrorist had versus the number of troops he brought with him. "This isn't good," he thought as he glanced back over his shoulder. "We're outnumbered two to one. They have at least twelve. I've got six." Thirty meters away, the men in the truck and his own driver stared back him. In this relatively calm state, they were a potent source of psychic energy.

He closed his eyes and drew additional energy from them. Had a fellow psychic stood nearby, the general would begin to glow from the amount of power he pulled inward. He used that energy to reach across the sound and start up the ferryboat on the other side. He slipped the ties off the piers and moved the controls forward. The boat started toward them from across the sound.

"Not bad control, James," he thought, "for a being a psychic less than a week!"

Some of the men who had patiently watched the general began to grow anxious. Sensing their impending mutiny, James grabbed the radio on his hip.

"Beery!" he radioed. "Assemble our men into a company. We'll need whatever equipment you can muster."

"Yes, sir," the sergeant responded. He grunted orders left and right. "Be ready for anything," he warned.

Out of the darkness, the men watched with amazement as the ferry slowed down and gently pulled up to the dock's edge... and no driver!

The corporal started to drive the truck onto the boat when the general signaled to the sergeant.

"Leave it!" the sergeant barked at the youth. "This job's on foot!" he told them.

"How did it come over with no pilot?" one of the men questioned.

"Must have an automated return," the general muttered and waved them on.

Oddly enough, the man who questioned accepted the general's answer. The men abandon the vehicles and ran onto the ferry. The general went up to the pilothouse. Using his mind, he kept his hands over the controls, yet he turned the vessel on by using his mental power to enter the control switches before he headed back across the strait for Fraser Island. In twenty minutes, they pulled into the dock on the other side of the sound.

"Stand back," General Pollack ordered.

His men watched as the older man deftly jumped off the boat with a pistol in his hand and bolted across the road. He disabled the sleeping sentry in the boathouse with his mind, only to find the pilot on the floor with his throat cut. Sergeant Beery ran in behind him and looked over his shoulder.

"Good bloody lord!" he said in a low voice. "Guess you was right, sir. They came this way alright."

"Yes, sergeant," the general said as he turned around. "Judging from their tracks, I believe they took over a house up the beach. It's probably close to the road so they can escape quickly. I suspect they're only using it for the night before they prepare for another attack up the road."

"Beg your pardon, sir," Beery said, his expression puzzled. "How do you know all of this?" the man asked.

The general trusted Beery. He wanted to simply tell him the truth, only he remembered Master Li's words, "tell no one about your power."

"Intuition," the general winked. "I feel it, just like I did that night back in Afghanistan. You were with me then, when the other men started to call me crazy. I just need to know one thing… Are you with me now?"

The sergeant stared back skeptically at first. Yet he saw an almost puppy-dog pleading expression on the general's face. His face broke into a big grin, "I'm with ya all the way, sir!" he said to his commander.

"Good," James said as he glanced around until he found some pencils and paper in a nearby table. "I want to follow a plan of attack," he said as he hastily drew some objects on the paper. "The house is just around the shore to the east and slightly north along the beach. I want two teams," the general explained as he indicated on the page. "One group will attack from the back of the house," he indicated, "the other group will go in the front. If I know my tactics, they'll have sentries on the beach and along the road that leads up to the house. Whatever you do, don't fire a shot. You'll alert the men inside. They may have bomb devices they can set off. We need to use stealth that will give us the element of surprise. Have you got a knife?" he asked.

Beery unsheathed a large blade. He nodded as he ran his thumb along its edge before he put it away.

"Razor sharp as always," he bragged.

"I knew I could count on you," James told him. "I want you to go in the back door. I'll go in the front door that faces the beach," the general told him. "Take out the sentry first and then position your men at the back door. Be ready to charge in when you hear some racket. That will be your signal. Let's go!"

The general seemed to move about with ease, the sergeant thought, as he and the general's men sprinted up the road. The general had more energy than he did. After a few hundred meters, Henry put out his hand.

"Sorry," Beery apologized, breathing hard. "I'm just a little out of shape."

This time, the general grinned at Beery. The two gray-haired men laughed at each other. The other men caught on and chuckled at the old men's dilemma until Beery cast a mean face in their direction.

"I can still wallop the likes of you!" he harshly whispered.

The other men's smiles quickly faded. After a minute, he nodded to the general and the group took off once more. Within a minute, they saw the lights on at a large oceanfront home.

"Why there it is, sir," Beery pointed out with a quiet whisper, "just like you said."

The general put his finger to his lips. He indicated to the men to stop behind a large group of bushes about fifty meters from the house. From this location, they noticed two men on the beachside porch, smoking and drinking beer... unarmed! He saw no sentry along the beach, though he still suspected one on the road in the back.

The general crouched down and pushed his finger into the sand.

"The sergeant will take one of you with him and head toward the back. Watch out for any sentries on the road. They may have them posted nearby," he quietly spoke. "Remember, we need the element of surprise on our side. No shooting! Use a blade," he indicated by making a cutting-the-throat gesture. "What time have you got?" he asked.

"Nearly ten o'clock, sir," Sergeant Beery told him.

James glanced down at his watch.

"Both times are identical," he noted. "We can't use communicators," the general told them. "They'll give away our position. Shut off your radio. I don't detect any motion sensors," he added, which caused the men to stir until Beery gave them a shake of the head, as if saying "ignore that!" The general continued his directives. "Move into your position, Beery," he ordered. "At ten, I'll start to move on the front of the house with these three. I believe if we move fast enough, we can take them by surprise. Agreed?"

"Whatever you wish, sir," Beery replied. "We'll cover the back. They're not going to get through us."

"Move out!" the general said.

"Come on!" Beery said as he grabbed his green corporal who drove the truck. The men silently crept away.

The two groups split apart under the cover of the brush with Sergeant Beery and the corporal heading around toward the back of the house. The general directed two of his men to crawl along the ground and cautiously approached the front deck to take out the two men there. They took out their knives, while the general and one private stayed back and watched. Just before they sprang into action, the two terrorist men on the deck moved back inside the house.

The general signed to the men on the ground to approach the front door on either side. One of the men scrambled past the front steps without being seen. He took up a position on the other side of the front porch. The general and the fourth man approached the front steps in a crouched position. He glanced down at his watch, ten o'clock.

He nodded to the other three men with him. The three slowly approached the front door head on. The men inside left it unlocked and partially open.

The general cautiously pushed the door open and slowly stepped inside, followed by his team. The terrorist group, the ones not upstairs sleeping, sat around the dining room table in the center of the house. They were setting up several explosive devices for the following day.

The general motioned for one of his men to move up the stairs once they were able. Then, he and his remaining men stepped in the light.

"Make one move and I'll drop you," he said as he pulled out his pistol and aiming it at the man he considered in charge. "Hands on the table where I can see them," he said.

The other three military men fanned out and searched the men at the table for weapons. One man, whom the general did not notice, sat in the shadowed corner away from the table. He started to pull a gun from his hip.

"I would not do that if I were you," Beery said as he calmly walked in from the kitchen.

The general nodded with his head to Beery to make his way upstairs.

"If any of you utters a word, just one, I'll shoot him," James said as he aimed his pistol at the head of the man in charge. "I'll shoot you next," he spoke with such conviction that the men did not move. "Beery move in quiet, take two men with you and bring the others down from upstairs," the general ordered.

"Yes, sir," Beery said. The men ascended the staircase. It was all Beery could do to control his delight with the situation. Everything that happened around them vindicated his belief in the general.

Beery silently crept up the stairs. His men fanned out. In seconds, James heard doors kicked open and shouting. Someone fired a couple of shots, they heard scuffling.

One of the men James covered started to move.

"One centimeter further and I'll pull this trigger," he said as he pushed the barrel into the forehead of their leader.

"Stop it you fools!" the terrorist man in charge uttered. "He means it!"

"Don't worry! It's alright, sir!" Beery called down. "We had a few that protested. They're a calm bunch now, though," he said as he pushed a group of men ahead of him down the stairs.

"Private," the general indicated the man to his left.

"Sir?" the private said, not taking his eyes off the terrorists.

"Use the house phone," the general said. "Call HQ," he ordered. "We'll need air support. Tell them I need helicopters. In fact, tell them I'd like six Chinook helicopters fully fueled and two extra tankers. Tell them we have the entire gang, the terrorist that destroyed downtown Brisbane. Give them our position. Do it now!"

"Yes, sir," the private said as he moved past one of the terrorists at the table.

Yet as he passed, the terrorist pushed the inexperienced young man to the wall, swung around and grabbed the youth's weapon while he put him in a choke hold. Before he could fire, the general dropped down and shot the man in the forehead. The general rolled and popped up next to the table. At the same time, he lowered his gun at the others. The shot terrorist released his grip of the young private's neck and fell backward, his brains scattered on the wall behind him.

"Anyone else want to try something foolish?" the general offered.

The terrorists coming down the stairs witnessed this extremely fast action by a man they thought, on the outside at least, appeared old and past his prime. Everyone on the stairs halted for a second.

"I'd do as he says," Beery fiercely stated from behind them, "that man's liable to kill every man here if he doesn't cooperate," the sergeant added as he pushed the men ahead of him.

After that, they did not have any trouble with Girard's men. Laying face down on the beach, the general had the terrorists lined up, bound, and awaiting extraction as soon as their air support landed.

"You were right about them bombs," Sgt. Beery informed his commander. "In the living room, they've got several ready to go, and many more in the middle of construction. Looks like they was going to attack more targets, sir. Wasn't they?" he asked.

"I'm afraid so," the general sighed.

"I'd like to go in and defuse them, if you don't mind, sir," Beery said as he cracked his knuckles.

"Go right ahead," James said, patting his back. "Do you still remember how to do that?"

"Do I..." Beery started. "I may be physically unfit for service," he began, "but that was me specialty, sir. I can defuse a bomb with me eyes closed!"

"Use both," James told him.

Beery grinned as he went back inside and utilized his demolitions skills. He dismantled the bombs while two of the privates in their company went back to the ferry. The young men crossed the straits, and activated the homing beacon in the truck. They brought the truck and the car over to the island.

Beery walked out of the house. It was after midnight. He watched with pride as the company of men surrounded his old commander. These young men looked on the general with increased respect. They listened to his every word as if he were full of wisdom. Berry could see the headlines now: General captures terrorists.

"I wish I could see old Sander's face when they give 'em the news," he thought as he gazed over at his commanding officer with admiration in his eyes.

He stepped in front of his men and added a pat to his commander's back.

"You'll make the morning papers, sir," he said to General Pollack. "Whatever you've got attached to that nose, sir," he said in a low voice, "I'm glad that I served under you... then and now."

The general half-smiled, his mind on other matters. He was not finished with his work.

"I appreciate that sentiment, Beery," the general responded. "I know you trust me..." he continued, "however, I have another favor to ask," the general said as he turned to his subordinate.

"I'm your man," Beery responded at once without question.

"We have one more stop..." the general said, just as the distant sound of helicopters broke the silence in the air.

CHAPTER THIRTY-NINE

DILEMMA

MASTER LI'S WARNING ABOUT OPENING the aircraft door arrived too late. The second the door opened, a waiting soldier threw a shock grenade onto the stairs. The shockwave knocked poor Villi back, as he received the brunt of the explosion. It might have killed him if the back wall of the interior hadn't cushioned the blow. Su Lin cried out but none of the psychics had any strength to help him. She started to sob when Cecilia reached over and whispered to her.

"He's alive," she quietly spoke, "I sense it."

Su Lin nodded back. She sensed it, too, although she also sensed his pain.

Just then, big brawny uniformed men poured inside the advanced flyer. While they paused to look around at the futuristic interior, they also knew their jobs. They took charge and forcefully pulled the youthful yet weak Rollo team members out of the aircraft and threw them down on the ground. They appeared strange to the other men – no uniforms, no weapons – the Rollo team resembled a group of college students on vacation. They wondered at first if they had the right party. Was this a stray aircraft? How could this group of weak individuals be described by Girard as an American strike force.

"Are you sure about this, sir?" one of the underling men asked the group commander that Girard put in charge of the mission.

"Girard gave me strict orders," he barked back. "Get them off that... that thing!"

The Australian men were not very gentle in their treatment. They dragged the whole group and even the old man off the plane when they could not walk. One soldier simply took the unconscious Villi by the wrist and pulled him down the stairs, depositing his body on the ground next to the group.

Su Lin sensed Master Li, even in his weakened state, lend some of his energy to the big Russian.

The man in charge had his men stand around the assembled the group and started to radio Girard as to what he should do next. Just at that moment, Girard arrived on the scene, his vehicle brought in a big cloud of dust behind him. The big man rushed over to take charge. Yet the sight of the strange aircraft stopped him.

"What the hell is that?" he wondered aloud.

"That's what they flew in," one of the soldiers commented.

Girard walked over to where the men had the prisoners on the ground.

"Cyrus was right not to worry," he thought as he looked over their appearance. "These psychics are no match for my men... though three of them have a decent build," he privately thought.

He noted that one of them on the ground was an older man – a rather frail white-haired oriental man by Girard's standards.

"That must be the chinaman," he thought.

To Girard, the frail old man seemed harmless. Yet, Girard recalled that Cyrus came across that way the first time they met in the bar during the football finals. One of his men prodded Villi with the butt of his gun while the other prisoners sat facing each other with their hands on their heads. The soldiers stood over them and pointed their gun barrels at their backs.

"Check them for weapons," Girard barked. He'd been expecting soldiers in uniform, not these weak pitiful forms.

When they frisked his body, the soldier managed to wake Villi. He sprang to life and started to rise when he realized their position and relaxed. He glared up at Girard who stood over him. The two men exchanged the looks that one enemy soldier would give to another. Neither man looked away.

Only the large dark hairy man represented a possible threat to Girard. He appraised all of them. The other two tall men – the oriental and the obvious American – although large, seemed too slight in stature to be battle hardened soldiers. The site of these weaklings appalled Girard. He expected an elite strike force equipped in the same fashion as his soldiers, not seemingly "college students."

"They're kids!" Girard said, disgusted. "Shame on you, old man," he directed toward Master Li, "for dragging these children out here on a hopeless mission. You should know better," he said, upset. "Put the men in that truck," he ordered. "Put the two women in that one," he said as he gestured to another truck. "Cyrus says no molesting the women...not yet at least," he added with a slight smile to his men. He saw how his men drooled over the two very attractive females. "I promise, we'll have fun with them later," he offered.

Girard picked Master Li up like a dishtowel and threw the weak old man over his shoulder. Michael and Villi started to move toward them in response, when an arm reached out and stopped them. It was not one of Girard's men, but Han. When the two psychics turned toward him, he pulled his hands to his chest and made some quick finger gestures while he shook his head. None of Cyrus' soldiers seemed to notice or understood the significance of his hand signals.

"Let's go!" Girard ordered. "Cyrus wants them brought back to camp in one piece...."

Girard's men knew exactly what he meant when he said that. Gingerly, each man pushed his prisoner in the back toward the truck.

Villi, who had recovered although weak, eagerly wanted to respond. He knew he could toss Girard on his ear with or without psychic power. However, Michael followed Han's suggestion. He cleared his throat and hand-signaled his friend Villi, "do nothing." He also signaled to the others except Li. He opened his mind to Li. His mentor started to immediately give him instructions as they moved toward the waiting trucks.

"...you must act quickly, Michael," Li linked to him, his connection barely discernable. "Tell the others..." he added before his link went silent.

"What's wrong old man?" Girard asked as he flung Master Li onto his bottom inside the truck that he designated for the men.

Somehow Master Li minimized the impact of his body on the metal flatbed.

"I'm not feeling well," Li responded, his words barely audible.

"Cyrus took your energy, didn't he?" Girard said in a low voice as his men waited behind him.

The moment Girard said that, Li used a blank expression as he tried to hide what he suddenly realized. Girard had just revealed an important piece of information. Cyrus slowly sapped their psychic energy as they flew across the desert in a meditative state. He knew in that moment the condition would only be temporary. He quickly reached out and started to pull psychic energy from the soldiers around him.

"Michael," Li openly linked as he stared at the ground. He purposely did not move or indicate his improving condition to Girard. "Cyrus induced our malady as we crossed the desert. New plan... listen to me... You and the rest can regain your strength back from these men," Li told him. "Spread the word. Don't tip our hand to Cyrus," he cautioned. "Perform the task gradually. Do not flex any energy. Fill up on psychic energy and stand by for further instructions. Understood?"

"Yes, sir!" Michael replied via his link. He passed Li's message on to the rest of the group. "Remember, keep a low profile..." Michael linked, "continue to behave as if we have no energy. Master Li said to start absorbing energy now," he told them.

"Think you can make it back to the camp in this truck, old man?" Girard asked of Li. He returned from his vehicle and placed a folded blanket under his body before he repositioned him.

"Thank you," Li barely whispered.

Master Li stared up at the man for only a second before Girard remembered what Cyrus told him, "Never look into his eyes." Girard quickly turned his head away. Li knew from that gesture that Cyrus alerted Girard to the ability of psychics entering their minds. Girard must have developed his own ideas about how it was done. The big man briskly walked away from Li and left him unattended in the back of the truck.

"I don't need to look into your eyes," Li thought, amused by Cyrus' surmise.

Meanwhile, his men herded and pushed the rest of the males in past Master Li still sitting on the truck bed. Villi, Michael, Han, Zinian, Zhiwei, and Chou sat crowded around their mentor in a circle and faced Master Li.

Girard glanced over at the open aircraft door. He thought about leaving two men to go over this advanced flyer. They might find useful weapons onboard. Yet, as he watched, the door to the aircraft automatically closed and the large flyer vanished before their eyes, as if it no longer existed. He wondered if one of his men may have triggered a bobby trap device. He did not wish to sacrifice any of them. He heard the men murmur when they saw the aircraft disappear. He bent down, picked up a rock, and threw it with all of his might at the space where the aircraft sat. The rock sailed through the space as if the ship had vanished (an illusion the ship used as a defense mechanism). This drew an even louder reaction from Girard's men.

"Everyone back to base camp!" he loudly ordered.

His words woke the men up and they filed into the two trucks. He walked over to his jeep. Despite his leader's weak condition when he left, he knew that Cyrus would wish to be notified of their capture. Girard glanced over at the youthful party loaded into the back of the two trucks. He picked up his radio to call Cyrus.

"Cyrus... this is Girard," he spoke into the device. After a few times of trying, he finally managed to reach him.

"Yessss..." the man sighed. "What is it?"

Girard practically beamed with pride in his voice.

"Yes, sir, we captured 'em... an old man and some young people," he informed him.

"You've got 'em? Any trouble?"

"No trouble," he began before Cyrus questioned him further.

"How many?"

"I counted nine..."

"Any weapons?"

"No, sir," Girard continued. "No weapons and no resistance, at all... too weak."

"Did you say weak?"

"Yes, sir, that's right."

"What about their strike team... hardened soldiers?"

"Soldiers? No, not like your men. In fact, I would... uh, consider 'em as... untrained teens..."

"What?"

"Yes, sir... that's right, teenagers... yes, sir... very young... high school or college aged, plus the old man. We'll be there in less than twenty minutes, sir," Girard said.

He put the radio down and yelled to one of his subordinates.

"Get the trucks movin'! We're headin' back to the camp," he told him. He wanted to return before the sun had set. The twilight settled over the desert. The shadows disappeared into darkness. Soon, the air would turn cool and the night creatures would come out in search of a morsel. Perhaps, Girard thought, his men could find some scorpions or a venomous snake and torture some of their guests. They might pass the women around tonight as fresh entertainment.

"Who knows what the night will bring?" he thought as he pulled into the lead with the two trailing trucks behind him.

The ride back was not a pleasant one for the Rollo group. Li and the other men sat on the floor of the truck between the two rows of stern soldiers guarding them. Their bottoms bounced off the metal floor as the truck tore across the uneven countryside. Dust and dirt flew into the back. The soldiers pulled up cloth coverings over their mouths. Michael and the others took their shirts and placed those over their mouths to avoid breathing in the copious amounts of dust and truck fumes in the air.

Han glanced over at Master Li, feeling the old man's pain with each hard bounce of the truck. Li winced as the truck brutalized his old frame. The truck's flatbed banged into his thin flesh and bones, despite the folded blanket underneath. Han started to reach over to help him when one of the soldiers threatened to stop him with the butt of his rifle.

"Stay where you are, Han," Li linked in his weakened state. "If you try anything, he'll strike you."

"Master Li," Han linked back, "You are hurt."

"I'll be ok, Han," Li said. "I can survive this. Continued to absorb energy."

The others, having overheard the exchange, stared at the floor, and bided their time. Han reluctantly appeared to look away while the guard checked on Li. Satisfied the old man appeared uninjured; he ignored Li and spoke to his friend across from him.

"Shootin' these guys will be a pleasure," he said to his friend as he pointed the barrel of his gun at Villi's head and pretending to pull the trigger. "Pweh!" he said as he made a sound like a firing sound. Then he wrinkled his nose. "What they really need is some hygiene! These guys stink!" he laughed.

"Hey, you ain't no bed of roses," his friend kidded. "They call this bunch of kids a strike force?" he questioned, "more like a strike farce," he grinned. The other soldiers in the truck laughed.

Michael linked to his friend sitting across from him.

"I know you want to act, Villi," Michael thought. "I do, too. Let's let Master Li decide the moment, ok?"

Almost imperceptibly, Villi nodded back. He kept his eyes downcast. He knew that if he even looked one of them in the eyes, he'd have to jump into action. He itched for the opportunity. A soft hand touched his arm. He glanced over and saw it was Master Li.

"You and I both know that you could take all of them down in less than two minutes," Li linked to him. "We have – what do the American's say – bigger fish to fry."

"As you will, Master Li," Villi linked back. "But I just want you to know… I hate fried fish. I like it grilled or braised…"

"I understand," Li replied and tried not to smile. "You'll have your chance."

"Yes, Master Li," Villi humbly answered.

The convoy continued to bounce across the countryside toward the encampment during the next twenty minutes, the truck's rough ride took its toll on Li's body. By the time they finally arrived, Li could hardly lift his legs. Han started to protest once more when Li quickly linked to him.

"Do not assist me in any way, shape, or form, Han," Li told him. "Keep pulling energy… maintain your diminished appearance. Under no circumstances, do I want any of you to act out in any manner that might tip your hand to Cyrus," he instructed and knew they had all heard the link. "He must believe we are weak, that our psychic ability is nothing compared to his, and that he is still the most powerful psychic on the planet. He must continue to think that way if we are to succeed."

As they pulled into the large encampment, they could feel Cyrus' psychic presence. Each one of them glanced in the direction of the large tent at the opposite end of the compound.

"Evil," Cecilia linked to Su Lin. "I sense a mind bent on terrible purposes."

Su Lin subtly acknowledged Cecilia without arousing the suspicion of the soldiers who watched them. The men in their truck made derogatory comments the entire trip. The two psychic women read the vulgar thoughts in their minds. Su Lin could hardly restrain from putting her foot into the men's faces. She and Villi often sparred for practice. Su Lin taught Cecilia many martial arts moves as well. The Rollo psychics knew that if they combined psychic energy with their moves, they could easily kill a normal human being. During sparing matches, they compensated their blows accordingly. As Su Lin sat on the floor of the truck, she breathed in deeply while she drew energy from the men around her.

"Clear your minds," Li signaled as the truck turned into the camp. "I will give you a signal in a moment. You must act swiftly if we are to be successful in our mission."

The truck parked in a space next to other trucks.

"Blocks up now!" Li signaled. "Don't let Cyrus pull any more energy from you," he instructed.

All nine psychics put up blocks with their newly drawn energy, yet doing so cost them dearly. Since they were so badly drained, they did not yet have enough time to fully charge.

Back inside Cyrus tent, the lanky youth realized he had made a crucial mistake. He used up too much energy from his own body when he attacked the space station. Even if he drew off energy from the other psychics or even his men, it would take him hours before he had that same level of energy he used to move the space station. He would not be able to utilize any psychic energy until tomorrow when he planned to fire on the asteroid. He had to wait until he could absorb enough energy.

He thought about the group of psychics that approached the camp. He had just enough strength to stand, but not enough to interrogate them. He did not want his men to see him in this state. He felt Girard's presence growing as he walked up the hill. The flap pushed back as the big man walked into his tent. Girard immediately gave his report when he saw Cyrus awake.

"Sir, the American strike team is by the main tent," Girard said as he stood nearby. "What are your orders?"

"Orders?" Cyrus questioned. He felt weak... very weak. "Put them in a secure place where you can have them watched," he advised. "Post sentries around them. I... I need more rest," he told his second.

"But, sir," Girard protested.

"Not now," Cyrus shot back. "I can't handle this right now... I'm tired... I need rest! Now, go away," he said as he dismissed him.

Girard walked back to the entrance and looked across the camp as his men pulled the strange group from the trucks near the main tent. He saw their frightened faces and noticed how they huddled together. He did have a punishment tent where he sent men that misbehaved. He and Cyrus tortured a few men in there and left the center table with its shackles in place as a reminder to those who might disobey. Cyrus had killed three men there… the men heard their screams and learned to fear him. Not enough room for nine people. Girard thought for a minute. He also had a medical tent with about a dozen cots. It was empty. He could shackle them to cots and assign guards at either end to monitor them through the night. He could hold them prisoner in there, he reasoned. Still, he did not trust them.

"I don't like this, but I'll comply with your wishes, sir," he said over his shoulder as he left Cyrus' tent.

He stormed down the hill and briskly made his way through the camp. The men kept their eyes on him. They knew when Girard was upset or angry. They could see his muscles tense beneath his tight t-shirt. His face had a scowl. His whole body looked moist as if he were under a strain. Their concerned eyes followed him as he headed toward the group of young people.

Meanwhile, Cyrus stretched out on his plush wide bed and breathed a sigh of relief. The day's results contented him. He struck a major blow against the Australian government and scattered the Australian Army in different directions. He captured his only real threat by robbing them of their power. Finally, he moved the space station into position so that when the key time arrived tomorrow, he only had to send a beam into space, which according to the scientist, would strike the asteroid and slow it down. He had about ten or so hours left before he had to create his energy beam and affect the asteroid's path.

"I'm sure I'll feel better in the morning," he thought as he closed his eyes.

Girard stormed over to the Americans. He addressed the old man.

"Our leader isn't ready to receive you," Girard grunted as he approached the old man. "But he'll take care of you in the morning," he added.

Master Li and Han exchanged glances. They wanted to conserve energy, so their fingers silently spoke their thoughts for them. Only the Rollo group seemed to notice the subtle yet rapid movements that silently spoke volumes.

Girard led them into the medical tent. He ordered each person cuffed by ankles and wrists to their cots. When they spread Su Lin out on her back, it stretched out her clothing and forced the young woman to reveal all of her voluptuous figure to the men. She was the most beautiful woman the men had ever seen. Girard paused over her cot and gazed down at her. Villi bristled but restrained from action. Su Lin twisted around and fought the shackles. Girard's men laughed.

"A feisty one," Girard muttered. "I like women with dark hair. It'll be a pleasure to make you perform for me," he told her.

"Don't!" Michael linked to his friend, Villi.

Even worse, they purposely placed Cecilia face down so that she had to turn her head to the side. One soldier started to smack her on the bottom. He raised his hand over his head when Girard reached up and grabbed the young man's wrist.

"Did you do that?" Villi linked to Michael.

"No…" Michael linked back, "but I believe Master Li did."

Girard let the man go and gestured toward a pile of blankets.

"Cover 'em up," he ordered.

Reluctantly, the soldier covered each person with a single blanket. They were not very thick blankets. Girard knew the temperature could be quite cold at night. Most of his men in the main tent had four or more of these blankets. If he lowered the flaps at either end, the tent would be warmer than the outside air.

"They'll survive," he thought as he exited, closed the flaps, and posted four sentries around the tent with orders to change after four hours.

"What will we do now?" Han linked to Li as they lay on their backs, side by side in the dark.

The others in the room waited for his reply.

"We must wait," Li told them via a mental link. "Be patient… try to maintain your consciousness…" he said, although he could barely sustain his own. "This may take some time until we return to normal power levels. Cyrus retired for the night. That gives us a chance to fully recover," he indicated. "Villi," Li asked, "what time is it?"

"Just after ten… local time," Villi answered.

Michael glanced over at Li. He thought it strange that Master Li had such a powerful block up. Was he the only one of their group who sensed it?

"We may have to wait until dawn before we act," Li continued to advise. "Slowly pull in energy through the night and hope we wake before he does," Li said. "If you feel tired, sleep in shifts. Maintain your blocks so he cannot drain your energy."

Master Li closed his eyes and no one, not even Han laying on the cot right next to him, could detect Li's energy level. Villi had to verify with Cecilia that he was breathing.

CHAPTER FORTY

CHECK AND MATE

GIRARD DECIDED TO RETIRE AND leave alone the prisoners inside the medical tent through the night. For a while, he lay in his tent and wondered if he acted wisely in regards to their capture. After all, they represented a threat to his livelihood. He wanted to interrogate them, ask questions about that futuristic aircraft, and find out what they knew about being psychic. He knew he could easily persuade some of them to talk, especially the blonde girl. As much as the darker oriental girl appealed to him, the blonde was almost too easy, he thought. He considered dragging her into the torture tent to make a point to both the men and the psychics as to who was in charge.

"A few pain-induced twisted limbs and she would all bark out what she knew," he thought. He nearly went back to their tent and implemented his plan.

However, Cyrus was not the only person fatigued. His day started before dawn and he even worked out with the men at midday to keep his mind off the Brisbane job. Earlier when he put the prisoners in the medical tent, he ordered his men "shoot to kill if one of them attempts escape." That was enough for him. By the time he laid down on his bed, not even the need for a woman stirred the big man. He closed his eyes and quickly fell asleep.

The camp grew very quiet. None of the men stirred from their cots. Time seemed to lose its meaning. The men slept very soundly including Girard. In fact, he had not slept this sound in a long time. He tried to wake, but could not open his eyes. He felt as if he were in a wrestling match. A strong force pushed against his will. He pushed back with all of his might.

Suddenly, he opened his eyes and fell out of his bed onto the boarded floor of his tent. His head struck the floor and nearly knocked the big man out. Rubbing his forehead, he slowly rose with one hand for support on the side of the bed. He glanced over at his bedside clock and then down at his wrist. Five thirty in the morning! His alarm failed to go off. Yesterday he wanted to sleep in. No today. He wanted to rise early.

"Shit!" he thought as he pushed up to his feel. "My alarm!"

He quickly pulled some clothes on, ran out of his tent, and dashed up the hill to check on Cyrus. He went straight past the guard who seemed in a daze. He found Cyrus, still in bed, and fast asleep. He shook him but Cyrus did not respond. He moved in closer to check him over.

"He's breathin' and his heart is beatin'…" Girard thought, "but somethin' doesn't smell right."

Suspicious, he left Cyrus' tent and looked out across compound. He noticed that the guards had changed their posts around the medical tent. Nothing appeared amiss. Wanting to personally investigate, he walked down to its location.

"Anythin' stirrin'?" he asked one of the guards outside the tent.

"Nothin'," the man said, "not a sound."

He noted that the locks they put on the doors were still in place. Satisfied, Girard walked into the main tent. He ordered three guards up to Cyrus tent. Before they could arrive, he thought he heard Cyrus cry out. He listened but only heard silence. He shrugged off the feeling and walked around to check on his men.

Up the hill, Cyrus woke up and felt sick to his stomach. Disoriented, he rose and went into his bathroom. He had a special flush toilet and sink installed in his tent. He also had an insulated tank that provided running water for his shower and small sink, including a wash basin he kept at his bedside. Inside his bathroom, he splashed some cold water on his face and looked in the mirror. Had he slept? He did not feel rested. He headed for his small refrigerator. He opened the freezer. The ice was low.

"Lissen forgot to fill my ice trays," he commented. "What time is it?" he wondered. "I thought Girard was gonna wake me. Where the hell is he?" he asked aloud. "Guard?"

No guard responded. He went to his table and saw the clock read 5:45 am.

"What?" he declared. "Girard!" he called out with his mind. "Get in here!" he ordered. Yet Girard did not respond. "Girard?" Cyrus tried again. He turned until he faced in the direction of Girard's tent. His mind traveled around the camp until he found Girard, sitting down inside one of portable the toilets near the main tent.

"Girard! What are you doing?" Cyrus demanded.

Startled, the big man nearly fell off the toilet seat.

"Hey! Take it easy! What's it look like doin? I'm takin a dump!" Girard shot back.

"Where are the prisoners?" Cyrus asked.

"Where I left 'em," Girard answered.

"And where's that?" Cyrus demanded.

"I put 'em on cots in the medical tent... sir," he said as he began to wipe.

"The medical tent?" Cyrus questioned. He reached out with his mind toward the medical tent.

At that moment, Master Li opened his eyes. He glanced over at Han and Michael. They were awake while the others had eventually fallen asleep.

"Wake up!" Li spoke into their minds. "Time for action!"

Using his power, Li pushed out a charge of psychic energy that rippled through the tent and woke the entire Rollo team. The shackles that bound them to their beds dropped off and fell with a metallic clunk on the floor next to their cots. All nine psychics stood up and stretched out their arms and legs. They felt that most of their power had returned to normal levels during the night. The group gathered around Master Li, each one an expert at keeping their blocks up, even in sleep.

"Action?" Han questioned. "What sort of action did you have in mind?" he linked.

"Cyrus is awake. Be ready to take evasive action on my command," Master Li told them. "Maintain your current level of blocks. He doesn't understand their complexity. He woke up about five minutes ago and he's been unable to precisely locate us. He'll assume that our energy levels are so weak, he cannot sense us. Therefore, we represent no threat to him."

Li surmised correctly. As hard as Cyrus tried to pinpoint their location, he could not sense the Americans. They were simply non-existent.

"Girard! I don't sense 'em. Are you certain they're there?" Cyrus questioned.

"Yes, we shackled and handcuffed each prisoner to their cot," Girard told him.

"I don't understand," Cyrus mumbled as he grabbed some clothes and pulled them on. "Either their energy level is so low I can't sense them, or..."

He ran to the opening of his tent. The guards normally stationed at the front of his own tent were missing. In the distance, he noticed the guards around the medical tent were also gone. In fact, as he looked around the compound, he didn't see any of the regular sentries on duty.

He reached up and pulled down on the heavy cord attached to the pole, which rang the alarm next to his tent.

"WHAAAA!" a loud alarm blared into the still cool morning air.

The alarm sent the encampment into chaos. Men jumped up from their beds and grabbed their automatic rifles while they tried to pull on their clothes. Cyrus did not see Girard anywhere. So as the men scrambled from their barracks, Cyrus started to bark orders with a bullhorn in his hand.

"They're trying to escape!" his amplified voice yelled. "Go and find them! They must be out there somewhere. Start with the medical tent!"

Only a handful of men responded quickly enough for Cyrus. Girard had trouble with his trousers and zipper as he scrambled out of toilet. Other men still slept in their cubicles as if the blaring alarm did not affect them.

"I see that plan of action backfired," Han commented when he heard the alarm go off. "Cyrus saw through your ruse," he pointed out to Master Li.

"It doesn't matter," Li said as he brushed off Han's remark. "I want each of you to draw as much psychic energy as you can from that troop tent before they come charging in here!" Li ordered.

The team responded to Master Li's request. Even Han saw the strategic advantage to this. Cyrus could not direct the men with his psychic energy once they were angry or excited. The psychics drew energy until they built up a reserve inside their minds.

"Perhaps it will give us a fighting chance," Han thought.

"Once Cyrus can sense our presence, he'll figure out our blocking technique and order his men in our direction," Li told them. "They'll be armed to the teeth with a variety of weapons. We don't have much time. Michael… Villi… disable as many soldiers nearby as you can," Li said as he drew in additional power. "You wanted to make a difference," he put to Villi. "This is a good time."

Villi managed to knock out several soldiers inside the tent with one thought, although such a big move cost him a great deal of energy. Cyrus noticed that few men responded to his alarm. Suddenly, Cyrus stopped pulling on the rope and shouting orders. He stood very still in front of his tent. His eyes looked across the compound at the medical tent. They hadn't escaped. They were blocking him somehow. He realized they never left the place. He started to shout at his men, but his bullhorn no longer worked. He slammed it down on the ground.

"Damn you!" he screamed once he realized he had been tricked.

He reached out for Girard to help him give orders to the men just as Michael anticipated his move and knocked Girard unconscious. The big man took two steps toward the medical tent. He spun around and went down.

"You just eliminated his queen," Han noted. "Nice move," he added. "I do believe your strategy is improving, Michael."

"Thanks, Han," the tall young man responded.

"It's only check, Michael," Li put in. "Cyrus has other moves. We're not close to checkmate yet. We've much to do."

Cyrus tried to directly attack Michael in retaliation only to have his energy deflected by Master Li. Frustrated and angry, Cyrus then ran down the hill into the compound, screaming.

"They're in the medical tent. Shoot the tent! Shoot the medical tent! Open fire and shoot!" he ordered.

Some of the men still unaffected and alert cocked their automatic weapons and pulled the triggers. Before the bullets started to fly in the direction of the medical tent, Master Li pointed out that none of them had the ability to deflect all of the bullets.

"Let's get out of here! They're going to start shooting! Find cover!" Li ordered.

Still suffering the effects of the brutal truck ride, Li managed to lift a portion of the medical tent opposite the main tent with his mind and headed as fast as he could run for a stack of packing crates nearby. The rest of the Rollo team quickly scrambled out of the opening. They simultaneously jumped just as the sound of rifle fire filled the air and bullets started to ricochet in every direction off objects inside the tent. Cyrus' men shot up the medical tent in short order. The bullets ripped the canvas material to shreds.

Someone reached down and lifted Master Li under his armpits. Strong arms carried him beyond the packing crates as those bullets could easily penetrate the wood. Soon, additional bullets struck the sand and objects around the American group with rapid thud sounds. His rescuer pulled Li behind a nearby metal storage shed. Bullets started to ping off the corrugated metal, yet some pierced through the cover and filled the shed with numerous holes.

Li glanced up at the person responsible for his safety.

"Oh, hello, Michael," he said.

"Master Li," Michael responded. "I'm glad to see you're safe. I can't lose my mentor, can I?"

"Not until you are master," Li finished his thought.

"Will I be master someday?" Michael asked.

"Someday... perhaps," Li linked to him. "Are you ready to go home yet?"

"After we stop Cyrus," Michael linked back.

Li smiled and rubbed his arm.

"You are stronger than I thought," Li commented as he pulled energy from some of the still dormant men. Michael followed his example. "Thanks for the rescue," Li told him.

"I'm going to work my way up the side," Zhiwei informed the others.

"Trying to flank their position. Perhaps I can take out a few of those shooters," he linked to the others.

"That won't be necessary," Li told him. "Be patient. They are emotionally overwrought. However, they are also overly confident. Their confidence will override their emotion. Let them come to us. As soon as they move within range, drain them of their useful energy and then knock them out," Li advised.

"Yes, Master Li," an echo of replies returned.

Spread out behind a variety of obstacles, the Rollo team waited on the ground for Cyrus' men to make the first move. Without Girard leading and giving commands, most of the men were confused as to where they were shooting and what was the target. They could see nothing inside what was left of the medical tent, whose fabric now hung as shreds.

"Li! Where are you?" an angry voice entered all their minds. "I know you're out there. You can't hide forever!"

Cyrus sent out a blanket call. He could not pinpoint one mind to attack, with all of them blocking. He could no longer sense their exact location, although he guessed from the appearance of the medical tent, they fled into the rest of compound.

"We might be able to use his confusion to our advantage," Han privately linked to Li.

"By all means, master strategist. If you have a plan..." Li began, when Han shared his idea with Master Li and the others.

"Li!" Cyrus called out again. "If you come out now, I will not harm any of your team!" he called to them. "Li!"

No one answered.

"I don't care who is over there," Cyrus called to his men. "Open fire on that entire end of the camp! Smoke them out! Use hand grenades if necessary, but do not moved too close..." he started to warn them.

Unfortunately, one brave soldier tried to sneak around the side and flank their positions. The moment he moved within range, nine psychics drained as much power as they could share and one of them quickly took the man out. He fell on the spot. The other men saw this.

"Idiot!" Cyrus yelled. "See? See what can happen! Now stay back or you'll end up like him!"

Cyrus heard a sound over his shoulder. He turned back to survey the area when he noticed a white haired old man peering from behind a nearby rock.

"How did that old man get over there?" he wondered. "They're up here!" Cyrus yelled to his men. "Come on!" he gestured toward the rock at the top of the ridge. "Over there! Get him! He has all the power. Throw everything you've got at him! Go! Go!" Cyrus ordered.

"Look!" one of the men cried. "I see him! Come on!"

Nearly every man with a gun ran up the hill in the direction that Cyrus indicated. Not as nimble, Cyrus tried to join them, but could not scale the steep hill as quickly as these fit, well-trained soldiers. However, he only ran about ten meters, when he suddenly stopped.

"Wait a minute!" he thought as he saw through the ruse. "That's one of my tricks. It's a diversion!"

In that instant, he felt Master Li standing right behind him.

"If you make any sudden moves or shout any orders," Li said quietly as he walked up, "I will be forced to kill you," he told the maniacal psychic.

Sweat broke out on Cyrus forehead. He wanted to countermand his order. Yet, he instinctively knew that with Li's incredible power, he had to focus his energy on the true enemy. He turned around just as Master Li reached his position.

"So, old man. We finally meet, face to face," Cyrus linked to Li. He saw a small, thin, white-haired, elderly man standing in front of him, dressed in nothing more than a flowing garment and some sandals. "You are older than I thought, and stupid to let me drain your life force that way," Cyrus linked, smug and secure.

"You are more foolish than I thought," Li retorted as he gazed at Cyrus with nothing but pity. "Do you truly believe that you can become powerful enough to rule the world? Why would you waste such a rare and precious gift on such a silly ambition? Don't you know that we stand to gain so much more by achieving our goals in secret?"

Cyrus leaned back his head and laughed.

"Now who is the fool? Secret? You think you can keep a thing like this secret? In this day and age?" the man challenged. "Li, you are more stupid than I thought. Now, you will die," Cyrus said with cold emotion, ready to make his usual death move.

Cyrus reached out and took Li by the throat with his energy. Before he could latch onto Li's flesh, Li deflected his energy away, barely, but he deflected it nonetheless.

"Still weak I see," Cyrus said.

He reached into his side holster to grab his gun. When he felt around, he realized his gun was missing.

"Looking for this?" Han asked as he walked up behind Master Li. He had the gun in his hand. Swiftly, he used his mind to pull the gun apart, flipping the bullets and parts off in different directions, along with the clip.

Cyrus glanced over Han's shoulder. He saw the other psychics advancing on his position. His face changed from one of superiority to one of alarm. He knew it was time to make his exit. He'd been out maneuvered. He turned and ran up the hill toward his tent and the safety of his men. Li and the others let him go.

"Help! Help me!" Cyrus cried as he ran. "They're after me!"

Han started to run after him when Master Li held up his hand.

"Let him go," Li said.

Han ignored Li and intended to use his mind to trip Cyrus.

"I mean it, Han," Li said quietly in a direct link.

"But Master Li," Han protested. "He is our target. He can rouse the men to further action against us."

The sky began to lighten around them. The twilight began to fade to the dawn of another day. Yet, the air seemed too still. The group sensed something strange about the eastern portion of the sky.

"Don't you feel it?" Li said quietly as he sank to the ground and sat in the sand.

"Feel what?" Han asked as he looked toward the east. He turned his mind to some distant point in the sky. Then he felt it. "Yes... I see what you mean..."

The air gradually filled with a loud, deep, bass-like, chopping sound. Coming over the horizon, advancing on their position very quickly, were five large Chinook Army helicopters moving their way. Cyrus must have felt their energy approaching, too. He halted from trying to round up his men and headed directly inside his tent.

"He's trying to escape," Li sensed. "He won't get far. We can do nothing more here." Master Li glanced up at his friend with a slight smile. "Han, the marines have landed. Let them mop up. We need to catch a rogue on the run. He'll be kilometers from here before those helicopters land. We cannot chase him on foot. To head him off at the pass," Li said smiling, "we'll need a bit of Chou magic. I believe we have sufficient psychic energy, but we should fill up with as much as we can carry before we leave. We need to take a vehicle or two and head back to the aircraft. We must depart this place as fast as Cyrus is. As a parting gift, foul up every gun on the base... do it now... the best you can."

The team stopped to perform a bit of mischief as they also soaked up the last bit of psychic energy they could squeeze from the place.

"Come on!" Li directed as he ran toward a group of parked army trucks and jeeps. "Villi... you drive," Li pointed out. "I believe the rest of us can squeeze into the back. At least we'll have seats this time. Drive as fast as you can, back to the aircraft. We'll manage."

"Yes, but I want you and the women in the cab," Michael insisted.

The team moved as Li directed. He sat up front squeezed in with Cecilia and Su Lin. Villi drove. The other five men sat on the soldier's seats in the back. Soon, a large truck sped away from the camp as fast as its wheels could travel.

In the command chopper overhead, one of the pilots called out to the head of this operation:

"General Pollack!" the man yelled over the sound of the chopper. "I have a truck moving southeast away from the encampment, sir," he informed him.

For a second, the general reached out with his mind and detected the strong presence of Master Li.

"Go get him!" he linked the words of encouragement down to the truck. Then he turned his power on the pilot who was watching the screen in front of him. "I don't see anything on your scope," he told the man.

"I could have sworn," the man said as he glanced down and saw nothing.

"Give me outside loudspeakers," the general requested.

"Go ahead, sir," the co-pilot told him. He connected the general's mouthpiece to exterior speakers.

"This is the Australian Army!" James bellowed. "If you surrender your arms, we will not open fire on you. Lay down your weapons and walk to the center of the camp with your arms raised over your heads," he ordered. "Keep your hands up where we can see them!"

His voice carried such command that the men on the ground immediately followed his directive. Sergeant Beery, who sat next to General Pollack, glanced over at his commander with renew respect for the second time since late last night.

"I'm ready to lay down my arms, too, governor!" Beery said, smiling. "That's some voice, sir."

"Just don't forget it, Beery," the general quipped, "I expect excellent service when we get back to Diggers."

"You'll get it, sir," Beery promised, "along with a promotion, I'll wager!"

The five big helicopters landed and the general's men rounded up Cyrus' men. They bound their hands with plastic cuffs while the major general walked the grounds. He sensed that Cyrus fled minutes before they landed. He would let Master Li take care of him. He was proud of his men's efficiency. He would give every one of them commendations for their excellent and unwavering service.

"This removes all the threats to our country except one," he thought as he watched the men board the helicopters. "I'd hate to be in his boots and face the likes of Master Li as an enemy," he spoke with as much reverence as Sergeant Berry would about his commander.

Grinning, General Pollack waited until every man was onboard before he ordered them back to their home base... after they transferred fuel.

Chapter Forty-one

Destination desert

Before Cyrus ran through camp to evade the landing helicopters, Girard regained his consciousness and his bearings. He noticed some soldiers struggle with jammed rifles while others seemed comatose. A small group ran past Cyrus tent and into brush at the top of the hill for no apparent reason. In all the confusion, he started out to search for his leader when he saw Cyrus standing up on the north hill surrounded by nine people. At that moment, the morning sunlight caught his eyes and Girard stopped to blink away the first rays of sunlight. When he looked again, the nine had vanished. Cyrus turned around and ran up the hill away from the camp toward his tent.

"What the..." he started to question just as he heard the sound of the helicopters. "I know that sound," he thought. "Why hasn't Cyrus..." he began when he realized Cyrus was running away. "What's happening?" he shouted.

Cyrus had an all terrain vehicle parked at the back door to his quarters. He hopped in and started it up. The scene around Girard quickly decayed further into chaos. As the big helicopters drew near, he did not think twice. He ran toward Cyrus, just as pale scrawny young boy started to rev up the engine.

"Cyrus!" Girard called out to him. "Cyrus! Stop! Take me with you!"

At the last second, Cyrus heard Girard's shout above the roar of the engine and the chopping helicopters. He stopped the vehicle and spun around in his seat. He watched as Girard ran toward him. For a second, he felt a tinge of guilt. The man had been loyal to him. Girard also helped him achieve his goal. Yet, all of that seemed part of the past as he saw his plan falling apart. Cyrus knew he would need to hide for awhile and rethink his strategy. He shrugged his shoulders and shook his head.

"Sorry old timer," he thought mentally to him. "Every man for himself today, g'day mate," he added.

Girard heard the sound of beating air growing louder. He knew that after all he had done, the military and the government would blame him for everything that happened. Cyrus would get away and leave him to face the consequences alone.

"Traitor!" Girard called out as Cyrus turned to leave. "Coward!" he yelled as he reached for his side arm. He whipped out his pistol, took aim, and started to squeeze the trigger.

"Coward" would be the last word Girard would ever utter.

"I told you when we first met," Cyrus thought to his mind, "it is a mistake to ever underestimate me."

Girard took aim and tried to pull the trigger but his finger would not budge.

"I should have eliminated you a long time ago when I first sensed your treachery," Cyrus uttered. "You won't have to wait for your military tribunal. Here is your judge, jury, and sentence carried out."

Girard's face twisted into a hideous expression of pain. He dropped the gun and ran his fingers over his face, screaming. He felt his skin burst into flames as Cyrus made him believe that fire slowly peeled away his skin and burned off his flesh. His blood boiled, his groin fried, his eye balls hardened like eggs in boiling water. Girard fell to the ground and screamed while he writhed in agony.

"I told you I could make you suffer," Cyrus seethed as he took out his anger on the defenseless man.

"Lay down your weapons..." a loud voice called out and continued to speak. Cyrus kept his focus on Girard. As the helicopters started to descend, he reached out and broke several of Girard's cerebral arteries. Blood gushed out of his ears, nostrils, and around his eyes.

"Die!" Cyrus said through gritted teeth while he finished the big man off when he internally crushed Girard's body.

Killing Girard made Cyrus giddy. He laughed as he wielded his power in such a cavalier fashion. With all four wheels spinning, he sprinted away and hoped he left a cloud of dust to cover his exit. Once he made his way out of the canyon, he headed north for the village where he stopped an escaping prisoner.

In the camp, Sergeant Berry commanded the mop-up while the general walked over to inspect Cyrus' tent and obtain any paper or documents he left behind.

"We'll soon have them all rounded up for you, sir," Sgt. Beery reported.

"Very good, sergeant, carry on," Major General Pollack said as he walked from Cyrus' tent with a treasure trove along with the infamous laptop computer under his arm. He waved his arm and called the sergeant to him. "I don't know if you realize what's going on here, Berry," the general told him.

"What's that sir?" Berry asked.

"We managed to capture all the men responsible for the tragedy in Brisbane," the general informed him. "However, these men were behind a terrorist plot against the Australian government. We must transport them back to the military prison at HQ," he ordered. "We'll send intelligence back here to examine… " he said as he indicated Girard's body, "what's left of their leader. This is now a crime scene. We'll let forensics take over."

"Yes, sir," Sergeant Beery replied.

The two hundred men boarded the five transport helicopters that the general procured for the effort – each chopper able to transport two platoons if necessary. Gradually, before they reached the base, he convinced every one of his prisoners that Cyrus never existed. Only Girard had perpetrated these crimes, just as the general convinced the bombers when he captured them. Later, he would also convince the coroner that Girard died of a stroke. No one would ever know anything about Cyrus. As far as the world was concerned, Cyrus Keaty never existed, just as the criminal himself wanted.

After he drove due north for several kilometers, Cyrus stopped his vehicle and turned around. A massive dust cloud rose from the desert as the five cargo helicopters bearing his entire army prepared for lift off. He bit his lower lip and sneered. He had been so close to victory, had it not been for this Li character.

"I swear… if it takes me to the end of time, I will destroy you," he muttered.

He put his vehicle back in gear and continued to head north. He made his way through the rough countryside until he finally came across the road that the soldier Blake found. He knew it would lead him to the service station run by the two idiots he so easily fooled. He would rob their till before he moved into the local town for more pillage.

A huge roar came up behind him followed by the chopping sound of the helicopters as they made their way over the horizon. Cyrus stared straight ahead and pushed his vehicle as fast as he could.

"I will seek my revenge on everything and everyone connected with your organization," he promised. "You will never see me coming. I will sweep in and take you out, one by one."

After several kilometers, he realized the road he traveled on was not a straight course. This was a different road. He had veered slightly to the west. Without a compass or any object on the horizon for a bearing, he took a road that did not lead directly to the station. If he took a different direction, he might run out of gas or become lost before dark. He pressed on through the day until he finally found a dirt path that lead in a more northerly direction. He turned the overland vehicle onto this dirt road and headed even faster toward what he hoped would be a town at the end of it.

After nearly an hour, he finally came to an eastbound semi-paved road. He was not certain how far west or north he traveled, or if he started east, how far he would go before he ran out of petrol fuel. He closed his eyes and cast his senses.

"Well, well, well," he smiled, "a trailer with a lone occupant! Won't he be surprised to see me?"

Cyrus evaluated that the man had food, water, and fuel for his vehicle – everything he needed to press on. The man even possessed an old truck. While it was not as reliable as the ATV he rode, it would go faster on the road and be more comfortable. He decided he would take that, too.

Cyrus revved the engine and started in the direction of the trailer when a white object moved into the shimmering heat waves of the road up ahead. After only a minute, he knew this was no mirage. The strange vehicle with its lone occupant silently moved straight for him.

"You've traveled far enough, Cyrus," a voice spoke to his mind.

As he slowed down, he noticed a tall man in a white robe stood on a floating platform of some futuristic design. It was not Li, but another man, taller, meatier, and wearing a long white robe-type garment that seemed to shine with a strange glow in the mid-day sun.

"How bizarre," he thought. "This must be a mirage!"

"I am not a mirage, Cyrus," the same voice addressed him.

The tall man rode his hovering device right at him. He would not yield and blocked Cyrus' way forward. All at once, Cyrus sensed a psychic presence on the man's right, followed by one on his left. Then he sensed psychics behind him. They were coming at him from all directions. His head spun around as his vehicle sputtered to a stop and then shut down. No matter how hard he tried, he could not start it.

"You aren't going anywhere, Cyrus," another voice added.

"We've got you covered," one more threatened.

"Don't try to run," a new voice spoke.

"You are surrounded," still another voice broke in.

Several floating platforms moved in around him. Each rider wore a bright shiny white flowing robe. They closed their circle tighter until hardly any space separated his ATV and their hovering silent platforms.

"Let's see," he said as he twisted around. "Eight very advanced platforms. You've been busy stealing alien technology and building things. This is perfect," he said as he stood up over his seat. "I won't have to seek you out after all. I can tear you apart right here, starting with you, missy," he said to Cecilia.

Cyrus should have started with Zhiwei or Chou, if he wanted to pick the weakest psychic in the group. But he thought like a misogynist. Cecilia had the power to fling his body into the air about a thousand meters and drop him over a pile of sharp rocks. She resisted that impulse. Instead she bowed and backed her platform away slightly as did Su Lin next to her.

"Scared of me?" Cyrus smiled at her apparent cowardice.

However, Cecilia only made room for one more platform to enter inside the circle, mounted by Master Li, dressed in similar flowing white robes, though his robes, in addition to their iridescent cloth, had a large green dragon on them whose figure wrapped around Li. Cyrus could feel the tremendous power that emanated from Master Li. For the first time in his existence, he realized the true incredible power of this seemingly small frail Chinese man and it frightened him.

"Your days of misusing your power are over, Cyrus," Master Li openly linked as his platform moved right in front of Cyrus' vehicle. "We will offer you two choices. I will let you decide. My team is willing to work with you. We know you've done some terrible things. We do not take life as casually as you do. We treat all life as being very special and precious, a rare gift in this dark realm called the universe. Even this planet is the rarest of creatures inside this end of the Milky Way, a floating Garden of Eden, an oasis in a cold vacuous space."

"Spare me the backroom philosophy, professor," Cyrus spat at him.

Master Li continued as if he had not heard his abusive remarks.

"If you fill your garden with toxic garbage, nothing will grow, not even weeds," he pointed out. "But, if you tend such a place properly, who knows what will flourish. We intend to look out for the planet Earth. Which path will you choose? Destruction or creation?"

"Li you are full of so much..." Cyrus sneered at him.

"You will not address me with your vulgarities," Li said and cut him off.

For the first time in his life, Cyrus felt psychic power control his actions, instead of the other way around. He could not speak, no matter how hard he tried.

"We don't have all day," Li said with a firm voice. "We must return and help the general undo part of the damage you perpetrated on society. Tell us... what is your decision?"

As Li linked his thoughts, Cyrus slowly slipped his hand down into his left pants pocket and fingered the gun he had there. He reached over and started the engine. He dropped the clutch, held the brake, and put the ATV into high gear. This action forced his wheels to spin in place which instantly created a large smoky cloud as cover. He whipped out the gun and emptied the chamber in Li's direction. The barrel of his gun flashed several times as Cyrus squeezed the trigger tight and repeatedly shot his pistol straight at Master Li. Bullets ripped through Master Li's flesh and sent the old man backward off his platform. When he finished, Cyrus dropped the empty clip, grabbed another, and slammed it in. He twisted in his seat and fired rounds at each of the surrounding psychics. He made direct hits on each of their heads. With his deadly accuracy, he aimed directly for their forehead, right above the bridge of their nose. The bullets entered their skulls and took them out, one by one.

Satisfied he had killed all nine, he disengaged the brake and started to take off, when something caught his eye. A pinpoint of light in the sky seemed to twinkle with a strange pulsing purplish light, a rather odd phenomenon. He could not look away from it. A sound began to grow in his ears… lub-dub, lub-dub, lub-dub… it was sound of his beating heart. He gasped for air. His hand no longer held a pistol. The cloud of smoke he created instantly vanished. He could not move.

"Help!" he cried. "Can't… breathe!"

Slowly the larynx in his throat began to close. He gasped for air. The air grew still. The sound of his heart began to slow as he tried in vain to inhale.

"How does it feel?" a voice echoed, "…to die by suffocation, struggling to breathe in those last moments of life… the life you snatched from your victims without remorse, without a conscience, without regret."

Cyrus frantically tried to look around him. The smoke, the gun, the killing… had all been an illusion. The gun he had in his pocket slowly lifted up and hovered away from him. He began to grow dizzy. The air swam with little objects that left tracer trails. His heart beat slower as he gasped his last breath.

"Time and again you demonstrate a lack of respect for life," Master Li's voice rang in his ears. "We offer you a chance for redemption and you choose death. So be it. You pronounce your own sentence. Team, withdraw."

"Last one back is a rotten egg!" one cried.

"No… first one back!" another answered.

"I told you they were fast!" one yelled.

"Look out!" another said, but it was all in fun.

Cyrus still faced skyward. He could not move or witness the event. He only heard the sound of laughter from young men and women while they chased each other with their hovercraft, until they disappeared over the horizon, playing a game of who would be the first to arrive at their aircraft. They left Cyrus' fate to Master Li. Cyrus continued to labor in his breathing.

The white light in the sky grew larger and larger until Cyrus' eyes widened in the realization that the object was really Master Li in all his glory, formed into a brilliant "spirit" body that floated down until it reunited with Li's body on the platform still in front of Cyrus. Li allowed him the ability to bend his neck, though he still could barely breathe.

"I have only killed once in my life and that is one too many," Master Li confessed. "Why must you choose death?"

"I hate you," Cyrus gasped.

"You are hopeless," Li sighed and shook his head, "and pitiful. I cannot let you abuse others with your power. Once this situation has passed, the WPO will hopefully operate in a new way to detect emerging psychics and properly guide them. The object lesson here is one of morality… for if we do not follow some overall guiding path that treats all with equal righteousness, then we may as well end this great experiment. I chose to have hope for humanity. Goodbye, Cyrus Keaty."

Master Li turned his back on Cyrus and slowly moved his platform away. Cyrus lashed out with his mind at Li, even as he struggled to breathe his last breath.

"Get you… I'll… I'll… get… you…" he uttered as his throat gurgled.

As the team headed back to the aircraft, Michael and the others sensed a power struggled between two psychic men. One repeatedly attacked, while the other easily fended off the attacks. This went on for nearly a minute, until quite suddenly, they could sense only one powerful psychic move in their direction.

Master Li opened his black card and sent out a general notice to members of the WPO around the globe: *"The threat from Australia is eliminated."*

CHAPTER FORTY-TWO

THE MAJOR (GENERAL) AND HIS MINOR, PART II

ONE WHOLE DAY PASSED, WHERE the Rollo psychics slept in their "bivouac" beds while the general "tidied loose ends." Fortunately, it did not rain during this period, although rain was scheduled soon in the forecast. Everyone expressed profound relief when rescuers found General Wallace in the Brisbane rubble. The middle-aged soldier surprised his physicians when he quickly recovered from his wounds. Although, with Cecilia's secret help, General Wallace soon found after her treatments that he never felt better in his life. Once he regained his status and had full communication access, he changed the hierarchy of the military overnight.

Chief of Staff General George Wallace saw the error of his ways and put a man in charge beneath him that he trusted. By unanimous vote of the joint chiefs, they elevated James Pollack to the rank of full general and placed him in charge of the army, a position long coveted by Gen. Sanders. Years later, before he retired, James would eventually take over as Chief of Staff, taking Gen. Wallace's place. He made the changes to the military he felt were long overdue – social changes, hiring changes, and promotion changes. He helped persuade lawmakers to pass bills that increased medical and educational support for all servicemen and women. His leadership led to the largest enrollment period the peacetime military ever had. They actually turned away too many recruits.

However, before any of that took place, James worked behind the scenes shortly after he returned to the base with Cyrus' army as his prisoners. He entered the military computer system, with help from his Galactic Central voice, and cleaned up the mess that Cyrus created when he pilfered the military supplies. When military intelligence processed the prisoners, no one in the company of men could recall any leader except Girard. They all blamed Girard for what happened. They said that he broke into the base and stole the items.

Later the same day, General Pollack presented additional evidence of Girard's duplicity in the entire affair when he showed them the plans the ex-felon created on his laptop computer. Maj. Gen. Pollack received high praise for his efforts from the top brass including the prime minister. As Sergeant Berry predicted, the headlines in papers all over the nation proudly stated, "General captures terrorists!"

At the end of that very long day which followed the terrible events in Brisbane, an exhausted James Pollack entered Digger's with Sgt. Berry, the two men informally arm in arm. The officers in the club gave the men a rounding roar of approval with a lengthy standing ovation. When the brouhaha finally died down, the two men proposed a toast with English whiskey.

"...to fallen comrades."

"...to fallen comrades!" the other officers echoed.

The military services lost 37 members in the Brisbane bombing. A private on staff read their names aloud while the members listened. As all glory from won battles quickly fades, a somber note of reality fell upon them and the day ended with silence. James returned home to find a welcoming wife that gave him what he needed most, love and support.

Two days later, inside the general's house...

"I don't care if the thing makes the best mousse in the world," Penelope said, close to anger, though still playful, "I insist on making dinner... my way," she told Chou regarding his fusor. "I may not be Running Elk, but I can cook a thing or two... if you will allow me."

She pushed everyone out of her kitchen. She would not accept any assistance except to fill a shopping list, which she gave Su Lin from the start. She performed all the baking, cooking, and only allowed Han's assistance to serve. Although after dinner, she accepted Su Lin's help to clean up. She did not interfere when Su Lin stocked her shelves, her refrigerator, and her freezer with fresh supplies from the fusor – enough food to last the couple a very long time.

"I am curious about... well, you know who," Michael cautiously wondered as the group gathered in Pollack's living room. "How did you anticipate some of his reactions," he asked Li.

Penelope promptly served tea at four o'clock that afternoon. She brought in a tray of baked goods to accompany her tea.

"Thank you, Penelope," Master Li said as he took a freshly baked cookie from the tray. She poured out a fresh cup of tea and added his honey with a slice of lemon. Li leaned back in the chair and glanced over at the man to his left. "Do you want to answer Michael's question Han?"

"You play poker, Michael," Han spoke as he sat forward. "We had an ace up our sleeve, an unknown element for Cyrus, but a known one to us – the general," Han explained. "His abilities already surpassed our opponent's."

"We weren't certain if he could penetrate through all layers of blocks," the general spoke up. "It was the one thing that would have alerted him to my arrival that morning had Master Li not anticipated it," he stated wistfully. "Han and Li both knew I was coming with reinforcements. They did not know how long it would take me to track down the terrorist suspects who attacked Brisbane. They relied on my incredible ability to locate enemies, which I demonstrated earlier in Afghanistan. I've had a notorious reputation in the military community for years, which I simply chalked up to instinct. I knew where my prey was and took action. I didn't know if it was related to my psychic ability back then… but Han expressed his faith in me before I left. He knew I could do it, all the time."

"Thank goodness… *he*… couldn't penetrate those blocks," Penelope added. "More tea, gentlemen… ladies?" she spoke.

"I'm only glad you planted that stuff when you did," the general linked to Han.

"Stuff?" Villi questioned.

"Why…. *His* plan, of course. Didn't you know? You must have suspected," the general revealed.

"Wait a minute… I don't understand," Cecilia interrupted. "Are you telling me this entire plan of…" she had difficulty saying his name, "*his*… was not really his plan… it was a plan by Han?"

"Precisely," the general told her.

"You traced his plan back to the astronomer?" Villi asked for a clarification.

"Li contacted me. We were revamping the computer system, remember? I had access to the most top secret computer system in the country," the general told them. "Once Master Li discovered Cyrus's idea, Li asked me to find out more information. I used the system to discover his two astronomy victims. We gave the information to Han. By the time you arrived, he figured out the rest. We also realized at that time, that uh, *he* was not aware of different psychic levels. He did not evolve through Galactic Central. He lacked the discipline and the focus, especially in blocking technique."

"So he never caught on that we knew about his plan to use the space station?" Cecilia guessed.

"He probably knew that we knew about that," Li muttered.

"Our coming to Australia must have surprised him," Villi realized.

"Unfortunately, he sensed my approach. That's why he altered the timetable for his attack on Brisbane," Li explained. "It was meant to throw us off, take the general out of the equation. I knew that it would only be a matter of time before James showed up. I liked his style..." Li added and smiled at the older couple.

"He does have style," Penelope sighed as she hugged his arm.

"When he made his last contact, Master Li let a few details flow in the opposite direction," Han threw in, "such as psychic absorption."

"It is unfortunate that we did not predict the diversion in Brisbane, the terrible act of a desperate man beginning to feel cornered," Zhiwei commented.

"I hate to think we might have prevented it," Li spoke quietly. "If only I had seen it in his mind. He's quite devious..."

"You mustn't take any blame for something devised by that monster, Master Li," Penelope boldly spoke up.

"I quite agree," the general added. "That madman was responsible for those deaths. Imagine the damage that would have happened if you hadn't interfered?"

"Just a minute... you said he let the psychic absorption slip in the other direction," Chou conjectured. "Does that mean you tricked..."

"Oh, I get it!" Michael spoke up. "The business with the space station... an illusion?"

Master Li smiled and nodded to his team.

"Li had to appear as if he was as weak as us on the plane," Han said. "You couldn't know. Cyrus... (Master Li cringed when Han said his name) entered every mind on the aircraft. Li implanted the illusion as he drew enough energy from our minds to perform his deed. Then Master Li made Cyrus believe he attacked the space station and did those terrible things, only they never took place. Li projected to Cyrus and the others it all happened."

"I wondered how you had enough energy to help Villi," Cecilia put in.

"Oh... I forgot to thank you for that," Villi added.

Master Li simply shrugged his shoulders and took a sip of tea.

"Thank goodness, it's over," Su Lin added the sentiment they all shared.

"What happened to... well, since we aren't saying his name... you know who?" Penelope blurted. She tried to avoid using his name like the rest of them.

"I thought Master Li killed him," James said as he turned to Li. He noticed Han half-smile and Michael, too. "You mean you didn't?"

Master Li cleared his throat. The team only learned the fate of the tyrant and scoundrel after Li shared it with them on their way back to the aircraft. Li turned to his Australian hosts and explained Cyrus' fate.

"Mr. Irving Warren is a waste treatment worker in the small indigenous community of Warburton, population 506," Li told them. "He cleans sludge from people's septic systems and will do so for the rest of his days. The town council had trouble finding someone to fill the position, which the state held open for twenty-eight years until Mr. Warren showed up and volunteered. During his free time, he helps Warburton's residents with anything, such as home maintenance. He never accepts payment. At night, Mr. Warren lives in a small shack on the outskirts of town, a place previously condemned, but now his home for the rest of his life."

"Amen," the team said in unison.

"Why didn't you destroy him… as he did to others?" Penelope asked with raised eyebrows. "After all the evil he did? What if he reverts to his former self?"

The whole Rollo team exchanged glances before they looked at Master Li to say something. The elderly sage took in a deep breath and sighed. This unanimously voted WPO position was difficult to explain, especially to non-psychics.

"We are not about revenge or death," Li said quietly. "We are about life and restitution. We believe in justice, not murder. We do not become the thing that is our opposite, simple because that is expedient. We stand for something that is grand… and to keep our sights set on that goal, we pledge our lives to carry out those principles, no matter the cost. Yes, I would agree with you that the families of his victims will have to pay with a life of sorrow and misery for the loss of their loved ones. Our organization cannot fill the void from that loss. We can help them deal with their tragedy over time with special events that will enrich their lives."

Penelope simply stared at Master Li. She found his explanation difficult to accept. In her mind, retribution should be an aspect of justice. Li rose and crossed the room to where James and Penelope sat together on the sofa. Master Li sat next to Penelope and spoke to her directly.

"Just as every member of the WPO stresses some special attribute, which contributes to our organization, I wish to make a small request of you," he said to her. "I want you to track down the families of his victims and suggest a form of compensation. That will be your mission, Penelope," Li said to her, "if you'll accept it."

"The family of every victim?" she timidly asked. "That would seem a daunting task."

"You must contact every single one of them," Li requested, "including those affected by bomb. Zhiwei created a probable list of victims that currently has over 2700 names on it. We expect that number to rise even higher when we learn the total number of the victims from Brisbane. You must research the background of each family and send your recommendation to the Tyler Foundation. The foundation will quietly arrange the benefits you recommend without question," he told her. "It is not enough to replace a lost loved one. With your help, we will try to compensate that loss, even if that means a lifetime of counseling and monetary assistance. We, meaning through your work, will make amends as much as we can. Chou will supply you with special devices to help speed up and simplify the process. You'll find them delightful and easy to use. We are counting on your good judgment, Penelope. Will you do this for us?"

The idea of being so sympathetic to these victims astounded her. She did not know what to say in response. The thought of being that considerate and philanthropic filled her heart with many emotions. She glanced over at James. He slightly nodded his approval. She turned and looked into Master Li's kind blue-gray eyes.

"I will try to do as you ask," she finally said as she choked up.

Master Li patted her hand, mumbled thanks, and went back to his tea. Penelope could not look at anyone. She turned her head to James, but she could not speak her feelings. However, the entire room knew how Penelope felt. She had worked in charity for many years. Never had any organization sought to recompense victims in this manner. A tear dripped off the end of her nose as she bowed her head. No one spoke or linked. Sensing the need to distract from Penelope's moment of emotion, Dr. Beaton-Tyler spoke up.

"What will you do now?" she asked the general aloud to break the silence.

James did not reply. He tried to console his wife. Penelope cleared her throat. She sat upright, turned to Cecilia, and forced a polite smile.

"The general has three years left in the military until his retirement," she said. "He is scheduled to attend a special ceremony in Canberra next Tuesday. He's to get some award…"

"… only the Victoria Cross," Han spoke up. "The highest military honor in the land, along with the Cross of Valor and be made a Knight of the Garter!"

"Yes… something like that," she blushed for him. The two held hands and gazed into each other's eyes. Penelope, born and raised in a military family, learned to place her feelings in check. She straightened her shoulders and dabbed her face with a handkerchief the general handed her. "Later, we thought about traveling, since money is no longer an object," she continued. "We would love to see the WPO headquarters in America. Frankly, I can hardly wait to see it."

"We look forward to your visit," Michael put in.

"Excuse me," Zhiwei spoke up, "general, I don't mean to pry. But I would like to address one last thing," he asked.

"What is it, Zhiwei?" the general responded.

"I'm still curious about that tracking ability," Zhiwei asked. "Mind manipulation for you was a relatively new concept. How did you so easily convince Sergeant Beery to come along with your idea," he asked. "Surely the sergeant must have doubted your reasons for traveling out of town."

"First, I searched the minds of drivers stuck on the blocked highway as we flew into Brisbane," James explained. "I replayed memory after memory. Whether they knew it or not, some people actually spotted the terrorists as they drove from the city and headed north. They simply ignored the fact that what they saw was important or unusual. When I saw a white van pass up car after car in a rush to drive north, I suspect that van held the terrorists. Therefore, I knew the general direction. It was simply a matter of tracking the van after that." He smiled at Zhiwei. "You forget. I headed up the procurement division. As I sat in the back of the car, I used one of the computers they gave me to call up military satellite images. Once I knew where to look, I quickly located the van. I correctly guessed that if we tried to attack their site or rush them with a large force, they would explode another large device they had already prepared. After we broke in, we discovered they had several ready to go off in case they were attacked."

"Secondly, I resorted to trickery," James confessed. "I altered the thoughts of my officers during our brief meeting. I knew Beery would be the most difficult. The damned Scot..."

"James!" Penelope admonished.

"...darned Scot then, is so emotional, it was difficult to break through. I knew I had to find an emotional way into his mind. That's when I remember the past... periwinkle," he winked at Penelope. "I knew that appealed to his sense of duty."

"That does it," she said as she pushed away. "Don't you think it's high time I heard about periwinkle?"

"Periwinkle?" Han perked up.

"I forgot to tell you the whole story," Li broke in. "His code name."

"Please tell us, general, about periwinkle," Zinian added.

Chou and the others sat forward to focus on the story.

"This took place early in my career. You might say this was my defining moment. I was only a captain. I volunteered..."

"Which I always found hard to understand," Penelope broke in. "Why, James?"

"They took a nuclear weapon, dear," James softly spoke. "What if they

313

chose Adelaide as the target. What about you, our families, or our friends? I couldn't let that happen to anyone…"

"A nuclear weapon…" Chou echoed.

"At any rate, when my commander revealed the plan to drop us in the eastern mountains of Afghanistan, they asked me what my code name should be," General Pollack said to the group and turned to Penelope. "I could only think of you… of what would happen if I never saw you again. I remembered it was your favorite flower and that we had it growing wild on our lot. So I told them, call me periwinkle," he explained. "I got ribbed for that one. Sergeant Beery is one of the few men left remaining from that company and the only one that knew my code name. When he reached for the note on the car, I had to stop him before he destroyed it. He was trying to protect my secret identity."

"You mean that's all there was to it?" Penelope asked him. "I thought it had something to do with what happened in Afghanistan," she said.

"Good 'ole Beery," the general commented, his eyes drifted, "such a loyal and dedicated man."

"Tell them the rest of the story," Li spoke quietly, yet loud enough so that Penelope could hear. "Tell us the whole story of periwinkle."

The general took a big gulp of tea and looked around the room.

"Where to begin," he started. "We had been on patrol for only a day, scouring the hills for our target, when the news arrived of Tamby's death. An Indian assassin took him out, but the Pakistani's recovered the weapon. We found out from some villagers. Imagine! They knew and we didn't! We were on radio silence. I was devastated. The news demoralized the men, especially when we knew they considered us expendable if anything we wrong. Remember, this was long before 9/11 in America. We had no allies in the region. Our mission was top secret. Yet, we never encountered any resistance going up into the mountains. It was when we started south to cross over into Pakistan that a large group of fighters, a fringe Afghanistan group, flanked our position. We didn't know… the following morning, they planned to attack and cut us to ribbons. Somehow, I sensed their position and their intent, though I said nothing to the men. I suggested a nighttime ambush maneuver on the enemy's position to Sergeant Beery. I was a very young and naive officer at the time," the general told them and paused. "Dear old Berry. He listened to me very politely, and probably thought I was daft. He probably thought we were going out for a walk and then return to the camp. Yet to his credit, he obeyed and came with me. As we neared the enemy's position, he began to trust me. I came through the front while he covered the rear, the same maneuver we repeated years later on Fraser Island. I surprised the enemy first before Beery got into position. I burst onto their campsite. They scrambled for their weapons. Before they could kill me, I fired through their ranks and took out six men."

"Six men!" Villi stated.

"Yes, my big friend, Villi. At first, I intended to offer them a chance to give up. But they were intent on murder. They cocked their guns and started to fire. So, I had to act. They fought hard to the last man. Well… I was a crack shot in those days," James recalled and then he pointed to his left chest. "This entire row is for accuracy and marksmanship," he said as he pointed to the ribbons. "At any rate, I suppose the intensity of my attack must have frightened the survivors. The remaining forces grabbed their weapons and ran for their lives rather than surrender. They ran smack dab into Beery. God only knows how their bullets missed me! Had we waited, we discovered from their lone survivor that they planned to attack us in the morning with a barrage of grenades. We found the grenades because one of our men spoke Arabic…"

"He might come across as an ignoramus," Penelope quietly spoke up, "but as I recall, the man who spoke Arabic is Sergeant Berry. He studied in Edinburgh… didn't he, dear?"

"Aye, lass," the general replied with his best Scottish accent.

James noticed that the room fell into silence. He picked up the story's end.

"After I killed those men, I stood there, trembling with fear, knowing I did a very foolish thing. I heard a burst of gunfire followed by Beery's voice. He told me to stay where I was. He was coming to me. He dragged back one frightened lone prisoner, when I happened to glance down. I noticed a small flowering plant growing up from the rock between my legs, the only color in that whole area. I pulled out the plant by the roots and wrapped it in one the dead men's headbands. Beery walked up to me at that moment. 'Beggin yer pardon, sir,' he observed, 'but that's a periwinkle, sir,' he told me. 'Must have brought you a bit of luck.' After that, if they wanted me for a special mission, they used the code word periwinkle. No one kidded me about the name after that mission."

The general looked about the room and felt everyone's gaze on him.

"You never told me that story," Penelope said.

"I didn't want you to know that I almost died that day," James told her.

"You've been in other skirmishes, dear. Why not tell me about that one?" she asked.

"I don't know," the general explained, "…perhaps because when I charged into their position, I was outnumbered fourteen to one. I attacked with such precision that they thought I had other men in the dark behind me. Seven survivors fled. Beery took out another four and captured one, while the other two scampered off into the night. Needless to say, they never bothered us again." He looked deep into her eyes. "I acted in a foolhardy fashion. I didn't want you to know how reckless I'd behaved. If I had failed…"

"But you didn't," Han said. "You took a risk to save your men, general," he pointed out, "just as you did on Fraser Island, based on your instinct as a soldier, a valuable asset for both you and your men," he commented.

"Yes, but under different circumstances…" the general objected.

"I believe your guidance had more to do with your ability than you give it credit, general," Master Li told him. "You broke into that base camp, you charged into that house, and your helicopters landed at exactly the right moment. Those events seem very convenient. Your ability to 'sense' has served you well. Personally, I'm grateful you listened to your instinct," Li said.

"Here, here," the others echoed.

"I'm glad you acted on your instincts, too," Penelope quietly added. She referred to the choice he made to keep the date the night they met.

The general blushed and squeezed her hand when he heard her thought.

Master Li glanced over at the clock on the mantle. He hand-signaled to Villi "begin take off preparations for the aircraft," a signal the others caught, too. "It's time we go home."

The general noticed Li's hand movements and questioned with his puzzled expression. Li tried to explain.

"We've learned to use sign language based on the hand signs used by the hearing impaired," Li told him. "Cecilia and Michael invented a few shorthand moves which they passed on to the rest of us. I will teach them to you when you come to Rollo, which we hope will be soon."

Master Li and the others stood up.

"On behalf of our group, I would like to thank you for your warm hospitality and extend an open invitation to America," Li said and bowed. "You and Penelope will always be welcome guests."

"Our pleasure, Master Li," the general responded and shook his hand.

"You are welcome here any time," Penelope added. "Bring your… house, too," she added which made the group chuckle.

"That house will be gone tomorrow," Zinian informed them. "I believe it is supposed to rain this evening?"

"Why, yes, Zinian," Penelope stated, "It is."

"It will melt like a cake in the rain," he said with a grin, "and fertilize the new grass seed, too, general," he added with a wink.

The Rollo group expressed their farewells to the Pollack's. Outside, the darkening sky began to send down the first drops of rain. With the aircraft packed and the temporary quarters headed for destruction, the American group prepared for takeoff, except for Chou. He lingered in the yard outside the ship, the first sprinkles of rain dripping off his short-cropped black hair.

"I'm to have the final word it seems," he said when he ventured over the Pollack's standing at their back door. "You'll need this," he stated and extended his hand to the general. "It's not a credit card," he told him.

"What is it?" the general asked.

"Place three fingers from one hand anywhere on the front," Chou indicated.

The general held it out in his left hand and placed three fingers from his right hand on the front.

"Recognize James Pollack," a voice stated. The card expanded in his hand until a large flat screen formed a 50 x 25 centimeter rectangular screen. The couple witnessed with amazement as the three-dimensional picture of Rollo appeared.

"What a beautiful place," Penelope commented on the image.

"That's Main Street in Rollo," Chou explained.

"The large structure in the background… Is that the WPO headquarters where Han and Master Li live?" James asked.

"Yes," Chou acknowledged.

The couple exchanged glances.

"We'll have to make that trip to America sooner, don't you think?" Penelope asked James. He smiled at her.

"Zhiwei and Master Li appreciate reports as often as you can send them," Chou told them. "Some members send us their thoughts or wishes daily. You may speak or link with the device which also records your image. Should you want to contact other agents, ask for the list of WPO agents. The device will show you how to communicate with them. Our agents love to use their cards, so use it as often as you like."

"How do I close…" James began.

"Just think to it," Chou told him.

James considered shutting down the device in his hand. The screen shrank to credit card size. The general put it in his shirt pocket.

"What If James should lose it," Penelope asked, "or worse, misplace it?"

"While you cannot activate the card, Penelope, you can move it around without causing its destruction," Chou explained.

"That's a relief," she said as she cast the general a worried expression.

"Interaction from anyone else will cause its instant destruction. Good luck, general… Penelope," Chou said as he sprinted through the rain toward the aircraft.

James and Penelope watched as the giant white bivouac across the yard melted into a pile of gray goo and quickly dissipated.

"So much for my dreams of owning a hotel," the general quipped.

The couple waved goodbye and watched as the huge aircraft quietly lifted straight up and turned toward the northeast.

"Master Li?" Villi called. "I'll need that bubble…"

Moments later, an object of incredible sophistication streaked toward North America at great speed.

The End of "The Voices Down Under – Book IV" of "The Voices Saga"

Up next: "The Proximate Voices – Book V" of
"The Voices Saga" due Spring 2011